# INEVITABLE

# INEVITABLE

Angela Graham

To all the hardworking mothers out there
who find time to follow their dreams!

# Contents

# Prologue

Everything about the sight in front of me was wrong.

Only an hour earlier, I'd blown an exaggerated farewell kiss to my boyfriend, Mark, as he backed out of the driveway, heading to work. Yet there sat his beat-up truck in its usual spot. Worry churned my gut, but instead of rushing up the porch stairs to check if he was all right and find out why he returned home already, I stood frozen, leering at the sight of the white Jeep parked in the neighbor's spot.

My chest tightened at the sight, a cold shiver of dread creeping up my back. The thunderous pounding of my heart rang through my ears. I recognized that Jeep. Every girl in town would agree it wasn't one you wanted to find anywhere near your man's vehicle.

I bit my bottom lip, gnawing on it anxiously when I felt Hilary's hand on my back. Hesitantly, I peered up to meet her tight, awkward smile.

"Maybe he wasn't feeling well, Cassandra." She shrugged her shoulders, but the concern clouding her usually bright-chestnut eyes as she glanced at the Jeep and then back at me was all I saw. "I'm sure it's not what you're thinking."

What *was* I thinking? Mark was the perfect boyfriend who'd given me five blissful, wonderful years. He was the man I was going to spend the rest of my life with—the man whose

1

arms I dreamed would hold me when I was old and grey, taking my final breath of life.

Suddenly enraged at myself for fearing the worst, I bolted up the metal stairs two at a time and gripped my front doorknob. I knew I was being silly, but the dread that had settled in my gut sent a series of doubts racing through my mind. With my feet planted firmly on the welcome mat, I closed my eyes and whispered a silent prayer that I'd find Mark with his infectious smile and a perfectly justified reason as to why he came back home. The knob turned in my clammy hand; the door was unlocked, as always.

My stomach rolled into a tight, painful knot as I tiptoed through the makeshift foyer. The apartment was nothing more than a large open room with exposed brick walls. There was a tiny kitchenette and a partition separating the bedroom, which was large enough for our king-sized bed and small dresser.

Fear froze me in place. I needed to see, but my legs refused to move any farther. They were suddenly stiff as boards, with cinder blocks instead of feet.

Erratic thoughts of the Jeep's owner nestled somewhere in there pounded in my head. A shudder tore me in two, and every fiber of my being screamed something was wrong. When I cleared my throat and opened my mouth to deliver what I knew would be a weak greeting, I was cut off by a loud feminine moan. It was followed by the gruff voice I was certain I'd cherish until I was a little old woman, surrounded by our grandchildren.

"Yeah…like that, baby."

I doubled over as the sound of his voice ripped the air from my lungs. As my knees gave out, Hilary's fingers dug into my forearms, attempting to hold me up.

"Come on, let's get out of here." Her whisper was dark with a violent rage. Despite her help to straighten me on my feet, the pain racked my body and mind overwhelmed every last shred of standing ability I clung to.

My head shook, tears pooling in my eyes as I fought back the urge to fully collapse and sob uncontrollably until the emotions numbed. *It has to be a bad dream. It has to.*

Anger—pure, unadulterated fury—built rapidly inside me, temporarily bandaging my heart and preparing it for war. I drew the strength I needed from it to stand straight and take the few short steps around the partition.

My hands balled into tight fists while my feet led the way until I stopped at the end of the bed. My face hardened, jaw locked as I took in the sight before me.

Mackenzie was on her back, proving every rumor about her was true.

"Ah Mark, yes, harder, you're so…CASSANDRA!" Her eyes opened wide.

Mark's head shot up and whipped to the side, his body panting as he looked over his right shoulder. His eyes bulged when he caught my crazed stalker glare. Cool steel filled my nerves. I didn't blink or flinch.

He shot off the bed, shoving Mackenzie's naked body aside as if to make her disappear. She skidded off the edge of the mattress and landed with a loud *smack* on the hardwood floor.

"It's not what you think, Cassie." He stepped toward me, reaching out to touch my arm.

The harsh snort behind me alerted him to Hilary's presence and he backed off, grabbing a pillow to cover his front. Mackenzie scurried around on the floor, clutching the sheet to her body, attempting to collect her clothes that were scattered around the room.

My eyes closed, and blood flooded my ears. Ever since high school, Mackenzie Taylor had been known for only one thing: seducing other girls' boyfriends. She disposed of them as quickly as she snatched them up. It was nothing more than a game for a girl with low self-esteem and an egotistical, bitchy attitude. I shot her a menacing scowl, then returned my focus to the bastard in front of me.

"Cassandra, please." Mark's voice dripped with desperation as he stepped toward me. I took an equal number of steps back, my face twisted in disgust.

"I'll be by tomorrow to pack my stuff." My tone was cold and clipped. "Don't be here."

I turned on my heel to leave, my bravado unwavering. The moment his hand gripped my elbow, something deep inside me snapped. I balled my hand into a hard fist—exactly as my grandfather had taught me—and whipped around, connecting it with his nose.

"Son of a—" Mark dropped the pillow and grabbed his face as he stumbled backward, falling over the bed.

Hilary turned away, her face a combination of proud from my actions and pale from catching him nude.

"What the hell is your problem!?" Mackenzie slipped into a pair of denim shorts that covered little of her ass, then bent over to inspect Mark's busted face.

*My problem!?*

I turned, a small grin curling my lips. Filled with pride, I took one menacing step toward her. She sucked in a loud, ragged breath and staggered back, nerves visible on her makeup-smeared face.

With my chin held high, I walked away without another word. I'd always been branded the sweet, perky blonde who looked for the good in everyone, but today I was no longer that girl. Today, I was a woman betrayed by a man unworthy of my affection or loyalty.

But the humiliation stung, ripping through me with no

remorse, teaching a painful lesson. I'd come home to grab a more comfortable pair of shoes for a day of shopping and found something much more painful than the six-inch pumps I'd been wearing.

The rumors around town, which I'd chosen to ignore, were true. I'd wasted countless hours fantasizing about our wedding, raising children, and the house we'd build together.

Hilary wrapped her arm around me, leading me out the front door and down the stairs. Nothing mattered in that moment. I only wanted to get away—away from the betrayal and the inquiring stares, which would surface once Mackenzie's side of the story began floating around our small town.

Luckily, I had a place awaiting me: a place I'd always considered home, even though I'd never officially lived there. The quaint house, situated deep in the country, was one my grandparents had willed to me a year earlier. Mark said it was too far out of town to move to, but that was exactly what I needed.

It sat vacant, waiting for me to begin the next chapter of my life…alone.

# Chapter One

## ONE YEAR LATER

"Slow down, I can't…keep up much longer." Hilary stopped abruptly, bent over, and grasped her knees. "Seriously, unless you plan on calling for help, this is as far as I can go."

With a snicker, I stood a few feet ahead of her, jogging in place. Hilary's breathing had been growing heavier for a while and I was quietly waiting for her to call it.

"I told you to stretch first," I said, watching her chug from her water bottle.

"I didn't think it would burn this badly." She looked up at the sky, her brows knitted together. "Not to mention this damn sun is killing me."

My legs stilled and I rested my hands on my hips. "Hey, at least this town has a hot paramedic or two, you know, in case you collapse from heat stroke." I rubbed my thumb and pointer finger over my chin. "Hmmm, sexy paramedics. On second thought, we should jog the entire way back."

She narrowed her eyes, collapsing onto her back in the tall grass of the meadow alongside the road with an exaggerated groan.

"Joking!" I held up my hands in defense.

She was beat, her face a deep crimson red and covered in beads of sweat. I'd never felt better; I was completely in my zone. No matter how close Hilary and I were, we couldn't be more different.

After a short sip of water to moisten my dry throat, I was eager to get moving again. "Come on," I said. "We'll walk back."

Hilary looked relieved, peeking through one open eye. "Thank God." She gripped her knees to pull herself into a sitting position, looking exhausted and completely out of her element. "I have no idea how you do this *every single day*."

"You'll get used to it." I grabbed her hands and pulled her to her feet. We both knew she would *not* get used to it, but I felt compelled to play along.

"Yeah, about that…I'm not so sure this is for me." She wiped the back of her arm over her temple and wrinkled her nose at the moisture it collected. With a somber sigh, she tilted her head back and scowled up at the bright morning sun. "I'll stick with the gym. Air conditioning and all—you understand."

"You're going to make me jog alone?" I feigned an exaggerated pout as we began walking back the way we came toward my house.

"Very funny. It has to be annoying having me slow you down. Besides, I look ridiculous in these tiny shorts next to you. Look at that stomach." Hilary leaned over, giggling, and slapped my abs. "I'm freaking jealous!"

"You're jealous!?" I continued walking but raised an eyebrow, gaping in her direction. "You know what I'd give to have an ass like yours?"

It wasn't a lie. My body may have been toned and tight from a mix of working out and good genetics, but next to her, I looked like a prepubescent girl. Hilary had the body of a grown woman, and the confidence to flaunt it. The girl stood

7

at least four inches taller than me and was built to suit any guy's fantasy. Deep down, she knew it too.

"What the hell am I going to do, huh? I indulge a little at the bakery for the first time in my life, and boom: ten pounds gained." She sighed. "It didn't really bother me until you-know-who decided to stroll back into town."

"Right, it must be *horrible* to gain a little weight and have it go straight to your ass. I think your fan club has enlisted even more admirers because of it." I chuckled, trying to reassure her. But still, ten pounds? I didn't see it. Hilary was being ridiculous. Her anxiety had less to do with the weight and more to do with Caleb, her childhood crush.

I offered a tight, supportive smile and continued down the road at a brisk pace, thankful she was picking up steam once again. The meadow beside us ended where the forest line began. The thick foliage and full branches of the tall trees offered occasional shade, but the heat beat down over my back, highlighting the sweat glistening over every inch of my exposed body.

Secretly, I loved it. The sensation of my stomach tightening when my legs stretched out and pounded against the rough pavement was euphoric. I could always get lost in the peaceful melody nature hummed in my ear. My day was never the same when I skipped my morning jog.

"So, speaking of Caleb, how long are you going to wait until you finally make a move?" I smiled, tugging out my loose ponytail and pulling it into a messy bun to keep my long hair off my back.

"Um, never."

"Seriously? You spent nearly every day in high school crushing on the guy, and he's finally moved back to town. What the hell are you waiting for?"

"Exactly—I spent every waking moment pining for a guy

that hardly even noticed me." Hilary looked down, wiping sweat from her stomach while we went around the first curve. "Even when he did, he looked at me like I was a child."

I offered a lopsided smile. "He's only two years older than you. Do you really think age matters anymore? You're all grown up now." I pulled my lips into an encouraging grin as I gave her an exaggerated once-over. "You're not a little girl anymore. You've got to go talk to him and make a move before someone else snatches him up."

She laughed, a soft smile settling over her thoughtful expression.

Now that Caleb was back in town, I was fully expecting my confident best friend to disappear into the insecure girl she became whenever he was near. It was an oddity growing up and watching how quickly her sharp tongue could get tied up, leaving her either stuttering or frozen when Caleb so much as looked at her.

We walked in silence for a few moments before I grew restless at her sudden lack of conversation. I hadn't seen Caleb since he'd moved away a few years earlier, but there was plenty of talk around town about his sudden return.

"I heard the restaurant will be opening next week. Caleb sent an invite for a grand-opening party."

"I still can't believe he bought the old place." Hilary took a drink from her water bottle. "It's a dump. My grandparents wouldn't even eat there the last couple of years."

I shrugged. "I'm actually excited to see what he has planned. The building looks amazing, and I heard he renovated the inside and added a bar."

From what I'd been hearing, Caleb was turning it into a full-blown restaurant with an expansive bar, and even had a dance floor built. The forty-minute commute to the city every time we wanted to go out would be no more. I was thrilled. I hated making the long drive just to have drunk guys spill their drinks on me and throw out cheesy pick-up lines. I went out to dance, and even that always seemed to get ruined. Guys never seemed to take the hint: Sometimes a girl wanted to dance alone. It was as though they assumed if you didn't come with another guy, then you were begging to be picked up. Not the case—at least, not for me.

Hilary continued walking, her expression indifferent. How was she *not* excited? She was the one who had to plead with me to go out with her all the time.

I jumped in front of her. "Come on!" She stepped back, pursing her lips to hide a smile. "A real bar!" I shouted.

She shook her head at my antics and walked around me.

"You know it's going to be great. We can go dancing. Plus, we'll finally have a decent place to eat in this town," I added, and watched her expression begin to brighten.

Just as we rounded the second curve that indicated we were less than a quarter mile from my house, a large moving truck sped by, blaring its horn. Hilary grabbed my arm and leapt off the road, practically diving into the grass.

We stared at each other and then at the taillights of the truck in disbelief before I fell back, panting.

Hilary stood up, brushing the grass from her purple shorts and shouting several explicit slurs. The near-death experience caused my blood to pump so fast, though, that the ringing in my ears blocked out most of her rant.

"What the hell!?" Hilary yelled, her arms flailing furiously. "Dumb son of a—*ugh*! He could have run us over!" She looked back at me, furious.

We'd just begun walking back to the road when two more trucks raced by, followed by a sleek black BMW with dark tinted windows.

"Where the hell are they going out here?" Hilary asked,

her breathing finally calm.

"I don't know," I replied, deep in thought. Why *would* moving trucks be out here at this hour? There were no other houses out this way besides mine, and—

"The Millers' Estate." I let out a puff of air, annoyed at my own forgetfulness. "I completely forgot—it sold early last week."

"Really?" Hilary asked, surprised. "I have to admit, I never thought anyone would ever buy that place. The house is practically a mansion. It's been on the market for what—four, five years? Why would someone with that kind of money move to Harmony?"

I shook my head and shrugged my shoulders. "Maybe they're on the run from the mob and need a place to hang out. This would be the town for that." I chuckled.

She looked over at me and laughed, swinging her arms as she walked. "That must be it."

Through my laughter, a tiny sting radiated within my chest at the idea of a new family living in that house. The Millers were the sweetest old couple, who'd built the place for their family over fifty years ago. I remembered my grandma saying how heartbroken they were once their children grew up and scattered around the country. Only one of their kids ever came to visit, and later helped move them into a retirement home.

"Well, it'll be good for you to have some neighbors. Your mom hates you living out here all by yourself. You do realize it would take the sheriff at least fifteen minutes to get out here, *speeding*, if you needed help?"

"Nothing bad ever happens in Harmony." I snickered. "Besides, my grandpa left me more than just his house: He also taught me how to shoot a gun." I tilted my head toward her, bent my knee forward, and pursed my lips, giving my best

*Charlie's Angels* gun-toting impression.

She laughed at me and took a long swig from her water bottle. "You're telling me—living out here in your grandparents' creepy old house—you don't ever get freaked out?" Hilary stopped walking and stared at me in disbelief. "The thought of you with a gun just makes me laugh, Cassandra. Sorry, but I mean come on, you weigh what—a hundred pounds?"

I raised my chin proudly. "One-twenty. Not that it matters."

Honestly, she was right. I always felt like a child when holding my grandfather's pistol during target practice. But still, it was registered and locked away in a safe under my bed, in case I ever needed it.

"The only thing that actually scares me is where I'm going to go swimming now."

"You still swim in the Millers' pool?" She shot me a disgusted glance.

I rolled my eyes. "Yeah. I help keep it clean, and in exchange I get to use it whenever I want."

"Don't expect a chance to say goodbye to it now," she teased.

I bit my bottom lip, annoyed I had another month of heat to endure with no place to cool off. At least I started my first year of teaching in a couple weeks, which would *hopefully* keep me distracted from the temperature.

Hilary and I were thrilled to both land jobs our first year out of college, and at the same elementary school. She'd quickly snatched up the second -grade position, which I'm sure had nothing to do with her godfather's position as principal. I, on the other hand, was about to give up finding a teaching job in town when Ashley Morgan—the newly married kindergarten teacher—announced her pregnancy and requested a year's leave of absence.

Three more weeks, and we'd officially be putting our higher education to use.

We climbed the last hill and rounded the final corner to find the moving truck parked at the top of the overgrown grass hill in front of the massive estate. The giant black wrought-iron gates separating it from the road were open.

"We should go introduce ourselves," Hilary said, grabbing my arm to stop me from passing the estate.

"Please tell me you're kidding." My eyes grew wide as I tugged my arm free.

"What? It's rude not to."

"No, what's *rude* is allowing their first impression of us to be like this." My gaze shifted between our bodies, soaked in sweat and undoubtedly giving off an unpleasant odor.

"Good point." She laughed, scrunching her nose. "Let's get out of here."

The moment we began walking away, my eye caught sight of someone stepping out the front door and walking down the porch stairs. The man was tall and lean with broad shoulders, and dressed in faded blue jeans and a black T-shirt that clung to his chest. My feet halted, giving my brain time to memorize the unexpected image.

The morning sun highlighted his golden-brown hair and the slight scruff over his jaw. My stomach clenched, and my breath hitched.

"Oh my God! Is that your new neighbor?" Hilary's shrill voice rang out and the man's head snapped to the side, his eyes staring straight down the driveway and landing on us. His brows rose as a seductive, crooked smile crept over his lips.

I couldn't put two thoughts together if my life depended on it, but my feet made me proud and somehow carried me at full speed away from the gate and to my own driveway next door. For the first time since I'd moved in the previous year, I was thankful I never got around to trimming the hedges that concealed most of the Millers' front yard. To my surprising satisfaction, though, I could still catch glimpses of him staring at us through the thin shrubs that were spaced too far apart for complete privacy.

The man was gorgeous—unlike any man I'd ever seen. Since Mark, no guy had caught my eye…not like that. For some reason I didn't understand, it terrified me.

Once I reached the end of my stone driveway, I pulled open the screen door, relieved Hilary hadn't changed her mind and tried to go talk to him. I felt disgusting—not the way I wanted to face a neighborly introduction. Hilary was laughing hysterically behind me, and I turned around to give her a piece of my mind the moment we stepped inside.

She choked back her remaining giggles and held up her hands to stop me before I got a chance to speak. "Relax, you look fine. Besides, he was all the way up the driveway. I'm sure he barely saw us."

*Oh, he saw us!*

I followed her into my kitchen and pulled two tall glasses from a cupboard. It was pretty damn evident that he not only saw us, but knew we were gawking like a couple of schoolgirls.

My stomach had just returned to its previous calm state, but the replay of his image sent it catapulting back through a wave of foreign emotion.

I wondered if he looked that good up close.

"So, how lucky are you!?" She smiled as I grabbed the ice tray from the freezer, glaring at her as I set it on the counter.

"We know nothing about him," I huffed, rolling my eyes and listening to the ice clink in the bottom of the glasses over her incessant cackling. "For all we know, he's married with five kids."

14

"Possibly...or maybe he's single and looking for a stubborn blonde schoolteacher to rock his world." She wiggled her brows in my direction and stood from her chair, crossing the small room to peer out the side window. From that position, there were no trees blocking the view to the Millers' back and side yards.

"*Rock* his *world?*" My voice dripped with repulsion at her choice of words.

"Well, it would do you some good. Loosen you up a little."

"I don't need to be...loosened up." I winced at my use of her words.

"When was the last time you went out with a guy, huh?" She craned her neck to look back at me and cocked an eyebrow.

My mouth snapped shut. She knew as much about my love life as I did. The only thing she didn't know was how much I missed being held—the simple touch of a man. I pushed the yearning away as I always did, refusing to dwell on it.

"Exactly. It's been a year since that asshole broke your heart. Time to get back out there and show off what the good Lord gave ya."

"Seriously?" I chuckled dryly, shaking my head. *So not my style.* Not that I had a style for picking up guys, but if I did, that wouldn't be it.

Her face lit up with a bright smile that showcased her perfectly straight, pearly white teeth. It spoke volumes, and I could tell she was on a roll now. Nothing I could say would make her stop.

"I say you go take a shower, let your unruly curls hang loose, and throw on one of those little whimsical summer dresses you keep hidden in the back of your closet—ooh, the one that looks like it was made from sheer vintage lace." Her grin grew wider. "Just strut on over there to introduce yourself, and you'll have him groveling at your feet in record time."

"Sure thing," I replied animatedly. "Why not?" I turned, pretending to follow her absurd directions, and burst out laughing when I halted halfway out the kitchen and turned around. "Oh that's right, I'm not a slut." I threw my hand in the air, giving her my best 'Oh, darn!' look.

Hilary turned her attention back out the window. "Well, don't say I never try to offer my assistance," she said with a short giggle.

I finished filling the glasses with water from the faucet and took a long, satisfying drink from mine. My dry lips and scorching throat stung for a brief moment as my body absorbed the liquid. I carried Hilary's glass to her and found myself staring out the window beside her.

There wasn't much to see besides an occasional middle-aged man wearing a blue polo and khakis lugging around boxes. There had to be at least a dozen movers filling the house with furniture.

"Looks like you were right."

I shifted my gaze to follow hers and noticed a small curly-haired boy wandering around the backyard. He was chasing a butterfly, running around without a care in the world. The picture he painted was adorable and sweet, and I found myself smiling when he jumped up, trying to capture the insect with no luck.

Despite the young boy's delightful traipsing around the yard, a pang of disappointment settled within me. I'd barely caught a glimpse of the man in the driveway. Why did I care if he had a family?

"Good for him," I said, pulling the curtain from Hilary's hand and letting it fall back into place.

She took a quick drink and walked back to the table, sitting down with her glass in hand.

"Once Caleb opens his new place, I'm sure you'll meet a nice guy to sweep you off your feet," she said.

"I'm done with men." I walked back to the sink and refilled my glass. "At least for a while." It wasn't a lie. My plans included fixing up my house and focusing on teaching. No man would fit into that.

"You can't be done already. You're only twenty-two years old! Way too young to be a man-hater."

I chose to ignore her, instead looking down at the melting ice in my glass.

"Come on—you've only had one serious boyfriend your entire life, Cassandra. Consider him your test run before meeting the perfect guy." Hilary maneuvered her chair to face me, causing a loud squeak to fill the small room as it slid across the linoleum. "Mark was a dick, but realistically, high-school sweethearts rarely work out. You have to put yourself back out there. Sheltering yourself in the middle of nowhere all the time is not the way to land a guy."

I raised my brows, giving her a cynical look. "Since when do you know how to land a guy? You never get past the first date." My voice was laced with amusement that I couldn't seem to hide.

"I'm waiting for Mr. Right." She grinned, but her voice faltered, and I caught a small glimpse of melancholy in her tone.

"You mean you're waiting for Caleb Townsend." I pulled out the chair across from her and sat down. It felt good to relax after our jog. I peeled off my shoes and socks using the tips of my toes. My bare feet tingled when the warm air hit them.

Hilary chugged the rest of her water and stood up,

ignoring my comment as she placed her empty glass in the sink. "I better get going. I need a shower, and then I need to pick up some groceries."

"Maybe you'll run into Caleb." I smiled, hoping to lighten her mood.

She rolled her eyes, but there was a subtle smile tugging at the corners of her lips.

I never thought a guy with a reputation for trouble like Caleb would catch her attention. But he did, and I'd been hearing about it from her ever since.

"I wonder if the little boy will be in your class," Hilary said, lingering in the doorway.

"Who knows? He looked too young for kindergarten." I hated to admit it, but a part of me hoped he wasn't in my class. Living next door to his father, who looked that amazing on moving day, would be hard enough.

She scoffed. "It's going to be interesting watching you with all those little kids, considering you're an only child and never even had a single cousin."

"Hey! I babysat."

"Mmm hmm, that's exactly the same thing." She laughed, walking toward the front screen door that allowed a cool breeze to fill the house.

"I'll see you Saturday at Caleb's grand opening, right?" I called out.

"Try Friday—I need your help finding the perfect dress. And I expect to have the full scoop on the new neighbors by then."

My gaze wandered back to the window when I heard the rickety screen door slam shut.

New neighbors—that would be a change I'd have to get used to. I wondered what the family's name was or, more precisely, what the gorgeous man's name was. He didn't appear to be more than thirty; maybe I was overstepping by assuming the little boy was his son. He could be his nephew, or even a family friend.

I looked down at my hands resting on the table and shook my head, laughing at my unrealistic-yet-wishful thinking. What was the matter with me?

After a few more minutes of enjoying the peace and quiet, I stood and walked to the sink, placing my empty glass inside. I was in desperate need of a cold shower—not just from the scorching run, but also from the sweltering image of the new mystery man forever engraved into my mind.

# Chapter Two

## FIRST IMPRESSIONS

I woke to the echo of hammering seeping through my open window. Rolling to my stomach, I buried my head in the cluster of pillows and groaned. I already hated having neighbors.

Slowly, the noise began to fade away, and my eyes slid shut. The haze of sleep was eager to claim me once more, and I was more than happy to comply when an unearthly roar filled my room, terrifying me wide awake. I leapt out of my once-cozy bed and whipped my head around to face the window, my chest heaving. The sound could only be described as a jackhammer, but what the hell would anyone need that kind of machinery for first thing in the morning?

"Ugh!" I stomped my foot on the cold floor, dragging myself out of the bedroom. My fingers ran through my disheveled hair, pulling out the knots they found as I headed down the short hall to find out what exactly was causing me to lose sleep.

I stopped in my tracks and grimaced at the grandfather clock in the corner of my living room.

"Damn." That couldn't be right—it read eight fifteen. My

internal alarm had always woken me first thing every morning at seven sharp for my run.

Annoyed, I brushed my hands over my sleepy eyes and sighed before continuing to the kitchen at the back of my house.

With a silent but wide yawn, I trudged to the window and pulled open the dull-green kitchen curtain decorated with faded embroidered flowers that I'd been meaning to replace. My gaze landed instantly on a young woman standing near the pool in the Millers' backyard.

Her long, light-brown hair lay stick-straight down her back. A trim body in tiny white shorts and a low-cut pink tank top told me everything I needed to know.

Damn it. Some people had all the luck.

She had to belong to the beautiful mystery man I'd spent my night dreaming about. No wonder I'd overslept—my internal alarm had been too busy enjoying the free show the nameless man put on for me last night. It'd been months since I'd experienced any sexual dreams due to the lack of stimulating men in my town, and this was by far the most memorable.

I sighed, wondering if someone had stolen my luck away. Perhaps I was suffering the consequence of a past life, doomed to watch everyone around me fall in love and live happily ever after while I baked birthday cakes for their kids—alone.

Whoever this girl was, she must have been amazing in her past lives because she had too much going for her. Even the estate she was now living in would fall under the category of 'dream house' for half the country.

She appeared to be barking out orders, one hand on her hip, the other pointing to different areas around the yard. I found her surprisingly irritating. It wasn't like me to be jealous, especially over a guy I'd not even officially met, but it wasn't just about him. I could never say it aloud, but a small piece of me envied her even with only one glance: gorgeous husband, adorable son, and a beautiful home. It was all I'd ever dreamed of.

I dropped the curtains and muttered, "Well, that's that."

It was official: Mystery man was off the market. There was no reason to waste any more time fantasizing about him finding me sunbathing in the backyard, wearing the tiny bikini Hilary had talked me into buying the previous summer. It wouldn't end with Mr. Hotness flirting and enticing me to join him for a dip in his pool; not only was he taken, but from the looks of it, the pool was being destroyed.

Just my luck.

⸻

Within the hour, I found myself falling back into my morning routine of jogging in peace. Hilary would never accompany me again—that I was certain of. In all the years I'd known her, I'd never seen her so exhausted. She worked out at the gym in the evening, which was the complete opposite of myself.

When I rounded the first corner, all thoughts of the Millers' pool and the flawless new neighbors had cleared from my mind. Everything was perfect. A dark cluster of clouds overhead shielded the morning sun, but I was grateful for the coolness it brought.

The fresh smell of dew and the morning air filled my nostrils with every soothing breath. Music blared in my ear, singing Adele on repeat.

A smile crept over my lips as I approached my usual turnaround point: the small road sign indicating 'You are now entering city limits.' My feet sprinted forward, quickening my pace. As I crossed the road to go back up the way I'd come, my entire body drained of all the serenity I'd felt moments earlier.

I continued jogging, but my steps grew slower and heavier as my eyes locked with his.

There he was: my new neighbor. The Greek god who'd filled my night with visions of endless passion was jogging, wearing nothing but a pair of dark-grey shorts that screamed designer and a devilish smirk. My gaze fell on his sculpted abs, and trailed down the perfect V that disappeared into his shorts.

Shaking my head to pull myself from my hypnotic state, I plastered the friendliest smile I could muster on my face and prayed it came off less awkward and contrived than I knew it was.

The catastrophic ripple of emotions whirling inside me left me dumbfounded. It wasn't like me to feel a pull like that toward any man—especially one who was possibly married. I reached down and slid my finger over my iPod, ending the music.

"Morning," he said, his eyes lit with amusement.

For some ungodly reason, I closed my eyes and continued jogging past him, too stunned to speak.

*Smooth.*

What was it about this guy that sent my body preparing for mutiny against every moral I swore I had? Thankful I'd passed him, I grew painfully aware he could possibly be turning around at the same location, which would put him directly behind me again.

My entire body went rigid. Damn, how long had he been behind me? The thought of having done something ridiculous or embarrassing with him unknowingly watching caused my ears to smolder and stomach to drop.

I'd never felt so self-conscious, and all I could do was replay the last half hour I'd spent running. Heat filled my body and a shudder shot up my spine, wrapping around my neck when the memory from fifteen minutes earlier replayed through my pounding head.

Noticing a puddle of water, I leapt over, arms fluttering gracefully over my head in what could only be described as a botched ballerina grand jeté.

I shuddered. What the hell was the matter with me? Thankfully I didn't expand on the thoughtless move, as doing so would've forced me to whirl around and see him sooner rather than later.

Instead, I continued jogging on, and...

*Oh, no.*

My blood ran cold, legs as heavy as weights slowing me down. Nausea shot through me and I flushed, cringing as my face grew hotter and, without a doubt, redder.

*Oh, God.*

I yanked out my ear buds with trembling hands and threw them over my shoulder, picking up my pace and trying not to collapse from humiliation. The memory of stopping to tie my shoes shortly after leaving the house hit me like a sledgehammer to the gut. After double knotting my laces, like a child, I'd stood, and...those damn shorts.

I blew out a ragged breath and bit hard on my bottom lip, recalling the moment I'd stood up and pulled free the shorts that were riding up my rear.

I wanted so badly for the earth to open up and swallow me whole.

I forced myself to believe he'd had yet to hit the pavement behind me when that had happened. The thought of him watching me remove a wedgie from my ass was too much to bear.

That was it. Not only did a flawless, confident beauty already have him, but I was the dork who danced over puddles and wore shorts so small they had to be physically removed from my behind.

*Yeah*, I thought, nodding my head. *No need to worry about impressing him now. Dear Lord, why did I have to wear this outfit today?*

I cringed, jogging faster and glancing down at my skintight shorts. They were a faded blue, with a pink stripe down each side. My mother had bought them when I joined track in high school...my freshman year. My halter top was nothing more than a grey sports bra, shrunken from multiple trips to the laundry room and showing off more than I intended on letting anyone around here see.

It was a rare occasion for someone to travel this road—especially at this hour. That is, until his moving truck nearly ran Hilary and me down...and now this.

I was pulled from my self-deprecation when I heard him clear his throat. *Oh no.* I looked to my left and there he was, in step beside me.

"Um...hi." I sighed at my lack of poise. Stuttering was not my usual conversation starter, but since we were both already aware of how giant an idiot I'd acted thus far that morning, I shook it off.

He was staring at me with a crooked smile as his gaze shifted shamelessly down to my chest.

I made a face I was certain he caught and pulled my top up, hoping to hide the cleavage spilling out that was capturing his attention.

A chuckle rumbled in his chest, but his face was impassive aside from the glimpse of light brightening his eyes before he looked straight out at the empty road ahead of us.

It was the sexiest laugh I'd ever heard.

Rolling my eyes, I continued my brisk pace, keeping my gaze ahead of me. *Okay, it wasn't that sexy.*

But trying to ignore the feelings creeping through my

25

body proved difficult. Every muscle worked overtime, trying to keep my pace while ensuring my figure appeared as attractive as possible.

*Give it up. He's married.*

A giant puff of air was pushed from my lungs when I laughed, relaxing. I was acting crazy. I'd never been one to get insecure over a guy, attractive or not, and I sure as hell wasn't going to start now.

"Do you always run this early...?"

"Cassandra," I said, answering the unasked question.

His lips pulled up in a ghost of a smile. "I'm Logan."

Finally—a name. Shifting my gaze to his hands moving in rhythm with his legs, I spotted an unadorned ring finger.

"So...?"

"Hmmm?" I was at a loss. What the hell was he asking now? Why couldn't we run in peace? It was bad enough having him look damn near lickable, and so close beside me.

"Do you run this early every day? You're in great shape." His gaze wandered down my body, lingering on my legs, and then back up as he grinned. "Very nice shape," he repeated in a gruff murmur.

I swallowed, blinking wildly, and looked down at my feet. *Keep them moving, one in front of the other,* I reminded myself. *He's nobody special.*

"Yeah. Every morning." I needed to get a grip, but the look in his eyes every time I glanced in his direction was absolutely mesmerizing. If I didn't know better, I would've sworn he was planning on snatching me up and devouring me in one giant bite. That look was powerful, and it left me breathless.

I wiped away the many inappropriate and vulgar thoughts that filled my mind and tilted my head in his direction.

"What about you? You seem in pretty good shape."

Finally, I could speak in complete sentences, and without a stutter.

His eyes lit. "Every morning. Although in the city, it was on a treadmill. This morning has been a very nice change."

I rolled my eyes. How long was he planning to keep this up?

"Right, well—"

My foot caught in one of the many potholes in the beat-up road and my body shot forward, arms flailing wildly. I knew what was coming, so I closed my eyes, scrunched my face, and waited for the impact.

Strong arms caught me around the waist, but it was too late to stop my one leg from giving out and skidding across the pavement, shredding the skin on my knee.

Logan's grip never faltered, and he slowly helped me up to a sitting position.

"I'm fine," I hissed, heat scorching my cheek. I was certain he was going to ask. I looked up, planning to deliver my best 'Seriously, I'm fine,' but the look of distress staring back at me left me frozen.

Pretending I wasn't hurt when his eyes were filled with genuine concern was impossible.

Hesitantly, I pulled my gaze away to focus on my knee. It was covered with dirt and oozing blood. I had a feeling I'd be picking pebbles out of it when I got home.

"That looks bad." He bent down to examine my wound; the muscles in his naked back flexed and glistened with a layer of sweat. He had to do more than simply jog in the morning to have a body like that.

His clean, masculine scent usurped my senses. He smelled exactly how I always imagined a real man was supposed to smell. Mark always sprayed on multiple layers of expensive cologne, masking his natural scent.

Completely mesmerized by his bronzed, taut skin, I didn't see him pull out a sleek black bottle.

I winced, biting back a groan of pain when he began spraying the icy water over my wound. The liquid ran down my knee, dulling the searing pain.

"Thanks," I mumbled, looking anywhere but into those captivating, hazy-blue eyes.

"You think you can walk back?" he asked, standing up. "You still have half a mile to go."

"I'll be fine." The thought of limping the whole way was disheartening, but what other choice did I have?

The smug grin I'd seen earlier replaced his concerned expression, and I couldn't help returning a smile when he reached out and pulled me to my feet.

I groaned as the pain ripped through my knee when the muscles pulled. My hands rubbed soothing circles around the area above the wound, but it did little to help.

"Hop on."

I looked up and saw Logan bent down, facing away. He slanted his head back and smirked.

"Come on, I'll give you a lift." His brows rose and he motioned his head for me to get on his back.

"You can't be serious!" I laughed nervously, waiting for him to stand back up laughing as well and telling me of course he was kidding.

"Get on, Cassandra." His tone was new—not playful, or even serious. It was demanding, yet gentle.

"Um…that's not really necessary," I choked out, stunned. The thought of wrapping my sweaty body around him was unbearable.

"You'll either get on my back, or I'll throw you over my shoulder." He stood and turned to face me, his expression giving nothing away. He was impossible to read.

I stiffened when I realized he wasn't joking.

"I don't—" My voice cracked, nervous laughter catching in my throat.

"All right, then, over the shoulder it is."

Before I could say another word or attempt to run—not that I'd get very far—he had his arms around my waist and my body thrown over his shoulder. He could pass for a firefighter, but I didn't need rescuing.

Panic set in as my eyes widened in shock. "Put me down!" I yelled, pounding my fists on his back as he began walking, clearly blocking me out. "I can walk!"

My mouth rested inches from his skin and his scent assaulted my nostrils at full force. *Focus, Cassandra, focus!*

Logan continued at a smooth, slow pace. He seemed to be enjoying himself too much to rush.

"You always this stubborn?" he asked, finally breaking the long silence.

"Pretty much," I mumbled through gritted teeth. My body had fallen limp in his arms, slung over his shoulder like a piece of meat. If only he had a cave to drag me into and ravish me until I forgot all about this humiliating stunt.

*Where the hell did that come from?* There was something about this guy that was so enticing, and I knew that was a bad sign.

He chuckled once. "Thought so."

When we reached my house, I sighed. *Finally*. He carried me up my driveway to my front porch.

I waited for him to set me down, but he didn't move. He just stood there, thinking or something. My body stiffened. I didn't like the idea of him thinking right then. I only wanted to run inside and slam the door in his face, no matter how much my body might disagree.

Looking back to see what he was doing, I gasped. He was blatantly staring at my ass that happened to be inches from his face. His searing breath hit the bare skin of my rear that peeked out from under my tiny shorts that were riding up once again.

"Put me down, you pig!" I yelled, smacking him on the back of his head.

He let out a deep, guttural laugh. His entire body pulsated, bouncing me up and down with the rhythm, before he finally put me down.

Once back on my feet, I straightened my shoulders, narrowing my eyes and pursing my lips.

"You should clean up that knee," he said, ignoring my look of disdain. All amusement was gone from his voice, but his eyes still danced with delight. "Hate to see those sweet long legs get an infection."

I rolled my eyes for the twentieth time that morning. What the hell was happening to me? I looked away and muttered, "Whatever. Thanks for the lift, I guess."

He turned around and headed down the driveway without another word.

Inhaling a deep, much-needed breath unaccompanied by Logan's delicious unfamiliar scent, I let it out just as I heard him call out.

"Anytime, sweetheart."

I looked over to see him standing at the end of the drive, a thoughtful smirk on his lips.

*Yeah, he was definitely behind me too long on my jog.*

Never again. From now on, I'd run in the evening.

# Chapter Three

## OLIVER

After showering and bandaging my knee, I spent the remainder of the day inside, blasting my favorite tunes to help block out the commotion next door.

Without any air conditioning, I was forced to open the windows to survive the intense heat wave that decided to hit right after lunch. I managed to remain busy to keep from replaying the morning's events over and over in my mind.

I dusted, vacuumed, and started a load of laundry before climbing the tiny ladder in the hall ceiling to pull down more of my grandparents' treasures tucked away in the attic.

When I'd first moved in, Hilary had helped me empty most of the old furnishings to make way for newer items more to my taste. It hurt to watch the house empty slowly, but I kept some of their art and knickknacks, and had yet to replace the curtains in a few of the rooms. It was beginning to feel more like home with the love of my grandparents built into the walls, wrapping me in a warm embrace.

After my grandfather died four years ago, my grandmother slowly faded away. His death was unbearable for her. It didn't help matters that her only child—my father—had disappeared years ago and didn't bother to show up for the funeral.

Every year, my father sent me a birthday card with a hundred-dollar bill and no return address. That was until my eighteenth birthday, when the card not only had an address on the outside, but a phone number written under his usual closing: 'Love you always, Daddy.'

I never called, but like I'd done with the many others cards before it, I stacked it in a small box and tucked it under my bed with the untouched cash still inside.

It was only a couple months after I received that card that my grandfather died. I asked my mother if anyone had heard from Martin, my father, but the look in her eyes told me no. He'd set himself up to be unreachable to everyone but me.

I felt the burden on my shoulders when my grandmother collapsed in her living room the night after she lost her husband. She needed her son, so I pulled out the child-sized shoebox and dialed the number.

A man answered on the second ring, and all I felt was sadness—no anger. I asked if Martin Clarke was there, and he said, "Speaking."

It was the moment of truth. I could've let out all my frustration and buried resentment at his ability to up and leave, but by that point, it didn't matter. My mother had done her best to raise me, and I loved her for it. I wasn't one to hold a grudge. He was Martin, not my daddy.

And I only had one thing to say.

"Your father died in his sleep last night. The funeral is this Sunday."

I hung up, feeling proud for doing my part—not for me, but for my grandmother.

I never told anyone I made that phone call, or that the number even existed. I debated telling my mother, but didn't want to let anyone down if he didn't show up. My mother's parents died in a car accident before I was born, but Martin's father treated her like a daughter—even more so given the disgrace of their son leaving her with a young child to raise on her own.

The day of the funeral came and went with nothing but tears and happy memories of my grandfather's long life. No one spoke about Martin, nor did he show up.

That was the final straw. I packed up all the cards with the crisp bills inside and sent them to the return address from the last birthday card.

My grandmother died in her sleep five months later on my grandfather's side of the bed, clutching a picture of her husband and son during happier times.

I didn't call the phone number that time. I no longer had it, and like before, he never showed up to the funeral.

So now, as I sat in the hallway with a box filled with my father's childhood mementos, it was easy to carry it outside and throw it on the burn pile.

—◆◆◆—

By the time the sun began to set, I had a spotless house and fewer items in the attic. It felt good. I sat on my back porch, finishing a plate of pasta I'd made for dinner and smiling at the beautiful array of colors in the sky. My nearly dry wash hung on the line, swaying in the breeze. The neighbors' horde of workers had retired for the evening, and my new patio chairs were comfortable enough to fall asleep in. Everything about that backyard was a happy memory. I sighed, completely relaxed.

The view from my property was nothing but a straight line of trees leading into the mammoth forest. My first and best childhood memories were made here, looking out at those trees. On the far left side of the lawn sat a tree fort my father and grandfather had built for my sixth birthday. They'd been grinning with excitement when my mother walked me out there, blindfolded, and they'd all yelled, "Surprise!" I still climbed up its ladder every spring and fall to sweep the cracked wood floor, dust away the spider webs, and make any necessary repairs.

My grandfather's toolshed was the one part of the house I never attempted to clean out. It was packed full of everything anyone could possibly need—not that I knew how to use ninety percent of his collection. Now, a screw gun or hammer and nails were a different story.

Feeling suddenly nostalgic, I set down my ice-cold glass of lemonade and began heading to my home away from home perched atop the fattest tree in the yard.

Glancing over at Logan's house, I scowled. The pool was destroyed, leaving a taste of contempt in my mouth toward his female friend for ordering it to be done.

He seemed overly flirty that morning, leaving me to wonder exactly what his relationship with the woman was. She could have been his decorator, for all I knew. There was no ring on his finger, but nowadays that didn't mean much.

Lost in my musings, I heard a *crack* sound out from the treehouse, followed by an ear-piercing scream.

Adrenaline shot through me, pushing me to run full speed at the tree and up the rickety ladder.

"Get 'im, get 'im, get 'im!" the small boy inside shrieked as he crouched in the corner.

I took a deep breath, relieved nobody was hurt, and followed his gaze to the corner across the tiny room.

"I tried scaring him away with that," he explained, pointing at a broom.

The boy began to stand. He was no taller than four feet,

34

and his mop of curls made it impossible not to smile.

I picked up the broom. Stiff with anxiety over what he was trying to scare away, I leaned down to find a small brown mouse trembling in the corner.

Poor thing. I'd never been a fan of the little creatures, but its giant ears and terrified shiver plucked my heartstrings.

"It's okay. He won't hurt you," I said, turning back with a smile. "We should get him back home, though. What do you say? Will you help?"

I watched as his concerned expression melted into a sliver of a smile.

"Will he bite me?"

"That depends." I smiled, standing back up. "Will you bite him?"

He giggled, shaking his head. "No!"

"Well, then, I think we're pretty safe." I laughed. "Can you hand me that box over there?"

He picked up the small wooden crate I'd once used to hoist up treats my mother would place inside for me to enjoy without having to climb down and handed it to me.

Crouching down on all fours, the boy returned to his spot in the opposite corner.

I reached under the table, staring at the terrified creature, willing it to stay still. *Please don't bite me.*

Surprisingly, I was calmer than I thought possible. This was very much out of my comfort zone, but considering I had no one else to help us, it left me in charge of stepping up.

My body tensed as I held the box out carefully—sympathizing with the horrified mouse frozen in fear, its eyes bulging—and dropped it over the creature.

"You got him!"

"We still need to get him outside, though." I glanced around, searching for something to slide under the box so I could lift it up, and found a square tin sign that had hung on the wall for years before it rusted across the top. My mother had had it made for me; it read 'Cassie's Castle.'

"Can you hand me that?" I pointed.

The boy stepped forward and handed me the sign. This time, however, he remained at my side, and even squatted down for a better view.

He began clapping, and a giant grin spread over his tiny face when I slid the sign under the box and pressed it to the bottom as I crawled backward slowly.

"Will he fall out?" he asked, his eyes wide with excitement.

"Not if I keep this pressed under here," I explained. "Let's go down and put him in the forest."

The climb down the ladder was not one I'd forget anytime soon. It was a struggle to maneuver holding tightly to the box while attempting to hide my terrified anxiety at the thought of the mouse running up my arm if I made a wrong move. Within minutes, we'd climbed down the ladder, and now stood at the edge of the tree line in my backyard.

"Ready?" I asked, watching him bounce up and down, nodding his head. *Adorable.*

Leaning down, I placed everything on the ground and stepped back.

"You can do the honors," I said, smiling down at him.

"Really?" His eyes grew wide with surprise.

"Yeah, all you have to do is lift the box," I said, noticing his apprehension.

He stepped forward, stood over the box, and glanced back at me. I gave him a reassuring smile, and his body noticeably relaxed.

When he pulled off the box, the mouse shot straight at him. His mouth flew open in a giant circle, spilling out a

36

laughable shriek.

The mouse continued past him and out into the sanctuary of the trees, leaving the boy jumping around, giggling hysterically.

"You okay?" I snorted. His laughter was contagious.

He nodded, grinning. "I've never seen a real mouse before. He was kinda cute."

"Yeah, he was," I agreed, but before I could say more or properly introduce myself, a woman's voice began yelling.

"Answer me, Oliver!"

"Uh-oh," he said, looking down at his feet.

I turned to see the stick-thin supermodel responsible for ruining my fantasies of Logan, as well as my pool. She was even more beautiful up close—exactly the type of woman Logan belonged with.

"There you are," she said, stopping abruptly a few feet away and staring between the boy I assumed was Oliver and me.

"We caught a mouse with giant ears and then I got to set him free!" Oliver grinned, looking back the way the mouse ran off. "You shoulda seen him!"

"Ew." Her face dripped with repulsion, and I couldn't help laughing.

She shot me a nasty look and I bit my lip, giving a tight smile.

"Hi, I'm Cassandra. I live here," I said, tilting my head back toward my house. "Oliver was just playing in my treehouse, and—"

"What?" she interrupted, her expression stern. "I told you to stay in your yard."

The look of despair in Oliver's eyes was one I recognized all too well. He was too young and innocent to have that amount of sadness written over his face. My chest tightened, and the sudden need to defend his actions pulled at my heartstrings.

"He was only here because I asked for his help. I'm not crazy about mice." I gave my most convincing apologetic face and hoped for the best. For the first time in my life, I'd lied without guilt. The smile on his face was worth it.

The young woman sighed. "Well, if you don't mind, Oliver needs to stay in his own yard. His father has enough trouble keeping his eye on him. The last thing he needs is Oliver wandering away."

"I really am sorry." It was all I could muster, because her expression shifted so radically from bitchy to protective and worried that I shuddered. Maybe my new neighbors weren't as perfect as I'd made them out to be.

Her expression softened, and she smiled down at Oliver. "It's fine. I just worry about him out here. He's only four, and living this far out of town—with no friends around to play with—it's not fair for him."

I nodded. It was true—there were no other small children living in the area. It was one of the few things I'd disliked when I'd stayed with my grandparents any longer than a night.

"I'm sure your son will find a lot of fun things to do out here. I always did when I was younger." I stopped talking when she began to laugh. Her face had turned soft and friendly.

I pulled my brows together, unsure what I'd said that was funny. Was there something on my face? My body stiffened, and I ran my hand over my hair self-consciously.

"Oliver's not my son." She was smiling; however, this time it was focused on Oliver, who was snickering as well. "I've gotten that a lot this weekend. I'm his aunt, Julia."

I sucked in my lips, giving a tight, embarrassed smile, and nodded. "Logan's your brother?"

The rate at which the smile dropped off her face nearly caused me whiplash. Instantly, her casual friendly demeanor was wiped away and the bitchy girl was back, glaring at me.

"You already met Logan?" she asked through gritted teeth. Her voice dripped with disdain.

I unconsciously took a step back. *What the hell just happened?*

"Um, yeah," I muttered, confusion undoubtedly written all over my face. "He seems...nice."

She puffed out a breath of air and crossed her arms over her chest. "Oliver, why don't you go inside and get cleaned up for dinner?" she said, her eyes never straying from mine.

I stiffened, waiting like a child to be reprimanded for something I was innocent of as my subconscious began screaming, 'Uh-oh.'

Refusing to be intimated, I broke her gaze and smiled at Oliver.

"Thanks again for your help."

"No problem. Maybe next time we'll catch a snake!" He grinned, and for the first time, I saw his father. It was almost the exact grin Logan had thrown me more than once that morning.

"Oliver..." Julia warned.

"I'm going." He pouted. "Bye, Cassandra." He waved as he walked away, leaving me face to face with his strangely terrifying aunt.

She stood my height—barely five six—and weighed no more than I did. I felt fairly confident I could take her if need be, as I was more athletic in stature than she was. Problem was, I still had no clue what the reason for needing to take her down was.

"Stay away from Logan," she hissed once the door slammed shut behind Oliver. "He needs to focus on his son, not you."

"I'm not—"

"Logan's not known for self-control. If you show interest in him, he'll waste no time luring you into his bed and, if you're lucky, possibly keep you around for a day or two. But that's all you'll get." Her tight expression and cold tone slowly began to soften, which I had a feeling was due to my stunned expression.

I was well aware exactly how unlucky I was in life, so I nodded dumbly, taken aback by her harshness. "All right."

"I'm sure you think I'm a bitch. I don't mean to come off like some crazed sister from hell, but you have to understand, my only concern is for Oliver. I saw the way he looked at you—he likes you, and he just met you. Oliver's not normally one to speak to strangers, let alone make friends with them." She dropped her arms from her chest and sighed. "Look, Logan plans on living here for at least two years, so the last thing Oliver needs is to have you pissed off at his father when he plays with your emotions and then drops you like last week's garbage."

"No offense, but you're really good at making your brother sound like a jerk—you do know that, right?" A nervous laugh escaped my lips, but I was completely serious.

"He's really not." She laughed softly, walking back to the house. I followed, listening intently to every word.

"Logan's an amazing brother and father. He's paying my tuition at school and all my expenses, and spends nearly every Sunday with our mother. The whole reason he moved here was because he wanted Oliver to be close to me while I went to school. I start this fall at the college in town. Logan just...doesn't let anyone besides family get...close."

Just as we stopped at Logan's back door, the realization hit me: If Julia wasn't Oliver's mother, than where was she?

40

"She broke his heart," Julia said, reading my mind. "Oliver's mother was everything to Logan. She left shortly before Oliver's first birthday and hasn't come around since."

My heart broke not only for Logan, but also for his innocent son. The sadness in his eyes now made even more sense, and I wished I could take it away for him. I knew all too well what it was like to have a parent disappear out of your life, never to be heard from again.

"I like Oliver. He seems like a sweet kid. I don't mind keeping an eye on him when I'm around. As far as his father goes, I'm actually known to have impeccable self-control." I laughed, lightening the somber mood we'd fallen into.

"It was nice meeting you, Cassandra." Julia smiled sincerely. "Once school starts up next week, I won't be around much. I'm staying at the dorms, so I'm glad you'll be right next door."

"I have to ask: Why would you move here to go to school? Harmony has the smallest college in the state. I graduated from there last month, and I have to admit it's nothing special."

"One guess," she said, smiling ear to ear.

I knew that look—it was the same one Hilary got every time Caleb was mentioned.

"Ah." I chuckled. "The things we do for men."

I left after we exchanged parting pleasantries of "Nice to meet you" and "We should get together sometime", and found myself whistling on the short walk to my own back porch.

Julia was lovely, and just the type of girl I'd want living next door to me. Although she'd be living in a dorm, she planned to be around, and I looked forward to getting to know her better.

Grabbing the warm glass covered in condensation from the heat, I felt a strange tingle flutter through my stomach. I

41

looked up across the yard, and there standing beside the house, feet away from where Julia and I had just been talking, was Logan.

I swallowed loudly, my gaze locking with his. I couldn't smile or look away. I was frozen, unsure if he'd heard any of our conversation.

He blinked and dropped his gaze to the ground, then slowly drew it back up at me. His expression was heavy in thought, and I knew he'd heard us.

A deep breath helped soothe away some of my nerves, and I was finally able to pull my lips into a kind smile.

Logan continued staring, his brows pulled in. Deliberately, that sexy smirk appeared, and he was back to the man I'd met earlier.

I laughed to myself, shaking my head as I walked inside, ignoring the growing attraction and flurry of emotions inside me that I knew I could never act on.

# Chapter Four

## THE MUFFIN MAN

The next day, I woke early and watched out my front-room window, waiting for Logan to appear for his morning jog. At seven thirty, he walked out his front door, shirtless and gorgeous, and stared over at my house.

I dropped the curtain in my front room, startled. I didn't want him to see me gawking. I really wasn't.

Okay, maybe a little.

He seemed to be waiting, taking his time to stretch. I peeked out again as subtly as possible, and caught his occasional glance back at my house. Every time he bent down to stretch another part of his toned body, I felt the image etch itself into my brain. *Damn him.*

Finally, after what felt like forever considering I was flushed with lust, he took off down the road.

I'd planned on becoming a night runner, but today I needed my morning jog more than my mother needed her coffee.

Grabbing the small duffle bag I'd stuffed with clean clothes for later, I sneaked out and hopped into my car. If I couldn't run here, I'd find somewhere else. There were lots of great trails in the area.

My biggest concern was getting out of the house after Logan left—not only because I didn't want to get talked into jogging with him, but because I knew if he challenged me I'd have gone with it. I hated my competitive side sometimes.

Also, because I wanted to see his face when I passed.

*HONK!*

Logan stopped abruptly, turning slightly to face my car. But if the horn had startled him, it didn't show in his expression. *Damn!*

I drove past, smirking. *That's right—chicks can smirk too.*

———◆———

By the time I'd finished jogging around the riverbed, which was located just inside city limits and less than two miles from my house, I felt not only satisfied, but proud.

Instead of driving back to my house and running the risk of seeing Logan again this early, I headed to Hilary's apartment.

"Thanks for letting me shower here," I said, sauntering out of the bathroom, hair wrapped up in a towel on the top of my head.

"Of course, but I still don't understand what the big deal is." She handed me a glass of orange juice and sat down with her coffee. "Maybe his sister was exaggerating."

I gave her a skeptical look and took a sip of the cool juice.

"You never know." She shrugged.

With an unconvinced eye roll, I set down my glass. "She seemed pretty sincere to me. But it doesn't really matter, anyway. I won't take a chance and have it turn sour, and then be stuck living next to him. Besides, Oliver's a good kid, and with school starting soon, I'll have a class of students to keep me busy."

"All right," she said. "If you think you can stay away from him, then good for you." She scrolled through her phone, looking semi bored.

"What's that supposed to mean?" I asked, appalled.

"I'm just saying it's been a while since you've been with a guy, and it's obvious you're attracted to him...so we'll see." She sipped her steaming cup of coffee, her finger still tapping at her phone, but the corner of her mouth twitched with the faintest smile.

*I'll show her.* I could be around Logan and resist any charm he threw my way. Besides, he'd given me no real reason to think he was interested in me. I imagined the women he seduced looked more like a plastic Barbie and less like a fresh-out-of-college teacher.

No matter the amount of attraction and pure lust I felt toward Logan, I'd stand my ground to not only protect my heart, which I knew would get hurt, but also because I felt I owed it to Oliver. He had a look that told me he needed people to look out for him. Between Oliver and my heart, I'd never let either get hurt.

———◆◆◆———

For some unexplained reason, I found myself in my kitchen the moment I stepped inside my house. I spent the afternoon baking two dozen delectable muffins with fresh blueberries. Due to the broken air conditioner, every window in my house was open. Today, it created a perfect scent, the breeze swirling with the aromas from my new oven. I was too cheap to get the air conditioner fixed, but top-of-the-line kitchen appliances were another story. It was heaven.

After dinner, I placed all the muffins—minus the four I'd already eaten and would regret the next time I slipped on my bikini—in a large basket I'd stored in the spare bedroom.

45

Walking across my yard, muffins in tow and seeing the sun was beginning to set, I realized I'd lost track of time. Arranging that many muffins to create a picture-perfect display took nearly as long as creating a flower arrangement, and still, I knew it could've looked better. My Martha Stewart OCD was showing again; I blamed that on my grandmother.

Glancing down at my watch, I saw it read eight forty-five. Interrupting bedtime for Oliver hadn't been my plan, but I was already here and the muffins were deliciously fresh.

"Just drop it," Logan's smooth voice called out.

My head snapped up, my feet halting a stone's throw from Logan's front door, which was cracked open. I knew his remark was not meant for me, considering it was followed by a very feminine moan.

"Don't you have a bed in this giant house?" the woman giggled, and I felt my gag reflex kick in. Time to abort my official welcome-to-the-neighborhood mission.

I turned to tiptoe away from the door, my focus so transfixed on getting out of there as quickly and quietly as possible that I didn't see the black urn filled with dead flowers behind me.

I bit my bottom lip hard, but the crashing of the vase against the cement porch sent my nervous system into overdrive, and all I felt was the searing gaze of someone in front of me.

"Cassandra," Logan said, his eyes lit with amusement, yet his expression indifferent.

My cheeks scorched, my palms digging into the rough handle of the basket.

Why did my name sound so incredibly sexy rolling off his tongue? I shook my head once, blinking wildly to pull myself out of the trance his state of undress caused.

He stood there under the porch light, wearing a pair of

46

light-wash jeans with the top button popped open and an unbuckled belt. His long-sleeved button-down shirt was rolled up to his elbows and hung completely open. I'd seen his bare chest before, but with a crisp white shirt exposing just a teasing amount, I was mesmerized.

I'd definitely interrupted someone tonight.

The naughty thoughts that crept through my mind in record time both appalled and fascinated me, as did my body's incredible reaction to them.

*Damn it. Pull yourself together, Cassandra!*

"Sorry, I didn't mean to…interrupt," I stuttered, looking anywhere but at him.

The woman, whom I assumed was responsible for his nearly nude state, had appeared at some point and was standing behind him. Her chest pressed against his back and her eyes screamed at me to get lost.

Pulling myself out of my thoughts, I recognized her from around town: Katie. She was a grade above me in high school. I remembered her as one of the annoyingly popular girls.

"It's not a problem, sweetheart. Did you need something?" He seemed oblivious to the woman rubbing her hands up and down his forearms, kissing the back of his neck. He raised his shoulder where her lips lingered, forcing her face away.

She frowned, looking both embarrassed and annoyed. His gaze never strayed from mine as his usual smirk crept slowly over his luscious lips.

*No, not luscious!*

"Hmmm?" I asked. All I could see was the perfect stubble surrounding his chiseled jaw and plump, kissable lips.

*Think, Cassandra.* Why was this so hard? I'd never had this reaction to a man before.

I shook my head again. "Right, I made these for you and

Oliver." Finally, something that pulled me back to reality: Oliver, his son. The son who needed me to stay off—no, *away from*—his father.

My arms had been like dead weights working against me, but suddenly I began finding my way out of my lust-fueled fog. I held out the basket for him to take, but his face was marred with confusion.

He glanced down at the basket, then back up at me. Was he debating whether he wanted them? I spent so much time making sure they not only tasted perfect, but also creating a brilliant presentation. I at least wanted Oliver to have them. Worry was settling in my gut. *Why did I come here? What was I thinking?*

Suddenly, his expression softened, and a smile pulled at his lips. It was unlike any others I'd seen on him before, or even the grins he gave during our disastrous jog. This smile was warm and genuine, and matched his equally soft eyes. I stood there with bated breath, practically swooning over him.

*Damn it.*

"Thank you. Oliver went to visit his cousin for the night, but I'm sure he'll enjoy one when he returns."

I smiled, appreciative for him stowing away his cocky attitude.

"Ooh, those look good!" Katie grabbed the basket from Logan, planting an exaggerated kiss on his cheek in the process, and disappeared inside the house.

I fought back the urge to race past him and tackle her to the ground, screaming, *"Not yours, slut!"* But instead, I did what I always did when faced with frustration: I gave a polite, tight-lipped smile and turned to leave.

A part of me wanted him to tell me to wait—not the logical part of my brain, obviously. There was nothing left to say, and even if there was, he was definitely off limits and I was strong enough to resist.

But after that sweet smile, it didn't matter what he had to say. I only wanted another excuse to stare a second longer. That was all I needed—one more second to capture his essence and lock it away for my dreams.

I hated that I felt like an irresponsible girl, but a man that good looking was a crime against women. How could anyone expect *us* to keep our hands to ourselves around that— especially when you added in his relentless charm and tempting allure?

"Cassandra."

I stopped, my stomach flipping violently and my ears smoldering. *Did he really just say my name? Why does he want me to stop?*

Everything inside me screamed to stay strong, keep walking, and pretend I didn't hear him. *Run away! He's a player, womanizer, and flat-out man whore, according to his own sister.*

But instead of doing the smart thing for once in my life, I listened to my body—to those urges kept dormant since my breakup with Mark over a year ago.

"Yeah?" I asked tentatively, turning back just enough to see him.

"Would you like to join us, sweetheart?" His lips pulled up, spreading into a wide grin. His eyes glistened under the porch light, filled with something dark and primal.

*Ew! No thank you!* Julia was right: complete player. *What the hell was I thinking?*

The smug look on his face remained unfazed as I scoffed and turned back around, heat undoubtedly brightening my cheeks. I left without another word, chastising myself for letting him see even the slightest shred of attraction I felt.

Never again. He was an arrogant jerk, and I wasn't about to be pulled into his clutches.

# Chapter Five

## THE POWER OF MEN

"You're sure I look all right?" Hilary asked for the fifth time in the last hour.

I glanced up from the sink in my tiny bathroom and grimaced. Nerves tainted her usually cool poise. This was not like her at all. I'd seen her get ready for numerous dates with attractive guys, and never once did she care about her outfit or how her hair looked. But an invitation to the grand opening of Haven, Caleb's bar and grill? Watch out.

"No, you don't look all right." Looking back into the mirror, I swiped on a hint of pearly lip gloss and glanced up at her reflected response. Her eyes were narrowed at me.

"You look hot!" I laughed. "What the hell is wrong with you?"

She cracked a slight smile that begged to shine brighter, but her body remained noticeably rigid. "I should have worn the green one," she sighed.

The dress Hilary was wearing looked absolutely flawless on her: a classic little black dress with a soft neckline that flared out in the skirt, showing off her long tanned legs.

I remained silent, swiping on a touch of smoky eye

shadow and deep-black mascara. I couldn't wait until the party was over and I'd have my friend back to her perky, confident self.

Hilary shoved me over and pulled the makeup from my hands just as I finished. I turned to scoff, but noticed the corner of her lips pulled up slightly. *About time.*

Backing out of the tiny room, I wondered why she was still standing in front of the mirror rolling on another layer of mascara. She'd started getting ready for tonight's party the moment she awoke…yesterday morning.

"The sales clerk said it brought out my eyes," she called out.

I sat down on my couch in the front room. Why she was still stuck on the damn green dress was beyond me.

"And I told you, the one you're wearing is perfect. Now stop worrying." It was all I was going to say on the matter. If only she knew the truth about her love-at-first-sight, must-buy-now emerald cocktail dress.

I had to admit, the moment she'd spotted it in the boutique window the previous day, I was equally mesmerized. The price tag was a bit steep for my taste—or, more accurately, my budget—but completely worth it for the right occasion.

The problem arose when Hilary sauntered out from the dressing room and my eyes flew straight to the tiny pooch the fabric created around her midsection.

Growing up, Hilary was naturally fit, but through college, her figure grew from toned to curvy. She fully embraced her new appearance, as did the local boys.

Over the winter—the last semester of college before graduation—she'd spent a little too much time inside stressed about exams and fueling up on junk food. Honestly, the weight was hardly noticeable, distributed evenly through her tall body. But the green dress somehow created a less-than-appealing illusion of a tummy she didn't have.

So I did what any good friend would do: I lied, telling her it looked great but that the black one we'd been looking at earlier was worth trying on as well. The lively sales clerk nodded along with a supportive smile and handed her the new dress.

Once Hilary disappeared behind the black curtain, I turned and gave an appreciative smile, finding the employee with a look of 'Close call.' That's right: Girls stick together. You don't send another female out there in a dress that accentuates every flaw she wants to hide. At least, I could never do that, and it was a relief to see I wasn't alone.

Hilary had walked out of the dressing room, twirled in front of the mirror, and watched the black dress flutter around her hips with a building confidence.

"Perfect!" I said, beaming. "Caleb will never be able to resist you in that."

With a relieved grin, I turned to catch the clerk's icy stare narrowed at Hilary.

I winced at the sudden shift in the room. It was distressing. You would've thought the busty, flame-haired clerk saw us robbing the place at point-blank range; her friendly, animated smile had been replaced with a nasty sneer.

"On second thought, I loved the green one," the clerk bit out, feigning sincerity. "It really brings out your eyes."

*Bitch.* I wanted to leap off the fluffy ottoman I'd sat perched on for the last twenty minutes and rip out her bobbed short hair. Looked like Hilary was in for some competition in the Caleb department.

Luckily, after the best murderous glare I could muster in the once-comrade-now-bimbo's direction, the girl retreated without another word.

What was it about men that turned females against each

other in less than a second flat?

Shaking the disheartening memory of our shopping trip away, I looked up to find the clock reading eight thirty. Time to get going.

"Seriously, you look great. Now let's go, or we'll be unfashionably late," I called out from the living room after slipping on my red pumps and grabbing my clutch. It was an accessory I always thought foolish to have in a small town like Harmony, but I couldn't resist. It was also the only thing in the expensive boutique I could afford.

My outfit was the complete opposite of Hilary's: whitewashed skinny jeans with a white tank top under a grey fitted blazer. I left my hair down, letting it air dry to show off my natural curls. Everyone always seemed to compliment me when I wore it that way. The red heels were as dressy as I was getting. It was a restaurant opening in Harmony, not Manhattan.

"Ready," Hilary said.

She stepped out, and for the first time all day, she stood tall: shoulders back, head up, a smile on her face.

There was my best friend; I knew she was in there somewhere. Hopefully I could keep the babbling freak from earlier hidden in its dungeon once she actually encountered Caleb.

———◆◆◆———

Twenty minutes later, we were parked in the back lot of the restaurant. Hilary had spent most of the drive either glancing in her compact mirror or fidgeting with her hair while shifting in her seat.

"Ready?" I asked, switching off the engine and turning in my seat to face her.

She nodded and smiled. "Why do I feel like I'm walking

into a firing squad?" She looked down, embarrassed. "Sorry. I don't know what the hell's happening to me."

"It's fine. I've grown used to your Caleb-induced freak fests. I was beginning to miss them."

We both laughed as we climbed out of the rusted red Volkswagen Beetle my grandfather had fixed up for my sixteenth birthday.

"Make me a promise?" I stepped around her, blocking her path just as we hit the sidewalk in front of the lively restaurant, which blared soft rock music.

Hilary stepped back, nerves clouding her expression, and gave me a tense smile.

"No matter what happens with Caleb—"

"I know, I know. I'm still gorgeous and perfect and deserve better if he can't see that. I got it already. I love you, but I'll be fine, really."

My brows rose, a smile tugging at my lips. "Actually, I was going to say I don't want to hear you moping around for the next week if nothing happens, but yeah, let's go with yours."

Her mood lightened and she was smiling brightly when we walked through the double glass doors held open by black painted cinder blocks.

"There he is," Hilary whispered the exact moment our feet stepped inside.

I held my lips together tightly, stifling my laughter. The excitement in her voice was refreshing.

To my surprise, I felt a pang of jealousy. The last time I'd felt that level of excitement was the day Mark and I had moved in together.

The thought of him forced my head to whip around, praying he wasn't there tonight. I'd done fairly well avoiding him after the disaster of moving out the day after I'd caught him cheating last summer.

He refused to leave the apartment that day, watching me the entire time, shooting off excuse after pitiful excuse for why Mackenzie had been in our bed. With him. Naked. But I'm not a moron. No number of excuses was going to stop me from throwing everything I owned into boxes and shoving them into the back of my friend's pickup truck.

Mark finally relented, and with the final box, he'd had the gall to sit on the floor, head hung low, and tell me he'd always love me. All I could think was that couldn't have been love. If it was, I didn't need it. Love be damned; I never wanted to feel that vulnerable and broken again.

Since that dreadful day last summer, we'd had very few run-ins, and not a single one resulted in a word being spoken between us. I only hoped tonight wouldn't change that.

I followed Hilary, smiling and nodding hello to the many familiar faces. It was a great turnout and, as I spotted Caleb across the room, I could see the pride written clearly on his face.

It was no longer the outdated diner I grew up eating in, having a mother who never cooked. The diner had practically been a second home when I was not staying with my grandparents.

That is, until three years ago, when the owner died and his son, Josh, ran the business into the ground. The place turned into a dump and, as rumor had it, Caleb won it in a poker game. Not only had he added an extravagant bar and dance floor, which was the highlight for most everyone my age, but he'd practically rebuilt the place from the ground up. I was proud of him.

Unlike Hilary, to me, Caleb was never anything more than the boy who lived across the street and scared off the bullies who dared me to eat a worm when I was six. We'd never been particularly close—more like distant cousins who got along when we were around each other.

Hilary turned on her heel, stopping me in my tracks, and whispered, "Oh my God."

I expected her to say more, but instead, she gripped my arm. A hiss poured out through my gritted teeth from the pain. I looked down to make sure her nails hadn't broken the skin. All clear, thankfully. The line to the ladies' room was crazy, so cleaning up a battle wound was not on my itinerary tonight.

"Is he looking at us?" she whispered.

I pulled my wide eyes away from her fingers, pouting over the fact that that they were still digging into my arm, and followed her gaze. Caleb was staring directly at us, smiling and holding up his wine glass, motioning for us to come over.

First things first: I needed to pry her manicured claws out of my skin. She finally noticed, and gave an apologetic shrug as she loosened her grip immediately.

I could only chuckle. I understood all too well. It'd been a long time since I'd felt that crazy enamored feeling, but I remembered it. All actions on her part tonight would fall under the best-friend clause: *Thou shalt not be punished when butterflies are controlling thy body.*

Weaving through the crowded room was not as easy as I'd anticipated. I somehow found myself leading, which was bizarre considering Hilary had started in front. She was now trailing behind, walking no faster than a sickly snail and just as pale. I could only imagine the emotions ripping through her as we grew closer to the one guy who'd unknowingly held her affections.

Caleb's father, who owned the local law firm, bragged for years about Caleb going off to college to later join the family business. Instead, he'd skipped town right after high school, never to be seen again.

His return came as a surprise to pretty much everyone in

town. The renovation of the diner went on for a few months without anyone knowing the identity of the new owner until he appeared suddenly two weeks ago. Now here he was, over five years after he left, and just as handsome as ever. His light-brown hair was shorter than in high school, but still covered his ears in a shaggy mop. Bright-green eyes lit his masculine face; he was no longer a boy.

He reeked of cool indifference in black trousers and a simple untucked white dress shirt, which was unbuttoned at the top. A black tie draped around his neck was loosened and untidy. The leather strings wrapped around his wrist were frayed and ragged, but they only added to his appeal; very few men could pull off the effortlessly attractive look like he did. His lean build was less muscular and more toned and athletic. He was tall and attractive, and looked like he'd just finished a photo shoot for *GQ* magazine, but still, it did nothing to stir any feelings inside me.

"Hey, Cassie. You made it." He still had that mischievous lopsided smile that made you wonder what he was up to. Caleb Townsend was always up to something.

"Surprised you remember me," I replied, smiling.

"How could I forget?" His lips twitched, attention turning to Hilary as he continued. "Cassie here once left the light on in her room after dark, and from across the street I could see her singing into her hairbrush, dancing on her bed."

Hilary giggled as her eyes locked with Caleb's, and all I could do was give a tight, annoyed laugh. I remembered the night vividly—or, more accurately, the next afternoon, when he came over to tell me to close the curtains at night after teasing me for at least ten minutes.

"She had moves." Caleb chuckled, looking at me and taking a swig of his drink.

I quickly noticed he was looking past me. I tensed the

moment I felt hot breath caress my ear from behind.

"I wouldn't mind seeing a few of those."

I knew that voice and that masculine fresh scent, and I could already visualize the smirk covering his gorgeous lips.

*No, not gorgeous. Not sexy. Not even attractive. Ugly! Hideous as a troll living under a rotting bridge.*

I turned slowly, my eyes connecting with Logan's.

*Damn it. Definitely not a troll.*

"Hello, sweetheart."

As expected, there were those tempting lips that made my insides shudder and quake. His eyes raked over my body, ignoring the aggressive glare on my face.

"I'm not your sweetheart," I scoffed.

The corner of his lips turned up even further as he sipped his drink: scotch, from the look and smell of it.

*Too close.* I stepped back.

"Do you mind not hanging out behind me?" My tone was harsh—just the way it sounded in my head, thankfully. I wasn't going to fall victim to his charm and let him watch me get all flustered. He had plenty of other girls to put on that show for him.

I folded my arms across my chest, eyebrows rising as I waited for him to move anywhere but directly behind me. Instead, he leaned into me, placing his empty hand on my shoulder.

My breath caught when his thumb rubbed small circles into my blazer. Thank God I'd worn that. His breath was again caressing the lobe of my ear again, his stubble so close it nearly brushed my cheek. He totally knew what he was doing to me.

"But it's so lovely back here…" he murmured, his voice gruff, "…sweetheart."

Before I could retort or slug him, he was turning and walking away.

58

I took a deep breath and turned my attention back to Hilary, who was now standing in front of Caleb talking, oblivious to my interaction with Logan.

"Second-grade teacher, really?" Caleb said to Hilary. "Lucky kids."

Hilary blushed, looking down at her drink. "I have to admit I was surprised to hear you were back in town, and that you bought this place."

"Wasn't my plan, to be honest. This place ended up in my hands, and I decided why not go back to my roots for a while?" He smiled.

"So you won't be staying long?"

"You never know. I was thinking about finding a good manager to take care of things here once it's running smoothly, but then again, I might find a reason to hang around a while."

"There's not really much in Harmony worth sticking around for." She frowned, oblivious to his deeper meaning and hungry eyes.

Caleb chuckled. "I have a feeling Harmony has a lot to offer this time around."

Hilary looked up to meet his eyes, and I suddenly felt awkward staring.

I turned around, surveying the room, and found Logan at the bar ordering another drink. He wore the sexiest pair of black dress pants that hung low on his hips, and his grey V-neck tee accentuated his muscles. His arms weren't massive, but they were enough to feel safe in if they were wrapped around my—.

I shook the thought away and choked down a giant gulp of the expensive wine I snatched off a passing tray. Only Caleb would serve free wine that tasted this good. I drank the remnants of the liquid and handed it to yet another passing waiter a moment later. The wine alone was worth coming out for, and would be my next reason to come back. Delicious.

"You should come with me," Caleb said, catching my attention when I noticed Hilary standing motionless, not answering him.

The beginning of the conversation was lost on me, so I had no idea what to say when her eyes flickered in my direction. I smiled, and my shoulders rose and fell.

"Um…yeah, I would love that. I mean…if you want…um…" Hilary's poise was slipping. It was time to retreat before she embarrassed herself.

"We should go say hi to some friends." I slid my arm through hers. "Congratulations again, Caleb. I'm sure you'll see us back often."

I was certain Hilary would be a regular customer at the establishment when not at school.

"It was good seeing you again, dancing queen." He chuckled and returned his gaze to Hilary, his expression soft. "I'll be in touch with you soon."

Hilary said nothing, only nodding with a giant grin as I pulled her through the crowd.

She was freaking out on the inside—that much was evident—when we stopped at the end of the bar. I asked for two more glasses of wine, but quickly noticed she'd had yet to touch the one in her hand.

*More for me.*

Glancing around the room, I felt good. I rarely drank, but there was something enticing about the unusual music, the crowded room full of smiling people, and Logan staring at me.

*Logan is staring at me!*

I whipped my head down and focused on the surface of the bar in front of me. Caleb really did do a good job with the renovations. I sneaked a quick glance up and found Logan with a straight face, eyes still locked on me.

I shot him an annoyed glare, but he only laughed.

"Can you believe it?" Hilary asked.

"Hmmm?" Had she said something?

"Caleb invited me to go see the end-of-summer parade with him next weekend."

She was beaming, and I couldn't help but smile. She deserved happiness, and ever since we were kids, the only time she lit up like that was when Caleb came around. I sometimes wondered if that was the reason she always liked hanging out at my house. Her home was a lot more fun; my dad was long gone, and my mother was a workaholic. What was fun about that?

"I think he has a thing for you."

I rolled my eyes when I realized she was staring at Logan. *Always the hopeful romantic.*

"Not happening," I snorted. Where were our drinks?

"Come on! He's cute, single, and he lives a few steps away from you. Why not just take a chance?"

"The list is too long," I muttered.

Hilary gave up and dropped the subject, turning away to talk with old friends we went to school with. I chanced another—this time subtle—glance in Logan's direction.

I regretted it instantly. He was no longer looking my way, wearing the mysterious smirk that made me wonder what exactly I secretly adored. Instead, I found him leaning against the bar, captivated by the familiar raven-haired woman in front of him.

My head dropped. I struggled to find my next breath as my stomach began filling with angry fireflies, burning to get out. I snatched the glass from Hilary's hand and swallowed it with one loud gulp.

"You all right?" she asked concernedly, surprised by my actions. We'd been friends since we were still in diapers;

61

whatever she saw on my face caused hers to contort in nearly as much panic as I was feeling. She turned to see what could've upset me, her forehead marred with worry lines.

"Cassandra." Her voice was full of the one thing I despised when she spotted Mackenzie pawing at Logan: pity.

I shoved past everyone in my way. I needed to get out of there. I felt like a caged animal, ready to tear apart anyone who got in my way.

The sight of Mackenzie was infuriating, but it had absolutely nothing to do with the fact that she was running her skanky claws up Logan's arm.

No, that had nothing at all to do with it.

My manic wave through the crowd caused me to bump into a man who stumbled backward and bumped into Mackenzie, of all people, shoving her right into Logan's open arms.

Perfect. I'd just helped her out.

Logan looked up at me with a quizzical expression, but all I could do was keep moving.

The moment I stepped outside, the warm night air filled my lungs. Finally, I could breathe.

"I'll drive," Hilary said, appearing out of nowhere.

I didn't argue as I pulled out my keys and tossed them in her direction.

# *Chapter Six*

## LET THE GAMES BEGIN

By the time Hilary dropped me off at home, I'd convinced her I was fine, and she left reluctantly.

After tossing my clutch and keys on the table, I headed straight to my bathroom to wash away my makeup and throw my hair into a loose bun. Drained, I peeled off my outfit and opened my dresser drawer. It was a warm, balmy night, so I put on a creamy, light slip before retreating to the kitchen for a glass of cold water. It helped quench the heat burning me from the inside.

Savoring the cool liquid, I closed my eyes and sighed. Tonight was a disaster. I'd made a fool of myself, and I'd hear about it for the next week.

I peered out the window toward Logan's house and sighed. The night had immersed us in darkness, despite the bright full moon.

The fact that I'd let the mere sight of Mackenzie not only ruin my evening but also bring up insecurities I'd buried deep inside over the past year left me furious. I was better than that—stronger. Why did I let that tramp get to me after all this time? The worst part was I still wasn't sure what bothered me more: seeing her there smiling and giggling, happily oblivious to the pain she'd caused, or seeing her with Logan.

Mackenzie could be with Logan right now, wrapped in his strong arms, lost in his fresh masculine scent and charming voice. I shook my head and groaned. Knowing Mackenzie, that's exactly where they'd be. But so what? I didn't care.

Okay, there may have been a little sting, but it was absurd. I didn't understand why it bothered me so much, but it only added fuel to the raging fire burning wildly inside me, seeking revenge on the bitch.

Logan meant nothing to me; I barely even knew him. He was nothing but an arrogant player who got off on watching me get flustered. He was toying with me.

And why wouldn't he? I'd given him quite a show so far. For some outlandish reason, his actions seemed to lead to that a lot since I'd met him. I'd never gotten worked up by a guy like that before. It had to have been from the lack of a man for so long—nothing more.

Deciding an internal debate over my feelings would lead me to no real answers, I chose to clear my mind with a peaceful stroll. As I opened my back door, I glanced up at the clock, not having realized it was already past eleven. The night felt like a blur, spinning out of control around me.

Barefoot, I stepped onto the warm, rough grass and smiled. There was something about nature that always reminded you how small you really were in the grand scheme of things.

Walking leisurely through my backyard, I was somehow pulled toward Logan's house and decided to take a peek at his pool. They'd destroyed it in less than a few hours the first day he moved in, and I wondered what the destruction encompassed.

As I grew closer, I gasped. Not only was the pool

completely restored and expanded to include a gentle curve for a cascading waterfall, an attached Jacuzzi, and a winding slide, but it was also filled with bright-blue water that shimmered in the moonlight.

I glanced up at the dark house settled behind it. The lights were still out. My eyes shifted between the pool and house as I anxiously kneaded the back of my neck. Damp skin and loose, dewy strands of hair met my hands, and my resolve faltered.

A slow, invigorating grin crept over my lips and surged through my nerves. There was no one around, and the sultry night air was beckoning me toward the cool water.

It was a dream. The pool was beautiful. I walked toward the edge and dipped my toe in, beaming. The temperature of the water was blissful—exactly like a perfect bath with a mild chill, which I found calming after the night I'd had.

My feet danced happily around the concrete edge of the pool, making their way to the deepest end. Reaching my hands into my hair, I pulled free the elastic band holding it in place, and smiled as golden strands cascaded down around my face.

After tossing the piece of elastic to the ground, I reached my arms over my head, stretching. Flutters soared through my stomach. The short gown I wore hiked up to my thighs, exposing more skin than appropriate, but nothing about sneaking into your neighbor's pool was exactly proper. I decided it was best to keep the gown on, seeing as I was already crossing the invisible line of my moral boundaries by just being there.

Without another thought, I dived straight in with a graceful splash, swimming under the water until I reached the other side. After emerging, I ran my fingers through my wet hair.

It was then that I noticed the flutter of curtains and a soft dim light coming from an upstairs window.

Someone was awake.

I shuddered, my hands flying to cover the thin fabric clinging to my breasts. I wore nothing except panties underneath the now-translucent cloth.

Gazing up at the window, training my eyes to see through the darkness, I watched the curtain open further to reveal the dark familiar eyes staring out, glistening in the shadowy light. Unable to make out anything else, it was enough for my body to shiver at the thought of him watching me. I knew those eyes: Logan's eyes.

I was faced with two options: I could do what he expected, which was to scurry around trying to cover myself from the clingy sheer fabric as I scampered home like a fool, or...

Tilting my head to the side slightly, I smiled and raised my brows. Slowly, I walked up the tiled steps, fully revealing my wet, barely covered state. My eyes never strayed from that window, from his eyes, as I stood under the moonlight with the most confident poise I'd felt in front of him thus far.

I was through acting irrationally around Logan. He was nothing more than a guy—a neighbor. I had a point to prove not only to him, but to myself. I was in control.

His dark eyes grew wider. I could see more of his face as he leaned closer to the window. Fog began to settle in front of him, awakening a need inside me I'd never dreamed existed.

With an unwavering gaze, I ran my fingers slowly across my stomach and up to the shoulder over my slip. Caressing the silky fabric of the strap, I bit my bottom lip and slid it down smoothly over my sun-bronzed shoulder. My lips twitched into a ghost of a smile.

Carefully, my finger hooked under the second strap, my breath ragged as my body reacted to the sight of his tongue darting out and licking his lips. My confidence grew with every movement he made, and without hesitation, I slid the strap down. I held the gown to my chest, not willing to fully treat him to an undeserved meal as I turned around to face the pool.

Laughing softly to myself at my brazen actions, I released my hand, allowing the slip to fall lasciviously down over my hips and pool at my feet.

I stood there, facing away, bare before his eyes in only a tiny white lace thong. Walking around the pool with my back still to him, I peered over my shoulder and shot him a crooked grin before diving back into the warm water.

With a deep inhale of fresh air, I looked back up at the window. The curtain was dropped, and the light was out.

I laughed a therapeutic, deep laugh, shaking my head.

My point was made and my body had enjoyed the soothing experience, so I stepped out of the water and grabbed my gown, disappearing into my own yard as quickly as my feet could carry me.

As I opened and stepped through my back door, a light appeared, illuminating Logan's back patio. It was soon followed by the faint sound of a sliding door opening.

I giggled, feeling proud, and retreated inside. I felt like my old self. If Logan thought he could intimidate me with his sexy charm, he was in for a surprise.

Two could play that game.

---

The next day, I woke to my usual internal alarm, bright and early, filled with a newfound energy. By seven thirty, I was dressed in a pair of pale-blue jogging shorts and soft-pink tank top: the most comfortable exercise outfit I owned. I tossed my hair into a high ponytail and didn't bother stopping in front of a mirror as I left my room to fill my water bottle.

I wasn't going to rearrange my mornings to avoid Logan

any longer. I'd never been that girl who got frazzled around a hot guy, and I sure as hell wasn't going to start now. He'd had his fun, but now it was time for him to meet the real Cassandra.

Leaving my iPod on the foyer table, I took off, enjoying the sounds nature greeted me with. The morning air was fresh and cool, with a hint of moisture. Perfect. I inhaled a deep breath as I jogged in my usual direction.

Within minutes, I heard someone behind me. I didn't need to turn back—I knew who it was. I wondered if he'd mention the previous night.

Half an hour later without a word out of Logan, I noticed one of the large potholes I regularly ran around to avoid. This morning I was feeling exhilarated and relaxed, so instead of jogging to the side of it, I did my infamous ballerina leap from the other morning. This time, however, I followed with a dramatic twirl. I smiled, and it felt good.

I didn't bother to look back during my twirl, so I wasn't sure whether he was laughing at me. He didn't make a sound, and I didn't care either way.

I was back to my old self.

The city-limits sign came into sight, and as I was about to cross the road to turn back, I heard his smooth voice.

"You seem to be enjoying your morning." His tone was soft and lighthearted.

I could feel his arm brush mine as he came up beside me. He was waiting for the nerve- racked Cassandra to show.

*Not happening.*

Against the pull of my body enjoying the sensation of his touch so close to me, I was able to keep my head. I looked to my right, staring him straight in the face, the bright sun behind him eclipsing his expression.

"Yes, I am," I replied, smiling.

I heard him chuckle as I raced forward, leaving him in my dust.

To my surprise and enjoyment, he never said another word, though I could feel he was still close behind me. He gave me the peace I treasured on my morning jogs.

Slowing as I approached my driveway, I smiled.

"Have a good day, sweetheart," he called out as I walked up my driveway. My body was surging with electricity, and I was pumped to get my day started.

"Tell Oliver I said hi," I called back before disappearing inside my house.

———◆◆◆———

Showered and in my car by noon, I stopped by the small grocery store on the edge of town. With school starting in two weeks, I needed to pick up a few last-minute supplies. My cart was full of cheap notepads, pencils, and red pens by the time I reached the tissue aisle.

"Hey, I tried calling you about twenty times this morning," Hilary said, stepping beside me while I stocked up on Kleenex. "Are you all right?"

I turned and smiled. "Yeah, sorry. I turned my phone off. Just needed a day to myself, but I'm good—promise."

She looked at me intently, studying my expression as if trying to decide whether she should push the subject. I cocked an eyebrow and made a face. She relaxed and turned her focus to the tissues in front of us.

"So Caleb called me last night," she said, as if it were the most natural thing and not something she'd dreamed of for half her life.

"I didn't know you gave him your number."

"I didn't." Her nonchalant expression began to falter, a smile tugging at her lips. "He said he has ways to find out things worth knowing."

"How cocky of him." I laughed. My cart was full, so I began walking toward the registers. "So what did he want—to prove his stealthy abilities at getting a phone number in a town of less than a thousand people?"

She rolled her eyes. "He's having a thing at Haven this Saturday and wants me to come and bring you along."

"What kind of thing? He just had his opening. I didn't realize Caleb was going to be livening up the town with parties every weekend."

"It's not a party, it's an…event." Her tone was soft and slightly embarrassed. What was she not telling me?

"What kind of event, Hilary?" She now had my full attention.

"Will you promise to come with me?"

"Not until you tell me what it is."

"Please? Caleb wants me to help out, and inviting all my single friends will really help him."

I frowned. So much for Caleb's interest in her, but she didn't seem to notice.

"Hilary—"

"Promise you'll come with me and I'll owe you one. Please?" She gave her best sappy face that made it impossible to refuse. *Damn her!*

"Ugh. Fine, I'll go," I grated. "But I'll collect this debt when you least expect it."

Hilary nodded with an excited grin.

I began unloading my cart on the register's conveyor belt and smiled at Miranda, the cashier. Having no idea what I'd just agreed to, I braced myself for the worst.

"Don't freak out…" Hilary began slowly. "…it's speed dating."

"What!?" I yelled more loudly than I'd intended, but to

my credit, that was far worse than I could've imagined. "Speed dating!? No, not happening."

"Come on, you can't back out now! You promised." Hilary smiled as she scurried away, retreating quickly toward the front doors. "I'll see you Saturday at eight. I'll meet you there. And wear a dress!"

I bit my tongue and turned back to Miranda. She was our age and single, and the look on my face must've been enough for her to read my mind.

"I'm not going." Miranda laughed. "I actually just started seeing someone."

I shook my head with a heavy sigh.

"That'll be sixty-eight dollars and thirty-two cents," she said. I handed her my debit card.

"Have a good day, Cassandra—and good luck." Miranda grinned as I walked out.

---

"Tell me again why I let you drag me to this," I pouted as Hilary and I stopped in front of a small table covered with pens and nametags. If only I hadn't been born and raised in this town, I could get away with writing a phony name. Alexandria had a nice ring to it.

I grinned, lost in thoughts of the possible personas I could conjure up for tonight's grueling event, when Hilary snatched the sticker in my hand and filled in my rightful name. She was no fun tonight.

"Owww," I said, exaggerating for full effect when she slapped the sticker roughly onto my upper abs. The low cut of my dress left no other place.

Pulling in my brows, I shot her a look of annoyance. "You know, I have better things to do than spend my Saturday night with a bunch of pathetic guys looking for a frivolous one-night stand, right?"

"Don't be so negative." Hilary leaned down to fill in her own nametag. "I'm sure most of the guys here tonight are looking for a deep, meaningful relationship."

I heard a snicker catch in her throat and couldn't help but smile. Maybe she'd be fun tonight after all. Standing up straight, she looked down at her strapless turquoise dress that was accentuated by her full breasts and frowned. There was nowhere to really place the sticker.

"I don't see the point in nametags," I scoffed. "We're not children. If you're old enough to go on a date, you should be old enough to *not* need a nametag." My short white summer dress looked silly sporting the bright-red sticker. It had taken long enough to persuade myself to put on the damn thing in the first place for this, and now it was marred with a hideous tag.

Hilary placed hers on her small tan handbag.

"That's cheating." I frowned. "If I have to look ridiculous, so do you."

I pulled it off her bag and slapped it on the center of her large chest. Her low-cut, flower-print dress now looked less sexy and more awkward, but at least we were going in as equals.

"Thanks," she grumbled. "Look, I never thought I'd be spending my night speed dating either, but Caleb asked and you know he's not the easiest person for me to refuse."

"Yeah, I've noticed you have that problem." I tried to stifle my chuckle when a large group of women began shuffling in the doors, pushing us forward.

Caleb was certainly going to be thrilled with the turnout. I grimaced. I'd never realized there were that many single people in Harmony.

"Are you going to make a move on Caleb tonight, or

72

continue playing the sweet friend who's eager to help out?" I asked. I hadn't seen Hilary since the supermarket on Monday, but I'd received multiple texts from her throughout the week about hanging out at Haven to lend a hand with setting up this event. "At some point, you have to confess you're in love with the man—preferably, before one of these bright-eyed, bushy-tailed tramps sinks her claws into him."

We walked toward the crowded room filled with singles, all holding drinks and wearing similar nametags. I cringed; this was not where I wanted to belong: among every other person incapable of finding love.

"He asked me to come here for speed dating. Does that sound like a man interested in me?" Hilary sighed.

"Whatever you say."

Sifting through my purse, I turned my phone to silent—not that I'd hear it over the music.

"Oh. My. God," Hilary giggled. I looked up to find her facing the bar. "Look who's here. Never thought a guy like *that* would need help finding a girl."

Great, so apparently I *did* fall into the box of people who needed help. I took a deep breath, preparing myself for a night spent talking to guys with cliché pick-up lines that still lived with their parents. I followed Hilary's gaze to see who she was talking about, and my eyes widened at the sight of Logan.

*Can I not have one night out without having to deal with this guy?*

He was sitting at the bar, staring straight at me wearing his trademark devilish smirk. He raised a glass of what appeared to be hard liquor in my direction, causing my body to stiffen and pulse to race. Wild flutters crept through my stomach, and my breath caught in my suddenly dry throat.

*Why did I still feel this way around him?* I'd jogged every morning, but hadn't seen him since the beginning of the week. I did notice him leaving about the same time I left to go run.

73

Instead of a bare chest, shorts, and tennis shoes, he'd been wearing a dark suit and tie.

He didn't even look in my direction the morning he drove right past me; it was as if my cold shoulder had turned him off. I was no longer any fun. I should've felt proud and relieved, but instead there was a tiny ounce of something unknown and bewildering tugging at my chest.

I was the one avoiding him, not the other way around. He'd be lucky to have me groping him in his foyer the way Katie did.

"Guess he's getting lazy with his pick-up efforts." I laughed. "He gets them served up on a platter tonight."

Logan cocked an eyebrow, and my insides took a dip. I grabbed Hilary's arm and pulled her into the nearby restroom.

"What the hell!?" Hilary snapped when I released her. I struggled to regain my composure, ignoring the stares of the few women standing around the mirrors. I hated that this one man caused my body to react like that. I'd spent all week feeling so proud of myself.

"Why does he have to be here tonight?"

"Caleb said he's a regular at the bar most nights." She gave me a wry smile. "Okay, what's *really* the problem? You think he's hot and you had that dirty, or shall we say delicious, dream about him, so why not get to know him?"

Oh, the things she'd have to say if she knew exactly how many dirty dreams about Logan I'd had. The things he did to me in my slumber were mind-blowing. I shook my head, groaning.

"What part of him being a dick did you not understand the other day?" I answered, throwing my hands in the air. "I'm not going to be another notch on his bedpost!"

"You're right, sorry." She shook her head as if suddenly remembering something. "Maybe he's just here having a quick drink? He's not exactly in need of a speed-dating service."

She gave me one last smile before turning to leave me in the ladies' room that was now unoccupied.

A deep breath, in and out, while I stood in front of the full-length mirror next to the bathroom door did nothing to clear the swarm of butterflies overwhelming my stomach.

"Okay, Cassandra, you can do this. He's not that hot," I whispered to myself while fluffing my hair and reapplying my favorite red lipstick. If he could lurk behind me and throw around his good looks, so could I.

———◆◆◆———

"Hey, Cassie! Thanks for coming out tonight," Caleb said as I approached the bar. Logan sat on the stool in front of him.

Before I could reply, my gaze wandered down to Caleb's arm wrapped around Hilary's waist. That was new. I glanced up to see Hilary biting her lip, staring back at me with wide eyes and holding back a giant grin.

"I'm sure we can find some poor schmuck in here for you to turn down," Caleb chuckled.

"Very funny, Caleb. I'm only here as a favor, so don't tempt me to leave."

"Relax. I just heard around town you're not the easiest girl to pin down a date with," he explained.

*Where did he hear that?* I rarely got asked out, but granted, when I did, I was pretty good at coming up with a reason why I couldn't—not because I wasn't looking, but because the right guy hadn't asked.

"Maybe it's because the people in this town aren't used to women with standards—something most women here tonight lack," Hilary replied, smiling at me. Her gaze shifted to Logan, and she shot him a cocky smile.

I couldn't help returning her smile. She never failed to

have my back, and I loved her for that. As much as I knew she was freaking out having Caleb's body so close to hers and actually touching her, she still wasn't afraid to speak her mind.

Caleb craned his neck to say something to Hilary, but my mind was too preoccupied with the feeling of Logan's eyes boring into me. I needed to say something or at least look at him, but finding the courage was a more difficult task than it should've been. Why did he have to look so amazing tonight?

He was still wearing a suit. The top few buttons were undone, as was his tie, and his jacket was thrown over the stool beside him. Thank the heavens above he was seated, since his trousers were sitting snugly below his waist and I had no doubt they'd show off the perfectly sculpted ass that had driven me wild the day he carried me home from our jog.

My heart began to race, and heat shot from the tips of my toes to the top of my head. *Breathe, Cassandra, breathe.*

I puffed out my chest, held my head high, and turned to face him.

"Hello, Logan," I said slowly before pressing my lips into a tight line that pulled up slightly on the sides to keep me from looking like a total bitch. My cheeks burned as I forced the smile; the thought of him knowing just how much he left me flustered drove me insane.

After a long, tense silence, he finally spoke. "You look stunning this evening." His words were low and smooth as his eyes locked with mine. They were deep blue, and clouded with something that pulled me in.

I swallowed hard, hoping nobody noticed as his gaze trailed slowly down my rigid body. The tension was thicker than ever, and I couldn't take another second of it. I was playing right back into his hands.

"So, what brings you here tonight, Logan?" I said his name more slowly and softly than usual, hoping to capture a hint of seduction to see his reaction.

He looked back up to me and lifted his drink to his mouth, smiling. "Beautiful women."

"I see." I finally glanced away from him, nodding for the man across the bar. "Well, I hope you have fun," I muttered quickly when the bartender stopped to take my order. I ordered a glass of wine—the same wine that had been served the week before.

"Allow me, sweetheart," Logan said, reaching for his jacket.

"Thanks, but I can buy my own drinks." I took my glass from the bartender and turned away, walking toward some old friends without another word. I did, however, put an extra sway in my hips for good measure.

I could feel his eyes on me, and I smiled. It felt good to have the upper hand for once.

"I don't think she likes you." I heard Caleb chuckle, and craned my neck back subtly over my shoulder to catch Logan grinning as I sashayed across the room.

# Chapter Seven

## FLIRTATION

Standing in a small group filled with women I went to school with, I finally began to relax. Maybe tonight wouldn't be all that bad. Surveying the room, I noticed there were a few men I'd never seen before, and most were around my age.

Hilary was still at Caleb's side, his arm wrapped around her waist, hand resting on her hip. She looked completely overjoyed and smitten. I was happy for her; she deserved a good guy, and despite the mystery of Caleb's extensive absence, he'd always been nothing less than a gentleman. He was that guy in high school every girl fawned over, even though few held his attention. But he always treated them with respect, which is why they continued to come around.

Living across the street from Caleb growing up, I'd seen many girls coming and going with giant, bewitched grins covering their faces. To my dismay, I'd also seen the loneliness in him when he'd hang out around the block, sneaking a smoke.

Logan was no longer at the bar; it was as if he'd just disappeared.

I recoiled. Why was I looking for him? The thought of

78

him leaving should've calmed my nerves a little, but instead I found myself wondering if he took one of the many single women there home with him already.

Caleb stepped away from the bar with Hilary at his side. She rang a small bronze bell in her hand, smiling.

"All right, let's get this thing started, shall we? Ladies, you'll each have a table to yourself. The men will be the only ones moving around tonight...at least, while you're still in my bar. They'll have five minutes at each table to convince you they're worth your time. Guys, if you want another five minutes, just stay put till the next bell chimes or the woman kicks your ass out of the seat.

"Now, some of you may find love—or at least a good time." Caleb cocked an eyebrow. "And others may end up with a drink thrown at 'em. I'm looking at you, Pauly." Caleb chuckled, as did half the room. "Either way, you're all here tonight buying my booze and I've got a beautiful woman on my arm, so I couldn't be happier." Caleb squeezed his arm tighter around Hilary's waist, pulling her into his side. A bright shade of red flushed over her cheeks.

I smiled, picturing her face the next time we were alone and she was able to unload her side of the evening on me. At least one of us was having a night to remember.

"Now let's have some fun, and remember: No hassling any of these fine ladies here tonight, gentlemen," Caleb finished, raising his glass while Hilary rang the bell once more. The room filled instantly with soft laughter and shuffling feet as the women found their tables.

Making my way quickly to a small table hidden in the far corner, I sat down and waited for the first guy to approach. My glass of wine was nearly empty, so I looked up in hopes of spotting a waiter. Instead, my gaze landed on Logan.

He was still there, and walking straight for me. My

stomach tightened, eyes locking with his, dreading the thought of being trapped attempting a conversation with him for five long minutes. I swallowed, the scorching heat rising in my body as he grew closer. Out of nowhere, a young man stepped in front of my table, blocking my view. I blew out a deep, soothing breath I hadn't realized I was holding in.

With a sweet smile, the guy pulled out the chair across from me, taking a seat and clearing my view back into the room. Logan had stopped in the aisle, his expression dark, glaring at the back of the young man's head. A curvy, redheaded woman sitting at the table next to him whipped out her hand and grabbed his arm.

I couldn't hear what she was saying to him over the chatter of the room, but without a glance up at me, he sat at her table with a smile. My stomach clenched again. I wasn't sure what it was—jealousy? I wiped the absurd thought from my head quickly and looked at the guy in front of me.

"Cassie Clarke, wow, it's been a while. Not sure if you remember me: Robert. I sat behind you in science senior year." He took a long drink from his bottle of beer and smiled.

Sipping my wine, I looked up over my glass with a smile. "Yeah, of course I remember. How are you?" I had no clue who this guy was, but he seemed sweet. He was no Logan, but—

I bit the inside of my cheek. What the hell was the matter with me? I shook all thoughts of my frustrating neighbor away, smiling uncomfortably back at Robert. His faded red T-shirt depicting a sci-fi show I'd never heard of, buzz cut, and abysmal attempt at a mustache weren't doing it for me. I was never one to be rude, though, so I tried to listen.

"I've been great. They just opened a new comic-book store one town over, so I've been stocking up on my favorites for the winter. Have you been there yet?"

Finishing off my wine in one final gulp, I raised my glass at a passing waiter, letting him know I needed a refill.

"Uh, no," I said, my chest rumbling from my stifled chuckle. He looked so serious. "I've never really read any comics before."

His eyes grew a little wider, as if intrigued. "Really!? Well, I could take you sometime. They have all the best there." His hands worked animatedly in front of him. "All the classics, and some really great new ones you should…" His voice faded into the soft melody of music playing in the background.

Scanning the area subtly, I rolled my eyes. Hilary was sitting at the bar with her stool facing Caleb's, her legs situated between his. She was giggling, and Caleb's face was buried in her hair as he whispered to her. As happy as I was for her, I still wanted to kill her for dragging me to this.

As I shifted in my seat, Robert continued on about the latest video game he'd purchased recently. It took everything in me not to look at the timer; it felt like the five minutes should've been up ages ago. He talked faster than anyone I'd ever met, which wasn't helping.

Nodding along, I allowed my gaze to drift farther across the room toward Logan. He sat with his chair backed away from the table, glass of liquor in hand, watching the woman talk. Whatever she was saying, he appeared entertained.

*He looks good tonight…too good. That man should not be allowed near suits—at least, not around women.*

Heat rushed up from my toes, prickling my scalp. *Where the hell did that come from?*

Logan's gaze swayed from the woman to his drink, and then landed on me. I turned my head and attention back to Robert quickly, taking a drink as I listened to him ramble. He looked nervous, poor guy.

"So yeah, my mom doesn't mind. Plus, I have the whole

basement to myself!" Robert wiped the back of his hand across his forehead, removing the beads of sweat before wiping it on his pant leg. "What more could I ask for, right?"

Slightly sickened, I realized I had no clue what he'd just said, and he was staring at me expectantly with a wide grin.

"Huh? Oh, that's nice." I smiled, giving a small nod and hoping there was no question in his current rambling.

I couldn't help glancing over at Logan again when Robert began going on about his favorite movies, and as I stole a quick peek over the rim of my glass, I found Logan staring directly at me.

My eyes locked with his. I wouldn't be the first one to look away this time. Challenging him, my brows rose as his did the same, mimicking me with an amused expression and thoughtful eyes.

A smile tugged at my lips as his expression sharpened into an impish grin. The moment he glanced at Robert, scrunching his nose, I lost my resolve. *Damn him.* Smiling, I shook my head slowly.

The mellow music flowed into a new song, and I watched his eyes flicker from mine to the dance floor. I followed his gaze, biting my bottom lip to control the grin aching to break across my face. Logan nudged his head to the dance floor, beckoning me with his eyes to join him there.

With one faint shake of my head, I mouthed, "Not happening."

He cocked an eyebrow and glanced back at the woman in front of him; she must've said something to him. He answered her with what appeared to be a single word, and then his gaze returned to me instantly.

He nudged his head back to the dance floor and mouthed, "Dance with me." The heat of his stare warmed something deep inside me—something I'd never felt before.

Subtly, I shook my head once, a smile playing on my lips. The woman sitting across from Logan whipped her head around, glaring at me. I burst out laughing, and my hand flew to my mouth in hopes of covering the fit of giggles that hit me out of nowhere. If looks could kill, I'd be in trouble.

Clearing my throat, I looked back at Robert, who'd stopped talking. "Sorry, I just saw someone that was…wearing a crazy outfit," I lied quickly.

He turned in his seat to see, but my hands reached out, covering his. His eyes flew to my hands and then up to me, a smile brightening his face.

"They just left. So, what were you saying?" I asked, removing my hands slowly.

The bell rang and I smiled, saying a hurried goodbye and hoping Robert noticed I wasn't interested in more time with him. Luckily, he got the message and moved to the next table.

Logan moved as well, sitting down at a booth with an older woman. I recognized her from the meat counter at the grocery store; she was in her late forties, with three grown children. There were five more tables separating Logan from mine. The idea of being trapped with him so close to me warmed my cheeks, as well as other areas of my body. What would he have to say to me after that night in his pool?

"Joe," the man now sitting in front of me said, pulling my attention to him.

"Hi, I'm Cassandra." I smiled softly, giving him my full attention. He reached out and shook my hand. I cringed at the clamminess of his, and quickly noticed his hard expression and shifty eyes. "So, have you ever done anything like this before?" I asked.

He was much cuter than the other guys there, but still nothing compared to Logan. I winced, hating myself the moment I thought it. Logan seemed to be everywhere tonight—even in my thoughts.

"No, my wife and I separated a few weeks ago, and my buddies said I should go out and try to meet new people," he explained, finishing his drink in one gulp and slamming the glass down on the table.

I flinched. He reeked of alcohol. "That's nice of them. Trying to give you a little push."

"I guess. I think they just want me out of the picture so they can fuck my wife!" His tone was cold and filled with irritation.

I sat there, stunned for a moment, unsure what I could say to that. He reached across the table, grabbing my glass of wine and finishing it off as well. My internal self-preservation alarm blared in my ears, and my feet scooted my chair back away from the table. Of course the one cute guy in here was a nut job.

"I doubt that's true," I replied, my voice cracking. "Breakups are tough, and—"

"Really!?" he interjected. "I caught my best friend spying on my wife sunbathing topless last week!" Joe's nostrils flared as he sat up further in his seat. His knee bounced up and down wildly. "You know, you remind me of her a little…blonde hair, blue eyes." His face contorted with the anger that was seething off him. "I bet you're a cheating little bitch, too!"

"Look, asshole! You have no idea—" I leaned into the table. His remark paired with the frustration from being talked into enduring the night had finally come to a head for me.

Joe jumped to his feet abruptly, his chair crashing to the floor behind him. I flinched back. "You women are all the same!"

"Hey, buddy," Caleb said smoothly, walking over with his hands in the air. His stern expression and my memories of him as a teenager told me he could kick this drunk's ass blindfolded. "I think you need some fresh air."

Joe brushed Caleb off, bumping into his shoulder as he stomped out of the bar. Caleb turned back to face me. "You all right, Cassie?"

"Yeah," I replied with a nod, my body coming down from the surge of adrenaline. "I could use a margarita, though."

Caleb chuckled. "On the house." He walked to the bar where Hilary was standing, her wide eyes full of concern.

"You okay?" she mouthed silently.

I shrugged and looked down at the table. I just wanted to forget the bipolar jerk, but I realized the bar was eerily silent. Looking back up at the other tables, I sighed. People were staring directly at me, whispering.

But Logan was staring at the door the bastard had just exited through. My eyes were drawn to his clenched jaw and rigid posture, which took me by surprise. Leaning into my table, I noticed clenched muscles leading to his tight grip on his glass. He looked ready to implode.

He turned his head slowly to face me, as if he could feel me staring at him. His shoulders deflated and his body relaxed noticeably, his eyes becoming softer.

"Margarita?" a waitress asked, holding out my drink.

Looking up at her, I smiled. "Thanks."

"Come on, let's not pretend it's the first time you guys have seen a drunk guy!" Caleb called out, chuckling.

The room erupted in chitchat and laughter, falling back into the motions of the event, but my mind was still on Logan. What was going on in his head? He looked ready to follow the guy outside and tear him apart. The thought that he might care was too much to process. As I sipped my drink, I saw him tip his head toward Caleb, who walked straight over to him.

The noise in the bar was too loud and his seat too far away for me to overhear. Between the look on his face and his head nod at the door, followed by Caleb glancing over to me, I had a feeling it had to do with the drunk. Was he planning on doing something? I hoped not. The guy just needed to go home and sleep it off.

Hilary rang the bell a moment later, and I heaved a heavy sigh as the next man approached.

The following three guys who sat across from me were nothing to write home about. Only one was decent looking, but he came off as a workaholic with a drinking problem. Not to mention his constant vulgar compliments and eyes glued to my chest left little to be desired.

Logan, on the other hand, appeared to be having a much better time. On multiple occasions I caught him staring, and most of those times he seemed to be laughing...at me. Was it that obvious that these men were boring the hell out of me?

The bell rang, and Logan took a seat at the table next to mine. He was a mere five feet away, and facing in my direction. The woman at his table was pretty and about my age. I'd never seen her around town before, but after sitting so close to her all night, I'd quickly learned she was both flirty and touchy with most of the men who sat with her.

"Hi, I'm Vanessa," the woman told him, her smile all teeth as she looked him over. I tried not to pay attention; Mr. Gifford, the town barber, was now seated across from me and ordering a drink.

"Logan. It's a pleasure," Logan replied, and I suddenly felt awkward eavesdropping. Mr. Gifford cleared his throat, pulling my attention back to him.

"So, Cassie, you look delectable this evening." The old man licked his lips slowly, his eyes taking me all in.

Swallowing the repulsion rising in my throat, I gave a painful, tight smile. "Thanks, Mr. Gifford," I said politely. Why was he even here? He was old enough to be my great-grandfather, for Christ's sake.

"Please, call me Sal, honey," he said, leaning in to place his hand over mine. I pulled it away instantly, shooting him an assertive scowl.

"So tell me about yourself, Logan," Vanessa said, her voice eager for information. My ears perked up, waiting to hear his answer as well. "Rumor has it you have a son. How old is your little boy?"

Logan sat quietly for a brief moment, appearing unaffected, swirling his drink in his hand before he tilted his head and caught my gaze from the corner of his eye. I straightened in my chair, pretending not to notice. "I'd rather talk about you, Vanessa. What do you do for a living?" Logan's reply came out cold and clipped—something I'd never heard before.

He didn't seem to want to talk about Oliver, and I found myself curious about that. But the sound of Vanessa's voice as she began chattering about how she was a chef at a restaurant a few towns over left me bored.

Logan twisted his neck to the side just enough to wink at me. I rolled my eyes back at him. He chuckled at my impassive move, and Vanessa stopped talking abruptly. Damn, why couldn't I stop staring? It wasn't like me. At all.

"What's so funny?" she giggled.

Looking back at Mr. Gifford, I didn't listen for Logan's reply. He was drinking a bottle of imported beer, his tongue lingering around the tip, painting a disturbing picture I'd forever have engraved into my brain. *Damn him.*

"So, Sal, what brings you out so late?" I asked, deciding to make the most of my final few minutes with him.

"I may be a bit older than you, honey, but that doesn't mean I don't know how to have fun," he slurred, his eyes dark and clouded as they traveled to my cleavage.

Choking down the bile that was itching to spew from my mouth, I closed my eyes, hoping to make him disappear. I took a giant gulp of my drink, working hard to swallow it against the pressure of revulsion. For the first time that night, I found myself wishing Logan was in front of me. Anyone would be better than Sal.

"I've been waiting to get to this table, you know," Sal said, grinning like a Cheshire cat.

I made a face, unsure how to respond to his comment. "Hmmm, really? That's…" *Gross? Disturbing? Completely inappropriate?* I gave an uncomfortable, tight-lipped chuckle and took another long drink, hoping to dull his image with alcohol.

"Why don't we get out of here and go on back to my place? I'll have you screaming my name by the time the sun comes up."

I spat a mouth full of margarita across the table, struggling to control my harsh coughing as I set down my glass and reached for the napkin in front of me to wipe my mouth with.

*Did he really just say that?* His wife had died not even a year ago—not to mention this was the same guy who used to give me quarters when I was a kid.

Sal seemed unfazed, but the sounds from the table beside me left me reeling. Turning in my seat, I grimaced. Logan's head hung back, shoulders bouncing up and down as he laughed hysterically. I shot him a threatening glare, but he was too busy trying to compose himself to notice. Vanessa looked confused and disgusted by the mess covering my table.

"Come on, baby, let me show you how a real man treats a lady," Sal said, oblivious to my revulsion and the liquid in front of him. He reached his hand under the table shamelessly, placing it on my knee. I froze, my body painfully still and eyes wide as his wrinkled, calloused hand slid quickly up my bare thigh.

Before I could react, Logan was out of his chair, standing behind Sal with his hands on the old man's shoulders.

"All right, Sal, I think you've had enough fun with Cassandra tonight."

Sal stood up, threw me a quick wink, and walked toward the bar.

"Thanks," I mumbled.

"Anytime, sweetheart." His face lit with hilarity, and I could see him fighting off a smile before he sat back down with Vanessa.

After grabbing a few napkins from the dispenser on a nearby table, I sat there trying to wipe up the drink that was dripping from the table's edge. The bell went off and I sighed. When would this night be over? Shaking my head, I placed the soaked napkins to the side of the table just as Logan sat down in front of me.

*Shit.*

I needed more time to prepare for this. Taking a deep breath, I sat up further in my seat, pulling at my dress to cover any cleavage. He'd already had enough of a show from me in that department.

"Hello, Cassandra," Logan said, his voice rough and sexy.

"Logan," I replied coldly, tilting my head for added emphasis. I was in no mood for games tonight, and if he kept talking like that with that look in his eyes, I'd only embarrass myself. I flagged down the waitress.

"I have to admit, I was happily surprised to find you here tonight. A woman like you doesn't need this to land a date."

The waitress stepped to our table and we both ordered another round of drinks. I ordered water, earning me a dubious look from Logan. Ignoring him, I watched the waitress bat her eyelashes and giggle as he asked for a scotch, neat.

"Water?" he asked as the waitress walked away, his brows furrowed.

"Scotch?" I replied with equal disdain. Truth was, I needed a clear head to deal with him. My body was far too attracted to him, and with the amount of alcohol I'd already consumed, my brain was slowly forgetting why he was off limits.

He chuckled to himself. "You never answered my question."

"I'm only here as a favor to Caleb," I replied.

"Of course. I've been told you're very…considerate." He appeared to want to say something else but looked away, sipping his drink.

*Been told?* Had he asked about me, or was he referring to my striptease in his pool? We sat for what felt like more than five minutes just staring at each other. I flushed and tried to avert my gaze to look around the room, but it only seemed to add to his amusement.

The waitress reappeared, and I couldn't have been happier. Before sipping my water, I asked, "So, what's Oliver up to tonight?"

"Home. Sleeping, I would presume, at this hour." He set his drink on the table. "So, tell me, how long have you been a teacher?"

*How the hell did he know I was a teacher?* He was definitely talking to someone about me.

"This will be my first year," I replied before quickly adding, "Oliver seems like a great kid. I bet you guys have a lot of fun hanging out."

Logan squirmed in his chair, his expression unreadable. I wasn't used to seeing him uncomfortable, and considering it was about his own son, I wasn't sure what to make of it. Was he being overprotective of Oliver, or did he truly not enjoy talking about him? I had yet to even see him with his son. I was left unsettled with my thoughts when he spoke.

"Yes, we do." His voice was strained and distant. "Now, tell me, how long have you lived in this small town?"

"Why don't you like to talk about your son?" I asked, looking him straight in the eyes. Frustrated by my evening thus far, I didn't care about overstepping boundaries. The alcohol in my system fueled my courage.

Logan took a slow, deep breath as he downed the rest of his drink and looked up at me. "I'm sitting in a bar on a Saturday night with a stunning woman. I'd rather not talk about my son right now." His lips pursed, telling me the subject was off limits.

As I opened my mouth to speak, the bell went off. It was for the best. I took a drink and waited for him to stand up and move to the next table. "Have a good night, Logan."

He continued staring at me with an impish smirk, and I couldn't help but notice he wasn't getting up. The man at Vanessa's table went around him and everyone began at their new spots.

"I think I would like another five minutes."

I sighed, rolling my eyes. *Seriously!?*

"Fine. What do you want to talk about?" I asked, irritated.

"I want to talk about you." His tone was soft and seductive.

Picturing him saying that to multiple women, I huffed.

"Wow, does that line ever actually work?" I grumbled.

"You'd be surprised." He chuckled, amused at my demeanor.

"How about this: I'll answer a question if you answer one of mine," I said, raising my brows.

Logan appeared to be thinking it over. "All right. Ladies first."

"Why did you move to Harmony?"

"The local newspaper. I bought it. I would have thought you knew that already, sweetheart." His eyes brightened.

"Oh, was I supposed to ask around about my mysterious new neighbor who enjoys lurking behind me like a creep?" I rested my elbows on the table, distracted by the soaked napkins still resting at its edge.

He chuckled under his breath. "We both know you don't think I'm a creep. I'm insulted." I sat quietly, my eyes cast downward as he continued. "Now, I believe it's my turn. Have you always wanted to teach?" he asked, sipping his drink.

I was surprised his question was both easy and painless to answer. "Yes. Why buy the paper?"

"As a graduation gift for my sister." He smiled proudly.

"She's just now starting college." With confusion heavy in my voice, I made a face at the absurdity of buying an entire newspaper for a freshman.

His brows pulled together. "Yes, and by the time she graduates, she'll have a job at a well-established and reliable newspaper."

"Right," I whispered, growing bored and bitter at not having my own big brother to look out for me. "Lucky girl."

"My sister has been very loyal to me over the past few years." His tone grew serious.

"Helping with Oliver?" I looked up, gauging his expression.

He sighed. "Yes, helping with Oliver."

The air grew thick and heavy. I cleared my throat and changed the subject. "So, you bought the newspaper. Does that mean you own others?"

Relaxing back in his chair, he smiled. "No. But I have many ventures, as does my family. Julia is going to school in hopes of becoming a journalist, and I happened to stumble upon an opportunity to buy *The Harmony Tribune*. I couldn't pass up the offer."

His voice grew huskier, a pleased smile playing on his lips as he added, "I have a very hard time resisting temptation, Cassandra." His gaze seared into mine, confirming we were no longer talking about the paper.

Dumbfounded, I struggled to think while heat settled into my cheeks. The longer we sat, the more his smile grew. He could see right through me, and it left me paralyzed.

The sound of the bell rang through the air, and Logan remained in his seat while the other men went around him once again. An annoyed growl escaped through my gritted teeth.

"Seriously, have ten minutes not been enough for you to see that I'm not interested?" I snapped.

"I have one last request."

"Let's hear it," I replied, rolling my eyes.

"Dance with me."

My breath caught in my throat. His words were demanding yet irresistible, and for some reason I'd never be able to explain, I nodded my head dumbly.

He stood with a hint of a smile and held out his hand. With my hand in his, he led us to the dance floor. Only two other couples were there, looking completely smitten with their partners. Logan's arm snaked around my waist, pulling me in close while his other hand locked around mine. Our bodies began moving together slowly as Michael Bublé crooned his version of "Always on My Mind."

Caleb's playlist tonight included every soft, romantic song ever written. It set the mood for finding love. No doubt Hilary had chosen this song; it'd been one of her favorites for years. Not mine, however, not for a long time. The only time I ever remembered seeing my parents dancing was to Elvis's version at a friend's wedding a year before my father left. They looked so in love, so happy. I closed my eyes, burying the painful memory back in its dark place. They weren't in love—at least, my father wasn't. I was just too young to have realized it.

"Are you nervous?" Logan asked, looking down at me, giving nothing away.

"No."

"You're a terrible liar."

I rolled my eyes. His hot breath caressed my ear as he leaned in. I inhaled sharply, heat scorching my ears with every breath he took.

"Did you enjoy my pool?" he murmured so delicately my insides melted. "Because I most definitely enjoyed the view. Although I was a bit disappointed to find you were more of a tease than I'd originally thought."

I winced. *Tease*!? I narrowed my eyes, acid in my voice as I hissed, "Don't worry. It's the last time you'll see me anywhere *near* your pool."

He released a hoarse, throaty laugh. Anger bubbled up inside me as reality crashed over me like a tidal wave of ice water. My body tensed as I halted my feet from swaying with him. *A tease! How dare he.*

My head cocked to the side. "How many women in this bar tonight have you slept with?"

He held my gaze, a small grin spreading across his lips. "I've only recently moved here—I should be offended at your implication that I have nothing better to do with my time than bed multiple women. Is that the man you think I am?"

With pursed lips, I narrowed my eyes. He was in for a surprise if he honestly thought I was buying his crap. "So, you haven't been flirting with me tonight in hopes of sleeping with me?"

His expression was stoic; unreadable.

"Do you want to sleep with me, Cassandra?" His tongue darted out, moistening his plump lips.

My stomach rolled, butterflies emerging from its dark corners. My mind fought with my body over the urge to grab him by the collar, drag him outside to the back alley, and let him ravish me until I forgot every reason why I'd regret it later.

"You didn't answer my question. Let's say, hypothetically speaking, I haven't been with a man in months, and..." I pressed flush against him and rolled my hips. "...I really wanted to see what you could do to me in that pool of yours. What would you say to that?" I purred, tugging my bottom lip between my teeth yet struggling inside to keep my assertive confidence.

Logan dug his fingers into my hips. His mouth lingered above mine, his breath a warm mix of mint and scotch. "I would say, 'Let's get out of here and grab a hotel room.'"

"Ugh!" I pulled out of his arms, shoving his chest. "I knew it. You really are an egotistical ass!"

He chuckled silently, eyes bright.

"A hotel? Really!?" I hissed. "I'm a woman, not a piece of meat. I have no interest in going to a cheap *hotel* for some one-night stand with a man who can't even talk about his own son without cringing. You can go around with your fancy cars and expensive suits, but you have nothing I'm interested in!"

With a sudden turn, I headed straight to my table and collected my bag. As I walked past him to leave, I leaned in and whispered, "And by the way, I enjoyed your pool *very* much. It's a shame you'll never get me that wet."

I whipped around on my heel, walking away with my shoulders back and head held high but completely shocked at my own words.

The moment I stepped outside, my hands slapped over my mouth. *Did I really just say that?* I couldn't for the life of me figure out what it was about Logan West that brought out that side of me. He made me feel strong, confident, and completely sexy.

As much as I hated it and was completely over him, I went home wearing a satisfied grin.

# Chapter Eight

## TASTE TEST

I always knew I'd be a teacher one day. I remembered fondly setting up a class with small chairs surrounding a giant maple tree in my backyard. It started with my dolls sitting for lessons, but within a few summers I had real friends in those chairs, listening to me ramble on and on about nonsense. They weren't the best listeners, but it taught me how to stand in front of a class with my head held high, ready to share the knowledge I had.

Walking up to the building where I'd be spending three days a week teaching, I smoothed my hand down my crisp black pencil skirt. It fell just past my knees and had a tiny slit up the back, showing off my tight runner's legs and pulling me into my new role as teacher. I tucked in my short-sleeved silky white blouse nervously, wanting to make sure I looked just right. I felt grown up and ready to take on the world.

As I strolled down the bustling halls of the elementary school surrounded by rows of dated green lockers, anxiety rang in my ears. I knew most of the parents coming to my class tonight, but it was different from a passing hello on the street—they were entrusting me with their children's educations.

Every window in the building was propped open, allowing a warm breeze to filter in to relieve some of the musty odor. Another year had passed in this town without a single dime allotted for air conditioning in the elementary school. Open house started in less than an hour, and the heat from the never-ending summer was overwhelming inside the stuffy old building.

My mood lifted as I entered my classroom, and the temperature no longer mattered. I took a long gulp of icy water from my new mug sporting the school's logo and set my tote on the desk. The room looked great, though it still needed a few more details. I walked over to the massive whiteboard that hung from the pasty yellow wall and took my time writing 'Miss Clarke' in perfect print for my new students.

I'd spent every afternoon there the past week, preparing my classroom for a year of expanding eager young minds. Vivid primary colors and scenes of animals in the wilderness surrounding the alphabet fully decorated the room. I placed the names of all fourteen students, written flawlessly on pale-blue card stock shaped liked clouds, on a small desk beside a large dazzling rainbow I'd created.

"Perfect." I smiled, glancing around the room one last time. The pride I felt standing beside my desk replaced the nerves building inside me. Walking toward my door, I pulled my hair tie free, letting my natural curls fall around my neck. It looked best down, even though I would regret it due to the heat. I gave my hair one more tousle for extra bounce and placed my hands gracefully at my sides, rolling my shoulders back.

Within minutes, students began wandering in, lugging

bags of tissues and antibacterial wipes. I greeted them with warm hellos and showed them to their desks. Most of them were soft-spoken and unwilling to let go of their parents' hands, but still seemed interested in their new environment. Over the next hour, I met all but one of my students and watched them each explore the room. Everyone seemed as excited to start the year as I was. Kindergarten was a thrilling new adventure for both students and their parents.

Standing in the hall, relaxed, I waited for the last student still on my list.

"Cassandra!"

Turning, I saw Oliver walking toward me, holding Julia's hand.

"Oliver, hi! How are you?" I smiled.

"Great! I just met my teacher, Miss Harper. She's really nice."

I nodded. Jessica Harper was the voluptuous preschool teacher down the hall.

"She's a great teacher. I'm sure you'll have a wonderful time in her class." Looking up, I smiled at Julia. "How have you been?"

"Good. I'm loving Harmony, by the way. I never thought such a small town could have so many friendly people."

"Yeah, that's one of the nice things around here. Everyone gets along, for the most part." I smiled. "Have you been keeping busy at school? I haven't seen anyone around Oliver's house all week."

The entire week had passed without a single peep from Logan's house—not even from a straggling worker around the property. It was strange, as if they all disappeared or I imagined them ever existing, although I was grateful to have my morning jogs uninterrupted.

The problem was no matter how much I refused to

entertain him in my thoughts, the moment I climbed into bed at night and closed my eyes, Logan assaulted my dreams. He was a constant, seducing me on the dance floor, our bodies flush against each other. But the moment I began to remove his shirt, he'd vanish. It was the same dream every night, and every morning I woke needing a cold shower and good scolding from the other half of my brain.

"Yeah, I've been busy with my classes starting, and Logan took Oliver to the city for the week," Julia said, pulling me back to the present.

I nodded. It was none of my business, so why was I asking? She seemed to pick up on the uncomfortable shifting of my feet and gave me a suspicious look. I cleared my throat, desperate to change the subject.

"So, how do you like living in the dorms? I stayed there my first year, but didn't exactly see eye to eye with my roommate." I leaned in. "She preferred drinking over studying. We didn't mesh well."

Julia laughed. "Yeah, it's all right. I get along fairly well with my roommate, but I'm honestly not there that much. I have a friend who has an apartment in town, so I've been hanging out there a lot." Her face lit up when she said 'friend,' and I couldn't help myself.

"Friend?" I asked in a teasing voice, raising my eyebrows.

She blushed and opened her mouth to speak, but was interrupted by her brother approaching us.

"Hello, Cassandra," Logan said, a faint smile on his lips.

"Hello," I replied with a quick glance his way before turning back to face Julia. Her lips were pressed firmly together, and her wide eyes screamed at me that this was not the time to discuss boys.

"Oh, Mr. West!" Oliver's teacher Jessica called out, pushing out her chest and tucking a side of her short hair behind her ear as she walked toward us. "Can I have just one more minute?"

Logan walked away from us to meet her halfway between the rooms and I scowled, catching the look on the perky strawberry blonde's face. It was the same one Hilary wore around Caleb. Jessica was a few years older than me, recently divorced with a toddler son, and notorious for being needy when it came to men.

Logan approached her, unaffected as she spoke in a hushed voice, a wide grin covering her mouth. Logan's brows rose at her words, a blush creeping over her cheeks at his reply. I wanted to look away as her hand caressed his arm, but was too engrossed when she handed him a small piece of paper, giggling under her breath. He turned around as Jessica sauntered back to her class with an extra sway in her walk. I stood there stunned, hoping that paper wasn't what I thought it was.

Julia didn't miss the exchange, and it was obvious she'd come to the same conclusion I had. Narrowing her eyes as Logan strolled back over to us with his hands tucked in his trouser pockets, she crossed her arms over her chest.

"What's that?" she seethed, gesturing her head to the small paper he was folding in his hands.

He only twisted his lips into a lopsided grin and tucked it into his jean pocket.

"I swear to God, Logan, if that's her phone number!" she hissed. I agreed, and felt my blood begin to boil as well—not because he'd probably be calling the number, but because it was extremely unprofessional of Jessica. Logan was the new meat in town, and damn, these women were flocking to him like flies.

"We'll discuss it later," Logan said, his eyes flickering down to Oliver with a hint of irritation.

"Mrs. Clarke?" An older woman with peppered-grey hair approached with a young boy beside her.

"Yes, that's me, but it's 'Miss,'" I replied, smiling. "Come on in."

"We'll let you get back to your students," Julia said, taking Oliver's hand. "See you around."

"Bye!" Oliver said, walking away.

"Goodbye. And Julia?" She looked back over her shoulder. "I expect to finish our conversation next time."

She shot me an exaggerated frown, shifting her gaze to Logan, but finally gave me a soft nod and subtle smile.

"Conversation?" Logan's eyebrows rose, intrigued.

"Calm your ego. It has nothing to do with you," I teased as I turned away and entered my class to meet my last student.

---

The first day of school went off without a single issue. The children had warmed up to me by lunch, and proved to be everything I'd hoped for.

One of my favorite perks about teaching kindergarten was having Tuesdays and Thursdays off. It was a luxury that gave me more free time to plan my lessons and work on clearing out and sorting the remainder of boxes from my grandparents' attic.

Logan was still a no-show for my morning jogs, which I didn't mind; it made them easier and more relaxing. I still couldn't help staring at his gate as I passed, though, wondering if he was in there watching me. The thought caused a swarm of heat to pool in my stomach. I shook it off, popping in my ear buds and singing along with the music as I took off running.

Friday after school, I straightened the stack of graded papers on my desk, wiped down the chalkboard, and pushed in stray chairs. As the clock struck four, half an hour after the kids had left the building, I grabbed my tote and walked out of my classroom.

As I passed the office, I heard someone call out, "Cassandra!"

I stopped, craning my neck through the open office door toward the secretary, Mrs. Wilde. She was sitting at her desk, holding out the phone. "I'm glad I caught you. You have a call."

*A phone call?* I tensed, staring at the older woman with a heavy feeling of dread settling in. *An angry parent, maybe?* Replaying the past few days, I couldn't come up with anything I might've done to upset anyone.

I stepped into the office with heavy limbs, and she handed me the receiver.

"Hello, this is Miss Clarke," I said nervously.

"Cassandra."

"Logan?" My nerves washed away, and I was left feeling relieved but confused. And then it hit me: *Did something happen to my house?*

"I went into the city for a meeting this morning and have been sitting in gridlocked traffic for over two hours," he explained, irritation in his tone.

"All right, and I need to know this why?" I scrunched my brows. Mrs. Wilde leaned in closer to eavesdrop. I turned around, walking as far as the ancient device's cord would allow.

"I'm unable to pick up Oliver, and Julia's not answering her phone. I was hoping you could help me out by taking him with you until I get back."

I stilled my posture. He wanted me to watch Oliver? I honestly didn't mind, but I was taken aback he was asking me. I barely knew the man.

"Don't you have a nanny?" I asked.

"No, I don't trust strangers with my son."

103

"Well, Logan, you might have failed to notice, but I *am* technically a stranger." I chuckled once.

"Logan? Is that Logan West by any chance?" a voice asked from behind me. I turned to see Jessica walking in, with Oliver at her side.

With a smile directed at Oliver, I tightened the receiver to my ear. God forbid Logan say something lurid and be heard by his son.

"Cassandra, please. I have no one else to ask." His voice was warm and soft, catching me off guard and leaving me no other choice but to agree.

I nodded, and Jessica's face lit up.

"Go have a seat in the hall, Oliver. I need to talk to your father a moment."

Jessica held out her hand for the phone, which I handed over instantly. I greeted Oliver with a smile and small wave as he walked out.

"Logan! Hi, is everything all right?" Jessica asked enthusiastically through the phone. "Oh, that's terrible. I hate traffic. People need to learn to drive." Her face went through about a dozen reactions as she listened before finally giggling.

I rolled my eyes, taking a deep, annoyed breath as I stepped to the door and poked my head outside. Oliver was sitting in the short row of yellow plastic chairs, his small feet dangling down and kicking at the air.

"Why don't I take Oliver back to my place? My son is with the babysitter there and would love to play with him. I could make us a nice dinner for when you get back," Jessica said, a giant grin plastered on her freckled face. But whatever Logan's reply was caused her expression to drop away slowly. "Uh-huh. Oh…all right." She whipped her head around, staring at me with narrowed eyes.

*What the hell did I do? What is he saying to her?*

Jessica nodded her head at his words. "Yes, not a problem, Mr. West. Goodbye."

I looked over at her, surprised at her tone and the sudden formality with which she'd addressed Logan. Whatever he'd said to her, it had caused her to talk like an actual teacher and not some enamored schoolgirl.

She held the phone to me, her face flushed. As soon as I took it, she walked out, and I heard her tell Oliver to have a great weekend.

"Yeah?" I asked, confused.

"Please don't make me beg. I really need your help. Tell me you'll watch Oliver."

"Quick question first: Why not let him go to Jessica's house? She is his teacher after all; you should trust her more than me. Not that I'm untrustworthy or anything, it's just she seemed overly eager to make dinner for you. I'm sure you'd have a wonderful time." I grinned, imagining his expression at my taunting words.

"I have no interest in having dinner with my son's teacher. And Oliver likes you, as does Julia and most of this town. That says a lot. And about that meal," his voice grew huskier, "if you'd like to prepare dinner for us, I'd be more than delighted to have a taste."

I rolled my eyes, but a smile pulled at my lips in spite of myself. "I'll watch Oliver, but there will be no meal—at least, not for you."

"That's a shame; those muffins you made were delicious. I've been looking forward to the next treat you have planned for me." His voice grew smoother, deeper. I could picture that annoying, seductive smirk of his.

"Goodbye, Logan."

He chuckled. "I'll be there soon. And Cassandra...thank you." I heard him hang up as soon as the words left his mouth.

My stomach flipped. His words were sincere and genuine, and I couldn't help smiling as I placed the phone back on its cradle.

"All right, Oliver, looks like you're coming over to my house for a while." I stepped into the hall and Oliver stood up, worry marring his brow.

"Is my daddy okay?"

"Yes, of course. He's just stuck in traffic. What do you say we go back to my house and find a game to play?"

Oliver nodded, taking my hand and following me out of the building.

---

By the time we arrived at my house, Oliver had persuaded me to make blueberry muffins with him. He dropped his backpack on my couch and we went straight to the kitchen. I smiled as he pushed a chair across the floor to the sink and climbed up to wash his hands. I did the same, and then began handing him ingredients from the cupboards.

Oliver dumped everything into a bowl after I measured it out, and with a giant grin, he began mixing. Flour and blueberry juice covered his hands. With Oliver's help, the batter was mixed and poured into muffin tins less than thirty minutes later. After pushing two pans inside the oven, I turned around to assess the room.

Flour was scattered over the countertop and floor. Oliver followed my gaze, laughing.

"It's a mess in here," he said, grinning as he grabbed a handful of leftover blueberries from a bowl.

"You're pretty messy too." Flour had somehow been wiped across his brow and through his curly hair.

"I'll help you clean," he said, jumping down from the chair, blueberries still in his hand. As soon as his feet hit the floor, a blueberry hit the back of my arm.

"Hey!" I yelled, turning to face him with my arms crossed over my chest. "Are you trying to start a food fight in my kitchen, Oliver?" My voice was stern.

He stilled, eyes growing wide with nerves. "Um—"

"Because I'll win!" I reached for a handful of blueberries and raced toward him.

He took off running, grabbing the entire bowl and sneaking around the side of the kitchen table.

I ducked as he threw one after another, missing more times than not. I managed to get a few good shots in, which caused him to burst into a fit of giggles.

As I pounced to the side of the table, Oliver raced around me and grabbed the bag of remaining flour from the counter.

I held up my hand. "Don't do anything you might regret, now." I giggled.

"Daddy says you should never have regrets." With that, he flung the bag up and down. I dived under the table to hide as flour rained down around me.

With a heavy laugh, I felt adrenaline seep from my body. It'd been too long since I'd had so much fun, and I'd never had a food fight before—especially not in my grandmother's kitchen.

My breath caught as a familiar, smooth voice filled the cloudy air.

"It looks like Oliver wins."

I peered up from under the table to find Logan leaning against the kitchen doorway, arms crossed over his chest, wearing an easy smile.

"I always win!" Oliver said as I crawled out, adjusting my rumpled skirt and stained top.

"You always win, huh?" I asked, avoiding eye contact with his father.

"Yeah, Uncle Jax tries, but I win every time."

*Uncle Jax? How many West siblings are there?*

I laughed, glancing up to Logan slowly. To my surprise, he was staring at his son with a smile. His gaze then traveled from Oliver back to me.

"So, are there muffins to be eaten, or are you wearing them all?"

I looked down, wondering how bad I looked when Oliver spoke. "They're cooking right now. Can we wait till they're done?" he asked with big, hopeful eyes.

"Sorry, but I need to get some work done at home, and you need a bath," Logan replied warmly. The tone he used with his son was something entirely new: soft and gentle.

"I'll bring them over when they're done," I chimed in, looking down at Oliver. "All right?"

Oliver nodded. "Okay, but don't forget."

I laughed. "I won't, I promise. Make sure you grab your backpack."

Oliver walked past his father into the living room, leaving us alone.

"I forgot to ask over the phone: Does he have any allergies?"

Logan's eyes held mine, his smile melting away into a serious line. He looked almost confused at my question. His eyes suddenly brightened after a fleeting moment. "No, no allergies."

His expression grew lighter, amused. My brows scrunched together when he leaned in and slid his thumb over my cheek. I stilled as my breath caught and my stomach rolled, wild heat racing through me.

He pulled back, and I noticed the blueberry his thumb had collected. My cheeks blazed as his eyes locked with mine and his lips parted. Sucking the blueberry from the pad of his thumb, he smiled.

"Delicious."

My tongue darted out automatically, wetting my lips. His smile grew as he watched me with intent eyes.

"Got it!" Oliver said, appearing beside me.

Swallowing loudly, I looked down at the small boy, who took a giant whiff of the fresh-baked smell seeping from the oven.

"Don't forget to bring them over later," Oliver said seriously.

"I won't." My voice cracked.

"Bye." Oliver waved, taking Logan's hand. I shut both my screen and solid wood doors after a quick wave and without another word to his father.

My body slumped against the door, and I let my head fall back slowly as I let out a heavy sigh. Heat racked my body; I knew only two things would help, and giving into Logan was not an option. That left me pushing off from the door and heading into the kitchen to watch the muffins cook while I fantasized about all the dirty things Logan could've done to me in the tiny room. The moment my stove beeped, I pulled out the pans and rested them on top of the racks covering the counter before heading into the bathroom for a cool shower.

Two hours later, after deciding a bath would better satisfy me and fixing a quick dinner, I tucked the muffins in Tupperware and walked next door.

After one ring of the bell, Julia appeared with Oliver at her side.

"You brought them!" he exclaimed, reaching for the bowl.

I smiled as he opened the lid and took a giant bite of the largest muffin.

"Mmm, they're yummy," he mumbled through a full

mouth.

Julia laughed. "He's been going on and on about these since I got here."

I chuckled, happy to see him enjoying them.

"Sorry I couldn't pick him up from school. I turned my phone off to study."

"Not a problem, I didn't mind. But I should get going. I still have a kitchen to clean." Truthfully, I wanted to avoid another run-in with Logan. There were only so many cold showers a girl could take.

"Wait, are you going to the carnival on Sunday?" Julia asked, and Oliver's face lit up.

"I don't know. I really wasn't planning on it." The end-of-summer celebration was the biggest event this town ever held. Carnival rides, parade, fireworks; a grand old time, they called it. I went every year with Mark, but this year I looked forward to staying home and ignoring it. "You *have* to come," Oliver pouted. "Please? Daddy won't mind, right Aunt Julia?"

Julia shook her head, trying to hide something in her expression. Had Logan told her about our interactions?

"You should come. I'll be there…and so will the guy I'm seeing." She whispered the last part, her eyes bright.

"All right, I'll meet you guys there around noon." I wasn't feeling particularly thrilled about it, but honestly had nothing better to do.

Something in my expression caused Oliver to frown. "You don't have to," he muttered. His shoulders hung low, defeated.

I stepped forward, crouching to his level and smiling. "I'll be by the fountain in the center of town at noon. I promise." I held out my pinky finger.

His smile reappeared and spirits lifted as he hooked his pinky with mine. "I'll wait for you."

110

"Tell Cassandra thank you, Oliver, then go finish your dinner."

I looked up and caught Logan's gaze as he stood behind his son. His jaw ticked, and something dark was clouding his eyes. I glanced to Julia, who shifted on her feet, picking up on the tense air suddenly surrounding us.

"We'll see you there," Julia said, taking the muffins from Oliver and leading him inside.

I nodded and turned to leave, ignoring Logan's inquisitive stare. Whatever he was thinking, I knew it wasn't humorous or flirty. He didn't look happy with my interaction with Oliver, and I couldn't understand why. Walking down from his porch, I felt his gaze on my back until I stepped down his driveway and heard him finally close his front door.

Blowing out a deep breath I'd been holding, I felt lighter but completely confused. As I stepped onto my own property, I stopped, exhaling deeply as I realized where I recognized that look from: My grandfather had given the same one to the few men my mother had brought around when I was little. I shook my head, continuing to my front steps.

Logan was always surprising me with what he said or did, but this time it made sense. I'd never seen his protective-father side, and to be honest, I was starting to worry he may not have one. But after that day, I knew there might just be more to Logan West than meets the eye.

Smiling to myself, I glanced over to Logan's house, wondering what he was really like behind the stone wall he'd carefully built around himself.

# Chapter Nine

## ONE STEP FORWARD

I finally found a spot to park my car along the crowded street five minutes before noon. It seemed every resident in town was there, walking down the sidewalks, surrounded by their children. Pulling my shades down from my head, I slid them on, weaving my way to the massive fountain in the center of the town square.

That afternoon was a record-breaking scorcher for the area. Even in cutoff faded jean shorts, a coral tank top, and cream ballet flats, I felt the heat beating down over me. In need of relief, I twisted my hair up off my back, flinging it over my front shoulder.

Approaching a row of caricaturists sitting behind their easels, I grew captivated by the exciting mood surrounding me and felt fully prepared for a day of carnival rides and cotton candy. I smiled to myself as the scent of fresh popcorn filled my nostrils. Memories of past times here as a child flickered through my mind, adding to my breeziness.

"Cassandra, you came!" Oliver yelled as I approached. He

raced toward me, grinning ear to ear, but it was Logan who caught my attention. His light-wash jeans and grey V-neck shirt were, for once, not drawing my attention—instead, it was his apprehensive expression that noticeably relaxed when he saw me. Did he really think I might stand up a four-year-old child? Insulted by the thought, I shook my head, smiling down at Oliver.

"Daddy bought me a bracelet to ride any ride I want all day." He held up his wrist. "And here," he said, pulling a matching yellow plastic bracelet from his pocket, "this one's for you!"

He put the bracelet in my hand and I looked over to Logan standing beside his son, his face unreadable. I smiled and reached into my pocket, pulling out the small coin purse I stuffed cash and my ID in to repay him. His hand covered mine, startling me.

"You don't owe me anything, Cassandra—I owe *you* for helping me with Oliver. Plus, we're hoping to convince you to spend the rest of the day here with us," Logan said, his soft expression melting the last shred of reluctance I'd built up.

I nodded, my lips curling into a tight smile, before tucking the wallet back into my pocket. Logan took the bracelet from me and turned my hand palm side up, snapping it in place on my wrist. I pulled my hand away, trying to block out the tingles humming along my skin.

"Where's Julia?" I stammered, looking around, hoping to see her appear. Spending the day with just Oliver and Logan left my stomach rolling.

"She said to tell you something came up, but she'd try to make it later," Logan explained. His eyebrows lowered and he looked away, then back at me with a quizzical expression. "She's been acting secretive lately. Any idea why? She seems to like you enough to tell you if she's hiding some college frat boy from me."

I snorted and looked down quickly, slightly embarrassed, before speaking. "Would it be so bad if she was dating someone?"

"Depends."

"On?"

Logan's lips pulled into a faint smile, but didn't answer.

"Come on!" Oliver pouted.

I smiled, laughing at his enthusiasm as he dragged me behind him through the swarms of people toward the edge of town, where the rides awaited us.

Up first was the Ferris wheel, which came as a huge relief since I'd had lunch moments before arriving. Oliver climbed up in the seat first so he had the best view to look out the side, and I followed. Having not realized what that meant, I inhaled a deep breath when Logan followed and sat down beside me. The metal seat was barely big enough for all three of us, which pressed me up against the one man who sent my body into overdrive.

*Breathe. Slow breaths, in and out.*

His left arm stretched behind the seat and rested on his son's shoulder. *A protective move?* The way Logan looked around me to smile at his son told me it was.

"Sit down, Oliver. It's going to start moving now," Logan explained the second a man with long red hair and an AC/DC shirt clamped down the metal bar.

Logan's thigh pressed against mine, and out of the corner of my eye, I caught the slight tug on his lips. I'd promised myself that morning that I'd enjoy the day and ignore any of Logan's flirtatious advances, so I did just that. I wasn't about to let him have the upper hand.

Relaxing back into the seat, I ran my right hand through my hair and then let it fall straight onto Logan's upper thigh. It was just high enough to cause him to react. He swallowed, his eyes shooting down to my hand, then up to meet my gaze.

"Sorry." I shrugged, squeezing my hand inches from his zipper before pulling back as if it were accidental.

He cleared his throat and shifted in his seat. Yeah, I could handle this man—especially with Oliver around.

After the Ferris wheel, we rode ride after ride for the next hour until I needed a break. The ground was spinning under me from all the swirling motion, and I could've sworn Logan had two heads at one point.

"Cotton candy time!" Oliver exclaimed, his hand locked in mine.

I nodded and let him lead the way to the nearest stand. Logan stepped around me to order, but I grabbed his forearm and pushed him to the side, catching him off guard.

"I'm paying," I insisted sternly.

Before he could argue, someone called his name from behind us.

"Logan, hi! I was hoping you'd be here."

I didn't bother to pay attention to the female voice babbling to Logan as I paid for the three sticks of cotton candy; at least a dozen women had hit on him so far that day. I handed one stick to Oliver and had frozen mid-turn to give Logan his bright-pink bushel of fluffy candy when I saw Mackenzie with her hand placed around his arm, giggling.

My head shot down, ice dripping in my veins as I closed my eyes. Everything around me grew quiet as I willed myself to think straight. I wasn't going to give her the satisfaction of humiliating me yet again. I righted my posture and stepped closer.

"Here you go." I handed Logan the stick of cotton candy before twisting to face Mackenzie with an exaggerated contrived smile.

115

"Oliver and I will walk around while you…have some fun," I said with a bite, staring back at Logan. "Take all the time you need."

Turning on my heel, I took Oliver's hand to leave, but Mackenzie's shrill voice rang out.

"This is Oliver?" She stepped toward us, ready to pounce on the poor child. "Hi, I've been looking forward to meeting you. My name's Mackenzie. I'm a friend of your daddy's." She bent down to shake his hand, but looked quickly back over her shoulder to Logan with a wink.

It was then I noticed her new position caused her tiny floral print dress to rise up, giving Logan a full view of her hot-pink thong. I made a face, repulsed. Logan chuckled, staring not at the desperate whore putting on a show, but at me.

Oliver stood watching her, but didn't shake her hand. Mackenzie didn't seem to care as she let it fall to her side. She looked almost scary, especially to a child, with her giant grin full of teeth surrounded by bright-red lips and black eyeliner. "Would you like to go ride the Ferris wheel with me?" Mackenzie continued. "Your daddy can come too." She reached for Oliver's hand, but he took a couple steps back, squeezing my hand tighter.

"I already rode that," he said. "I want to play games with Cassandra now."

"Are you sure?" she asked with a hint of desperation. She smiled back at Logan as she stood back up, not willing to admit defeat. Logan's expression darkened as he stared at his son, reading him. "I can take you to play some games. I'm pretty good friends with some of the guys running them. I can get you a prize at every one, whether you win or lose."

His brows pinched. "I don't want a prize if I lose. You have to earn it. Right, Daddy?"

Logan nodded and walked over to take his son's other

hand. "Let's go play some games...with Cassandra."

I bit my bottom lip, holding back my smile as Logan led us away without another look back at Mackenzie. She stood with her arms crossed over her chest, her eyebrows furrowed.

—◆◆◆—

Game after game, Logan won while Oliver and I found our only success with goldfish. Between us, we won four tiny goldfish. I had no idea where I was going to put them at home.

"One more game," Logan said, smiling. He walked over to the darts booth and handed the man a twenty. Taking two darts, he placed them in my hand.

I sighed. "Seriously, you're wasting your money."

"That's for me to decide," Logan said.

"Pop that one—the green one!" Oliver cheered, pointing to the center balloon.

I held up the dart and threw it straight at the green balloon, blowing out a heavy breath and watching as it fell before making contact.

Logan chuckled and Oliver slugged him playfully in the gut. "You said it's not nice to laugh at girls!"

He raised his eyebrows at him, looking stunned yet pleased.

I smiled. "Yeah, it's not nice!" I added.

Logan held up his hands. "My apologies. Here, let me show you." Logan stepped behind me, causing every nerve in my body to come alive as he placed his arm around my waist to hold me still. His other hand covered mine over the dart.

"Focus on the green balloon," he murmured.

My eyes fluttered shut. I was trying to find my bearings when I felt his chest connect with my back. I couldn't think, couldn't breathe. I needed him to move away from me before I either turned around to maul him or passed out from lack of oxygen. I cleared my throat and threw the dart, failing to hit anything but the wood of the frame around the balloons, then quickly wiggled out of his hold.

Stepping away from him, I turned to face him and shrugged. "Why don't you try?"

Logan looked at me, gauging my expression as the man in the booth held out two more darts. I grabbed them, thankful to break eye contact, and handed them to Logan. He won three games in a row. Oliver shrieked each time, applauding wildly. When Logan finished off twenty dollars' worth of playing, he chose a giant stuffed pink flamingo.

"Here you go, little man." Logan smiled, handing it to Oliver.

"Cassandra can have it. She didn't win anything but fish." He giggled and Logan joined in, holding out the prize.

"Well, sweetheart, we'd hate to see you go home empty-handed."

"Ha ha," I laughed dryly before attempting to yank it from his grip.

But he didn't release it—instead, he pulled me into him. As I felt his hot breath run over my ear, he whispered, "Thank you."

I stepped back when my breath caught and watched his gaze flicker to his giggling son. Oliver was having a blast, and I was happy to be a part of it. I nodded once in understanding to Logan before grabbing Oliver's hand and skipping away for another game.

"I'm hungry," Oliver complained around six o'clock, so I led him toward the grassy area near the parade route while Logan disappeared to retrieve something edible without sugar in it.

"The parade should start soon. My mother is in it," I said, stretching my legs out in front of me. The aroma of freshly cut grass mixed with that of the food trucks was heavenly.

"Really?" Oliver's eyes grew wide, staring at me.

I nodded, smiling. "She works at the sheriff's department, and every year she helps build a raft."

"Wow! Do you get to ride on it?" he asked, sitting up on his knees, intrigued.

"When I was younger. You know, I—"

"Cassandra!" I turned to see Caleb and Hilary walking hand in hand, heading straight for us.

We'd only seen each other briefly after school the past few days, but she surprised me by showing up on my doorstep the morning after Caleb's speed-dating shindig. She was so eager to spill every detail of her evening by his side that she braved my morning jog with me. Turned out, Caleb was even more of a gentleman than I'd realized: To Hilary's extreme disappointment, he'd kept his hands to himself and didn't make a move.

She'd been hoping their date to the carnival meant she'd finally have a taste of his luscious pink lips—her words, not mine—and if I had to listen to her describe those lips one more time, I swore I'd reconsider our friendship. The girl had it bad.

I smiled. "Hey, I was wondering when I'd run into you guys."

"Caleb's been dragging me around to every single ride they set up here," Hilary complained, but it was clear she couldn't be happier.

"You know you loved it." Caleb chuckled, brushing a strand of hair from her cheek.

Hilary blushed and smiled. "I'm glad you decided to come. I didn't think you would."

"Yeah, Oliver convinced me."

"So you're here with Logan as well?" She turned a

suspicious eye on me.

"I'm here with Oliver, and since Logan is his father, yes, he's here."

"Logan's a good guy," Caleb said, releasing his hand from Hilary's and grabbing Oliver, tossing him up over his shoulders. Oliver squealed wildly as Caleb raced across the field.

"I'm glad I ran into you," said Hilary. "I have something to tell you, and please don't be mad."

Frowning, I turned my attention away from Caleb and his mimicking of gorilla sounds. I laughed. "Well, it's too early for you to be knocked up with Caleb's lovechild, so what is it?"

"Caleb hired a new guy at the restaurant. He's really cute and nice, and—" She stopped, sucking in a deep breath.

*Oh God, what did she do?*

"And?" I sat up straight, realizing where this was going.

"He asked about you. I told him you're single, and…he wants to get together with you next Saturday night." Her words flew out quickly, as if that would help persuade me to agree.

"No," I said, shaking my head.

"Come on! He wants to have dinner at Haven, that's all."

I sighed, kneading the back of my neck. "Hilary…"

"You have to admit, it could do you some good. Maybe give you a carefree night to release some of that pent-up frustration?" Her brows rose. "It could possibly help put an end to your indecent dreams about Logan. Unless you'd rather…" she leaned in, grinning, "go to him for help with that. I'm sure he wouldn't mind."

"You're terrible, you know that?"

"So is that a yes? He's really cute. I swear you won't regret it."

"Hope you like corn dogs," Logan said, walking over with

120

Caleb and Oliver.

"Fine, I'll go," I whispered. Maybe it *was* exactly what I needed.

"Great. We'll see you guys later," Hilary said, smiling at Logan and Oliver.

Caleb took her hand after saying goodbye and they walked away, back to the busy street.

"This looks perfect," I said, taking the enormous stick of fried food and a bottle of water from his hands. "Thanks."

"I only have so many hands, so I hope you don't mind sharing some fries."

Logan and I sat with Oliver between us. He placed a basket full of large French fries with ketchup squirted on the side in front of us.

"Looks good." I smiled, snatching one and taking a bite. *Delicious.*

"Her mom made one of the floats for the parade!" Oliver said before stuffing his mouth with a giant bite of his corn dog.

"Is that so?" Logan looked behind his son to me.

"Yeah, and I was just thinking I should go find her before it gets too dark."

"You have to finish your food first," Oliver said, "and promise to come back."

Logan and I laughed at his assertive tone, but I agreed quickly.

I finished my corn dog and sent a short text to my mother, asking her to meet me by her raft. Logan and Oliver walked with me for a while, but introducing my mother to Logan was not in my plan.

"I'll be right back," I said, walking away to greet my mother.

I could see her standing by her float, dressed in her sheriff's uniform and talking to a guy I didn't recognize.

"Hey, there you are," she said, smiling at me. She pulled me in for her usual hug, then stepped back with a scrunched brow. "You must be Logan West. I've heard a lot about you."

*Damn, there goes that plan.* How had I not realized he'd followed me? My mother could talk your ear off like no one else, and knew all the most inappropriate questions to ask.

"A pleasure to meet you, Mrs. Clarke," Logan replied, shaking her hand.

"Call me Felicia." She smiled, looking him up and down.

*Here it comes.* I knew my mother well enough to know now was the time to retreat, but I still had a favor to ask first. But before I could get a word in, she was absorbed in Logan.

"So, how are you enjoying Harmony?" she asked. I narrowed my eyes at her, but she only smiled, staring at Logan and ignoring me.

"It's lovely. I was actually born here."

My head cocked to the side, and I gazed at him. That was a piece of information I never knew, and suddenly I found myself wanting to know more.

"Really?" my mother asked.

He nodded. "We moved to the city when I was still a toddler. I don't remember living here, but so far I'm quite taken with your town."

"Yes, it's a nice place to live. I grew up here, as did Cassandra." My mother finally looked at me, and I noticed the spark in her eye. I grimaced.

"So, are you and Cassandra here together on a date?" she asked bluntly.

"Mom…" I mumbled under my breath. I placed my hand on Oliver's shoulder and spoke up. "This is Oliver, Logan's son. I'm here hanging out with him."

My mother's smile grew wider. "I see. Well, you know, my daughter is single, and I may be biased, but everyone in town agrees she's gorgeous. She just needs a good man in her life." Logan smiled as my mother stepped closer to pick a piece of grass from the side of his shirt. My ears smoldered as she continued. "Did you know she bakes and loves kids? She even enjoys cleaning. A natural-born housewife."

I rolled my eyes, heat rising in my cheeks. Logan nodded along, glancing at me from the corner of his eye with a crooked smile as my mother recited my girlfriend-material qualifications. This wasn't the first time, but it was by far the worst.

"I also caught her and Mark, her horrible ex," my mother made a face after speaking his name, "down at the river skinny dipping once. So my daughter is no prude."

"Mom!" I shrieked, humiliated.

She shrugged. "What? I worry about you, and Logan here seems very nice and handsome." Her smile grew when she looked back at Logan. "Do you plan on having more children one day? I would love a few grandchildren running around, but Cassie's still a little young; she needs to enjoy a healthy relationship first."

I cringed, focusing my attention on the ground, hoping to hide the flush I was sure covered my entire body.

Logan chuckled. "Cassandra's lovely. I've definitely enjoyed getting to know her." His lips turned up in a handsome smile, his gaze shifting toward me.

"She's my friend," Oliver spoke up, reminding everyone he was there.

"Yes, I am. Which reminds me: I need to ask you a favor," I said, glaring at my mother.

"And here I thought you just wanted to introduce me to your handsome new neighbor." She laughed once, completely aware of her actions.

Plastering a tight smile on my face, I held up a finger to

let Logan know I'd be a minute before grabbing her arm to lead her a few feet away. Talking softly, I asked my question, and smiled when she agreed. My mother walked away without another word; she'd said enough, and I turned back to face the impatient child looking around for something to do.

"All right, so I have a surprise for you." I crouched down in front of Oliver. "How would you like to ride on the float in the parade with the sheriff and his special furry friend?"

My mother appeared just then with a large dog from the canine unit at her side.

Oliver's eyes grew wide and he took off running toward the dog, eager to pet him. "Can I, Daddy?"

"Of course." Logan nodded, smiling.

"All right, let's get you up there. The parade will start the moment the first firework goes off, so say goodbye to your father and Cassandra," my mother said, helping Oliver onto the float.

Logan and I waved goodbye and began walking the short distance down the grassy path to find a clear spot. We found a quiet place a little ways from the road, but with a perfect view to see Oliver when he passed. I crossed my legs under me, unable to find anything to say; my mother had said enough. The longer we sat, the more Logan looked mentally preoccupied. Between his rigid posture and silent treatment, I could sense something was bothering him.

"Oliver will be fine. He's surrounded by a dozen officers and the toughest dog in town." I nudged his side playfully with my elbow.

He glanced up at me, frowning.

"We'll meet him at the end of the parade route. My mother will keep him close. Try to relax," I added, reassuring him.

His worried expression deepened as he continued to stare

at me before suddenly looking away. "Oliver had a lot of fun today," he finally said, gazing at the street ahead.

"He still is." I smiled, hoping to see Logan do the same. Instead, his eyebrows furrowed, and a heavy sigh escaped his lips. Something was definitely wrong.

Before I could pry, he cocked his head to the side, staring quizzically at me.

"I'm glad Oliver likes you, and that you're...kind to him, but..." He looked down, fidgeting with his hands placed over his knees in front of him. "Please don't make any more promises to my son, Cassandra."

"Logan, I—"

"Just don't," he said firmly, closing the subject just as the fireworks began filling the sky.

Oliver rode by, waving to the crowd and wearing a giant grin, my mother at his side. He looked enthusiastically happy, but I had a feeling that wasn't always the case. Logan's tense posture told me there was a lot I didn't know.

I placed my hand over Logan's resting in the grass beside me, but kept my focus on the parade ahead of us as I swallowed the lump in my throat.

"I won't let anything happen to him when I'm around. And I won't make any promises to him that I can't keep—you can trust me on that."

I could feel Logan's gaze on me, but he said nothing. There was nothing he needed to say. Oliver was a good kid, and I understood why his father needed to protect him. It couldn't be easy being a single father, or a child without a mother.

As I removed my hand, his fingers gripped mine for a brief second. Inhaling deeply, I pulled away slowly to wave back at Oliver, trying to ignore the new feelings growing inside me.

# Chapter Ten

## TWO STEPS BACK

Spending the entire day with Oliver and Logan at the carnival had opened my eyes. They were a family—just the two of them. I understood how hard it could be with only one parent, but Logan was doing a better job than most men would. My sympathy for him made it easier to ignore the woman sneaking out of his house while I prepared for my jog the next morning.

I didn't recognize her as she walked to her car just after five in the morning, clutching her pink heels, her hair disheveled and with mascara streaked down her face. I shook my head, popping my ear buds in and jogging past his property.

The week passed with Logan occasionally catching my attention while picking Oliver up from school, but otherwise we went our separate ways. Oliver, on the other hand, enjoyed hanging out in my treehouse, and after a little persuading he managed to talk me into fixing it up.

Truthfully, it wasn't exactly safe the way it was; between the rotting floorboards and rickety ladder, it was an accident waiting to happen. To my complete surprise, on Tuesday morning—my regular day off—I opened the door to two burly men dressed neatly in maroon polo shirts and khaki shorts.

"Um, can I help you?" I asked, standing in my doorway, fresh from my morning shower.

"We're here to help with the treehouse in the back," the tall man explained. It was then that I noticed the toolbox in his hand.

I shook my head, scrunching my brows. "I didn't—"

"Mr. West told us you'd be home today, and to help any way you needed on the place."

"Oh," I muttered, taken aback. It made sense, since it was his son playing there. Instead of walking next door, insisting I could do all the work myself, I smiled politely. "Go on around back, and I'll be out in a moment."

By the end of the day, my old hangout looked brand new. I painted the old furniture bright blues and greens while the men did the real work. Oliver came over just before dinner, making a beeline for the new sturdy ladder.

"Wow, this is great!" he exclaimed, climbing up.

I followed behind him, smiling as he took a seat at my previously hot-pink table. "Blue is much better." He grinned.

Oliver helped me hang some of the old signs from my childhood, and then ran home for dinner, explaining he'd bring over some of his artwork to hang later.

Later came and went with no sign of Oliver, so feeling pleased with the events of the day and wanting to thank Logan, I walked next door and rang the buzzer. After waiting another minute, I rang it again, and then turned to leave. *Maybe they went out.*

The moment I stepped down the first step, the door opened. I turned back, smiling, expecting to see Oliver or Logan. Instead, there stood a tall, blonde supermodel—at least, she could pass for one. She wore nothing but a silky black sheet wrapped around her barely twenty-one-year-old body.

She giggled back at someone in the house before turning to me. "Oh, you're not Zoey," she panted. Her heavy accent was foreign to my ears. I watched her expression drop to disappointment.

At a loss for words, I saw the lights of a car approach and watched another perky blonde wearing a men's button-down shirt as a dress saunter up beside me.

"There you are!" The first girl giggled, licking her lips.

"Come on, ladies, I don't enjoy being left waiting."

Logan's voice filled me with disgust. I rolled my eyes, hoping Oliver was no longer home, and turned to leave.

"We're coming, baby. There's some girl here who's not with us. Should I tell her to leave?"

"She's *definitely* not with us dressed like that." The second girl laughed, her accent matching the first's. She looked me up and down, then smiled wickedly. "Unless this is a country-bumpkin roleplaying thing you got going on. I bet you've got some great tits hiding underneath there."

Insulted and stunned, I scoffed and looked down at my oversized cutoff denim overalls and white tank top. With a shake of my head, my blood boiling, I snapped, "Enjoy yourselves, ladies. Make sure he pays you well—he's got the cash."

With that, I turned and stomped back down the drive.

"Cassandra!"

I stopped, standing by his gate, and looked back to see Logan standing in his open doorway, his perfect body bare aside from a pair of black boxer briefs. He was staring straight at me, his face illuminated under the glow of the porch light. He tilted his head just the slightest and opened his mouth, but then shut it tight again. There was nothing he could say.

I sighed, disappointed, and continued home with a new sense of sadness for Oliver.

Logan West was a pig. That wasn't going to change, no matter how much I wanted to believe differently.

——◆◆◆——

The next day after school, Hilary showed up ready to drag me out of the house to go find the perfect dress for my blind date the following night. Reluctantly, I agreed.

"So, what do you know about this guy?" I asked as we entered the small boutique sporting a giant sale sign in the window.

"Not much, but Caleb says he's a hard worker," she replied, holding up a low-cut, red dress that looked more streetwalker than first date.

"No." I made a face, shaking my head. "Absolutely not."

Hilary shrugged, hanging it back on the rack, and continued her search. I'd already explained on the drive over what I was looking for: sexy and sweet, but not too revealing; in other words, nothing that reeked of desperation.

"So, what's this Kurt like?" I asked, wandering toward a rack of shoes.

"He's…cute."

I looked over at her, narrowing my eyes. "You *have* at least met him, right?"

"Of course!" Her voice sounded insulted, but then she added in a whisper, "…Once."

"Once!?" I gasped, and my entire body grew rigid. "You said he asked you about me!"

"He did, which is when I met him." Her voice was soft. She was aware she was busted.

"Hilary!" I placed the nude heel in my hand back on its shelf and turned to leave.

"Hear me out, please." She grabbed my arm to stop me.

"You have ten seconds."

"Kurt came into Haven looking for a job a week ago. Caleb said he knew the guy from a friend, and agreed to take him on when he explained he'd been having trouble affording an apartment. He noticed you during the speed-dating night and asked me if I'd help set something up." She sighed, releasing her grip on my arm. "Caleb insisted if you guys went out that you do it there so he could keep an eye on you, but Kurt seems innocent enough."

I exhaled deeply through my nostrils, lips pressed tightly together. I shook my head and looked slowly around the brightly painted store. *What am I getting myself into?*

Hilary must've caught on to my resolve because a small smile crept over her lips. "Look, he seems nice, all right? And I think you'll have at least one or two things in common. Maybe he won't be Mr. Right, but he could be Mr. Right Now. You need to have some fun, Cassandra. You were with Mark for *five years*—time to date a little and see what's out there."

I looked her straight in the eyes. "Fine, but he better not be some creep or perverted old guy." She laughed, and I couldn't hold the frown on my lips any longer. I chuckled and brushed past her, grabbing the heels I'd picked up earlier.

"How old is old?" I heard her ask a moment later.

"Hilary!"

"Just kidding!" she laughed as I threw a sandal in her direction. "Trust me. Just don't overthink everything he says and tomorrow night will be fine."

A mischievous spark shimmered in her eyes, which I took as my cue to hurry up and pick an outfit.

"So, shall we head over to the lingerie department?" Her voice lit with amusement.

I rolled my eyes and grabbed the four possible dress

options we'd placed on a rack. Without a reply to her absurd comment, I slipped into the small fitting room.

In truth, it'd been over a year since I'd last had sex. Even though I refused to have a one-night stand with my charming neighbor, maybe relieving some pent-up tension with Kurt wouldn't be the worst thing. I missed it more than I'd ever let on—not just the sex, but also the safe and tender feeling of being wrapped up with someone I couldn't get enough of. With Mark, it was always rushed, but there were those few special times afterward where he would cuddle up behind me. They were rare—he enjoyed a cold beer and a loud sports game after sex—but I cherished them more than anything.

Maybe Kurt could give me that, at least for one night. I sighed, switching my thoughts away from anything depressing, and shook the ridiculous notion from my head with a laugh.

"Any luck in there?" Hilary called.

Pulling back the curtain, I revealed the little black dress that hugged my body in all the right ways but didn't scream 'slut.'

"Wow. Yeah, that's the one." She grinned as I twirled in front of the long mirrors.

I agreed. It was perfect.

"So, I have to ask…did something happen with Logan?"

My head shot up, confused as to why she'd even ask. *Did Logan say something to Caleb?*

"No. Why?" I continued staring in the mirror, but my thoughts no longer had anything to do with the dress.

"Nothing."

"Hilary…" I warned, turning to face her, arms crossed over my chest.

"Fine." She sighed, looking around nervously. "Caleb said Logan was at Haven last night and that he was really down on himself—completely the opposite of what Caleb is used to seeing. He even went home alone."

I marched back into the fitting room. I didn't care, nor did I want to hear more.

"He was also asking a lot of questions about you," Hilary continued through the curtain.

Curiosity prevented me, against my better judgment, from changing the subject.

"Like what—if I charge by the hour?" I bit my lip. *Why did I just say that?*

The curtain flew open and Hilary rushed inside, shutting it behind her.

"What?" her voice was dripping with repulsion.

"Ugh, nothing." I finished dressing, ignoring her impatient stares.

"Obviously it's something, so either tell me or I'll be making a pit stop at Logan's."

Unsure of what to tell her without freaking her out, I slid on my flats and moved to walk past her. She blocked my way.

"Talk. Now," she demanded.

I told her everything about what I saw, and all she could do was stare at me in disbelief.

"So you think the man hired prostitutes?" She shook her head. "Half the women in town want to sleep with him. Why pay for it?"

"I have no idea." I made a face. "But I just want to forget it happened, so can we please not talk about him again?"

She nodded and allowed me to exit the dressing room.

"This is just another reason why you need a date: something to get your mind off how shitty men can be and remind you how much fun you can have with a good one."

She was right. What was I doing waiting for my knight in shining armor? Men were all the same, and I was a fool to think I'd be surprised by any of them. I was fresh out of college, and while there, I'd never lived the true college experience.

I bit my bottom lip, butterflies fluttering wildly inside me. Tomorrow night, I'd have some fun, one way or another.

---

After I paid for the dress and heels, we headed to my house and relaxed on the back porch. I promised Hilary I'd let down my guard and give Kurt a fair chance. Who knew? Maybe we really would hit it off. She was thrilled, and to my complete shock, she pulled a box of condoms from her purse and tossed it on my lap.

"What the hell!?" I shrieked. "You gonna set up a health clinic?"

"Hey, better safe than…well, knocked up."

I tossed them back. "Yeah, I'm good."

Hilary reached back, slid open the screen door behind us, and tossed the box on my kitchen counter.

I'd opened my mouth to complain when she smiled. "Is that Oliver?"

Sure enough, Oliver was skipping toward us. Hilary looked pleased when I shot her an irritated silent glare that clearly stated, "Abort condom conversation."

I turned my attention back to Oliver and grinned to myself. Something about the small tot always made me smile.

"Hi, Cassandra," he said as he stopped in front of us.

"Hey buddy, this is Hilary. You met her at the carnival last week."

"I remember. Caleb is your friend, and he's awesome!"

She giggled, nodding in agreement with him.

"So, how have you been?" I asked, placing my glass of water on the table beside me.

"Great! Sorry I couldn't come back over last night. Daddy

had an important meeting, so I had a sleepover at my cousin's."

"You stayed over on a school night?" My voice came out sounding as disturbed as I felt.

"Yeah, Daddy said his clients were from out of town." His face melted into a slight frown. He looked down, and the smile was back instantly as he held up a paper bag he'd been holding. "But I brought over my artwork now, and Daddy even helped me pick out awesome frames to hang them."

I couldn't help smiling. Logan was a grown man—who was I to care what or whom he did in his free time? His clients, as he called them, were definitely from out of town, so at least it wasn't a total lie.

"All right, let's go hang them up." I stood up. "I'll race you!" With a playful grin, I ran past him.

# Chapter Eleven

## LOWERED INHIBITIONS

I stood outside Haven for what felt like forever, my entire body painfully alive and rigid. My hands were clammy, and trembled as I ran them down my short black dress and pulled on my best confident smile.

My feet carried me at a snail's pace through the door as the unnerving need to turn around and run echoed through my mind. This was an enormous step for me, but one I needed to take to put myself back out in the dating world. Just the word—dating—terrified me beyond justifiable reasoning. Mark had been my first and only boyfriend; what was I supposed to know about dating and what men expected?

"Cassandra?" A tall, dark-haired man stepped away from Caleb, who was leaning against the bar with a clipboard in hand.

Caleb winked with a soft smile and headed off behind the bar.

"Hi, you must be Kurt," I said, holding the smile on my face as smoothly as possible. My cheeks stung from the force it took, but it was the only way to control the bundle of nerves racing through me as he drew closer.

I was going to kill Hilary for this. The man was at least thirty-five, and considering this was my first real date ever, he was not what I'd expected. I'd never even considered dating someone more than five or *maybe* ten years older, let alone almost fifteen years.

I had to admit, though, she wasn't lying about his looks—he *was* handsome, in a rugged sort of way. His long hair hung just past his jaw and was tucked behind his ears. I couldn't help noticing his eyes, which were an intense, deep-grey shade that clouded with a dark glimmer when he did a quick once over of my body. He was dressed in simple beat-up blue jeans and a plain white tee. The man was all muscle, with a large, amateur-looking tattoo on his forearm.

I knew Hilary's intentions were more to help me dip my toes back in the water than find a steady boyfriend; the condoms sitting on my kitchen table proved that point. And judging by Kurt's cool demeanor, he looked plenty experienced in helping a girl do just that.

"Wow! I knew you were pretty, but…" He tilted his head to the side, his lips curling up into a crooked smile. "Seeing you up close, gorgeous is a more fitting description."

I smiled, biting my lip as heat spread over my cheeks. "Thanks, you're not too bad yourself." *Okay, I can do this.* He took my hand, placing a small kiss on my knuckles. I felt my confidence grow as he guided us over to a small table in the corner.

He was making tonight easier than I'd expected. He was sweet, attractive, and after a few drinks I'd have the courage to open up and try to get to know him a little. One fun date could possibly be the best thing for me. Part of me wanted to hit it off with Kurt just so I could officially move on from my past with Mark. Then the bastard would no longer be my only lover.

If we heated things up tonight in *that* department, it would also help soothe some of the ache I felt whenever I spent time around Logan. As much as I hated to admit it, Logan did things to my body I couldn't explain, and until I put out those flames he kept igniting for good, I was bound to attack his perfect body sooner or later. And that was not an option.

Against all rational thought, in the back of my mind I found myself thinking if all I wanted was a night of passion, maybe giving into Logan for just sex—with a mutual agreement that it never be spoken of afterward—could work. Nobody would have to find out, and nothing would need to change.

I shook my head to clear the absurd idea. *What the hell is the matter with me?* I couldn't stand the complication that would cause, with us being neighbors. Not to mention I was completely repulsed at his little ménage à trois the other day. I was definitely *not* his type.

Sitting across from Kurt, I held up the menu, debating what I was in the mood for—well, aside from a careless one-night stand, preferably with my arrogant neighbor.

"So, what made you want to work here at Haven?" I asked, lowering my menu to catch his gaze. It wasn't the most appealing job in town—not like Logan's, anyway. I berated myself inwardly for thinking of him yet again.

"I, um, recently moved to town. Needed a job, and Caleb was nice enough to offer. It's nothing permanent...just until I find something else."

I nodded with a small smile. The waitress came over to take our drink order, and Kurt ordered a bottle of wine. The man was reading my mind.

"So, I hear you're a teacher." He pushed his menu to the edge of the table. I caught his gaze and found myself being drawn into him.

I swallowed; something in his expression was sexy, yet dangerous. It was new and exciting. "Yes, kindergarten." My voice cracked. Where was the damn waitress with our drinks? I needed that wine to help me relax, pronto.

"That sounds...interesting," he chuckled.

The waitress finally appeared, setting down the bottle and two wine glasses.

"Thanks," I mumbled, watching as Kurt filled my glass. I downed the entire thing quickly, looking up through my lashes, slightly embarrassed. He gave me an impressed look before refilling my glass, a soft smile dancing on his lips. It was nothing like the smirks Logan threw my way. My head fell slightly, annoyed he was still in my thoughts, and I took another sip.

I really needed to stop thinking about Logan. It would never work, and based on the reputation Logan had built in the short time he'd lived here, it was painfully obvious he wasn't capable of having a meaningful relationship. There would never be anything between us, not the way I would need it. I'd only end up with a broken heart. I wouldn't do that to myself.

Here I was with a handsome, mysterious man sitting in front of me, giving me compliment after compliment throughout the night; I needed to focus on him. I could tell Kurt was attracted to me, he made it obvious and I had no doubt he would come home with me and show me everything I'd been missing sexually if I gave him the go ahead. It could be an enjoyable night, I reasoned, lifting my glass and taking another large sip to dull my screaming conscience. I was going to need a lot more to drink before this night was over.

——◆◆◆——

By the time dessert was in front of me, I was feeling free

as a bird flying high in the clouds. Nothing mattered, and for the first time in weeks, Logan was out of my head. Kurt was full of ridiculously silly jokes that kept me giggling as I downed glass after glass of wine. In all my life, I'd never experienced more than a mild buzz from drinking; always the responsible one. But tonight, I could see the appeal of alcohol.

Kurt seemed nice, and the longer we sat there chatting about frivolous nonsense, the more I was fighting with myself as to why this was a bad idea. I deserved it after everything that had happened with Mark. I'd spent so much of my life dedicated to him, only to be let down. Everyone around me easily let go of their inhibitions the second an attractive person entered the room, so why not give it a try for once in my life? It was time to live a little.

With another sip of wine to settle remaining nerves, I reached across the table and placed my hand over his, running my thumb across knuckles. His face lit up instantly with a smile, and he responded by brushing his fingers against my palm and giving my hand a gentle squeeze.

"Can I give you a ride home?" he asked after the waitress had collected our plates. I'd told him earlier that a friend brought me due to car trouble, which wasn't entirely true but made it easier—at least, that's how Hilary explained it when she'd dropped me off. Tonight, I was taking a new Cassandra out for a test drive, hoping she didn't crash and burn.

"Yeah, that would be nice."

He released my hand to pull out his wallet, placing some cash next to the bill while I finished off my fourth glass of wine.

"Hello."

My jaw went slack and all air spilled from my lungs as the familiar husky voice hummed through me.

"Logan." Kurt twisted in his seat, noticeably irritated.

"How are you?"

Logan's gaze burned into me from above but I kept my head down, eyes focused on the empty glass twirling in my fingers.

"Hello, Cassandra. How are you tonight, sweetheart?"

Closing my eyes, I inhaled a deep silent breath and put on the best smile I could muster before looking up. My breath caught at the intensity in his hazy-blue eyes.

"Hey, what are you doing here?" I narrowed my eyes, not wanting to be interrupted by him of all people while on a date. Grabbing the bottle, I attempted to pour myself another glass of wine with shaky hands. I was officially drunk and slowly feeling the effects.

Kurt took the nearly empty bottle quickly and poured the remainder into my glass. Both men watched expectantly as I wasted no time tipping it back and swallowing in one large gulp.

Kurt cleared his throat. "Logan is here most nights," he snickered. "Good for business, Caleb says. You should see all the women who flock to this guy. They can't seem to get enough of him."

"I'm sure," I mumbled, gazing back up at Logan, his eyes still holding me in their sight. "Well, don't let us keep you. I'm sure there's some pretty little tramp hanging around here waiting for you to take her home." Apparently, I wasn't a friendly drunk. I rolled my eyes, swallowing the repulsion I felt thinking about Logan taking home one of the town's barflies.

Logan's searing gaze held steady as he ignored my remark. "So you had a nice dinner?" His tone was soft, despite my insult.

*Why is he still here?* His voice was smooth and void of emotion, confusing me. But for some reason, I just felt angry. He had no right to stare at me like that. Was he judging me?

*Ha! He's hardly one to pass judgment.*

"Yes, it was great. I was just about to take Cassandra home," Kurt said as he stood from the booth. "We'll see you around."

"I see. Well, then, have a good night." Logan finally tore his eyes away, staring down at the tile floor, giving no clues as to what was going through his mind. It only added to my irritation. I ran my hands through my hair as he turned, walking back the way he'd come.

"You ready?" Kurt asked, offering a crooked smile.

I smiled, biting my bottom lip nervously. This was it: I was officially going to step out of my comfort zone and live on the outside for a night. He really was cute, and his lips were devilishly plump.

"Yeah," I murmured, placing my empty glass on the table. Kurt reached out and took my hand, helping me up. He was sweet, and the perfect gentleman.

"Oh, I almost forgot," Logan called out, turning back to face us. His darkened eyes stared down at my hand intertwined with Kurt's, but he held his unaffected composure as he spoke.

"Caleb is in the back." He inclined his head toward the double metal doors beside the bar, looking straight at Kurt. "He needs to speak with you before you leave."

"I'll be right back," Kurt told me after a moment's pause, placing a small kiss upon my knuckles before releasing my hand. The icy stare he shot at Logan when he shouldered past him was impossible to miss.

I waited until Kurt disappeared into the backroom, then crossed my arms over my chest. "Why are you here?" I asked, glaring at Logan.

"Are you going home with him?" His voice was strong and demanding—something I'd never heard from him before. His jaw worked hard under the skin, waiting impatiently for my answer.

How long had he been in the bar? Had he been watching me? How had I not noticed him? I grimaced. Usually I could sense when he was around. It had to be the alcohol in my system.

"He's driving me home, yes, and whatever happens after that is none of your business."

I reached down to the table to grab my purse but stumbled backward, groaning when Logan swept in and caught me around the waist before I fell.

"You're drunk, Cassandra." He sighed, holding me in his arms. His masculine scent filled my head, and I found myself unconsciously leaning further into him. His hand ran up my back, and I jolted back to reality. It would be a long time before I drank that much again.

I pushed against his chest, pulling out of his grasp and fighting to straighten myself. "Seriously!? This has nothing to do with you!"

He grabbed my hand, steadying me. "Shall I remind you you're a teacher in this town and someone my son holds in high regard? I'm sure you don't want to start rumors about the company you keep, or how you act at the local bar. Getting wasted doesn't seem like your style."

"Again: None. Of. Your. Business," I hissed, snatching my hand out of his. "Whether I want to take him home or not is up to me; it has nothing to do with you. I don't tell you who you should sleep with."

Logan froze. "Don't." His voice was suddenly full of more emotion than I could process in my inebriated state. His expression was hard—almost painfully so. He lowered his eyebrows and reached his hand out to touch me, but dropped it back to his side hesitantly. I watched his internal battle over his next move.

142

"What?" I sighed, completely annoyed, my brows scrunching in confusion.

"Please, Cassandra," he said. "You can't trust him."

He sounded so genuine I almost thought it was a different man in front of me instead of the narcissistic playboy I was used to dealing with.

"What are you talking about?"

"Did he tell you where he lived before moving here?"

"No, why?" I looked up and noticed Kurt heading back over to us, frowning.

Logan leaned into my ear and whispered, "Don't leave with him, please." His hot breath sent shivers down my spine when his lips brushed past my cheek. I could taste the bourbon he'd been drinking.

"Caleb said he didn't need anything," Kurt hissed through gritted teeth. He glared at Logan and snatched my hand. I winced at his tight grip.

"I guess he changed his mind." Logan's jaw clenched, his eyes glued to my hand wrapped once again in Kurt's.

"Right. You ready, Cassandra?" Kurt asked, running his free hand through his dark hair.

I looked to Logan, whose eyes were pleading with me. I sighed, too drunk to think properly. It was all too much drama for me at this point. The thrill was gone.

"I…um…I'm sorry, but something came up. I need to go. Another time, maybe." I pulled my hand away, and without a glance at either man, I grabbed my purse and rushed for the door.

I gasped the moment I stepped outside, the cool air hitting me like a much-needed breath. It felt good as I stood there trying to process what had just happened.

"Cassandra!" Logan's voice rang out behind me.

I took off walking, heading down the dark sidewalk,

focused on crashing at my mother's house. She lived down the block and worked nights. I figured I could have Hilary pick me up in the morning, and my mother would be none the wiser.

Logan followed me, his footsteps heavy against the cement. I had no idea why I'd listened to him. I should've ignored him and gone home with Kurt as planned. The only thing I knew for sure was that I'd had way too much to drink and needed to sleep it off.

"Cassandra, wait!"

I turned around, stomping my foot. "Why are you doing this to me!?" I yelled, throwing my hands in the air, the effects of the alcohol dominating my actions. "What could be so wrong with him, huh!? Answer me, damn it!"

Logan stood motionless, stunned by my outburst. He opened his mouth, but shut it almost immediately with a look of apprehension covering his face.

I narrowed my eyes and puffed out a breath of air as realization set in. "Right, so if you can't screw me, no one can?" I shook my head in disgust and turned on my heel, continuing down the sidewalk.

"Cassandra, it's not like that." He ran to catch up with me. "The reason Kurt's not right for you is..." He sighed, stopping in front of me. "...is because he just got out of prison."

I stepped back, shooting him a sharp, cynical look. "You're lying."

I stalked past him, bumping into his shoulder. A loud, irritated sigh came from behind me, as did the stomping of his feet. I quickened my pace, but was pulled up abruptly when strong arms snaked around my waist.

"Why would I lie to you about that? You can ask Caleb."

I grunted, smacking his arms, attempting to free myself. "You expect me to believe Caleb gave a job, at his coveted bar, to an ex-con?" I hissed. I tugged at his hands, but his grip was tighter than my drunken strength.

"Believe whatever you want, Cassandra. I'll make sure Caleb explains it to you once you've sobered up." Logan twisted me around to face him, his hands still gripping my hips.

"Why was he in prison?" I asked, my energy fading.

"Attempted murder; a fight over his girlfriend at the time, or something like that. I don't know all the details, but you understand why I couldn't sit back and let you go home with him—especially after I watched you drink yourself into a stupor."

"*Excuse* me!?" I yelled. *How dare he!* I began thrashing in his arms, his insult generating the strength I needed, and hit him hard against the chest. "I am *not* drunk! Now let me go!"

His hands flew to my forearm, pulling me closer. "Let me drive you home. That's all I'm asking. I just need to make sure you get inside safely."

My shoulders slumped, body exhausted as adrenaline evaporated from my system. "Logan, I just want to go to my mother's and—"

"Let her go!" A voice boomed from behind us.

Seconds later, Logan's hands were ripped from my body, and he was thrown back into a small shrub. I heard a loud thud as he crashed down over it.

"Logan!" My hands flew to my mouth. I tried to run to help him, but Kurt stood in front of me, blocking the path.

"You all right?" Kurt asked, his voice full of anger more than concern.

My hands moved from my mouth to my forehead. I shuddered, groaning. I regretted drinking so much, and suddenly felt the urge to heave with each wobbly step I took. "Yeah, he wasn't hurting me."

Anger washed over his face, sharpening his features. I

stood there, frightened when he leaned into me. "So, what is this? You agree to go to dinner with me, but you're screwing him?"

I flinched at his harsh words. I stepped back, and tried to look over his shoulder when I heard Logan curse. I wanted to go to him. The thought of him in pain was nearly unbearable.

"I just want to go home. Logan and I weren't doing anything," I muttered, unsure what else to say.

Logan stood up, brushing himself off as he approached us. "I was just going to take her home," Logan said calmly, trying to diffuse the situation, but his voice only upset Kurt further. He turned to stare at Logan.

"Right, I've heard what you do to the women you take home." He snickered, looking back at me as if I were nothing but trash. "Although I'm surprised you weren't planning on fucking her in the alley behind the bar. She must be real special." Kurt narrowed his eyes at me.

"Look, you have everything all wrong, but to be honest, I'm too tired to deal with this. I'm going home—alone!"

"Cassa—" Logan began, but what followed was an earth-pounding thump.

I turned in a panic to see Logan stumbling forward, his hand holding the back of his head. I watched in horror as Kurt charged at him again.

"No!" I lurched forward. "Stop!"

The moment I stepped between them, I caught Kurt's fist right in the face. My head flew back and I lost my balance, sending me hard against the sidewalk. Pain radiated through my lip as blood filled my mouth. Tears sprung from my eyes and my hands covered my injury as I sat there shell-shocked.

"Son of a bitch!" Logan roared, his voice raw and unhinged. In a flash, he tackled Kurt to the ground. His fists crashed into the man's face over and over until the sounds of

146

police sirens and Caleb's voice rang out.

# Chapter Twelve

## TLC

Logan fell back at Caleb's feet as the officers jumped out of their squad car and raced to the scene. I sat on the grass watching, my head buried in my knees and back against a tiny tree.

"You're under arrest!" one of the officers barked, pulling Logan to his feet and yanking his hands behind his back.

"Wait, this was all Kurt. Logan was only protecting Cassandra," Caleb explained, still catching his breath from running over.

"Cassandra?" The officer looked to me expectantly.

"Yeah, it's true," I replied, wincing at the pain when my lips moved. I ached everywhere, but cringed at the realization I'd be sporting a nasty bruise the next day.

"We had a feeling he was going to give us trouble," the other officer said, standing over Kurt's unconscious body. "He's got a record that had us concerned at the station."

I exhaled and glanced up at Logan. He'd been telling the truth, just trying to look out for me, and I'd gotten him hurt and ruined his night. All I'd wanted was a night as an average twenty-two-year-old, but had I taken Kurt back to my house, hidden in the woods where we'd be practically alone, who knew how that would've ended.

I recoiled as I imagined the terrifying possibilities. This was the exact reason I never drank. So much for lowering my inhibitions for a night.

"Holy shit!" Caleb muttered, looking down at me. "I swear to God, Cassandra, I had no clue. I knew him from a friend. We hung out back in the day and he told me he'd been in jail, but that it was all a misunderstanding." Caleb ran both his hands through his hair and rested them on top of his head. "He said some guy was sleeping with his fiancée and attacked him when he confronted him. Kurt told me he messed the guy up pretty bad, but that he didn't start it." Caleb sighed and dropped his hands and head. "Damn, I should have had him checked out."

I shook my head in disbelief. He walked closer, leaning down in front of me.

"I messed up, but I swear I never thought he was capable of hurting you. You have to believe me." His hooded eyes filled with concern and regret.

"The officer needs a statement," Logan said, tapping Caleb on the shoulder.

Caleb let out a deep sigh and turned away, shoulders deflated, to talk to the officer.

Logan crouched down in front of me and gently pulled my chin up to examine my face. "The medics need to check you out—make sure nothing's broken," he said lightly, brushing his finger down my nose and over my top lip.

I hissed through the pain.

"I wanted to fucking kill him," Logan murmured, more to himself than me. "I shouldn't have let you get between us. You should have left—went back to the bar and got Caleb or something." His voice grew louder, angrier. "Why the hell did

149

you step in—"

"What's this?" The officer snickered, gaining our attention. He bent down, retrieving a vial that was peeking out from Kurt's pocket. "Cocaine. Looks like he violated parole in more ways than one tonight."

An ambulance pulled up and paramedics appeared moments later, lifting Kurt onto a gurney.

"Will you be pressing charges, Mr. West?"

Logan turned to look at me, his jaw working hard as he took in my appearance. I shook my head once, causing his frown to deepen.

"No," he answered, looking away. "The coke should be enough to lock his ass back up."

"What about you, Cassandra?" the officer asked, holding his pen and notepad.

I shook my head again.

"All right, then. If you change your minds, just stop into the station." He smiled and, after taking a few notes, climbed into his squad car. "Have a good night—and put some ice on that pretty face, Cassandra."

---

After the scene cleared and the crowd disappeared, I sat on the sidewalk, leaning against a fire hydrant and feeling the weight of the night's events. It was eerily quiet. I refused everyone's offers to drive me home. I just sat there, watching and waiting until I had my chance to speak with Logan.

"You okay?" My voice was soft—nothing more than a breath in the wind.

He was leaning against a car, rubbing the back of his head. He said nothing, just stared down at the patch of grass in front of him.

"You should get your head looked at. You might have a

150

concussion," I said more loudly, noticing the dried blood on his hands. Kurt had hit him pretty hard, but Logan refused to go to the hospital. One of the paramedics did, however, manage to get a quick look after Logan had made sure I got a damn-near-full physical. He was relentless, and it took everything I had to prove I'd be fine. Luckily, it wasn't a broken nose. The maniac's fist had caught more of my lip, and the pressure there was already building beneath the skin.

I sighed agitatedly when he still didn't answer me. "I'm sorry, but how was I to know the man was a psycho? You should have told me before watching me drink so much." The alcohol was long gone from my system, between the rush of adrenaline earlier and the pain from a grown man punching me in the face.

"And you would have believed me?" he snapped, looking my way for only a brief second before dropping his head. I hugged my knees closer against my chest and rested my chin on them, watching Logan shake his head in thought.

He looked at the grass and then tipped his head back, staring at the full moon. Finally, he pushed off the car and offered a hand to help me up from the grass.

"Probably not," I mumbled honestly. I stood and stepped back to see his face under the glow of the street light. "But that's *your* fault. You're always hitting on me, or making me feel…I don't know. You just get in my head. I never know what's real and what's a game."

Our eyes locked for a long moment before he spoke. "You're right." He wiped the blood off my cheek softly. "I'm sorry."

His arm wrapped around my waist, and he helped me down the sidewalk to his car.

The ride to my house was painfully quiet. I wasn't sure if he was angrier that I got hurt or that I hadn't let him take me home before things got out of hand. Either way, I could tell he was pissed. His hand was tight around the steering wheel, grinding into the leather.

The moment he turned off the ignition, Logan was out of the car and opening my door for me. He caught me off guard when he swept me into his arms and carried me to my front door.

"I can walk, you know," I said, trying to climb down.

"Shut up and unlock the door."

Accepting defeat, I tugged the keys from my purse and reached down, sliding my house key into the lock. He was definitely mad.

After we walked inside, he laid me on the couch and headed straight into the kitchen. The sound of drawers and cupboards opening and closing made me stifle a laugh until I heard him place a glass on the kitchen table.

Everything became instantly quiet, and it took only half a second until my posture stiffened. *Shit!* I'd left the condoms Hilary gave me on the table. The silence persisted for what felt like hours. Seconds ticked by as minutes until I heard a *swoosh* of air, then a loud thud. The sound of water running brought me out of my flushed state.

I lay back, exhausted, knowing there was nothing I could say. I closed my eyes, embarrassed and broken.

"Drink this."

I opened my eyes to find Logan sitting beside me with a tall glass of water in one hand and a wet washcloth in the other.

"Thanks," I murmured.

He waited quietly as I took a sip, but as I leaned forward to set it down, he frowned.

"Drink more," he insisted. I brought the glass back to my lips, obeying without complaint. I wasn't used to having a man tell me what to do, but this was different—he was trying to take care of me. It was…nice.

It took nearly five minutes for me to consume the entire glass, my swollen lip burning each time it made contact with the icy water, but Logan waited patiently beside me.

Once I finished, he took the glass and set it on the coffee table in front of us. I watched with fluttering nerves and hooded eyes as his hand reached out, pulling the bloody strands of hair from my face. With his other hand, he slid the washcloth gently over my chin, across my mouth, and around my cheeks. His eyes studied every place the cloth cleaned. My stomach filled with swooning butterflies eager to thank him with each tender caress to my skin.

"How do you feel?" he asked, his voice low and raspy, as he set the washcloth on the table.

I swallowed. How could I answer that? Every emotion I'd ever experienced was present at the moment. I felt confused, terrified, and completely taken aback by his kind actions.

"Does it hurt?" he pressed further.

"Huh?" I stuttered, attempting to find my voice as I blinked. "Um…yeah. I mean, no…it's fine. It's feeling better." I attempted a convincing smile, but the pain flared back up in my lip. "Thanks."

I sat quietly for what felt like forever as Logan retreated to the kitchen with the soiled washcloth and empty glass, and replayed the tender touches he was capable of giving.

"I want to start over," Logan said as he entered the room with a piece of French bread and the refilled water glass.

"Start over?" I cocked my head to the side, staring at him in disbelief. *How can we start over now, after all our interactions over the past month?*

"Yes." He sat down, handing me the items. "I want to really get to know you, and if that means starting over as friends, then I'll take it. I want you to trust me, Cassandra." He looked away in thought for a moment, then back to me. "I'd never hurt you."

Was this happening? Could I honestly forget everything I knew about him? My insides screamed for me to give it a try, and before I could debate it, I nodded.

"All right. I'd like that…friends." I took a sip of water, processing the thought of a friendship with Logan West, and set the glass down to pick at the bread. "I can't forget how much of a playboy you are," I admitted openly, "but with everything else, it would be nice to have a clean slate."

"Thank you." He smiled, his eyes brightening. "Now finish that, and then I'll help you into bed."

My brow arched up. "When you say 'help me into bed,' you do mean alone, right?"

"Well, there is always the option of friends with benefits." He chuckled softly, his chest rumbling.

"Don't push your luck."

# Chapter Thirteen

## OLIVE BRANCH

I woke with a shudder the next morning. My face was buried in my pillow, which pressed against my painful broken lip. Groaning, I twisted to my side and held a hand in front of my mouth, not brave enough to touch the tender gash. I pulled myself up and fell back against the cream-linen-upholstered headboard Hilary and I had tackled as a DIY project earlier in the summer.

*Hilary*, I thought, closing my eyes. *How could she set me up with someone who'd just gotten out of prison—someone who could've done God knows what to me had I taken him home?*

With my eyes closed, I inhaled through my nostrils and exhaled slowly, attempting not to move my mouth. I repeated the movement twice, the deep cleansing breaths calming the growing anger inside me. I stretched my arms high above my head before padding across the floor toward the bathroom.

The shower worked wonders on my body. Exhaustion made me refuse one the previous night, even though Logan had offered to stay in case I fell, but I'd just wanted the night to end.

My body rested against the cool tile, warm water

cascading over me as my mind drifted back to Logan. His unprecedented kindness left me both grateful and confused. There was so much more to Logan West than he led on, and with each new glimpse I received, I was left wanting more.

After my hair was twisted up in a fluffy white towel, I wiped the fog from the oval bathroom mirror.

"Ugh!"

I leaned forward over the sink to examine my swollen lip with a giant gash running down it. My fingers ghosted over the area, and I flinched when it stung even under my own touch.

I fell lazily onto the corner of my bed, still draped in nothing but a towel, and picked up my phone I'd set to silent last night. I rolled my eyes when I saw eighteen missed calls and fell back against my pillows, scrolling through the list. Twelve were from Hilary, and the rest from my mother.

There were also a few texts from Hilary. Each asked a variation of *Are you all right?* and *Can I stop by?* As I continued scrolling through the messages, my phone lit up with a new text. With an irritated scoff at Hilary's persistence, I opened the message, surprised to see an unknown number.

**Good morning, sweetheart. Hope u are feeling better. If u need anything, please let me know. See u tomorrow morning at school –Logan**

I stared down at the message, rereading it, wondering how he had my number. My lips curled into the faintest smile as I hit *Reply*.

**Thanks. I'm sure u r in a lot worse shape than me. Did u have Julia check on u last night? U promised.**

I hit *Send*, then saved his number in my contacts. Almost instantly, I had a new message.

**Yes, and as you can see I survived just fine :)**

I smiled and typed back quickly.

**Good, I could only imagine the mob of angry women**

156

**coming after me if anything happened to you.**

I didn't have to wait long until my phone lit up.

**Now that I think about it, had I been truly hurt, I would have greatly enjoyed u nursing me back to health.**

Another text dinged before I could reply.

**U in a naughty nurse's outfit would heal any man's ailment.**

I chuckled and rolled my eyes as I began typing.

**Friends, remember. No more enticing seduction routine.**

**Enticing? Really? Do tell more.**

**U wish. You've enticed more than your share of women in this town. I won't be added to that list.**

I smiled, shaking my head at his flirty banter.

There was no instant response after that. I'd meant it playfully and began to worry I'd insulted him, which wasn't my intent. Rereading my own text over and over, I realized how it could've been received. The longer I waited for my phone to light up with his reply, the worse I felt. It took over five minutes, and I preferred to think he was merely busy and not offended.

**Of course not.**

Shit, he was hurt. Great start to a friendship.

**Sorry, I didn't mean anything by that. You're charming and hot, of course women would want to sleep with u.**

I hit *Send*, then reread my message. Okay, that sounded better in my head. I was just feeding his ego now. My phone dinged immediately.

**So u think I'm hot. ;)**

Yeah, completely added to that damn ego of his.

**I've seen hotter.**

**I sincerely doubt that and for the record u haven't**

seen all of me.

**And I never will. Although I saw enough when we were jogging. If u cared about women at all you'd wear a shirt.**

**Did u find it distracting, sweetheart?**

**Again, I've seen better.**

**Well, I haven't seen anything sexier than watching you jog ahead of me. Highly impressed.**

I froze, staring down at the tiny screen. We were treading dangerous waters. It was so easy with Logan—*too* easy—to go down that path, but I wanted to see more of the man who'd looked out for me the previous night.

**Well, FRIEND, I need to start my day. And that will not include jogging this morning. Still a little sore.**

**Have a wonderful day. If u need anything at all, call.**

**Thx. Tell Oliver I said hi.**

I placed the phone back on my nightstand to finish charging, then walked over to my dresser in search of my favorite pink cotton shorts and a tank top. Today would be all about relaxing around the house.

---

I'd walked out to the kitchen and placed a bowl on the table to prepare breakfast when I quickly realized the box of condoms was gone. It didn't take long to look in the trash can and find them sitting on top of Friday's newspaper. I cringed, flushing at the idea of Logan seeing them, but the idea of him throwing them in the trash was slightly bewildering. Why did he care?

I dropped the lid and decided to forget it ever happened. So what? Logan knew I had sex—or that I was considering having sex, anyway. Not now, though. I was officially off the market until I met a guy who could prove he was worth my time.

The moment I curled my feet up under the blanket on my petite couch with a bowl of Fruit Loops in my lap, a loud knock vibrated at my front door.

"Seriously?" I sighed, rolled my eyes, and headed for the foyer.

It could only be one of two people: Hilary or my mother. At that moment, I would've rather dealt with the latter. I was still too pissed at my friend.

One glance through the small peephole left me debating my options when I saw Hilary, with Caleb at her side. Worry and nervousness radiated off her, while he looked distraught. His hair was disheveled, and dark bags highlighted his usually sparkling, mischievous eyes.

With a small, calming breath, I opened the door slowly.

"Oh my God!" Hilary shrieked, her hand flying over her mouth. "Are you all right? God, I…I am *so* sorry. Please, can I just come in? I haven't been able to sleep at all since Caleb told me what happened to you last night."

I held the door open, moving aside for Hilary to enter before stepping back in the way to block Caleb from following.

"I'll talk to you later," I told him calmly, unable to deal with both of them so early in the morning.

"Cassandra, I truly am sorry," Caleb whispered, unable to hold my gaze. "I should have looked into his background. I had no clue the guy was dangerous, I swear."

"I know. We'll talk later, I promise." I shut the door slowly, feeling worse.

I stood behind the closed door for a few silent moments before turning on my heel to find Hilary staring back at me, her eyes hooded and face pale. She wasn't lying about not sleeping. I'd never seen her look that bad before.

"I can't freaking believe this. I had no idea," she said, her hands working animatedly as she spoke. "If Caleb had told me the guy had been to prison, I never would have tried setting you up with him. You know I want to see you start dating, but God, not with a guy like that."

I walked past her and plopped back down on the couch, pulling the blanket over my lap. I curled up comfortably and grabbed my bowl of cereal.

"Come on, say something," she pleaded, walking toward me.

I took a large bite of cereal, chewing slowly, and watched Hilary take a tense seat across from me in the armchair.

"Your lip looks…bad. Do you want me to get you something for it? I can run to the pharmacy."

I took another large bite of cereal. Hilary sat squirming in front of me, waiting for me to speak. She sat up on the edge of the chair, her shoulders slumped forward, hands fidgeting.

"Listen, you know I love you. You're my best friend!" Her voice raised an octave. "I would never set you up on a date if I thought the guy would hurt you. You have to believe me!" Her eyes glistened with unshed tears.

I swallowed my last bite of Fruit Loops and leaned forward to set the empty bowl on the table in front of us. As I leaned back, I gave her a small smile.

"I know," I said sincerely, tilting my head slightly to one side. "I just wanted to see how much groveling I could get out of you."

"You're horrible! You know that, right!?" Hilary scolded, throwing one of the small pillows at me.

I laughed as I caught it, wincing at the pain shooting from my lip. I placed the pillow behind my back as I settled further in the sofa.

"I deserve it," Hilary sighed. She leaned back into the chair, looking relieved I was finally talking. "I was so worried.

Caleb came over at midnight, banging on my door to tell me what happened. He feels horrible. He thinks it's all his fault, and I—"

"It *is* his fault!" I interrupted loudly, furrowing my brows.

"He never meant for—"

"Stop defending him, Hilary!" I yelled. I stood up, unable to sit while reliving it. "Caleb screwed up, and Logan was attacked because of it!"

"Caleb thought the guy just had a run of bad luck in his past. He was trying to help him out by giving him a job."

"I get that—I do—but that doesn't mean he should keep the guy's past hidden from potential dates. What if I would've brought Kurt back here, like I was planning?" I asked, raising my brows.

"I know. I feel terrible." Her hand slid listlessly across her forehead and down her long hair. "How did Logan get involved last night, by the way?"

"He showed up at the bar. He wanted to protect me—unlike everyone else."

"That's not true; Caleb just didn't know everything. He wanted to see the good in Kurt. Is Logan all right?" Hilary asked, genuinely concerned. "Caleb said it was a pretty nasty fight. Rumor has it Kurt is still in the hospital."

"Yeah, Logan sent me a text earlier. And as far as Kurt is concerned, I hope he rots in prison." I frowned, walking back over to Hilary. "I know this wasn't your fault. And I also know that Caleb would never put anyone in harm's way. I'll talk to him, all right? Just not today."

Hilary nodded and stood up, pulling me in for a hug. "I'm just glad you're all right."

---

Hilary and I spent the rest of the morning and afternoon

hanging out like a couple of teenagers. We buried ourselves under a heaping pile of pillows and sheets, snuggled on the couch, and watched reruns of our favorite shows.

"Seriously, Dan and Blair? Ugh!" I scowled, fast-forwarding through their joint scenes.

Hilary popped an Oreo in her mouth, giggling at the look of loathing covering my face.

"I agree—Chuck and Blair all the way, although he really needs to stop sleeping with everything in heels." She giggled again before taking a giant swig of milk and maneuvering to face me. "Speaking of rich playboys, what's going on with you and Logan, anyway? I thought you were completely done with him after interrupting his night."

"I was. I mean…I am." I didn't know how I felt anymore, so instead of dwelling on it, I snatched the bag of Oreos from Hilary's lap. I shot her a fierce look when I realized the bag was empty. "Okay, you are *so* going jogging every morning this week."

"Don't try to change the subject," Hilary scolded. "I think it's sweet he was looking out for you. From what Caleb tells me, the guy really isn't so bad."

"Logan showing up last night was anything but a romantic gesture," I scowled. "But if he hadn't, I hate to think of what might have happened. I drank way too much to help me relax, but a part of me wonders if I really would have been able to go through with anything if Kurt and I were alone. It's not like hooking up with a guy on a first date is something I've experienced before. And if I tried to stop things with Kurt once we were back here…" I stopped myself, closing my eyes, trying not to think the worst.

"I never should have pushed you to go out," Hilary muttered, her voice full of shame.

"Looking back on last night, I'm grateful Logan was

there," I said, a small smile tugging at my lips. "I saw a side to him that was so different than what he lets everyone else see. He's a good guy—it's just hidden under many, *many* layers of head games and irresponsible behavior. He helped clean me up, and even refused to leave until I was tucked into my bed." I chuckled, remembering how stubborn he could be.

"That doesn't sound like the Logan Caleb normally talks about," Hilary said, raising her brows.

"I know. It caught me completely off guard that he may actually have a heart buried in that chest of his."

"His gorgeous, perfectly chiseled chest, you mean?" Hilary teased in a sing-song voice.

"Yeah, he definitely has the sexy part down, but we decided to be friends—start over and try out a real friendship." After the texts that morning, I was painfully aware of how hard being friends with him was going to be. My body craved his. It was strange and unnerving, and I just hoped my brain was able to outweigh the natural physical urges I felt around him.

"Can you do that? I mean, you said you've had *how* many naughty dreams about the guy?" Hilary giggled when I cocked my head to the side, narrowing my eyes at her.

I chucked a pillow across the couch at her, laughing. "I know," I said, blowing out a breath, "but it's complicated. Between not wanting to hurt Oliver and Logan's reputation for sleeping with most single women in town, a friendship is all it will ever be."

"Well, I think he likes you, so if 'starting over as friends' is what you guys want to call it, I'll support you. Just be careful," Hilary said before turning the television volume back up.

◆◆◆

I woke to loud banging on my front door. I peeled my eyes open and looked over to see Hilary passed out on the other end of the couch. *The Gossip Girl* theme music played from the television.

With a soft yawn, I threw back the blankets and sauntered sleepily over to the door, rubbing my eyes. I glanced over at the clock on the wall, shocked to see it was after 8 p.m.

I knew who it was, so I didn't bother with the peephole. The moment I opened the door, my mother brushed past me furiously.

"What the hell is the matter with you!?" she yelled. "I have been trying to call you all day!"

Hilary sat up, her eyes groggy, and slipped on her shoes quickly. She shot me a sympathetic smile as she walked to the door. "I should go. I'll see you at school in the morning."

I nodded, turning my gaze back to my fuming mother. Her tense expression caused me to step back. She looked livid, and it took a moment to realize she was staring not at me, but my lip.

"I'm sorry I didn't answer my cell or call, but I just needed to unwind today," I explained, hoping to draw her attention away.

It didn't work. She reached out and cupped my cheeks gently, inspecting my injuries.

"That piece of shit," she mumbled, and dropped her hands. I could see the pain crossing her face.

I shifted my weight, then headed back to the living room and began picking up the empty food wrappers. After flicking the television off, I asked, "Shouldn't you be at work?" My mother always worked nights, so I was surprised to see her at this hour.

"I've been working double shifts for the past week. I just left the station, but have to be back in four hours." She sighed heavily, leaning against the wall. "Don't avoid the subject, Cassie. What happened?"

164

"I'm sure you already read the police report," I muttered.

"Damn right, I did! What the hell were you be thinking going out with that man?" She pushed off the wall and began pacing the room.

"Mom, I know you worry about me, but I'm fine, all right?" I left the room, throwing the last of the empty water bottles in the trash. I came back out, waiting for her rant to continue.

Watching me, her eyes softened. "Why don't you come home for a few days? You can sleep in your old bed."

"And have my mommy in the next room with a pistol, waiting to protect me?" I laughed, folding the blankets on the couch.

"Exactly." She grinned, falling into the small chair across from me. "I know you're all grown up, but I'm still your mother. It's my job to protect you."

"I know. Now go home and get some sleep. You look exhausted."

"Of course I am. I spent my entire shift trying to get ahold of you."

"Well, as you can see, I survived and will live another day to keep you on your toes." I smiled.

She sighed, accepting defeat on the subject. "Fine, but keep ice on that lip. And don't forget you still need to come down and give your full statement. Don't think I'm letting that son of a bitch get away with hurting my baby girl! Logan West was there earlier."

I stilled, surprised to hear that since he'd said he wasn't pressing charges.

"By the way, that Kurt guy was just released from the hospital. They're transporting him back to prison as we speak."

"I just want to forget it ever happened."

"I know, honey." She hugged me. "I love you."

165

I squeezed her tightly. She was always the best at giving hugs that melted away my problems.

"I love you too, Mom."

I opened the door and watched her walk reluctantly out to the squad car parked in my driveway.

After closing the door behind me, I walked to the bathroom to get ready for bed. I had work in the morning, and the more I thought about it, the more against going in I felt. What would the kids think if they saw me like this? I looked absolutely frightening. There was no possible way to cover it up.

I snatched my phone from my bedside table and sent an e-mail to the principal, letting him know I'd need a substitute for the next day. For some reason, I also sent a text to Logan.

**Hope your day was as relaxing as mine.**

I hit *Send*, and he replied less than a minute later.

**Spent it with Oliver and my mother. He talked us into taking him to the zoo.**

I smiled.

Where did u find that much energy after last night?

Not much of a choice with a 4-yr-old. For the record, my energy level has never been an issue ;)

I rolled my eyes, but chose to ignore the last part of his text.

**Hope u had fun. I'm guessing u did all that after stopping at sheriff's?**

**Your mother got a hold of u I take it? She was a wreck trying to call u when I went in. And yes, I'm pressing charges.**

**Why go through all the trouble. They got him for violating parole. That alone will lock him back up.**

**One thing you'll quickly learn about me is that I don't allow people I consider a close friend to get hurt.**

**He will regret hitting u.**

I sat there, gnawing on my bottom lip as I typed. Now we were *close* friends? We'd only been something other than neighbors for less than a day.

**Well, his fist was meant for u not me.**

**He could have stopped it if he had any self-control. I've never hit a woman nor have I ever come close, even during bar fights.**

Bar fights? Okay, so there was a lot about him I didn't know. We were definitely not close friends. I rolled from my back to my side and began typing.

**U been involved in many bar fights? Let me guess, u screwed either someone's wife or their daughter?**

After hitting *Send*, I typed another quick message.

**Or u offended other patrons by wearing a ten thousand dollar suit in their bar.**

I chuckled softly, but the image of Logan beating on Kurt, leaving him unconscious and bloodied, reminded me of the glimpse of rage I saw in him. A shudder ripped through me.

I opened his text the moment it dinged.

**Let's be clear, I've never slept with a married woman, as far as I'm aware, and never would. Marriage is not something I would ever disregard so easily. As far as daughters, well, if they're consenting adults, I don't have an issue. But no, never fought over a woman. U were the first ;)**

I grinned, feeling giddy, and tried to squash it quickly. Friends—nothing more, I reminded myself.

**I'm honored. So I take it your suits were the issue then?**

**Men can get quite jealous of an impeccably tailored suit, sweetheart ;)**

I laughed, but as I did, a yawn spilled out.

**Uh huh. Perhaps someday you'll share some of your sordid past. For now, I'm sleepy.**

**Perhaps. Goodnight, Cassandra. Sleep well.**

# Chapter Fourteen

## OPEN-DOOR POLICY

I woke before sunrise the next morning and started the day with a long bath. After I climbed out, relaxed and ready to take on the world, I slipped into my favorite light-wash jeans with the knees worn out and pulled a yellow tank top over my head. After popping some extra-strength Tylenol, I decided to spend the entire day locked inside cleaning, hoping to take my mind off everything. I threw my hair up into a loose bun as I strolled out of my bedroom and cranked up the music on my stereo.

Within an hour, I was lost in the beats of Maroon 5 and dancing around my living room as I dusted each and every corner of its massive built-in bookshelf. I sang along like a madwoman, the meds covering the sting in my lip, occasionally gripping the duster like a microphone. Kurt be damned—I felt good.

Pleased with myself after finishing the bottom shelf, I stepped back to admire the perfectly polished structure.

"Looks good."

I jumped, chest heaving, and saw Logan watching me from the other side of my screen door. He oozed with sex appeal in a perfectly tailored black suit and grey tie. I caught myself staring before stalking across the room to turn down the blaring music.

Still panting, I turned around, giving a pointed look to the man now entering my house as if he lived there. One night's help hardly gave him free rein of the place.

"Ever heard of knocking?" I snapped, my breath heavy from singing. I regretted my tone instantly when I saw the sweet smile waver on his face.

"You weren't at school when I dropped Oliver off. I was worried—thought I would come check on you. That is what friends do after all." His lips curled into an easy smile, but it melted slowly into a frown when I stepped forward and his gaze dropped to my injured lip.

I knew he blamed himself for me getting hurt; it'd been obvious that night. I'd never forget the look on his face when Caleb pulled him off Kurt's limp body. He'd been acting on adrenaline and pure rage.

I smiled, releasing the tie in my hair and letting it fall down around my face, creating a curtain over that side of my mouth as I turned my head. "Right, well, thank you, but as you can see, I am doing fine—just catching up on some housework."

"So, can I come in then?"

It was a ridiculous request, considering he was already standing in my foyer. And besides, how could I deny him when he looked at me like it'd physically hurt him if I said no?

"Um, sure," I answered with a nod, chuckling under my breath. "Can I get you something to drink—glass of orange juice, water, anything?"

"No, thanks."

He looked around the room he'd stood in just the other night. It was strange seeing him there in the light of day; he felt out of place in the tiny living room. I'd bet his suit cost more than my furniture.

"So what are you up to today?" I asked, walking into the kitchen and pulling out a chair to sit. I gestured for him to do the same. "A day of boring meetings at the paper, I assume?"

He smiled as he took a seat across from me. "Not today. I'm on my way to meet my realtor."

"Are you moving?" A twinge of grief shot through me.

"No." He chuckled once, looking away. "Just looking to buy a small home for Julia so she can live off campus next year."

"You're...buying her a house?" I asked slowly, dumbfounded, my face twisted in confusion.

He chuckled again, placing one hand on the table in front of him, and looked up at me. His tongue darted out, moistening his lips slowly.

"I consider it an investment. She can live there for free with a few roommates who pay rent to cover some of the expenses. She's a good kid, and I know she doesn't want to live in the dorms next year. I love my sister, but I'm not exactly fond of her living in my home. It'd be good for Oliver, but annoying for me."

I opened my mouth to speak, but was stopped by a dry lump that had formed the second he'd licked those damn lips. I stood and walked to the sink for a glass of water.

"Yeah, I can understand that," I managed to get out before taking a sip. "Especially after witnessing your little ménage à trois party the other night."

He cleared his throat, and when I walked back to the table, I noticed his posture had stiffened.

"It was unfortunate that you stopped by when you did."

"Yes, it definitely was." I shook off the disgusting image of him under those women. "Although I was relieved to hear

Oliver wasn't home," I scoffed.

"One thing you should know about me, Cassandra: I love my son. He is my first priority." He leaned in further against the table, eyes locking with mine. "I may not have the best track record with women, but I treat them with respect and give them exactly what I can offer."

"Which is?"

His tongue darted out once again, and a flutter of nerves sent a chill through my body.

"Anything they ask for…in the bedroom." His voice was slow, rough, and enticing.

I dropped my head, heat creeping up my cheeks. God, what I bet he could do in the bedroom. Heat pooled in places I'd never felt before. I cringed at my body's response.

Looking back across at him, I gave a tight smile. "So, do you have any other sisters or brothers?" I asked quickly, changing the subject.

He nodded, his eyes lit with amusement.

"Care to expand?"

"Not really." He shrugged, still watching me with an uneasy intensity, as if he could read my mind. "Julia's my only sister, and I have two brothers. Not much more to say."

"Sibling issues?" I laughed. "I wouldn't know anything about that."

"You're an only child, I take it?"

I nodded, resting my elbow on the table and tilting my cheek into my palm. "So you bought the newspaper to give Julia for a graduation gift, and now a house. Kind of wish I had a brother."

He chuckled once. There was something in the way he laughed that soothed me, as if it could heal me from the outside in.

"Well, she *is* my only sister. Plus, my brothers are not

really around much to help her."

"What about your parents?"

"They live in the city. My mother is oblivious to anything financial, and my father prefers us to earn our own money. He refused to pay for Julia's schooling when she failed to achieve a scholarship." His jaw ticked but his expression smoothed a second later, replaced with the hint of a forced smile pulling at his lips.

"I'm not good at understanding fathers." I shifted in my seat and ran my fingers over the grains in the wood of the table.

"I heard about your father. Caleb told me he left when you were young."

"It was a long time ago," I grumbled, uncomfortable talking about it. "So what do your brothers do? They live in the city with your parents?"

"My older brother Lawrence is happily married, and yes, he lives in the city. He has a son a year younger than Oliver." He smiled to himself. "And Jax is...exploring life. Having fun."

"Having fun?" I snickered, cocking an eyebrow.

"Yes." His tone spoke volumes. *Jax must be the wild one in the family.*

"Well, you're lucky to have them."

"Sometimes." He grinned teasingly.

A comfortable silence settled between us as we sat there. It was nice—Logan West was a surprisingly normal guy, aside from his deviant sexual behavior. In another life, I could see myself enjoying that side of him as well. But that wasn't the case; we were as different as night and day in this life.

"Thanks again for checking on me, but you better get going. I'd hate to be the reason you left your realtor waiting." I stood from my chair. It'd been a pleasant conversation, and I didn't want to ruin it with heated stares and unnerving sexual tension.

"Anytime for you, sweetheart. I'm just glad to see that you're all right." With a strained look in his eyes, he stood and walked toward the door.

I followed, smiling as he turned back to face me. His hands were shoved deep in his pockets. He wasn't ready to leave just yet; I could see it written all over his expression.

"You know, this is a lovely home you have." He looked past me. "It has that female touch."

"Well, I *am* a female."

"That you are." He grinned, licking his bottom lip before shaking his head and looking away quickly. "Would you mind doing me a huge favor?"

I raised my eyebrows, waiting for him to continue, wondering where this was going. Oh, the favors I could do for him.

*No—bad thoughts!*

"I've never been too good at the whole house-hunting thing, to be honest. I mean, I know what I like, but women have very particular tastes."

"That they do." I smiled, awkwardly, waiting for the question.

"Would you mind…accompanying me today? There are four different houses I need to look at, and I have no idea which would be best for a girl like my sister. You would be helping me quite a lot."

I could tell he was trying, and since he hadn't resorted to his old flirtatious head games, I nodded in agreement.

"Why not?" This was it, a real attempt at being…friends. "I must warn you, though—I can be brutally critical."

"I would expect nothing less from you." His smirk lit his face with delight.

174

"Fine, give me twenty minutes to get dressed."

"I'll give you fifteen, since the realtor has already been waiting for ten." He chuckled as I sprinted out of the room.

# Chapter Fifteen

## EXPOSED

"Don't look at me like that! I'm telling the truth—all of them were horrible choices." I laughed, sitting across from Logan in a booth at a small diner outside of town.

"Come on, one of them has to be fit for Julia." Logan sighed, picking up his menu. "My real-estate taste can't be that bad."

I gave him a pointed look, covering my grin with my menu. "I'm trying to be gentle, I swear, but why would she want to live next to a golf course—and in an obvious bachelor pad?"

"Fine, that one may have been a bit masculine, but—"

"A bit!?" I scoffed, a muffled giggle slipping out. "There was a giant mirror on the ceiling in the master bedroom!"

"Fair point." He smiled, lowering the shiny menu. "I do have to admit I'm not keen on the idea of having a full sports club filled with men hanging out that close to my baby sister, but the third option… that had promise." His smiled faded when I made a disagreeing face. "What was wrong with that house? It's not far from a shopping plaza. Isn't that what girls like?" he added quickly, hoping to sway me.

Offended, I let out a puff of air and placed the menu down in front of me. "Your sister will not be shopping at an auto-supply store or The Military Surplus, I assure you."

"There were a few women's clothing stores," he defended.

"Believe me—I've met Julia, and she won't be shopping at any of them, either."

"What do you suggest then?"

"Honestly, I think you need to keep looking. Why not ask Julia to pick it out herself? It'll be her home, after all."

The waitress walked over wearing a bright-yellow apron and cheerful smile with a pad in hand, ready for our order.

"Where's the fun in that? I, myself, have always enjoyed surprises," he said, smiling up at the young woman with a large, round pregnant belly.

After placing our orders of simple burgers and fries, we were left alone once again.

"So, I wanted to thank you for hiring the men to help with the treehouse. I'll admit, at first I was planning on sending them away. But they were great, and I couldn't have done all that work on my own." I looked down, heat rising in my cheeks. "That was why I came over that night—to thank you. I didn't mean to interrupt your—" I shook my head, chewing my bottom lip, and added quickly, "Oliver said he'd be coming back over."

Hesitantly, I looked back up and caught a flicker of something clouding his eyes before he blinked it away. He looked down at the table, then slowly back at me with his confident, dazzling smile firmly in place.

"My pleasure. Oliver enjoys it over there. I've been meaning to check it out myself, but didn't want to intrude...especially after the other night, considering your run-in with—" He tilted his head and lowered his eyebrows before changing the subject. "Did you hang his artwork?"

I nodded, and he gave a tight, almost uncomfortable smile.

"Oliver was excited to show you his pictures. I took him to pick out the frames the moment he came home from school. He told me you painted the inside of the treehouse green and blue; I hope they matched well."

"They did, thank you. He was thrilled to see them hanging up. And just for the record," I leaned in to whisper, "you having prostitutes over is something I'd like to forget and place in the start-over, clean-slate file." I made a face as I sat back up in my seat.

The waitress appeared beside our table. She placed a glass of Coke in front of Logan and water with a slice of lemon in front of me, then walked back toward the kitchen.

Logan watched me intently for a few moments before asking, "We're friends, right?"

"It seems like we're getting there," I said, not looking up from my glass.

"Then as your friend, I want you to know that you can ask me whatever it is that's on your mind, even if it pertains to my sex life."

My cheeks flushed and my stomach clenched in a tight knot. What was I supposed to ask him: *How often do you pay for sex?* The man shouldn't be paying anyone for that. Every woman in town wanted to sleep with him—including myself at times. I blinked the thought away the instant it hit me.

"All right, why pay for sex?" I whispered, embarrassed to speak the words.

He chuckled. "I have never paid for sex, Cassandra. Those ladies were old friends I met overseas, and occasionally they visit the States on vacation." His eyes took me all in, causing my throat to go painfully dry. I swallowed loudly, unable to pull my gaze from his. "They know what I like and what I am willing to offer. There are no strings attached—just consenting adults having a pleasurable time. They called me that afternoon saying they were in the city and were interested in coming by."

He waited for me to say something, but I just sat, stunned at how quickly I'd jumped to the conclusion of prostitutes.

"I called my brother to make sure Oliver could spend the night there, which he was more than happy to accommodate," he continued. "He gets along great with his cousin."

I nodded, slowly understanding. "So they weren't—"

"No, they were friends. No money involved. I did, however, buy them takeout and a few bottles of fine wine."

I laughed coyly, unable to meet his eyes as I fiddled with my straw. I was relieved he wasn't as much a pig as I made him out to be, but he was still far from a saint.

"Now, tell me—have you dated anyone recently?" he asked.

The waitress set down our plates and he lifted his burger, taking a bite.

"My last relationship didn't end very well." I dipped a fry into the small bowl of ketchup. "What about you?"

"I don't date."

"So I've heard." I laughed, biting into the hot fry.

"Will you come out with me again if I schedule more houses to look at?"

"On one condition."

He smiled, waiting for my demands.

"I pick the listings we go see. No more golf-course sex dens."

"Fair enough. I would hate to waste your time." His eyes beamed with mischief that left me both excited and unsettled.

We both sat there silently, enjoying our meal, no longer

needing small talk. It was a comfortable silence I don't think either of us was in a hurry to end.

"You ready, sweetheart?" he asked after the waitress removed our plates.

I nodded, taking one last sip of my water before sliding out of the booth.

"Logan!"

I turned toward the familiar voice and saw Julia...with Mark at her side.

My stomach sank at the sight, but it was his hand wrapped around her waist that sent blood rushing to my ears, muffling the voices around me. Every inch of my body stiffened, and my skin buzzed to life.

"Hi Cassandra!" she greeted me.

My voice abandoned me, leaving me standing painfully still, searching my vocabulary and drawing a blank.

Her gaze flickered to my split lip. "Oh my God! What happened?"

The urge to speak was overwhelmed by my stunned disbelief that Mark was truly standing in front of me. It had been so long, and now...of all the days...and with Julia.

I couldn't breathe. In a moment of panic, I inhaled a sharp ragged breath, which only worsened my struggle.

Logan spoke, but it was only mumbles in the background. Whatever he said, Julia offered me a sympathetic smile that only added to my torture. Mark was really here, and seeing me with a busted face. He'd probably laugh when it got around town that it was my own fault—I'd practically walked right into Kurt's fist. My shoulders began to ache from my rigid posture, and it took all my strength to lift my foot and shift my weight. I needed to move—to do something to prove this was really happening.

Julia's high-pitched voice broke through my agonizing

haze, and I managed to hear at least part of the conversation going on around me.

"...introduce you guys." Julia was speaking to Logan—at least, I assumed she was.

"Logan, this is Mark. We've been seeing each other for a few weeks now." I swallowed, my throat painfully dry. *Breathe, in and out,* I reminded myself over and over as Julia continued. "Mark, this is my wonderfully sweet big brother, Logan."

Mark held out his hand for Logan to shake and my gaze fell upon it. The mere thought of Mark and Logan ever touching caused my stomach to plummet. Suddenly lightheaded, I reached out to brace myself on the edge of the booth. Logan's warm hand was on my back instantly, steadying me, but I couldn't pull my stare from Mark's extended hand to look up. *Oh God, I must look like an idiot.*

"Glad to finally meet you. Julia talks a lot about you." Mark's voice ripped through me. Memories of that once-soothing tone haunted me, drawing out my fury.

Logan never shook Mark's hand, but I was too queasy at that point to read into why. The moment Mark pulled it away and tucked it back around Julia's waist, my legs began to quiver and shake. I couldn't stand there any longer.

"I gotta go," I blurted out and raced past them, my heart pounding heavily against my chest, head blaring for me to move faster.

As I pushed with all my strength against the door, I stumbled, nearly falling to the pavement. A giant gulp of air washed over me, filling my lungs.

"Cassandra?"

I couldn't look back. I needed space—from everyone. I ambled forward, desperate to find my car and disappear.

*My car? Damn. Logan drove.*

I shook my head and buried my face in my hands as I

181

leaned over the hood of a stranger's beat-up truck.

"I'm…I'm sorry, you should go back in," I stammered, failing to keep myself together. "Get to know Julia's boyf—" I couldn't say it. The anger and disgust consumed me more and more the longer I remained there, so I stood up straight and began walking.

When I reached Logan's vehicle, I stopped and closed my eyes, attempting to calm my shaky breath before facing him.

"Cassandra, talk to me," he murmured, reaching out his hand and placing it over my shoulder from behind me.

"I'm fine." My voice cracked, so I cleared my throat. It was awkward and loud, but so had the last five minutes been. "Please, just take me home." I fought to hold my composure.

Logan opened the passenger door for me. My gaze focused down at the pavement when the beginning of warm tears began prickling my eyes. *Damn it, not now.*

I climbed inside, relieved when after a hesitant moment standing at my door, Logan shut it and walked around to the driver's seat. He glanced over at me once he was situated in his seat, opening his mouth, but he closed it again and started the engine. He sighed as it purred to life, putting it in gear without a single word.

I shifted in my seat awkwardly, staring blankly out the window and pretending not to notice his worried glances. Twenty long, grueling minutes of complete silence left me trapped in my self-deprecating thoughts.

As we pulled into my driveway, I sat numbly while he turned off the engine. A few minutes passed before I turned in my seat and noticed his hands still gripping the steering wheel. Unable to find the right words to break the unbearable tension I'd created, I only felt worse. He continued staring out the windshield for a moment longer before finally speaking.

"Cassandra…"

"I hate him," I muttered unexpectedly, appalled at my own words. I'd never said it aloud before, and now it just spilled out. Tears stung my eyes, but I fought them, wiping my fingers across my eyelids.

"Talk to me," he murmured, reaching out and taking my hand gently.

"Mark and I…we were together over five years," I began, inhaling sharply and turning to look back out my window. I couldn't bear to look at him. I wasn't even sure why I was telling him anything. I supposed after spending the morning together and getting to see a different side of him, I felt comfortable. Plus, I wasn't ready to go inside and be alone with all the pain.

"I was young and in love. He was all I thought I would ever need." I stopped as a stray tear rolled down my cheek. I hated that Mark still brought out this reaction. I was over him, I was certain of that, but the sting from his actions was still there.

"He destroyed everything we had…everything we were together…I never thought…" I shook my head, berating myself silently for being such a blind fool back then.

"I thought he loved me…*God!*" I cried out, another tear betraying me as it made its escape down my burning cheek. I wiped it away immediately, forcing myself to hold it together in front of Logan, but I could feel my walls crashing down.

"I'm such an idiot!" I sobbed, tears finally falling. I closed my eyes tightly and inhaled a giant breath, refusing to shed another tear for the bastard. My nerves slowly began to calm, and my sight grew clearer.

Logan's hand gave a sympathetic squeeze, and I turned to look sheepishly up into his beautiful blue eyes. They left me breathless; I'd never felt more at home. His features were soft and tender, his eyes intense and warm.

183

"You don't have to tell me," he whispered, and it was exactly what I needed to hear. For some reason I'd never understand, I felt safe there in his car with only him, away from the world. My head rested back against the upholstered leather, and I released a ragged breath.

"Cassandra, listen to me." He released his hand from mine and brought it up to my chin, reminding me of the damage to my lip. I attempted to pull my face away, but he held firm. "Look at me."

Opening my eyes slowly, I gazed up at him and his reassuring smile. It was so soft, and full of an unknown shyness I never would've thought him capable of.

"Mark's an idiot. He didn't deserve you. You are one of the most beautiful and kind women I have ever met, and I assure you, I have seen more than the average man in my travels." His easy smile brought one to my lips, the melancholy beginning to fade with his words.

"Things don't always work out the way you plan, but I swear to you, you are everything that any smart, deserving man could ever ask for." He grazed his thumb across my cheek over my dried tears. His lips sealed tightly together before he pulled his hand away.

"Thank you," I breathed, emerging from my fog. "I should get going. It's getting late, and you need to pick Oliver up from school soon."

After I unbuckled my seatbelt, my body felt lighter; in fact, I felt better than I had in months. I hadn't realized I was still in need of closure—and not by seeing Mark again, but by having a man remind me I was worth everything I always believed I was. And Logan wasn't just any man, but one who truly meant it. I would be forever grateful. It was as though a dead weight had been lifted from my shoulders.

The moment I turned to open the door, Logan reached

out and caught my wrist.

"Would you like to have dinner with—"

"No," I interrupted, but held a sweet smile firmly on my face to ease any harshness. "I told you: friends only."

He grinned, and I frowned at the amusement on his face.

"You should let a friend finish. I was about to ask if you would like to have dinner with Oliver and me this week."

"Are you sure that's a good idea?"

"Oliver would love it. We never have dinner guests other than family. What do you say?"

Hesitantly, I replied, "All right, I'd like that. How about Wednesday?"

Logan had helped me regain my stolen confidence in men; I owed him at least a friendly meal. Plus, Oliver would be there, and he always brightened my day.

"Sounds perfect. Come around six."

I stepped out of the car and turned back. "Goodbye, Logan. Today was actually not too bad," I teased.

"Goodbye, Cassandra. Put some more ice on that lip."

I watched as he drove away, leaving me feeling like a new woman. I was proud of myself for never giving in to his constant flirting over the past month, and instead was much happier with the growing friendship we were creating.

I smiled to myself while unlocking my front door, realizing Logan might just be a good friend after all.

# Chapter Sixteen

## MISCONCEPTIONS

My feet shifted from side to side, my nerves jolting to life as I knocked lightly on the impeccably carved front door. I'd stayed home from school the last two days, and luckily my lip was no longer swollen—just a little red around the cut. With a gracious smile and dressed casually in a pair of dark fitted jeans with a grey cardigan over a white camisole, I waited on Logan's welcome mat. The breeze had a slight bite to it as August drew to a close.

The door creaked open slowly, revealing an infectious grin shining from the small boy inside. I relaxed, smiling back.

"Cassandra! You came!"

"Of course I came." I laughed when he grabbed my hand and tugged me inside through the foyer and down a long hall.

The house was unlike how I remembered it the few times I was there with the original owners. A creamy beige paint replaced the old floral wallpaper, and hardwood floors now covered the formerly carpeted living room.

The farther we went into the house, the more an intoxicating aroma caused my smile to broaden. I inhaled, closing my eyes as I took in the delightful scent pouring out of the kitchen as we rounded the corner.

"Daddy, Cassandra is here!" Oliver exclaimed more loudly than necessary when we stopped in the massive gourmet kitchen.

"Good evening, Cassandra." Logan smiled, turning away from the stove to greet me.

His simple white tee clung sinfully to his sculpted chest, capturing my attention. My gaze wandered down to his light jeans, worn through in the knees and hung low on his waist. I dropped my head, embarrassed to look back up, knowing he was watching me gawk at him. I closed my eyes for the briefest moment to get my wits back in check, and willed the blood that had pooled in my cheeks to disperse. As I opened my eyes once again, I noticed his bare feet. The man made something as simple as cooking the sexiest thing I'd ever witnessed.

I looked back up and grinned. "Wow, you're actually cooking?" I teased, laughing once, hoping he wouldn't mention my prior blatant staring. The image of Logan holding a giant wooden spoon, standing over a steaming pot at the stove, was one I wanted to store away for as long as I lived.

"There is a lot about me you don't know, sweetheart." He winked.

I opened my mouth to give a snappy comeback, but was interrupted.

"Yeah, like how big of an ass he can be!"

I turned to gaze at the man standing in the doorway. He looked about my age, maybe a bit younger, and judging by the charming smirk dancing across his lips, I knew he was definitely related to Logan.

"Hi." I stepped closer to him, smiling. "I'm Cassandra."

"Jax. A pleasure," he replied smoothly. He took my hand and placed a lingering kiss upon my knuckles, causing me to flush, my stance uncomfortably rigid.

I smiled hesitantly as his gaze locked with mine and he released my hand. I was pulled from the moment when I swore I heard a low, throaty growl slip from Logan. With a subtle shake of my head, I stepped back into the room toward Oliver.

"Well, Cassandra, not only do you have my nephew running around yelling at me to put on a clean shirt, but it seems you've inspired my brother to cook again. You must be quite the lady."

He leaned against the doorframe, his eyes raking down my body, then back up. He flashed a sinful crooked grin.

My head shot down and I stared at the rustic tile floor, feeling the blush creeping over my cheeks once again. I couldn't imagine making Logan do anything he didn't want to.

"They're good guys." I smiled softly, thankful my voice came out smooth and strong. I looked up and over at Oliver, who was waiting impatiently for me to follow him.

"Come on, Cassandra, we can go sit down. Daddy will bring us our plates when he's done." Oliver took my hand.

"Yes, please make yourself at home," Logan said with a soft smile on his lips before returning his attention to the stovetop.

Oliver led the way to the formal dining room.

"You can sit next to me," Oliver puffed out, exerting all his strength to pull the antique upholstered chair out from the table.

"Thanks." I sat in the chair and watched him repeat his actions on the seat beside me. "You know, Oliver, you can call me Cassie if you like."

"Is that your name? I thought it was Cassandra." His forehead was marred with confusion when he was finally up in his chair, his head barely clearing the top of the enormous table.

"It is, but my family and close friends call me Cassie. You

can call me whichever you prefer."

"Cassandra is pretty," he said, looking at me and tilting his head, "but I want to be your friend, so…I'll call you Cassie."

I smiled at his thought process. "Great."

My eyes took in the room, roaming over the fine cabinet in the corner and up above the table. My mouth fell open and I gasped when I saw the dazzling crystal chandelier above me. Sunlight beamed in through the window, glittering off hundreds of differently shaped and cut crystals. Dropping my head back further, I was drawn to the breathtaking mural on the ceiling.

"This is a beautiful room," I breathed, enchanted. My gaze held firm, absorbing every detail the extremely talented artist had painted.

"We don't eat in here very much. Daddy says it's only for our special guests."

I relaxed back in my chair, unable to peel my eyes away from the painting above. A pale-blue sky with beautiful smoky clouds parted to reveal what looked like the heavens above. A magical kingdom, carved from gold, peeked down. It was gorgeous.

"My daddy painted that! I helped, too. I handed him the brushes, and I even painted that over there." I glanced in the direction of his finger and saw a small yellow sun in the far right corner that an obviously young but talented child had painted.

"Wow, you did a wonderful job!" I smiled sincerely. The entire work was a masterpiece.

"Yeah, he takes after his old man," Jax said as he entered the room followed by Logan, who was juggling two wine glasses and a small tumbler. Jax took the seat across from me while Logan placed the tumbler of water in front of Oliver and proceeded to sit on my other side at the head of the table.

He handed me a glass, then looked down sheepishly when he noticed my eyes flickering back down from his mural.

"I didn't know you painted," I said softly, surprised to see him shift in his seat. "It's beautiful." I took a small sip of water as he smiled gently in return.

Logan was an artist—and a damn good one. And even more surprising was the fact that he was shy about it. I couldn't believe this was the same man who'd flirted endlessly and tried to seduce me into bed. My inner self laughed as I realized just how complicated he was.

Logan gave a subtle, crooked smile. "Like I said, there is a lot you don't know about me."

He then stood and left the room, returning minutes later with our meal. It looked amazing, and I still couldn't believe he'd cooked it.

"How long have you painted?" I asked. I found myself eager to learn more about this side of him.

"Yeah, yeah, Logan can paint. But tell me more about you, Cassandra," Jax said. "Do you happen to have any single friends you'd like to bring by sometime?"

"He's kidding, of course," Logan said, shooting a threatening glare at his kid brother. "He's young, and full of raging hormones."

I laughed, but covered my mouth with my hand, suddenly remembering I was sitting beside a four-year-old.

"Why don't you go wash up for dinner, Oliver?" Logan said, catching my uncomfortable glance at his son.

Oliver sighed, looking down at his plate of food, but did as he was told. He hopped down from the chair and sulked out of the room.

"You're one to talk, brother," Jax went on after Oliver had disappeared around the corner. "I've seen all the girls hanging around your bachelor pad in the city. I'm sure living in the country hasn't changed that. Am I right, Cassandra?" Jax eyes were solely on me now. "Living right next door, I'm sure you see a string of scantily clad vixens coming and going at all hours of the night when Oliver visits Lawrence."

"Enough, Jackson!" Logan sneered, his hands balled into fists on the table.

I took a bite of the most amazing mushroom risotto I'd ever tasted and smiled across the table. "So, what do you do, Jax?" I asked, trying to diffuse the tension building between them. After another bite, a small moan slip passed my lips. Logan could really cook.

"I travel. I enjoy meeting new people, new women, and showing them a good time."

*Definitely related to Logan.* I nodded, unimpressed, and placed another forkful of risotto in my mouth, savoring the taste.

"There's not much else at the moment to do with my time," he continued.

"You could try finding a job," Logan said, irritated. "Or perhaps join our sister in college."

Jax took a swig of the soda in front of him and grinned wickedly in my direction. My mind was still too wrapped up in the delightfulness in my mouth to care much about his smoldering expressions.

"College is no place for me, unless it's at the coed parties. As for a job, I'm planning on talking my big brother here into employing me at his little paper in town."

I raised my eyebrows, my mouth stuffed with food.

"Lawrence and Father both turned you down at the head office, I take it?" Logan grumbled.

"No, I just thought I might want to see what this small town has to offer for a while." He looked me up and down in my chair, and gave me an approving smirk. "And judging by the gorgeous woman sitting across from me, there seems to be a lot."

Like earlier, I heard a faint growl coming from Logan, but I simply ignored both men, losing myself in the meal Logan had so wonderfully prepared.

Oliver rejoined us, and the table talk turned to treehouses, movies, and books. Turned out Logan not only cooked like a chef and painted like a master, but also enjoyed reading classic literature. Today was full of one surprise after another.

We finished our meal and I stood to help clear the table, but Logan's hand covered mine, removing the plate from my grasp.

"I have someone to take care of those. Oliver, what do you say we show Cassandra the library?"

I couldn't help the smile that grew on my face at the idea of a library. Just the word made me feel giddy.

"And on that note, I'm out." Jax stood up and slipped around the table, stopping behind me. I turned to face him while Logan stood watching warily. "It was a pleasure to meet you, Cassandra. Piece of advice?" He leaned in closer to my ear. "Keep those panties of yours on if you ever want another invite to dinner around here."

With that, he shot Logan a smug grin and said a quick goodbye to Oliver. I stood there, stunned and slightly embarrassed. Logan had a hell of a reputation among his siblings.

"What did he say?" Logan asked as we walked out of the room, following behind Oliver.

"Nothing important." I shrugged, offering a half smile, but his expression was clear: He didn't believe me.

Entering the room behind Oliver, I was flabbergasted. The man had an actual library in his home. No wonder he'd had so many moving trucks there that first week.

"This is…wow!" I giggled, grabbing a book sitting on a small round table next to one of the four armchairs in the room. A large upholstered coffee table rested in the middle, and Oliver climbed up on it, lying on his stomach. He rested his chin in his hands and stared up at me.

"Daddy makes me read a lot." He sighed, his feet swinging in the air.

I smiled, looking up from the book in my hand: *Treasure Island.* "How horrible of him!" I scrunched up my nose.

He chuckled. Logan sat across from him in a chair, watching me.

"We just started that one the other night. We take turns reading a page," Logan explained, smiling proudly at his son. "His reading is on a third-grade level."

I smiled back and placed the book down, impressed. As I perused the shelves, a yawn spilled from my lips, and I looked over at the clock on the table. It read eight fifteen.

"I should get going." I turned to face Logan.

He stood, as did Oliver, and walked me to the door.

"Thanks for dinner," I said. I ran my hand over Oliver's mop of dirty-blond waves.

"You can come every night," Oliver replied with a bright smile that lit his sleepy eyes.

"Thank you, I'll keep that in mind."

"He's a bit forward, but I happen to agree. Any time you want some company, let me know," Logan said.

I wasn't sure if I should read into the double meaning, so I simply nodded and walked out the front door, feeling great about our new friendship.

——◆◆◆——

It was later that week when I went outside to watch the sunset that I heard Oliver singing and knew exactly where he

193

was. I smiled, walking to the treehouse and climbing the freshly repaired ladder. With each step up, I was grateful the repairmen only fixed it up and didn't replace it. There were too many memories attached to it.

When my hands rested on the floor of the treehouse, I looked up, preparing to say hello, and froze. Oliver wasn't alone.

"Hello, sweetheart." Logan smiled. "I have to tell you, it's exactly as I imagined in here."

He looked enormous in the cramped space, but in the center of the room—where the roof peaked—he could almost stand up straight.

"Thanks," I said when Logan reached down and held out his hand to pull me up.

There wasn't a lot of room, which left me nearly on top of his feet as we stood staring at Oliver. My breath caught when his hand brushed against my bare knee. My cutoff shorts rested mid-thigh. I backed up a step, narrowing my eyes down at his hand.

He chuckled, knowing what I was thinking.

"Look what Daddy made!" Oliver held out a wooden frame and I took it, sucking in a deep breath when I saw the sketch it held.

It was of Oliver and me in my backyard. I was standing over him while he squatted down with a box in his hand at the edge of the tree line. My gaze shot up at Logan.

"You saw us?" I said, surprised.

He nodded, watching me carefully. The sketch was from the first day I met Oliver, when he'd released the mouse.

"Daddy said it was a good thing you were there to help me save the mouse. He's with his family now."

I looked over at Oliver, who'd taken a seat at the small table. He snatched a piece of construction paper and the tin of crayons. I smiled. He was at home here.

"This is…amazing. I should go get a hammer and nail."

"Already ahead of you—here." Logan took the framed sketch from my hand. Our fingers brushed together, awakening forbidden sensations. The moment his eyes met mine, my breath caught. I could see it on his face—he felt it too—but he stepped away, turning his attention to the nail already on the wall in front of Oliver at the tiny table.

"Perfect," I whispered.

Logan turned back to me, picking up his hammer. "Well, I have some work to get done. I should be going," he said.

I moved to allow him access to the ladder, but he halted his steps and looked over at me.

"I'll send you a text later with a few more listings for Julia. Let me know if you think they're worth checking out."

"All right." I nodded.

He smiled, descended the ladder, and disappeared. I stared at the flawless sketch hanging proudly on the wooden wall, unable to control the grin creeping over my face.

# Chapter Seventeen

## ALL BETS ARE OFF

By the end of September, Logan and I were in a good place. He and Oliver showed up the weekend following our treehouse visit, requesting my assistance in teaching Oliver to fly a kite. It wasn't something that took much of a lesson, but I was honored they'd asked.

We spent the day in the town park, where Oliver gave me a beautiful laser-cut butterfly kite. He explained how his daddy told him I'd love it, and I did. The day went off without a hitch; even the flirtiest of the single women at the park couldn't hold Logan's attention for more than a polite second. It was peaceful, and even included a picnic Logan called in from Haven that Caleb personally delivered.

After that, Logan was busy reinventing the newspaper while school became my main focus. On occasion, I'd find him lurking outside my class when he picked up Oliver. Our brief conversations or friendly nods were always followed with a swoon-worthy smile from him that left me breathless more often than I cared to admit.

To my surprise and slight disappointment, he never again joined me for any of my morning jogs. I considered asking why, but figured his mornings were full with more important things. The town had been rallying around with support for the changes to the newspaper, and for once, I actually enjoyed reading it. It was delivered every morning like clockwork. I never bought a subscription, but I wasn't surprised to find it on my stoop the first time. Logan, of course, would want to brag about the paper's turnaround, or perhaps just share in its success. I had to admit, he was doing an impeccable job making it appealing for all ages.

The first Saturday of October, Logan was at my door by ten in the morning, ready to take me to see a house I thought might be worth checking out. After looking at a few houses in person and viewing dozens through texts and e-mails Logan had sent over the last few weeks, one place finally caught my eye. I was hopeful it'd be perfect for Julia—it was less than two miles from campus, and overlooked the river that ran through the back of town.

"Explain to me again, Cassandra, why you believe this house would be perfect for my baby sister." Logan stood in the center of the master bedroom, unimpressed.

The two-story brick home had been completely renovated from top to bottom. It was fit for any female with its modern-yet-classic allure, including pale-grey walls throughout with bright-white molding surrounding them. Nearly every room included a crystal chandelier and plush, creamy-white carpet. It was fresh, clean, and sparkly. What girl *wouldn't* like it?

"First of all, it's gorgeous!" I squealed, skipping toward the mirrored double doors on the far wall. I sucked in a deep, excited breath as my hands grasped the doorknobs and pulled the doors open.

My jaw fell open. I was in heaven. The massive walk-in closet featured a luxurious center island for accessories, with enough shelves around the room to fit an entire boutique.

Jealous was an understatement.

"Forgive me, but 'gorgeous' is not the word I would use to describe this place," Logan said, standing behind me. "Over the top comes to mind—ridiculously excessive, perhaps—but by no means gorgeous."

"Ugh, and your house isn't?" I scoffed. My fingers danced across the marble top of the island. "Looks like you're just going to have to trust me then." I smiled and glanced over at him, ignoring his scrunched brow. "I promise: If you buy this house, Julia will love it."

"And if she doesn't, then what?" Logan asked, walking out of the room. *What a buzzkill.*

With an eye roll and irritated sigh, I said a quick goodbye to the closet, blowing it a woeful kiss before following. I'd always been modest, and living in a place like that had never been something I'd thought about. But I could still appreciate it for what it was: breathtaking!

Logan was speaking with Paula, the realtor, in the foyer. As I stepped off the bottom stair, I suddenly began to worry. *What if Julia* did *hate it?*

No. I shook my head, refusing to believe any woman could *not* love a place like this. It was a dream house for anyone who appreciated the finer things in life, and based on the way Julia presented herself, I knew this place was made for her.

Logan looked up at me, surprised when I grabbed his hand and led him into the living room. His hand was warm and soft, and the thrill of dragging him away added to my playful mood. The room was enormous, of course, with a glass fireplace in the center that created the illusion of two rooms.

"How about we make a deal?" I gave his hand a squeeze; my body resisted the idea of releasing him, but I forced myself to pull my hand away. The gleam in his eye and bemused smile left me giddy. I grinned, certain my plan would play out in my favor. "You buy this house for Julia, and if she hates it—which she won't—I'll be at your beck and call for an entire weekend. Two whole days."

Logan's eyes lit up at my proposal, his eyebrows rising. I had a feeling he was the type of man that enjoyed a good wager.

"And if she loves it?" he asked.

"Then it looks like you'll be my little whipping boy for a couple days. I've been meaning to have my house painted—not to mention, you're a pretty amazing cook." I brought my forefinger to my lips. "Hmmm, all the possibilities." I giggled playfully.

The thought of Logan shirtless, holding a paint roller in his hand and up on a ladder outside my house, was something I wanted to see...outside of my dreams.

"Yes, plenty of possibilities," he added with his trademark smirk.

I rolled my eyes and knocked him in the shoulder. "Don't be a pervert!" I whispered, unable to hide my smile.

"You insult me, sweetheart." He feigned a pout. "It's your mind that appears to be the dirty one."

After I directed a sharp glare at him, he chuckled, and we walked back out into the foyer where Paula waited, her feet shifting impatiently.

"It appears I'll be making a purchase today," he told her.

Paula's face lit up. "Great! Let's head back to my office and start talking numbers to make an offer." She held the door open for us.

"I'll stop by later this afternoon. Miss Clarke and I have lunch plans." His hand rested on the small of my back, heating the skin through my navy cardigan as he led me through the threshold. My stomach fluttered to life.

I raised my shoulders, chastising my body for betraying

me. "Actually, Hilary sent me a text earlier. She needs to meet me in an hour," I explained. My sole focus was on his hand and how good it felt—how natural. But I willed him to remove it. As right as it felt, I knew it was so wrong. We were two very different people, and I needed more than he could offer me.

We stood in the circular drive, looking up at the house once more.

"A quick bite, at least," he insisted.

"Sorry, I need you to drop me off at my house soon. No time for lunch, but maybe next weekend." I stepped back, and his hand fell away. With a quick goodbye to Paula, I smiled and offered him a slight shrug.

The few other times we'd gone out with the realtor, after walking through different houses that would never work for Julia, we always ended up at the diner or Haven for lunch. It had become our thing, but today I'd made plans. Hilary had been complaining that I rarely saw her outside of school lately, so a girls' day was severely overdue. It was to start with an afternoon of lunch and pampering.

"As you wish." He smiled, giving nothing away. I hated that he could be impossible to read when he wanted to. "But at least join Oliver and me at Nichol's Farm tomorrow. He wants to find a pumpkin before they're all picked over."

I laughed. "He does, or you do?"

"I'm not going to lie: Carving jack-o-lanterns is a pastime I greatly enjoy. So will you join us?"

"How can I say no to a day with Oliver and farm animals?" I smiled and walked to the car. I gripped the passenger-door handle and looked up, smiling at Logan standing beside me. "But I'm not carving mine yet. Halloween isn't for another three weeks."

His hand came down, resting over mine on the cool metal handle that suddenly seared into my palm. His breath was

200

warm and thick behind my ear. I closed my eyes when his chest connected with my back. My breath caught, my body humming to life.

"I've never had much patience, Cassandra. When I want something, I take it as soon as it's available." He opened the car door for me and I slid inside, blood rushing to my cheeks as he stared down at me with dark, hooded eyes. A small smirk played on his lips. "The pumpkins are ready for harvesting, so why wait?"

With that, he shut the door, leaving me to process his words for a few minutes while he said goodbye to Paula. Why did he have to make it so impossibly hard to resist him? I watched him slide into the driver's side and stiffened, realizing the tension would be unbearable the entire ride home if I just sat there wondering what exactly he'd meant.

"You better hurry up and get me home, mister." I smiled over at him, trying to take my mind and body's response off his possible double meaning. "Or you'll have Hilary to deal with."

"Yes, ma'am." The side of his lip quirked up as he pulled his aviators down from the visor and slid them on casually, taking his sweet time before revving up the engine. I couldn't help but giggle when he looked over at me with a mischievous grin, his hand on the shifter, and shot out of the drive and down the road.

# Chapter Eighteen

## EXPECTATIONS

The next morning, Oliver was at my door, adorable and cozy in a grey wool coat. The weather was beginning to take on a slight chill, which I welcomed happily; fall had always been my favorite time of year. Logan drove while Oliver sat in the backseat, replaying his week at school. The old Nichol's Farm was located on the other side of town, and had been there long before I was even born.

Once we pulled into the dirt parking lot, I unbuckled my seat belt, but was stopped from opening the door when Logan turned in his seat to face me rather than climb out. I sat, confused at the crease over his brow.

"What?" He had something to tell me that I wouldn't like. I could see it written all over his expression.

"Julia and Jax will be meeting us here," he said, but not in his usual tone. *He should be happy to spend time with them, right?*

"Awesome!" Oliver opened his door. "Where are they?"

My attention was still focused on Logan, realization setting in at what his somber expression was telling me: Mark.

He tilted his head, eyes soft. "I'm sorry. I told her about today, and when she called earlier, she said he'd be coming with her."

I looked away and opened my door, but his hand shot out, holding my arm gently.

"I told her he wasn't invited, but my sister is not one to listen to me—or anyone, for that matter." He sighed. "I'll talk to him and make sure he stays clear of you, if you'd like."

I shook my head, nibbling on my bottom lip anxiously. "No. Thanks, but it's all right."

He nodded once, gauging my reaction. I gave him a smile, and he returned one full of understanding and warmth.

We walked through the parked cars with Oliver between us, swinging in the air from our arms, giggling each time we lifted him. As we approached a red steel barn, we stopped near wooden crates filled with produce grown on the farm. I thought of my grandmother and smiled. At least once a month when I was younger, she'd bring me along to purchase anything in season.

"Stay here for a moment. I'll go pay," Logan said, tossing Oliver up once more.

I nodded, and took Oliver's hand to let him see the row of pumpkins behind us. They were set out for anyone who didn't want to go out in the field to find their own.

"Over here!" Oliver called out, catching me off guard.

I turned, plastering on a thin smile when I saw Julia and Mark approach. Jax was strolling up behind them, his red ball cap on backward and a tall, thin brunette on his arm. My smile grew. He was definitely Logan's little brother.

I suddenly felt a little out of place. It seemed this was more of a family outing, and everyone was paired up with dates. I wasn't Logan's date by far, but I wondered how it must look to the others. Did they think he and I were seeing each other? I cringed, realizing that with Logan's reputation, they must think I was sleeping with him. I felt out of place instantly.

Why *was* I there? I was just a neighbor.

"Hey, sweetie, you ready to see some smelly farm animals?" Julia laughed, her nose scrunched. She picked Oliver up for a giant hug and held him tightly in her arms.

Mark looked over at me and opened his mouth to speak, but snapped it shut after I shot him a threatening glare. He cleared his throat, shoving his hands deep into his hoodie pockets.

"Hi, Cassandra. I love your sweater," Julia said, smiling. I wondered what she knew about Mark and me.

"Thanks. Hope you don't mind me coming today."

"Of course not—the more the merrier," she said with a sincere smile. "Logan seems to enjoy having you around."

"We've been getting along pretty well."

"I'm sure you have," Jax snickered. I looked down, embarrassed. So they *did* think I was sleeping with him.

"Ignore him." I looked up to see Julia roll her eyes at Jax. "He's just not sure how to act around you after Logan threatened to disown him if he so much as flirts in your direction."

An awkward, broken chuckle caught in my throat. "Why would Logan care who flirts in my direction?" My gaze dropped to the ground, a bemused smile playing on my lips.

She raised her eyebrow, as if she knew something I didn't, then shrugged. "Who knows?" She grinned. "But you're the first girl he's brought around us, and—"

She was cut off as Oliver wiggled out of her arms and planted his feet back on the ground. We laughed, watching him adjust his coat in a huff. He looked up at Mark curiously.

"Hey, buddy." Mark squatted down to eye level with him. "My name's Mark. Hope you don't mind me tagging along today."

"That's all right," Oliver said shyly.

"Here you are," Logan said, appearing beside me and handing a wristband to Jax, his quiet date, and Julia. The air between us all grew thick and uncomfortably heavy when it became clear he didn't have one for Mark.

"I'll, uh…I'll be right back," Mark said awkwardly, leaving to purchase his.

Logan ignored him and leaned down to snap a band on Oliver's wrist, then stood and took my hand.

"I can do it," I said softly.

He said nothing, his fingers placing it on my wrist and locking it in place. His thumb lingered a moment longer than necessary, and he looked up at me slowly.

I pulled my hand away and smiled sheepishly. "Thanks."

"You sure you're all right with him being here?" he whispered, nudging his head in the direction Mark had retreated.

I nodded once, losing myself in his eyes. They were so enticingly blue and filled with nothing but concern, calming my nerves. I smiled, letting him know I really was fine.

"Come on, let's go check this place out," Jax said. He threw Oliver up onto his shoulders and jetted off toward the gate. His busty date followed.

"Careful!" Logan yelled.

Jax continued on with Oliver giggling, begging him to go faster as they raced for the first, smaller barn filled with chickens. Mark came back out a moment later, an orange bracelet on his wrist, and took Julia's hand.

As we began to walk, Logan's hand brushed the small of my back. I stiffened, but after glancing over at him and his reassuring smile, I relaxed against his touch. I never dreamed I'd be spending the day with Mark after everything that had happened, but with Logan at my side, I forgot all about him.

"Let's go catch up before Jax has Oliver sneaking into

one of the pens." Logan grinned.

———•◆•———

"Yuck! I hate farm animals—especially being this close to me," a young woman I'd never seen before complained in front of us. Wearing knee-high boots with nearly six-inch heels, she held up both hands disgustedly and maneuvered around a tiny puddle of mud. Her short blonde bob and bright-red lipstick stood out against the background of rust, dirt, and livestock.

We walked behind her silently, watching the hens go about their day. It was easy and comfortable being with Logan. Oliver and Jax were a barn ahead of us, and to my relief, Julia and Mark had gone with them.

As we continued through to another barn, my tolerance for the blonde bimbo and her two friends who were equally out of place but much less aggravating was wearing thin. Each time we stopped or Logan made a comment, she was there, hanging on every word. Her roaming hands rubbed his arm or touched his hand when he rested it on the wood pens.

It was driving me to a breaking point. I wasn't jealous, really, but I was about to rip her manicured claws off him if she did it again. It was just him and me; you'd think she would assume he was my boyfriend. Unless...

I winced. Logan was a six-foot-two Greek god, and I was...well, me. No wonder she acted as if I didn't exist. Next to him, I didn't.

"Oh my God!" she squealed, hands flailing wildly in front of her when one of the cows nudged her arm. I bit the inside of my lip hard, seeing red when the little skank turned around and flew into Logan's arms. She buried her head against his chest, her hands taking full advantage of having him in her grasp.

With a shake of my head, I continued walking. Better to leave than say something I'd regret. I had no reason to be upset anyway. Good for Logan. She looked like an easy lay.

Within seconds, Logan's hand was folding around mine. I flinched, wrapped up in my own head.

"I think the others aren't too far ahead. Oliver probably has them stopping to stare at every moving creature," he said as if nothing had happened and it was completely normal to hold my hand.

Did he really not feel the electric current that surged through me with his touch?

With the raw irritation of the blonde still fresh in my mind and my feelings that were in no way justified, I pulled my hand away.

"I was just going to get a bottled water. Stay here, and I'll catch up with you later." I then leaned in and whispered, "She likes you—might as well have some fun." I nudged my head back at the girl lingering behind us and turned to leave.

His hand shot out, grabbing my arm and pulling me back. He looked almost angry when he spoke, his voice gruff and stern. "I'm not interested in having fun with her, Cassandra, so if you want some water, I'll go with you."

I tried to hide the smile tugging at my lips, my heart swelling despite my brain telling me not to read too much into it. With his hand on my back—where I secretly felt it belonged at all times—we turned around and exited the barn.

"Daddy!" Oliver called out. He was standing beside Jax and his nameless date. They were in front of an outdoor pen full of pigs.

As we approached, Jax picked up a handful of straw lying on the ground and stuffed it down the back of Oliver's coat. I stopped, pulling out my camera to snap a picture of the hilarious face Oliver made before he grabbed a handful and threw it at his uncle. I smiled, watching them as they stopped abruptly, exchanged a few hushed words between them, then ran toward Logan.

Jax's busty friend walked toward me, giggling.

"Hi, I'm Cassandra."

Her laughter died down and she smiled. "Marissa."

"So how long have you and Jax been seeing each other?"

She grinned, turning to look back at him. Jax was dodging Logan's attempts at throwing wet straw. "We met last night at a frat party."

"Oh." I gave a tight, uncomfortable smile. "Well, I've only met him one other time, but he seems…fun." It was how Logan had described him originally, and watching Jax run around like a young boy, I could tell he was definitely the playful one in the family.

She nodded, giggling. "Yeah, a lot of fun."

Definitely the type of girl I pictured Jax with.

We stood for another moment, laughing and staring at the boys until she turned to fully face me. "So you're the one Jax's brother warned him about. You're a lucky girl. Logan is gorgeous."

I cocked my head toward her, unsure how to respond, so I simply offered a small smile. Jax must've told her, but I wasn't thrilled about being known as *that* girl.

"I, um…I guess. Seems like everyone's making a lot of assumptions. Kind of silly, considering Logan and I are just friends."

"That's not how Jax explained it."

Both annoyed and semi-interested, I asked, "And how exactly *did* Jax explain it—that I was sleeping with his older brother?"

"No, he told me you were a family friend and the first girl in a long time his older brother went out of his way for." She shrugged. "Jax seemed pretty happy about it, and on the drive over, Julia gave him the third degree about not scaring you off."

I sucked in my bottom lip to conceal my growing smile. "Well, like I said, we're just friends."

She made a face that told me she didn't really care either way before turning her attention back to the boys.

I took picture after picture, unable to stop giggling the entire time. I'd never seen Logan like that before. He looked young, happy, and carefree. After dodging handfuls of muddy hay, Logan raced after Oliver. The young boy was squealing with laughter when Logan snatched him up and dangled him over the pigs.

"You win! You win!" Oliver cried, a giant grin still covering his face.

"Ah, don't give up so easily," Jax laughed, smashing a pile of hay into Logan's hair and grinding it in.

Logan set Oliver down and tugged the hay out of his hair. He then scooped up as much as he could hold and turned toward his kid brother, but stopped suddenly and glanced over at me. My giggling ended abruptly when I saw a flicker of mischief cross his eyes.

I backed up, shaking my head. "Don't even *think* about it."

He stalked toward me, a grin spreading over his lips slowly. I held up my hands when he was a mere foot away. Stepping back slowly, I turned to run, but his strong arms locked around my waist.

"No!" I yelled, giggling. "No, no, no!"

His hand flew down the front of my sweater, hay scratching between my breasts, but the electricity of his touch as his hand slid down to my navel and back up overwhelmed any other sensation. I stumbled forward out of his grasp, pulling on my sweater to let the hay fall through, and noticed Oliver doubled over, laughing hysterically.

"*Really*!" I puffed out a deep breath. Oliver turned and ran off to another barn, Jax and Marissa snickering beside him. Logan was still there, staring at me while I pulled out more and more of the water- and mud-saturated hay. Through my frustration, his hearty laughter was music to my ears. How could I be mad when he looked so stress-free and cheerful?

"Like some help, sweetheart?" His laughter died to a soft chuckle as he drew closer. He stopped in front of me, his chuckle now completely gone and gaze intense as he picked out a piece of straw that had somehow found its way into my hair.

Heat flooded my body, awakening the dozens of butterflies in my stomach. They fluttered wildly as his hand slid slowly from my hair down to my cheek. His touch was soft and unbearably gentle. I knew it was wrong, yet I leaned into it. His warm palm cradled me, creating a need I'd never felt before. My body stood rigid, on full alert, attempting to put out the burning fire building inside me.

Logan's eyes flickered down to my lips and then slowly back up. I knew what he wanted, and for once, I couldn't find the reasoning in my brain to stop it. His other hand reached up to caress my other cheek gently, holding me attentively in place.

*Just one small taste*—it was all I wanted as his lips grew closer. I wasn't sure who was moving, but I could see it coming. I closed my eyes, inhaling his breath that was only a whisper above my lips. It was sweet, warm, and minty: exactly as I imagined it would be.

Bravely, I placed my weak hands on his forearms as he closed the gap between us, ghosting his soft lips against mine. His kiss was demanding, his lips parting mine, and almost

210

immediately his tongue darted out, looking for access. My head began pounding, my fingers gripping his coat, wanting to continue on this roller coaster of emotions and foreign touches.

His hands moved from my cheeks back into my hair, one gripping the back of my head while the other continued down around to my backside. The moment he squeezed my ass, pulling me flush against him, I pushed away, gasping for air. I stepped back, needing to put more distance between us. My eyes wandered around the ground, looking anywhere but up at him.

"Logan, we can't," I breathed, pulling myself back to reality.

Every part of me wanted to kiss him back with the same passion, but I knew he couldn't give me what I needed. I wanted a real relationship with a shot at a real future. Logan was sweet and gorgeous and said all the right things, but I couldn't let myself forget he was also a notorious playboy. I was nothing more than a small-town teacher, searching for my epic love—not just hot sex with a friend. Even if I'd gone home with Kurt before I learned he was psychotic, nothing would've happened. I just wasn't that type of girl.

With a deep breath, I looked up, knowing Logan would only grow bored of me within days if I ever gave into him and it would ruin everything. I'd rather have him as my friend than endure awkward encounters after a few passionate nights together.

"Take a chance, Cassandra," he murmured. With a smile, he ran his tongue across his lips slowly and took a step closer. I stood there, wanting so badly to say, *Yes, please take me now,* but I couldn't. His hand ran over my shoulder, blazing a trail up my neck. I closed my eyes for only a second, trying to contain the vibrations humming through me.

211

Logan leaned in to my ear, placing a gentle kiss on my lobe. "Let me show you what you've been missing—a night you'll never forget."

I sighed and looked away. We weren't anywhere near on the same page with life or love.

I smiled softly and met his gaze. "Exactly: The word there is 'night.' What happens after that, huh?"

"You know I consider you a friend. Why does that have to change? We get along. I enjoy your company, and would very much like to take you to my bed. Does that need a label?"

"That's not what I'm looking for, Logan."

He ran his hands through his disheveled hair. Tiny pieces of straw were still caught in his locks. "I am not the relationship type of guy. You know this already." His voice was gruff and unsteady. I could see what he wanted clearly in his eyes, but it wasn't enough.

"I know, but I'm the relationship type of girl." After a soft squeeze to his hand, I pulled away to catch up with Oliver.

# Chapter Nineteen

## REVEALING

After spending another hour walking from barn to barn, showing Oliver the many different animals, we were ready to find our pumpkins. Jax carried Oliver up the small wooden stepladder into a large wagon filled to the brim with hay. It was a short ride out to the pumpkin patch located at the back of the farm. Logan was behind us on his phone—"a business call," he'd explained before answering it—but the look on his face made me wonder otherwise.

Mark stood beside the wagon to help Julia up, then held out his hand for me. With a glare that clearly said *Don't touch me*, I stepped up slowly, balancing myself as I climbed over the ledge and took a seat next to Marissa. Oliver sat between Jax and Julia in the very back, eager for the tractor to start moving.

"Sorry about that," Logan said, sitting beside me. He stretched out his legs, crossing them at the ankles.

"Everything all right?" I asked, squinting from the sunlight as I looked over at him.

"Mmm hmm." He nodded, looking past me to Oliver.

The rigid straw poked at my ankles, digging at my jeans and irritating my skin, but childhood memories of riding in that

213

very wagon left me smiling despite it. Oliver let out a loud, cheerful sound when the tractor began pulling us along the dirt trail.

Logan sat quietly, looking out into the field, his eyebrows low and forehead marred with worry lines. He caught me staring, and his expression softened into a sweet smile. I returned it, and rested back against the rickety rails.

His tantalizing scent of nature and fresh soap was enticing—especially when combined with the taste of his lips, which still lingered on mine. Without thinking, I ran my tongue across my lips slowly, savoring the final trace of him.

As tormenting as it was to refuse him—and my body's desires—I was proud of finding the self-control to end things. Looking back, I had no clue how I'd managed to pull away. The memory of his hand in my hair while the other traced down my back and cupped my ass still felt amazing. I hadn't been touched like that in so long. I smiled to myself, knowing later that night Logan would be in my dreams, ready to show me exactly what could've been.

My body flinched when something pulled at a strand of my hair, jerking me from my lustful reverie. I tilted my head, brows furrowed, and caught Logan holding up a piece of straw.

"Just trying to help," he explained with a delicious crooked grin.

I smiled, narrowing my eyes at his flirty expression. I was relieved my rejection hadn't offended him; we seemed to being falling right back into where we were before the kiss: friends.

"Sure you are," I teased.

I looked over at Oliver, ignoring Mark's eyes on me when my gaze flickered past him.

"You having fun, Oliver?" I asked.

"Yeah, today is the best day of my whole life!" He sat on

his knees, wide-eyed, taking in the new environment. Julia's arm was wrapped around him.

It took less than five minutes for the tractor to come to a stop. We were surrounded by hundreds of pumpkins, large and small.

My camera was in my hands, ready to capture any moment worth remembering. So far, I had at least a dozen photos of Logan from behind; I couldn't seem to restrain myself. The man filled out a pair of jeans in ways that were purely sinful.

I walked around and snapped a picture of Oliver and Jax bending down to examine a tall pumpkin. I laughed when Oliver's face twisted in disgust.

"Yuck!" he shrieked. He kicked the pumpkin over, exposing the rot on the bottom.

"Keep looking," Logan said, walking up behind him. "You'll find the perfect one."

Jax took Oliver's hand, leading him farther into the field. Logan turned back to me.

"Did you find a pumpkin, sweetheart?"

"Not yet." I flashed a smile, then walked away to find the right one. It took a few minutes of searching before I bent down to life one that looked to have potential. It was covered in mud on one side, but I had a feeling it would be perfect underneath. I wiped away the dried gunk with a tissue from my coat pocket and smiled. I looked forward to cleaning it up and displaying it on my front porch.

Lugging the pumpkin my arms, I walked back to the wagon.

"I see you found a lovely one," Logan said, helping me up into the wagon.

After helping Oliver inside, he climbed in behind us. I burst out laughing at the pumpkin he had in his arms. It had to be one of the biggest on the lot.

"I did," I managed to get out through my laughter as I sat down. I stared between him and his ridiculous pumpkin, stunned he could even lift it. "Okay, I have to ask: Why would you want one that big?"

"I told you, I enjoy carving." He smiled, running his hands over its curves.

"Cassandra, are you going to carve yours, too?" Oliver asked, glancing at my pumpkin.

"Maybe next week. I like it the way it is for now."

He seemed pleased with my response and turned around, looking back at the field we were leaving behind.

My gaze wandered over to Mark and Julia laughing happily. She was sitting between his legs holding a petite pumpkin—shiny and perfectly round, with a long curly stem—Mark's hands resting on her thighs. Julia looked down at the pumpkin as if it was the finest in the field—much like how she looked at her boyfriend.

Mark caught me staring and his eyes locked with mine. We'd never talked after the day I moved out. I avoided him at all costs, and living in a small town, that was not an easy task. Hilary had heard his job transferred him to the city for a few months in the spring, which I assumed was how he'd met Julia. I shot him a threatening scowl, then looked away.

What were the chances she would be dating *him* of all people? I liked Julia; she had that air about her that at times screamed spoiled, yet she was surprisingly friendly and sweet. Unfortunately, I worried her new relationship would put a damper on our friendship.

Once we returned to the farm, Logan helped me out of the wagon, then Oliver. I walked off to the side, waiting, and rolled my eyes at the scene of Julia and Mark posing for a photo together. His arm was wrapped around her waist, pumpkins resting at their feet while his lips lingered on her cheek.

What surprised me in that moment more than anything was that I felt no jealousy—only concern for Julia. I hated the idea of her being with a guy who was capable of breaking someone's heart so easily.

Oliver was up on Jax's shoulders as he and Marissa walked toward me. I smiled. Never before did I think I'd see the day that I could look at Mark, cozy with another girl, without feeling violently ill.

It felt liberating.

—◆◆◆—

I woke the next morning to a text from Logan, which wasn't unusual. It'd become one of my favorite parts of the morning.

**House is bought and paid for. Hope she hates it so I can spend a weekend tormenting u.**

I rolled my eyes, hit *Reply*, and began typing.

**She'll love the house and then you'll be spending a long weekend as my little bitch!**

I placed the phone next to my pillow and lay back with a smile, waiting for his response. I knew it'd be instant; it always was. My smile grew wider when the familiar ping sounded and I picked up my phone, laughing as I read his text.

**I'll be your little bitch any day, sweetheart! Now get your fine ass up and have a splendid day at school.**

—◆◆◆—

Two weeks later, Oliver and I were playing in my backyard, making mud pies. It was his idea, and I'd learned by then I had trouble telling him no.

"What would happen if you took a bite?" Oliver

snickered, packing the soggy dirt into a rusty old muffin tin I'd found in the treehouse.

"Try it and let me know." I smiled, using a stick to draw tiny designs on my mud-covered hands.

"No way!"

I was wrapped in my winter jacket and my back rested against a tree, legs out. The moment was completely tranquil.

"Come on, just one bite?" I taunted, grabbing the plastic spoon and digging into our mess.

"You're crazy!" He giggled.

"And you're a mess."

His shirt was covered in dried mud, and grass stains adorned his knees. The sun was starting to go down and I still had papers to grade for tomorrow's class, so I stood up, wiping the seat of my jeans.

"Let's get you home." I pulled him to his feet.

Oliver helped clean up the bowls and utensils covered in our creations before heading home. I walked over with him, wanting to see him inside safely.

"Daddy's in his office. You should come say hi," he said. He opened the glass door on his back porch.

I'd only seen Logan in person twice since the day at the farm, so I decided to go say a quick hello. We stepped out of our muddy shoes, and I followed him up the steps.

"Daddy's office is over there," Oliver said, pointing down the hall before disappearing into his bedroom.

As I stared down the hall, my nerves began buzzing to life. I was alone in Logan's house, and he wasn't expecting me. God knows what I might walk in on.

The hardwood floor, covered with an ornate rug, creaked as I passed multiple doors. I followed a light shining from inside a room whose door was partially open. Logan's voice boomed from inside. Shifting my weight anxiously, I peeked in to find him standing behind a dark-mahogany desk, staring out the window.

He held his cell phone to his ear, his other hand shoved deep in his trouser pocket. He was still in his work clothes—a dark suit—but his white button-down shirt was untucked.

"The answer is no." Logan's tone was cold and clipped, and I was thankful I wasn't on the receiving end of it. "I don't know who you slept with to get this number, but you better lose it!"

He turned with a growl and I scurried away from the door, not wanting to interrupt. I tiptoed back to Oliver's room, my stomach clenched and ears scorching, and knocked gently.

He opened the door, wearing a clean shirt but still in need of a good scrubbing.

"Your dad's busy. I'll say hi another time," I explained, keeping my voice hushed. "Make sure you get a bath tonight."

"Wait, you want to see something?" Oliver asked suddenly. He was beaming, excited to show me.

"Another time, sweetie," I whispered, glancing down the hall toward Logan's office.

"Oh, okay." His smile fell. "Goodbye."

His forlorn expression broke my heart. He began shutting his door, but I reached out, holding it open.

"All right, let me see." I smiled, and his eyes brightened instantly as he perked up.

He grabbed my hand, then whispered, "We have to be very quiet, though. It's a secret."

I sighed, looking around nervously as he led the way down the hall to a room opposite Logan's office.

"It's in here," Oliver whispered, pushing open the last door in the hall and flicking on the light.

After a quick look behind me, I stepped tentatively inside the room. My jaw dropped as I took in the sight of dozens of paintings stacked against the wall. They were mostly landscapes and a few portraits of Oliver, as well as blank canvases. Two easels sat in the middle of the room, a metal stool next to them, positioned in front of a window. I walked farther inside, stopping at a large worktable with rows of brushes, tubes of paints, and other miscellaneous supplies scattered across the top.

"Here it is," Oliver whispered, standing in the corner and tugging at a white blanket covering a pile.

I walked toward him slowly, my feet heavy with worry. Would Logan be upset we were in here? It looked so personal.

I noticed a pair of his jeans thrown over a chair in the corner. They were splattered with dark colors of paint, and the image of him wearing them and nothing else flashed before me. I couldn't help but wonder what he looked like when he painted.

Oliver finally had the cloth removed from the painting and dropped it to the floor. I blinked a couple times, clearing my mind as I stood beside Oliver.

"This is my mom," he explained, his usual playful self fleeting as he gazed down at the portrait resting against the stack of other large canvases behind it.

The painting was a single portrait of the woman. It was extraordinary. She had long, glossy-black hair that fell around her shoulders. Her features were soft, yet held a toughness to them, her smile barely visible. She looked serious—almost sorrowful. I winced when I noticed her eyes. *Oliver's eyes.*

"She's pretty, huh?" he asked, looking up at me proudly.

"She's beautiful."

"What are you doing in here?" Logan snapped. "You know this isn't a playroom!"

Oliver and I turned around, but Logan's gaze was on his son, as if I didn't exist.

"I wanted Cassie to see Mommy."

Logan's jaw ticked and his nostrils flared. "Go to your room—now!"

Oliver looked at me, his face flushed bright red. But before I could speak, he burst into uncontrollable sobs, his tiny hands covering his mouth as he ran from the room.

I stood there, flabbergasted and angry. Logan stomped toward me, his eyes filled with rage, and grabbed the sheet from the floor. Without even a glance at the painting, he threw the sheet back over it.

"I've told him countless times to stay out of here when I'm not with him!" Logan yelled, his back to me.

"You were a bit harsh," I said, finally finding my voice, too angry to be afraid of him. "You need to go speak to him. He only wanted to show me her painting."

Logan turned to face me, tilting his head slowly to the side, glaring at me. He inhaled a deep, ragged breath, but as his eyes met mine, I watched his expression begin to soften slowly.

His shoulders slumped after a few moments, and then he walked past me to the window. The air was thick and uncomfortable as I waited for him to speak.

With nothing left to say, I was about to leave when I heard him sigh.

"That was her—Oliver's mother, Natasha—on the phone," he grumbled. I stared at his back, watching his fists tighten at his sides. "She wants me to bring Oliver to see her in London. Can you believe her? She hasn't seen him since his first birthday!" A deep, throaty snarl came next, and as if he couldn't bear to stand still, he began pacing the room.

I watched silently, waiting for him to continue. The anger and hurt radiated off him in waves. I shoved my filthy hands in my pockets and listened.

"She just left us one day. After everything, she just *left!*

221

Ran off with some rich son of a bitch—someone she thought could give her a better life." He knocked over one of the easels and I jumped back, startled. "I'll never look at her the same again. Oliver deserves better than that!"

"He does, but she is the only mother he has." My voice cracked and I swallowed, clearing my throat. "You have to see it from his point of view."

Logan stopped and turned, staring at me as though I'd said something absurd. "So what are you saying, Cassandra? I should take him to London to see her? Allow him to spend time with her, fall in love with her, just so she can leave him again?"

"No," I said softly, shaking my head, "you're protecting your son, and you should continue doing what you think is right. Just remember she is the only mother he will ever have. That's all I am trying to say."

"You don't think I know that? It took me nearly two years before I could look at him and not see her. He's my son, my…everything." He looked down. "I'm aware he sneaks in here. I've stood in that doorway, as well as in our old home, and watched him sitting on the floor, staring at her painting. Sometimes he'll tell her about his day. He has such hope that she'll come back."

Logan sighed. He dropped his head down and ran his hands through his hair, locking them together behind his neck.

"He doesn't even remember her," he murmured. "He romanticizes this idea of her appearing at our door and making us the perfect family."

I watched him walk back to the grand window and stare out into the setting sun.

"I'm sorry," I murmured, wishing I could help in some way. "She called you and wanted to see him—that's a step. Maybe one day you'll be able to trust her with him again."

"At one time, I wanted to believe that. But now…it's been so long. I can't…" With his back to me, I found myself desperate to see his face—to comfort him in any way he'd allow.

"Do you still love her?" I asked boldly, crossing the room to stand beside him.

He remained silent, closing his eyes for a moment. His face looked pained, and I regretted asking. I was trying to be a friend, but part of me wondered why he kept the painting.

Logan placed his hand on the wall, leaning against it. He looked tired. "I haven't seen her in over three years." He looked up at me. "A part of me wonders if I ever truly loved her to begin with, or simply loved the idea of her. We were young, and she was so vivacious." His chest rumbled for a split second as he looked out the window in thought. "She gave me everything a young college kid could want: sex, affection, and what I believed to be loyalty. She was beautiful. Every guy I knew wanted her, but she was mine."

He was quiet for a few moments as I stood there, unsure what to say. Logan was in love with Oliver's mother, and she'd broken his heart. It explained so much.

"I knew she was unhappy. I could see it every morning I left for work, and when I'd return, eager to spend time with her and our son, she was always out. Oliver was left with the nannies more often than not. Natasha even refused to change him—said she wasn't a hands-on type of mother. Thanks to my father entrusting me with the family business, I was able to make a name for myself. By the time Oliver was born, employing a nanny or two was manageable."

"Did she work?"

He laughed—a deep, guttural sound—and leaned further against the wall, looking over at me and shaking his head.

"No, she didn't work—not once she was pregnant,

anyway. I was barely twenty-one, and even though it wasn't what I wanted at the time, a family was something that had always been in my plans. I dropped out of school and took care of her every desire, gave her everything she wanted, but it wasn't enough." He looked away, staring as the sun disappeared into the skyline.

I placed my hand over his and he tilted his head toward me, his eyes hooded. "I'm so sorry. For what it's worth, you're an amazing father, Logan. Oliver is lucky to have you."

After a long moment of silence with our eyes connected, he blinked, then looked over to my hand resting over his on the wall. He pulled it away, and I stepped back.

After another long pause, he cleared his throat and offered a tight smile. "I should go check on Oliver. I'll see you out."

We walked out of the room and down the hall silently. I fidgeted with my hands as we descended the stairs, fighting to find the right words.

"I'm sorry if I overstepped. I—"

With his hand on the doorknob, he hesitated before looking up at me.

"Cassandra, you are…amazing. Oliver adores you, and I…appreciate having you in my life." His hand lifted to my cheek slowly, tucking a fallen piece of hair behind my ear. My breath caught, and his eyes locked with mine. His thumb caressed my cheek for a brief moment before dropping away. "Truth be told, I've never really had a friend that was a woman. They usually hang around only for my money or sex…sometimes both."

A soft chuckle shook his chest and I smiled, standing still, aware of every move he made and every breath he took.

"I also never speak about Natasha to anyone. You did not overstep. With you, I welcome it like a breath of fresh air, but it's still very new to me."

"Thank you for trusting me," I said, a soft smile on my lips. "I want you to know, I'm here if you ever want to talk about anything. I won't judge you." My smile grew to a grin and I sucked in my lips. "Okay, I might, but I won't hold it against you," I laughed, hoping to lighten the mood.

Logan grinned, his body visibly relaxing in front of me. "Thank you for that."

"No problem, buddy." I punched his forearm, giggling. He laughed louder as he opened the door.

"Tell Oliver I said good night." I stopped mid step out the front door, turning back with narrowed eyes, but a soft smile played on my lips. "And that you're sorry."

He nodded, smiling, then glanced up at the top of the stairs regretfully. "Good night, Cassandra. And enjoy your bath."

I looked down, remembering the state I was in and that my shoes were on his back porch.

"Oh, I will." I gave a flirty smile and headed home barefoot.

—◆◆◆—

The next day, I woke ready to see my class. Monday mornings were as welcomed as Fridays. I rumpled the quilt away from my body, stretching my arms high over my head. I pulled my crazy hair out of my face, twisting it over my shoulder. Per routine, I reached out to my nightstand, snatching up my phone.

I smiled, seeing his name listed with two new messages.

**I have an amazing son. All was set right after I agreed to let him stay up late eating ice cream & watching The Muppets movie.**

I scrolled to the next message.

**I did however refuse the dance number he requested & luckily he fell asleep before I was forced to give in. See you around, buddy ;)**

I laughed out loud, visualizing what it would've been like to watch Logan break out into a dance move from *The Muppets*. My fingers typed quickly.

**When you're ready for the showtune dance number I better be there to see it!**

I only had to wait a minute for my phone to ding with a new message.

**I would not hold your breath, sweetheart.**

# Chapter Twenty

## HELP YOURSELF

"So what's going on with you and Logan?" Hilary asked, tucking her legs under her body as we sat on her petite red couch and munched on cold pizza she had left over from the previous night.

I'd been reluctant to go into details about Logan previously when we'd hung out, but when she called this morning demanding that we talk, I knew it was time to spill. Somehow, Logan and I had become closer than I was with any other guy friend I had, and that had a lot to do with Oliver. He was over playing every weekend.

October and November passed in the blink of an eye, and I found myself waking up every morning to sweet *Have a good day* texts from Logan. He'd finally lain off the seduction, but he never turned down his charm. The man could find a sexual innuendo in almost everything we did together.

I didn't mind—he wouldn't be Logan without it—but there was so much more to him than anyone realized. Not only was he paying for Julia's education and had he offered Jax a position at the paper—which he eagerly accepted—but he was also extremely charitable. He and Oliver spent time volunteering at the animal shelter, which I happily joined them in, and donated money to multiple organizations. The more time I spent with him, the more I couldn't understand why he created a fortress around himself. Every time anyone in town tried to get close, he became more guarded. I was one of the lucky few he allowed inside, and I was grateful for it.

With my back against the arm of the sofa, I took a giant bite and watched Hilary stare at me, waiting impatiently.

She was dying for any, and preferably all, information she could pull out of me, but it was fun to drag it out a little longer. It wasn't like she'd been briefing me after every interaction she and Caleb had. After their date at the carnival, she'd suddenly become tight-lipped on the subject of all things Caleb Townsend—not that I really minded.

I took a long drink of water, savoring her irritation, then smiled coyly. "Logan who?" I took another large bite from my slice, avoiding Hilary's narrowed eyes and pursed lips.

I laughed, swallowing. "He's a friend. What's the big deal?"

"I gathered that much on my own without your explosive confession," she grumbled sarcastically. "Come on—time to share a few juicy tidbits about the elusive Logan West."

I shook my head and shrugged my shoulders. "Turns out he's not so bad. He's actually nice—sweet, even."

"That's all you have to say? You've been hanging out with him for the past few months!" Hilary chuckled, shaking her head. She took a bite of pizza and relaxed into her side of the couch. "You know, Caleb says Logan rarely goes down to Haven anymore to drink."

"That's none of my business. What he does in his free time isn't going to affect my friendship with him."

"Oh really? So what if I told you Caleb also happened to notice that when Logan *is* there, he turns down every offer from the slutty barflies?"

This was news. I hadn't noticed the lack of disheveled women sneaking out his front door in the early morning, but now that I thought about it, I couldn't remember the last time I saw a woman there. Hilary noticed my thoughtful gaze down at my plate, and a smug grin was covering her lips when I looked back up. I shook off what the news might mean.

"He probably has some other bar he picks them up at." I laughed, pretending not to care.

She shook her head, still smiling. The girl knew me better than anyone.

"Caleb thinks Logan is dating someone and just wants to keep it quiet." Her brows rose. "But I think he has a crush on a certain blonde teacher." She slapped my knee and stood, walking into the kitchen with her empty plate.

What if he *was* dating someone? Would he tell me? It's not like I'd ever asked, and I knew there were still a lot of things about him I didn't know. What if it was Mackenzie?

*Ugh!* I cringed. It was obvious from the previous interactions I'd witnessed between him and Mackenzie that she was interested. Logan made sure to keep Mark and me apart when Julia brought him around, and I wondered what exactly Logan knew about my past with the tramp.

I chuckled to myself, rolling my eyes. It wasn't my business. If Logan wanted to share something with me, then he would.

"So just friends, huh?" Hilary asked, walking back out with another slice and slouching down on the couch.

I sat up and looked her straight in the eye. "Why would I lie to you? Logan is fun to be around and Oliver is a great kid. I would never want to hurt him by fooling around with his father."

Hilary nodded but still seemed unconvinced.

"I was over there just last weekend watching a movie in the theatre they have in their basement. You have *got* to come watch a movie there. I mean, it's amazing, and—"

"Cassandra, what happened when you were there?"

"We watched a movie—*Jurassic Park*, to be exact." Poor Oliver had only made it halfway through before he'd run terrified from the room. Bad choice of movie. I scrunched my brow, but understood her question. I puffed out an exasperated breath.

"Oliver sat between us, for goodness sake. It's completely platonic, I swear."

Hilary scoffed and picked up her glass of soda. I was not letting up until she believed me. I was determined for her to understand that what Logan and I had was strictly a friendship.

"Honestly, I don't even think Logan feels that way about me anymore. I can't remember the last time he blatantly hit on me. It's been all house-related talk—I'm helping him furnish Julia's secret new place, which is only so I'll win the little bet I have going with him."

"Logan West wants to sleep with you. I can see it clearly every time he's around." Hilary laughed, looking at me like I was blind.

I groaned, setting my plate on the coffee table. "I am not kidding. Last week, I bent over right in front of him to tie my shoes, and I glanced back and he wasn't even looking! Not even a friendly appreciative glance. I work hard for this ass!"

Hilary's eyes flew wide open, and she chuckled while attempting to choke down her drink.

"Oh my God, Cassandra!" she shrieked. "You glanced back! So, what, you were *hoping* he was checking you out?"

"No! I just...I don't know. But trust me, the man no longer wants to sleep with me—which is good, since I'm spending Christmas with him."

"Christmas?" Hilary raised her brows.

"Yeah, I'm sending my mom on a cruise with some of my grandparents' savings I inherited, so I'll be alone. Logan helped me pick out the cruise line and set everything up for her. It was actually Oliver who invited me over, though."

"So you're going?"

I nodded. "I think it will be fun. I mean, you should have seen the shorts I was wearing! He didn't even give the tiniest glance or single perverted remark. It was…bizarre." I laughed.

"You're crazy!" She giggled. "What are you going to get him? For Christmas, I mean."

"I have no clue." I'd been thinking about it ever since Oliver had invited me. "What are you getting Caleb?"

"Nothing!" Hilary shook her head. "We're just friends too."

"Sure you are." I giggled. "For the record, Caleb has never *not* checked out your ass."

"Yeah, I know," she said softly. "I like him and I know he likes me, but…he won't make a move, and I'm too terrified he'll reject me."

"I don't get it. Maybe he's afraid to?"

We both burst into a fit of giggles, unable to keep a straight face. Caleb had never been afraid of making a move on a girl.

"Maybe you could…ask Logan?" she asked hesitantly. "I mean, I know he and Caleb talk a lot."

"All right, I'll see what I can pry out of him. But if he confirms that Caleb is waiting for you to make the first move," I said, pointing my finger at her, "you better do it!"

---

The next morning, I pulled myself from bed and headed into the bathroom. There was only one week left until

Christmas, and today was a Saturday to take it easy and hang out with my mother before she left for her cruise.

Once I'd grabbed my purse, keys, and phone, I opened my morning text from Logan.

**Have a wonderful day with your mother, sweetheart**

After sending back a cheerful but quick reply, I was in my car, headed to Haven. I spotted my mother's short, dirty-blonde hair in the back of the restaurant instantly. I smiled and headed over, looking forward to spending the day with her.

Stopping a few feet away, I noticed a middle-aged man with a trimmed mustache wearing jeans and a grey polo sitting next to her. He was the same guy I'd seen her talking to at the carnival in August. Hesitantly, I walked over and gave her a quick hug, eyeing her guest warily.

"Cassandra, dear, this is my friend George." Mom smiled more brightly than usual, and I shook his hand reluctantly.

"It's a pleasure to finally meet you, Cassandra. Your mother has told me so much about you. I feel like we've already met."

I nodded, pulling on a tight polite smile before shooting my mother a confused glance that clearly asked, *Who the hell is this guy?*

I took a seat across from them in the booth and awkwardly waited for her to explain. Christmas was always about mother-daughter bonding, so this year, with her going on the cruise, spending today together was a huge deal for me.

Once I realized my mother was too busy swooning over the man beside her to ask how my week had been going, I sighed. "So, George, do you work with my mother?"

He looked at her and smiled. "No, we met at the prison when she was bringing in some scumbag. I'm a guard there. The prisoner tried to cop a feel from your mother, and I stepped in. She felt she owed me for my help, so she agreed to have coffee with me after our shift."

"I did not feel obligated." My mother giggled, pulling his hand into hers. "I had been secretly eyeing you for a while." I felt a small wave of repulsion hit me as I watched my mother nuzzle her nose against George's. I swallowed, looking anywhere but across the table.

Mom had dated when I was younger, but none of the men ever lasted long and, thanks to my grandfather and his shotgun, they rarely got to know me. By the time I was a teenager, she'd stopped dating altogether, her sadness undeniable. She just gave up on finding the right guy.

"So, you work at the prison? Must be an interesting job." What was I supposed to talk about? I had no clue what else to ask. Luckily, the waitress finally decided to stroll over after taking her sweet time. My mother leaned over, planting a long, lingering kiss on George's lips.

I made a face and muttered, "I'll take a vodka—straight."

It was just past noon and I rarely drank liquor, but I was going to need it if I was expected to endure any more of my mother's touchy-feely, happy-couple time with this stranger. I wanted her to be happy—I really did—but preferably in the privacy of her own home and not on the day we were supposed to spend bonding.

"Vodka?" my mother cut in, insulted, then looked up to the elderly waitress. "She's kidding. Bring her a Coke."

I rolled my eyes, then met my mother's disapproving glare. I never felt more like a child as I looked up at the waitress and nodded for the Coke. I let out a heavy sigh, holding up the menu to block my sight.

"I hope you don't mind me coming along today, Cassandra," George finally said.

"No, not at all. We were just going to spend the day at the salon and then go to a movie. Hope you don't mind chick

233

flicks." I peeked over my menu, hoping he'd take a hint.

"Actually, George and I wanted to have lunch, and then we can go to the movie. I need to skip the salon today, honey. We, um...sort of made plans for tonight." She looked up at me, her eyes pleading for me to understand and let her off the hook.

My menu dropped from my hands, smacking on the table. "What? But you're leaving for your cruise tomorrow." My voice grew an octave higher, full of frustration and hurt.

Her expression softened. "I know, and that's why we made plans tonight. George is going with me. We were going to stay at a hotel closer to the airport tonight so you wouldn't have to drive me so early in the morning," she explained, offering me an apologetic smile.

I blew out a deep breath, looking away from both of them, choosing not to think about what was going to take place in said hotel room. I didn't want to ruin their time together. My mother deserved to be happy.

I caved. "Yeah, no problem. I'm glad you'll be going with her." I looked at George and gave him a friendly smile.

"Thank you, Cassandra. I hope we can spend more time together after the holidays. Your mother is quite the lady. I plan on sticking around as long as she'll have me." His voice was optimistic, which brought a genuine smile to my face.

I sat there listening to them fill me in on their brief time together while I picked at a large chef's salad. Every time my mother giggled, I was filled with too much happiness for her to be truly annoyed.

George pulled out his wallet to pay after the waitress dropped off the bill.

"No, let me get this," Mom cut in, grabbing her purse.

"Felicia, I've told you already: I enjoy spending my money on my honey."

I chuckled and then excused myself to the restroom, not needing to watch their playful banter.

As I walked past the bar, I heard a familiar husky voice hum through me.

"I'm not asking this time. It's important—damn it, Julia!" Logan growled into his phone.

I detoured toward him and took the seat next to his at the bar. I smiled when he looked up from his burger and fries. His hard features softened, his lips curling up into a broad smile as he took me in.

"Fine, go spend the weekend with your girlfriends, but I am rethinking your Christmas gift!" He slammed his phone down, took a deep breath, and then turned on his stool to face me.

"To what do I owe this unexpected pleasure?"

"I'm having lunch with my mother and her new boyfriend."

Logan's brows rose at my tone.

"Boyfriend? Good for her."

"Yeah, I know, but still a bit icky for me," I pouted, snatching one of his fries.

"Icky? Such a childish word for an educated woman like yourself." He chuckled, watching me roll my eyes.

"So what were you yelling at your sister for? Let me guess: She stole your credit card before jetting off on a luxurious shopping spree in Paris?"

"Not quite. I have an important business meeting tonight out of town, and she just called to let me know she was halfway to Hawaii for the weekend. My sister can be quite fickle at times."

"She's young."

"She's a pest, but I do love her, so now I have to find a babysitter last minute."

235

"I told you, you should consider getting a nanny." I grabbed the ketchup and popped the lid, pouring a little on his plate. I stole another fry, dunked it once, and tossed it in my mouth.

"You know I don't trust just anyone with Oliver." He watched me take over his plate, amused. "Please, help yourself, sweetheart." He chuckled as I grabbed yet another fry and coated it in ketchup.

"Sorry, I had a salad. I'm still hungry." I popped it in my mouth then pushed his plate closer to his chest, holding up my hands to indicate I was done. They were yummy, but a bit salty. My eyes flickered to his soda, then up at him.

Logan grinned. "As I said, help yourself." He handed me the glass.

"Thanks." I brought it to my lips and took a long sip of ice-cold lemonade. I sighed, savoring the freshness in the cold of winter. My eyes caught his and I swallowed loudly. He was staring at me with his head tilted slightly to the side, his casual expression hardening to something primal and raw.

I'd shared drinks with plenty of boys before, but it'd never felt like this. My stomach clenched, feelings awakening, sending a heat wave straight through me. It was such an innocent action between friends, but between Logan and me, it felt intimate.

I pulled my gaze away, took another sip, and swallowed before setting the glass back in front of his plate. "I can watch him," I said, breaking the thick tension hanging between us.

Logan inhaled a short breath, blinking a few times. He turned back on his stool, facing the bar, and took a bite of his burger. Swallowing, he looked over at me with a cocked eyebrow.

"What? You don't trust me because I stole a few fries? Geez." I laughed and punched him lightly on the arm.

Logan grinned as he shrugged playfully. "I wouldn't want to interrupt your time with your mother's new beau."

"Oh, please interrupt." I gripped his forearm. "I am *begging* you to interrupt!"

Logan laughed. He picked up his drink and took a small sip, his lips covering the lipstick mark I'd left behind. I shuddered, heat scorching my cheeks. Placing it back down, he tilted his head to peer over at me.

"I'll drop him off at your house in an hour."

"Great, I'll head home and dig out some board games and movies. What time will you be picking him up?" I asked, jumping down from the stool.

"It will be late—after midnight. Will that be all right? I have to take a private plane to New York for the meeting."

"No problem. I'll see you and Oliver soon."

I smiled, snatching one last fry with a quick wink before turning away and heading back to my table, no longer needing to lurk around the restroom waiting for time to pass.

"Ready?" my mother asked, standing from the booth as I approached.

"Change of plans: I have to babysit for a friend. Why don't you guys catch that movie, and we'll get together when you get back from your cruise?" I grabbed my coat and purse from the booth.

"Oh, all right." My mother stood, looking dumbfounded while I gave her a quick hug and George a small smile before heading out the door.

I'd never been so thrilled to babysit in my life—anything would be better than sitting through an entire movie in the dark with my mother and George.

# Chapter Twenty-One

## PUPPY LOVE

I looked around my living room nervously, realizing every board game I owned was labeled twelve and up. This was not going to be as easy as I'd assumed. I hung out with Oliver often, but not all day and night.

With a defeated sigh, I slumped down on the couch and pulled out my phone, quickly pressing a number from my favorites list.

"Hello!" Hilary answered in her usual cheerful voice.

"Hey, I need your help," I said, shifting and tossing my feet up on the other side of the couch as I stretched out. "I'm babysitting Oliver in like twenty minutes and have no idea what to do with him all day. Logan said he won't be back till after midnight."

"I thought you were spending today with your mom."

"Yeah, I'll tell you all about that later." I chuckled. "So, any helpful suggestions with Oliver?"

"It's your lucky day, Miss Cassandra," she sang. "The town's annual Christmas in the Park starts at three."

I sat up a little, hopeful. "Any idea what they're showing this year?"

"Kids' classics, like every year, until sunset."

"Perfect." I grinned, relieved. "You want to meet us there?"

"Only if I can ask Caleb to join us."

"Yeah, of course. I talked with him; we're all good."

I'd met up with Caleb a couple days after he'd showed up at my door with Hilary. His constant apologetic texts were too much, so I met him for lunch at Haven. After a nice meal and a few minutes of me scolding him for hiring a psychopath, we hugged it out. It was impossible to stay mad at him for long—especially since he was genuinely full of concern and regret.

With a quick goodbye to Hilary after agreeing to meet up by the fountain, I hung up and tossed my phone across the couch. A second later, there was a knock on my door.

*Perfect timing.* I stopped at the small mirror in the foyer for a quick check, running my hands through my hair. *It's only Logan,* I reminded myself as I grabbed the handle and opened the door.

My smile faltered when I found a gangly teenager with spiky bright-red hair standing on my welcome mat. Looking him over, my eyebrows pulling in, I noticed a large box at his feet. The bright-blue shirt he wore featured the image of a frightening snake wrapped around text that was too worn to read.

"Are you Cassandra Clarke?" he asked, staring down at the clipboard in his hand.

"That's me." My eyes traveled from him to the box, noticing the small holes in the sides. Curious, I furrowed my brows.

"Awesome. Sign this."

He placed a giant X on the slip of paper, then shoved the clipboard and pen into my hands. I shot him an unimpressed eye-reprimand before signing my name to accept the package.

"Who's it from?" I asked, handing it back to him.

"Don't know, don't care. Have a great day and wonderful holiday." He saluted me with a forced but smug grin before turning quickly on his heel.

I watched him climb back into his rusty old pickup and drive away, his stereo blasting some good-old Ozzy.

I shook my head. "Rude, much?" I grumbled, squatting down to pick up the box. My hands gripped each side, and I was just about to lift it when it shifted.

Stumbling back, I stood frozen, unsure what to do. Obviously it was some sort of animal, but who would get me that? Warily, I lifted my foot and nudged the box gently, hoping to hear a sweet meow or really anything other than a slithering hiss.

The box shifted again from side to side and I flinched back, inhaling a deep breath and blowing it out, my hands resting on my hips.

Did I really want to open the box when I was unsure who'd sent it? The last thing I needed was to come face to face with a large snake—or worse. I knew I'd pissed Mackenzie off at the carnival when Logan walked away, ignoring her, but that was almost three months ago.

"Problem, sweetheart?"

I looked up to meet the eye of a rather amused-looking Logan.

"What's that?" Oliver asked, squatting down to peek through one of the holes in the box.

"I have no idea, but I'm pretty sure it's alive," I replied, scrunching my nose at it.

Logan shook his head, chuckling at my childish behavior, then stepped forward and opened the top of the box easily.

"A puppy!" Oliver squealed.

The little chocolate Lab looked up at us with big brown

eyes.

"A dog?" I breathed, semi relieved but still confused. *Who would send a dog?* I watched as Oliver pulled the puppy into his arms, cradling it like a baby.

The small dog pawed at his chest, and I knew instantly whom it was from.

"My mom," I murmured, a slow smile spreading over my lips.

"Your mother sent you a puppy?" Logan asked, smiling down at his son.

"My grandparents gave me a Lab a week after my father left us. He was hit by a car when I was sixteen." I shuddered as the traumatic memory of saying goodbye to my faithful companion all those years ago replayed in my mind.

"I'm sorry," Logan said softly. "There's a note." He handed me the small piece of paper taped on the underside of the box flap.

*Thank you again for sending me on what I am sure will be the best vacation of my life. I wish I could be there with you on Christmas, but I saw this little guy in the pet shop downtown and knew he would put a smile on your face—not to mention keep you safe.*
*I love you,*
*Mom*

I looked up from the note, smiling.

"Well, looks like I'm a pet owner." I chuckled softly, watching how sweet the little thing was with Oliver.

"Come on in," I said, reaching down to grab the empty box, but Logan was quicker. I smiled, letting him get it, and went over to help Oliver up from the grass. Logan snatched up the dog with his other hand and followed me into the living room.

"I wanted to thank you again for helping me out tonight," Logan said, placing the box by the door and handing the pup back to Oliver.

"No problem. Do you mind if I take Oliver downtown for the afternoon? They're playing a marathon of Christmas cartoons until nightfall—figured he might enjoy it." I shrugged.

"Yes, he would like that. Wouldn't you?"

Oliver was too occupied chasing the little guy around the living room to answer.

"Great!" I smiled.

"What are you going to name him?" Oliver asked.

"Oh, um…" I'd never been any good at choosing pet names. I once had a cat I'd feed on the back porch when I was a child. I named her Kitty.

"Can I name him?" Oliver asked quickly. His pleading eyes were as big as the puppy's and just as adorable.

"Oliver, I'm sure Cassandra would like to name him herself."

"No, it's fine," I said, giving Oliver a small smile. I sat down beside him on the floor, and the puppy jumped into my lap. "So, what do you think we should name him?"

"How about, um…" Oliver stared contemplatively down at him for a long moment before finally looking back up with a giant grin.

"Stout," he said quickly.

"Stout?" I tried to repeat it as nicely as possible, not wanting to hurt his feelings for coming up with such a strange name.

"No! I said Scout," Oliver whined. I gave an apologetic smile, but between his young age and slight lisp I sometimes had trouble understanding him clearly.

"Scout," Logan repeated, trying out the name. The puppy jumped to his feet and turned to look up at Logan. "He seems to like it."

I smiled, watching Logan bend down to rub the puppy's back.

"Well, Scout it is, then," I said.

"All right, I had better be going. Don't want to be late. Be good for Cassandra." Logan gave Oliver a quick hug and whispered in his ear.

"I love you, too, Daddy," Oliver replied, dropping back to the floor next to Scout.

I walked with Logan to the front door and reached inside the small side-table drawer.

"Here. It's a key for when you come to pick him up tonight."

A small smile played on his closed lips. His eyebrows rose as he stared straight at me. "You're giving me a key to your house?" he asked as he took it. "I must say, it seems you are rushing a bit for my taste, love. But if you insist."

I smacked his arm playfully, rolling my eyes.

"You said it would be after midnight, which means we'll probably be asleep. Just come in and wake me up."

Logan slid the key into his inner coat pocket.

"Have a safe flight."

"Take care of my son, and yourself." He waved goodbye to Oliver one last time before heading out the front door.

After I closed the door, I turned back to Oliver and smiled, but it only took a second for me to realize I had no food for Scout.

"Do you want to take Scout with us to watch the movies?" I asked.

No answer was necessary as his face lit up. He grabbed the puppy and raced to the door.

—◆◆—

Oliver and I stood by the large fountain in the center of town, waiting for Hilary. We'd stopped at the pet store on the way to pick up a navy-blue leash and everything else Scout could need. I hadn't anticipated the rather large expense of owning such a little puppy, though part of the reason for the higher-than-expected bill may have had something to do with Oliver throwing a *few* too many chew toys into the shopping cart.

By the time we returned the bags to my car and put the leash on Scout, I had to hurry them along to meet up with Hilary. More and more children with parents at their sides flooded to the park, taking up the best spots on the lawn. For December, the weather wasn't too bad. Harmony rarely experienced freezing winters.

I pulled out my phone, ready to call Hilary when I saw her approaching. Beside her were Caleb and another guy I didn't recognize. He had neatly trimmed brown hair and was wearing khakis and a black wool coat.

"Hey, Cassie, sorry I'm late." Hilary gave me a quick hug and smiled down at Oliver. "Caleb got caught up at Haven."

"No problem. We had to pick up some things for my new dog."

"New dog? He's yours!?" Hilary grinned. "Oh my God, he's adorable. He reminds me of the black Lab you had when we were kids."

Hilary squatted down, holding his head in her hands, petting him. Caleb mimicked her movement, running his hands over Scout and enjoying Hilary's playful smile as she made silly faces at the puppy.

"You do know he's a dog and not a baby, right?" Caleb chuckled.

"He's just so cute!" Hilary cooed before standing up. "So I'm guessing you don't remember Luke, Caleb's younger brother. He just moved back to town."

"Oh my God, I didn't even recognize you!" I gasped, looking him over again. Luke was my age and had gone to school with me until fifth grade, when his parents separated and he moved away with his mother. Caleb stayed with their father and visited Luke and their mother on the weekend, but Luke rarely came back to spend time with his dad. When he did, he always stayed inside by himself, so I rarely saw him.

He smiled. "I could say the same for you. You're all grown up." He buried his hands deep into his coat pockets, a sheepish smile curling his lips. "I hear you're a teacher at our old school with Hilary."

"Yeah, kindergarten." I nodded. He had the softest green eyes: so innocent and sweet. Luke had always been the complete opposite of Caleb: shy and soft-spoken. As kids, he was always sitting in class or on his porch with his nose in a book. Even now, over ten years later, that bashfulness hadn't changed.

"What about you? Own a bar like your brother?" I smiled, nudging his arm with my elbow to loosen him up.

"No, I leave that line of work to Caleb—if you want to call it work." He smiled, and Caleb made an insulted face.

"Better than working for dear ol' Dad," Caleb chuckled.

We all began walking over the large grassy area, my hand wrapped around Oliver's and Scout tucked in Hilary's arms. She shot me a suggestive eyebrow wiggle, slowing her pace behind the guys, and mouthed, "Cute, huh?"

I shook my head, looking back out in front of me, but couldn't deny Luke had grown into a fine man. He was the embodiment of the all-American boy next door. His features were chiseled and sharp, and when he looked over, smiling at me, I lit up at his familiar dimples. He was still lovable Luke, just all grown up.

"I always wanted to be a lawyer—follow in my dad's footsteps and keep the practice in town going as he gets older."

"You just didn't want to deal with disappointing him like I did," Caleb cut in. "He persuaded you to do right by our family, and you caved."

I curved my arm through Luke's, smiling up at him to diffuse the tense staring contest between the brothers. "I always thought you'd be a professor or scientist. You are definitely the smart one." I gave Caleb a sly wink, which he snorted at.

"That makes me the handsome one," Caleb said, wrapping his arm around Hilary's waist.

We stopped in the field off to the side, but still close enough to see the screen. I pulled out a large blanket from my tote. Luke helped me lay it out while Hilary and Oliver played with a very energetic Scout and Caleb went over to the concession stand to purchase snacks.

"Hey, buddy. I got you some hot cocoa, and extra butter on the popcorn." Caleb waited for Oliver to sit down crossed-legged on the blanket before handing the goodies to him.

*Frosty the Snowman* appeared on the big screen first, silencing the yapping of the crowd instantly.

I smiled, sitting beside Oliver and watching Scout snuggling against his ankle. Caleb sat on the other side of him, with Hilary between his outstretched legs, her back pressed against his chest. I noticed his hands resting on his own legs, but his thumbs caressed her outer thighs.

*Definitely more than friends.*

"So, you go to my brother's bar much?" Luke asked in a hushed whisper as he scooted closer to me.

"More for the restaurant side than the drinking side." I tossed a small handful of popcorn in my mouth and held the bag out to him.

Luke took a few pieces and smiled. "Well, maybe I'll see you there sometime."

Oliver raised his finger to his lips, shushing us with narrowed eyes.

I gave him an apologetic smile before turning back to Luke, who held his hands up in defeat. We both stifled a laugh and turned our attention back to the giant talking snowman dancing across the massive screen.

# Chapter Twenty-Two

## PILLOW TALK

As the second film began, I asked Hilary to keep an eye on Oliver for me while I excused myself to use the restroom.

I was weaving through the clusters of people resting on blankets and folding chairs when I heard a muffled voice calling my name in the distance. I turned hesitantly, unsure if it was meant for me, and saw Mark standing on the other side of the massive lawn right beside a scowling Mackenzie.

The blood drained from my face, my stomach churning. Whipping back around, I tried to push myself faster through the crowded area without tripping over the dozens of limbs laid out on the grass.

I didn't want to deal with him, and by the look on his face, I had a feeling whatever he wanted wasn't good.

"Cassandra!" his infuriating voice blared louder.

He was catching up to me. Adrenaline began coursing through my veins, and my head began to throb. Why did he want to talk to me all of a sudden? And why the hell was he with Mackenzie and not Julia? I'd spent countless hours debating whether it was best to keep my mouth shut and not say anything to Julia about my past with him, and decided it

248

was. Mark may have cheated on me, but I wanted to hope, for her sake, he wouldn't do the same to her.

I quickened my pace so much that I was sprinting, my heart beating erratically. I sucked in a giant breath mere feet from the bathroom door and blew it out in a giant puff, relief washing over me as I rushed inside.

The first open stall was all I could see; everything else was a blur. I made a beeline straight for it and slammed the door, sliding the bolt in place with trembling fingers.

While struggling to catch my unsteady breath, I dropped my head and rested my hands on my hips. Seeing Mark while around Julia and Logan was tolerable, but this was different. There was no one here for him to put on a show for and try to impress.

"Cassandra?" His voice filled the restroom, and my head shot up. *Damn it! What does he want?*

I heard a woman complain about it being the ladies' room, but then the main door creaked shut.

I took a small step away from the door and the back of my knees bumped into the porcelain bowl. As quietly as possible, I bent down to peek under the door, staring straight at a pair of size-twelve combat boots. They stood sorely out of place against the dull-pink floor tiles.

I inhaled sharply. "Go away!"

"Cassie, we need to talk."

"Then you should have tried at the farm…while your girlfriend was around," I hissed through the door.

I was no longer his naïve little Cassie. I watched his feet step closer, stopping directly on the other side of the stall door.

"Why the hell are you hanging around with her brother? I've heard all about him." He snorted. "Logan's only using you for sex, you know."

My blood boiled. *How dare he.*

249

"Go to hell!"

"Look, I like Julia, all right? And having my ex-girlfriend hanging around just because she hopes she can fuck my girl's brother into monogamy is kind of a bitch."

"How did I ever love you?" I muttered, feeling more sad than angry. Had I really been that blind?

"Can we just come to an agreement on this already?"

"Agreement?" I snapped. The anger rushed back through me as if it'd never dispersed.

"You do whatever you want with Logan—I won't get in the way—but can you just not hang around when Julia and I are there?"

"Screw you!" I thrust open the lock and pushed the stall door open, smacking him hard in the chest with it in the process. I stalked toward him, my lips pursed tightly and eyes narrowed. I felt my nostrils flaring and blood pounding in my ears. I was ready to let him have it when a loud pounding on the restroom door rang out.

"Did you lock the door?" I gasped, staring wide-eyed at him.

"I just wanted to talk to you, damn it." He ran his hands through his hair, groaning. "I loved you, Cassandra, I did, but I fucked it up." He stepped closer, his expression softening. "I just want us both to move on and be happy. Julia's a sweet—"

The pounding on the door vibrated through the room more loudly than before, then I heard Luke's voice calling my name.

I narrowed my eyes at Mark, too angry to form any more words. Instead, I brushed past him and unlocked the door.

Luke was on the other side, his fist mid-pound and his eyes full of distress.

"Is everything all right?" Luke stared warily past me to Mark.

250

"Yeah, thanks," I grumbled. The weight of the situation left me exhausted.

Luke threw Mark a threatening glare before placing his hand on my back, leading me away to our spot on the grass.

Once we neared the blanket, I saw Oliver resting his head against Hilary's legs. I slowed and turned just enough to give Luke a small appreciative smile. No words were needed; he returned the smile with tenderness in his eyes and watched me sit back down beside Oliver.

Hilary leaned over and whispered, "We saw Mark follow you. Want to talk about it?"

I shook my head. "No, there's nothing to say." I kept my gaze straight ahead on Rudolph and The Bumble flickering on the big screen.

———————

With Scout snuggled tightly in my arms, I walked beside Luke, who had a sound-asleep Oliver slung over his shoulder. Six whole cartoons had held the young tot's attention. It was just past eight; the sun was setting, which was the cue that the older movies were about to begin. Oliver had passed out during the final kids' film, which was a relief.

Luke walked around the car and secured Oliver in the booster Logan had placed in my backseat. After he latched the seatbelt around Oliver's waist, Luke shut the car door and looked over the top, where I was standing on the other side.

"Thanks for helping me get him back," I said. "I couldn't bear to wake him up. He was exhausted." I leaned down, placed Scout in the backseat with Oliver, and shut the door.

"He had a lot of fun," Luke said, walking around the car. "Caleb tells me he's the son of one of your friends."

"Yeah, his dad had a business trip tonight." My stomach knotted as he stood there smiling, his hands in his pockets.

Thinking of Logan sent a sudden, distressing wave of worry through me. *Did he make it to New York safely?* I hadn't checked my phone. I then began to wonder what he'd have to say about my incident with Mark.

Surprisingly, I would've rather talked to him about what happened than Hilary. He always listened to every single word I had to say, no matter how much I rambled, and his eyes never showed even the slightest bit of judgment.

"I'm glad I came out today." Luke's gruff voice pulled me from my thoughts of Logan.

I nodded, smiling awkwardly and dangling my keys through my fingers. "Yeah, it was fun. I haven't watched *The Little Drummer Boy* since I was a kid."

Luke leaned forward and opened my door for me.

"Have a good night, Cassandra."

"You too, Luke."

I climbed inside, giving him one last friendly smile before waving to Hilary and Caleb across the street, whose hands were intertwined.

⸻

Once I was home, I carried a sleeping Oliver inside the house and placed him on the couch softly. Scout jumped up beside him and cuddled into his side while I covered them both with a blanket. I couldn't help smiling as I looked down at them. They were absolutely adorable and perfect.

With a silent yawn, I walked down the hall to my bedroom and yanked my sweater over my head, tossing it into the hamper. I opened my dresser drawer and reached in, randomly pulling out the first set of pajamas my fingers touched: a white long-sleeved button-up sleep shirt. It fell just past mid-thigh but was warm against my chest, and I hated wearing any type of pants to sleep.

My hands ran down the front of the thermal material, closing each button quickly as I wondered what time Logan would be landing.

After washing my face and throwing my hair into a loose ponytail, not caring how I looked, I put on some moisturizer and grabbed my blanket and pillow from my bed. The recliner, which I rarely used, would work fine, and I could better keep an eye on Oliver if he woke.

As I curled into the overstuffed chair and draped the blanket over my legs, I grabbed the remote and flicked on the television.

---

Logan walked across the living room, his chest and feet bare, his unbuckled jeans riding low on his hips. I stood from the recliner and dropped my blanket, confused by the determined look in his eyes.

He was in front of me instantly, pulling me into his arms with a low throaty growl. My insides shuddered, awakening a primal need I'd kept buried for far too long. I waited for him to speak—to say anything, tell me what'd brought this on—but his lips were sealed.

I glanced across the room to the couch and saw Oliver was gone, as was Scout. *Did Logan take him home already?* Before I could ask, his hands snaked up my back and through my hair, finally cupping my cheeks. His thumbs smoothed the wrinkles I felt on my brow from my bemused expression.

"Logan—"

He leaned in and my heart pounded, blood racing through my veins as I inhaled his fresh, clean scent. His lips scorched my skin as he placed a blazing trail of kisses from my ear, down my cheek, and to my jaw. Before I could comprehend what was happening, he claimed my lips.

253

I gasped and he used it to his advantage, darting his tongue inside my mouth, battling with mine. My entire body surrendered to him, giving in to the desires I'd tried to keep at bay for months. A shiver raced up my spine and wrapped around my neck, sending my body further into overdrive.

Logan's strong hands moved down my back slowly, tracing each and every curve before gripping my ass and lifting me up. Not missing the opportunity, I wrapped my legs around his waist, kissing him with a passion I'd never dreamed I was capable of experiencing. My body yearned to be one with his. I groaned dejectedly when his lips strayed from mine, his tongue gliding down my jaw and toward my chest. He took a few steps forward, slamming my back against the wall. My hands dug into his soft, wavy hair.

"I want you," I moaned, grinding against him in need of friction, his lips blazing a trail back up my body.

"Please...Logan..." I breathed, resting my head back against the wall to give him further access to all the places his tongue wished to travel.

"Sweetheart..."

"Don't stop, please," I begged, squeezing my legs around him more tightly and crossing my ankles at his back, locking him against me.

"Cassandra, for the love of God, wake up. You're killing me here." His voice vibrated through me, but his lips were still silently kissing my neck in the heat of passion. I pulled back reluctantly, staring at him in confusion.

Slowly, the vision of a shirtless Logan teasing my body began to blur away, leaving behind only his pleading voice. The haze lifted and my eyes jerked open, landing on a suit-clad Logan staring down at me with dark, hooded eyes.

"Logan!" I jumped forward in the chair. "You scared the hell out of me." I sat up fully, my hand covering my pounding heart as adrenaline ripped through me.

At some point, my blanket had been kicked to the floor and, shifting in the chair, I noticed my pajama shirt had risen up from my tossing and turning. I maneuvered quickly, pulling it down and reaching for the blanket to cover myself fully.

I felt the sting in my cheeks and slumped back against the chair, closing my eyes and taking a deep breath.

"Sorry to wake you." He shifted his weight from one foot to the other, his expression flustered.

"Your flight okay?" I asked, opening my eyes slowly.

He nodded, then looked over to Oliver. "Did everything go all right tonight?"

"Yeah." I yawned. "I'll call you tomorrow and fill you in on his day." I stood, holding the blanket around my body.

He nodded again, his expression leaving me further perplexed. I watched as he walked to the couch and lifted Oliver into his arms. Scout jumped down and began yapping at Logan's feet.

"You can keep the blanket around him," I said when he tried to unwrap his son.

"I'll bring it back tomorrow."

"No rush." I chuckled uneasily.

I walked him to the door and opened it for him.

"Thanks again, Cassandra. I'll see you on Christmas at noon, right?"

"Of course." I gave a small drowsy-but-still-sexed-up smile and watched as Logan walked out, turning back once more after stepping outside.

"Sweet dreams, sweetheart." He shot me a cocky grin, and my insides quaked.

He knew. He'd possibly even heard me. My blood ran cold, but I held his gaze, not giving him the satisfaction. I had no clue how much he'd heard, but the smug grin on his face and twinkle in his eye told me it was enough to paint a pretty good picture for him.

I bit my lip, my heated palm gripping the doorknob.

"Good night, Logan. Hope your dreams are equally pleasant."

# Chapter Twenty-Three

## CHARMED

I stood before the familiar oak door, where a fresh wreath with a bright-red bow hung proudly. It was just before noon on Christmas Day. Scout stood between my feet, tail wagging, yapping to be picked up. The pup was completely spoiled.

Logan had told me to come over whenever I liked, but I wanted to give him and Oliver their morning alone together. They'd spent the previous two days in the city with their family, but he hadn't failed to deliver his morning texts, as well as an occasional text throughout the previous day. Eager to read what he was up to, I couldn't get to my phone quickly enough. But with each smile or laugh, the more I realized I was getting in too deep.

Even after having been at Logan's home a handful of times over the last few months, my stomach still fluttered to life when I leaned in and pressed the small buzzer. It wasn't an uncomfortable feeling—I'd never been more at ease with a man before, even Mark—but the more time we spent together, the harder it was to remember why he was all wrong for me.

Within seconds, the door swung open.

"Cassie!" Oliver stood in red-and-white-striped pajamas,

his wavy hair still tousled from sleep. "You came!" He opened the door wider for me to enter.

"Of course I came. I promised you I would, didn't I?"

"Scout!" Oliver reached down and scooped up the pup, rocking him in his arms.

"I hope your dad doesn't mind I brought him along. Thought you might want to see him again. He misses you."

"I missed you too, buddy." Oliver placed a small kiss on the puppy's head, then turned and began skipping back inside happily.

With a soft laugh, I closed the front door and followed him. The perfect aroma of fresh pine and cinnamon filled my nostrils. I smiled. Green garland covered with glass balls and bright, colorful lights flowed down the banister, and a small tree decorated with homemade ornaments sat in the corner of the foyer.

I'd never dreamed Logan would decorate his home so lavishly for the holidays. He'd told me it was his favorite time of year as a child, but I'd never realized just how much he truly enjoyed celebrating it.

My eyes widened and my smile grew into an excited grin as I stepped into the enormous living room. Torn pieces of wrapping paper in every color imaginable completely covered the plush beige carpet. Toys of every shape and size were surrounded by scattered-about ribbons and bows. And in the corner stood the most magnificent tree I had ever laid eyes upon. My gaze traveled to its top, where a mercury-glass star rested only a mere inch below the ceiling.

My feet led me closer to the glorious sight, as if in a trance. The tree was decorated with a remarkable eye for great taste, sporting a mix of fragile antique ornaments, glittery glass balls, and simpler items made by a child. It was, in every way, my dream Christmas tree.

I stood in front of it and reached out, running my fingers over a small glass frame that held a picture of Logan. He was holding his newborn baby, Oliver. The soft look in his eyes and relaxed, blissful smile on his lips was something I'd only seen once or twice before. He looked years younger, still baby-faced himself, with his gaze focused intently on his young son. The joy in the photo was undeniable.

"Daddy chopped it down himself!"

Startled, I jumped, the ornament falling from my hands. I inhaled a sharp breath and watched as it swung back and forth on the wide branch.

"It's perfect." I blinked a few times and stepped backward to take it all in, smiling at the thought of Logan chopping down such a massive tree. The image of him out in the woods with his son, searching for the right one, made my heart swell.

Against my control, my brain somehow turned the sweet image into something much more lustful. My tongue darted out, moistening my dry lips as I pictured Logan's firm, toned muscles bulging deliciously through his snug shirt as he swung the ax against the tree trunk.

I shook the thought from my head when Oliver started laughing at Scout, who was rolling around with a long piece of velvety ribbon. I crossed the room and sat on the long sofa, feeling light and happy.

A few days earlier, Logan had invited me to go with them to help pick out the tree. It seemed lately he was inviting me to hang out more often than not, but I'd been busy with Hilary, finishing up our Christmas shopping. It was for the best; I wasn't positive I would've had the restraint to keep my hands to myself if I had to watch him perform such a masculine undertaking.

Instead, Hilary and I had endured a long day of pushy shoppers and rude clerks that ended with dinner at Haven—a

259

dinner I'd presumed would consist of only her and me, but to my surprise, Caleb and Luke joined us.

It was a setup—that much was clear the moment they approached our table and Luke slid into the booth beside me. Caleb shot me a small smile and impish wink, his arm quick to wrap around Hilary.

Luke was a great guy. He was cute and sweet, with a reliable career. Yet there was something missing when I was with him. I couldn't quite put my finger on it, but that mind-blowing, all-consuming hunger devouring me from the inside out when Logan was around left any other man unexciting. It was the feeling I experienced every time I was around Logan, and as much as I denied it, I secretly yearned for more. No matter how much I fought it, there was something primal in the way I craved him. It was the most exhilarating, yet scariest, thing I'd ever felt.

I decided at the time not to tell Logan about Luke. Since the day I'd watched Oliver, we'd only communicated via text. The Luke conversation was one I'd wait to have in person—not that there was really anything to talk about. I just didn't want him to think I was dating someone when I wasn't. It was irrational thinking—Logan was only a friend—but I still worried about his reaction. But it had nothing to do with the sick feeling I had in my gut when I thought about Logan dating lately.

No. Nothing at all.

"Will you come with us next year to help pick out a tree?" Oliver lifted Scout in his arms and plopped down in front of his new train set. "It was so much fun. You should have seen all the trees in the forest to choose from." He flicked a switch on the large black train and watched it speed around the giant circular track in the center of the room. Scout leapt from his lap and began chasing after it.

"Sounds like a lot of fun. We'll have to see." *Will I still be a part of their life a year from now?* The thought filled me with soothing warmth.

My body relaxed back into the sofa as I watched Oliver giggling while he tried to yell at Scout to get off the track. I laughed. I couldn't imagine not being around Oliver or Logan. We spent so much time together, whether it was hanging out in my backyard or cuddled up watching a movie. They'd somehow become more than just friends to me. We'd developed a connection, and it pained me to think it could be gone one day.

"Hello, sweetheart."

My body remained pressed into the sofa, relaxed. I craned my head back to greet him, and my breath caught instantly at the sight of his bare chest. A pair of black cotton pajama pants hung delectably low on his hips.

My eyes blinked involuntarily, blood rushing to my cheeks, and I turned back quickly to face the rumbling train on the floor. I tried to clear the inappropriate thoughts racing through my head. Logan always knew exactly what to do to catch me off guard and get me flustered.

Damn him.

Finding my bearings, I shifted in my seat and gave him an unimpressed eye roll.

"Too late—we both know you like what you see," he teased, cocking an eyebrow. He threw on a white cotton shirt I hadn't noticed he'd been holding, and I swallowed at how it clung to his sculpted chest and chiseled abs in all the right ways—or wrong ways. It was so unfair to feel this attracted to someone I *knew* could never give me what I wanted.

"You wish." I chuckled, narrowing my eyes at him. "Since when do you greet your guests shirtless, anyway?"

"Oliver woke me up at five this morning wanting to open

gifts. I was just about to take a quick shower when you arrived."

"Well, don't let me stop you. I'll play with Oliver while you're in there." I turned back to face Oliver. His face was twisted in frustration as he tried to change the track's shape.

Logan chuckled lightly, no doubt at his son's determination, and watched me as I stood from the couch and walked over to help.

——◆◆◆——

A half hour passed and I was still sitting on the floor, playing with the train set Oliver had received from Santa as Scout chased it.

Oliver let out a deep, hearty laugh when Scout jumped in front of the train, blocking its path. I began laughing as well when Scout let out a small yelp and leapt out of the way after the large caboose ran into him.

A sudden prickle tingled my skin, pulling my attention away. I lifted my head and found Logan leaning against the entryway, watching us with a faint smile on his lips. His hair was still damp, and he was wearing a pair of dark-wash jeans and a fitted black V-neck shirt. He looked perfect, and I had a feeling he knew it.

I smiled, feeling the same as he looked: peaceful.

Logan stepped into the room, his lips pressed in a relaxed line, and sat on the sofa a few feet behind Oliver and me.

"You're gonna stay to watch a movie with us tonight, right?" Oliver asked, not looking up from the package of cars in his hand. Scout sat in his lap, exhaustion setting in.

"Of course."

Not only did I have nothing better to do since I was alone for Christmas, but I loved spending time with Logan and Oliver. It was quickly becoming one of my favorite activities.

262

"Great! Daddy wanted to watch *Rudolph*. I told him we already saw it last week, though. I think he wanted to come with us." Oliver ripped into the package, removing each car one by one. "It was so much fun, and Luke was the coolest."

I nodded nervously and chanced a glance at Logan.

"Maybe next year we can all go together," Logan said, his tone unreadable.

"Oliver, this is for you." I grabbed a small gift with a bright-green bow from the tote I'd brought. I wasn't in the mood to discuss Luke.

Oliver sat up straight, dropping the toy in his hand and grinning.

"Wow, thanks!" He ripped into the paper, and I watched as his smiled melted into a bored frown when he saw what was inside. "A book?"

"Oliver," Logan scolded, offering me an uncomfortable smile. I smiled back with a shrug. I'd expected that reaction.

"Thanks," Oliver pouted, setting the book aside and crumpling up the wrapping paper to toss at Scout.

"Forgive him. He's—"

I began to chuckle, ignoring Logan's apology.

"Of course I got you a book. I love Dr. Seuss—plus I want you to be the best reader our school's ever had. But I also got you this."

With my hand still in the bag, I pulled out a larger gift. Oliver beamed, excitement dancing in his eyes as he ripped it open.

"Legos!" Oliver squealed. "Thanks!"

A satisfied smile pulled at my lips as he tore into the box and began scattering the tiny bags of small pieces in a circle around him.

"Are you going to help me?"

I nodded, reaching back into my bag to find the small gift

263

wrapped in silvery-grey paper and topped with a blue bow. "Give me a minute," I whispered, leaning forward.

I stood and took a seat next to Logan on the sofa. "This is for you." I smiled coyly, handing him the gift.

After endless nights spent searching online for the perfect gift to give the guy who had everything, I'd found my answer when Hilary and I went to the bookstore.

Logan raised his brows. "You didn't have to, Cassandra."

"Yes, I did. I'm not sure how, but you seem to have wormed your way into my life against all my reservations." I laughed once, nibbling my bottom lip.

He flashed me a smile, then looked down at the gift.

I sighed, looking down at my hands. "Seriously, over the last couple of months you really have become a good friend to me." I looked up, meeting his gaze. "Plus, I'd be sitting home alone eating my last box of Twinkies if you hadn't invited me over today." I grinned, nudging his arm to lighten the mood.

Logan's expression remained stoic, his gaze searing into mine as hot and confusing as earlier. His hand reached out, and my body flooded with the warmth that only he seemed capable of generating. I flushed from the heat as the back of his hand brushed delicately over my cheek for the briefest second.

"Thank you," he murmured.

There was no denying we both felt the electricity that flowed between us. I could see it in his eyes and soft expression.

"Open your gift," I breathed, desperate to break the tension.

Without another word, Logan unwrapped the gift slowly, as if savoring the moment.

"A book." He smiled genuinely. "Thank you, Cassandra, truly."

"I know how much you love to read."

Logan held the book in his hands, his laughter filling the room as he read the title aloud. "*How to End Your Player Ways in Thirty Days or Less*. How thoughtful."

I shrugged. "I figured you might be interested in…" I leaned in closer to whisper, "…slowing down on the number of women you bed every weekend." I giggled, when out of nowhere, a pang of jealousy ripped through my chest, surprising me.

Logan held the book in his hands, looking down at it in thought. I sat there, no longer able to laugh as I watched him flip through the pages. His lips pulled into a thin smile, but there was something deeper in his expression.

*Had I offended him*? I pushed away the thought. Logan was impossible to insult.

I reached for the book, flipped it open, and whispered, "You should check out Chapter Four: 'How to Let a Girl Down Properly after a One-Night Stand.'"

Logan raised his head slowly; his hooded eyes looked almost disappointed. In an instant, his expression smoothed into a broader smile, but it was too late. I could tell he hated my gift.

He cleared his throat, tilting his head toward me. He sat staring at me for a long moment before finally speaking.

"You know, I've actually been so occupied with business and all I haven't entertained any women lately." His was voice rough; serious.

I wasn't sure how to respond. I bobbed my head up and down, unable to find my words. What did that mean—that he wasn't sleeping around anymore? Was it wrong to feel relieved?

He set the book on the couch between us, and a sting of regret filled my chest. Hilary had told me that Caleb commented on Logan not going around banging any so-called 'hotties in heels,' but I hadn't really believed it. Why would he stop?

"Oh," I muttered coyly. "Well, perhaps you'll find something useful in the book anyway." I swallowed the large lump that had formed suddenly in my throat and moistened my dry lips slowly. I felt horrible. He looked defeated, like I'd just slapped him across the face. I'd expected it to be a funny gag gift, with him making some snide comment or perverted remark. We'd tease each other about it and move on with a good laugh. So far, the complete opposite was happening. I'd never felt like more of a bitch.

I reached back into my bag and stared down at Oliver, who was lying on his stomach, elbows propping him up, feet dangling in the air. His full attention was on building with his Legos, completely oblivious to the adult conversation and thick tension a few feet behind him.

"I got you something else, as well." I pulled the second gift from my tote beside the couch, feeling suddenly awkward.

Logan smiled, but it still didn't reach his eyes as he untied the ribbon. "Let me guess." He shook the box, and then whispered, "Condoms?"

I slapped his arm and rolled my eyes.

He chuckled, taking his time opening the package. The moment he had the box opened, his smile melted into something dark and secretive.

My stomach dropped. *Does he hate this as well?*

"Cassandra...this is—" he started, staring down at the mahogany frame in his hands.

"I took it myself. Do you like it?" Why was I so nervous all of a sudden?

He set the frame—which held a photo of Oliver and him in the midst of their straw fight at the farm—on the table beside the couch and looked back at me, smiling. It was my favorite picture, and one that now hung proudly in my kitchen.

In it, both their faces were relaxed and lit with humor. It was peaceful, and made me smile every time I walked past it, which was how I knew it was the right gift.

"It's perfect. Thank you, truly."

He stood, picking up the book I'd given him and placing it on the coffee table with a thoughtful sigh. I swallowed, watching him walk across the room to the tree, where he bent down to retrieve the lone present on the thick quilted tree skirt.

"This is for you." Logan smiled softly, handing me the snow-white gift bag filled with silver tissue paper. He sat back down beside me, staring over at Oliver.

"Thanks, but...you really didn't have to." I pressed my lips together in a tight, awkward smile. "I'm grateful you invited me over today. That was more than a gift in itself." I sighed heavily, my shoulders slumping forward. "I'm sorry about the book. It was stupid," I mumbled, running my fingers over the tips of the tissue paper.

He looked up from Oliver with his eyebrows raised, his lips pulled up in a reassuring smile. "Open the gift, Cassandra."

I bit my bottom lip and gazed back down at the stunning gift bag. It was almost too beautiful to open. Feeling no rush, I pulled out the sparkling tissue slowly and sucked in a ragged breath as I pulled out a long black velvet box.

I glanced up hesitantly to find Logan watching with curious eyes. His usually confident demeanor wavered when I noticed his lowered brow.

With bated breath, I opened the lid.

"Oh my G—Logan, it's..." My eyes grew wide, jaw falling lax at the sight of a stunning charm bracelet with diamonds set in what looked like platinum between each charm. I exhaled, my fingers ghosting over a little silver tennis shoe.

I looked up, tears stinging my eyes. Logan reached out

267

and took the bracelet from my hands, his eyes never straying from mine.

"The first time I ever laid eyes on you, you were jogging with your friend Hilary," he murmured. I lowered my gaze back to the tiny shoe and smiled.

"The first time I ever had the pleasure of hearing your voice," he said, tilting his head in thought, "you ended up tripping and needed bandaging." His finger brushed over the tiny silver Band-Aid.

Tears pooled more heavily in my eyes. His gift was unlike anything I'd ever expect. I wasn't sure what to think or feel in that moment.

"The first time I knew you were more than a pretty face," he said with a smile, his thumb caressing my cheek for the briefest moment, "you brought Oliver and me muffins." His voice cracked, and I bit my bottom lip as he touched the tiny muffin.

The burn of a stray tear as it slipped down my cheek pulled my gaze to my lap. I wiped it away quickly.

Next, he held up the miniature swimming pool and I laughed, looking up at him.

"This one speaks for itself, sweetheart." His smile widened into a broad grin. "It was a night I'll never forget…and one I wouldn't mind experiencing again next summer."

My head shot down, heat creeping up my cheeks. I shook my head, chuckling.

"This," he said, holding up a music note, "is for the first time we danced." He lowered the bracelet and looked me in the eyes. "I wanted you that night, Cassandra—more than I've ever wanted any woman. But I'm grateful every day that you wouldn't let me have my way." He sighed. "We wouldn't be here today if I'd slept with you then."

He looked back down, frowning. "I can't image you not being here today."

My heart swelled, helping me find my voice.

"The pumpkin patch," I said, running my fingers over the shiny jack-o-lantern.

"Yes, the first day I realized I wanted nothing more than to protect you—from your ex, and from anyone else that could hurt you."

I smiled, his words soothing every part of my soul.

"The carnival." I smiled, remembering our day together. The charm was of a Ferris wheel, and the only one that was gold.

Logan took my hand and clasped the bracelet around my wrist. He looked up at me, my hand still in his.

"The first day I knew Oliver was falling in love with you."

I smiled, tilting my head over to Oliver. His Lego creation was nearly finished. Logan's fingers clasped my chin gently, pulling me back to face him slowly.

"I was scared, Cassandra—terrified." He sighed, his expression pained. "The following few days after the carnival, I brought home women trying to…push it away." His hand fell, releasing my chin.

My face scrunched in confusion. "Push what away—me caring for your son?"

"No." He shook his head gently. "My feelings for you."

I closed my eyes and inhaled deeply to keep the tears at bay. "Logan—"

"I get it. I do. I'm not good for you. But just know, please know…" he began, a smile brightening his face slowly, "…you're important in my life, Cassandra. You're my best friend."

# Chapter Twenty-Four

## FAMILY

That afternoon was full of laughter. Playing with Oliver's many new toys and having a wonderful meal I helped Logan prepare, I found myself lost in a haze of possibilities.

It had been a lovely day, and the growing feelings spreading throughout me began to settle in a small crevice of my heart. The relentless urges to reach out and grab Logan, crush my lips to his, and hold on for dear life as he had his way with me took everything I had to resist.

The longer I remained so close to him, the harder it became to see reason. I was constantly reminding myself we were better as friends. As lovers, our relationship would be undoubtedly short lived...no matter how passionate it might be in the heat of the moment.

In the end, I feared his notorious reputation would reign supreme, and I'd walk away with nothing but a broken heart.

During dinner, I caught myself staring a bit too long from the corner of my eye as Logan helped Oliver cut his food. He was an amazing father, and witnessing that melted away even more of my doubt.

When the dishwasher was finally loaded after I'd flat-out

demanded Logan step back and let me clean up, we made our way down to the theatre in the basement.

I couldn't help smiling as Logan stood in front of the professional-grade popcorn machine, waiting for it to fill. It not only reminded me of childhood memories spent around the television, but also gave me the sweet feelings of making new ones. The buttery aroma filled the room, and the popping of the kernels began to slow just as the opening credits began to play on the enormous screen that took up the entire wall.

"Hurry up, Daddy!" Oliver didn't ever bother to look over at his father, instead staring expectantly up at the screen. Scout sat peacefully in his lap, pleased with all the attention Oliver had showered him with throughout the day.

I looked around the room that I'd been in only twice previously. There were two rows of recliners in front of the screen, but in the center of each row was an overstuffed sofa with pillows and a massive plush throw draped over the back.

I sat with Oliver in the middle of the first-row sofa while we waited for our popcorn impatiently.

"Your daddy is becoming an old man, you know," I joked loudly enough for Logan to overhear. "He is slower than we are at getting things, huh?"

"Yeah," Oliver chuckled, shooting his father a goofy grin. "He is slow like my grandpa."

I laughed, petting Scout and shooting Logan my own crooked grin.

"I'm coming, I'm coming," Logan drawled, glancing over at us. He scooped the fresh popcorn into three small tubs, and I laughed as he juggled them all in his hands as he walked toward us.

"You're lucky I didn't do anything to yours, sweetheart. So impatient." He grinned, handing me one.

"Like what? You wouldn't dare spit in my popcorn, Mr.

West!" I feigned shock, adding a dramatic edge to my voice.

"Well, I *am* a gentleman, but you'd be surprised what I could come up with to teach you a lesson in patience," he said with a playful smile as he sat on the other side of Oliver, "as well as respecting your elders."

I giggled. "Do your worst—I dare you." I popped a piece of the delicious popcorn into my mouth and smiled at him.

Logan chuckled as Oliver glared first at his father and then at me. "Quiet! It's starting."

I bit my lip in an attempt to control my laughter at Oliver's feeble attempt at authority.

The movie began, and after settling in through the first twenty minutes or so, I felt something hit the side of my head. I jerked forward in my seat, laced my fingers through my hair, and removed the offensive kernel.

With a tilt of my head, I glowered at Logan. He was wearing an impish grin and had a 'What-you-gonna-do-about-it?' glint in his eye.

I fought so damned hard not to smile, but as his taunting expression broadened, so did my lips. His beautiful sapphire eyes gleamed with mischief.

Regaining my self-control, I squinted my eyes, pursed my lips, and picked up the kernel. With luck—and to my satisfaction—I shot it back at him, hitting him square between the eyes.

A loud, guttural laugh rumbled in my chest, earning me a threatening glare from Oliver.

"Sorry," I whispered. Shooting one last triumphant smirk at Logan, I turned my attention back to the movie.

Oliver snuggled into my side, Scout sleeping soundly at his feet while *Home Alone* continued playing across the screen. I'd seen it multiple times as a child, which made me more aware of my surroundings then the film. To be more exact, I was all too aware of Logan's intense gaze burning into my side.

I tried to ignore it—perhaps it was all in my head—but judging by the heat racing through my veins and prickling the tips of my ears, I was positive I could feel him staring.

Chancing a quick glance, I shifted my head subtly to the side and peered over at him.

As I'd expected, his body was positioned to look more at me than the screen. I swallowed the knot forming in my throat, but once my eyes locked with his, I found no power to look away. His entire expression was full of something I didn't recognize; it wasn't full of the lustful stares he'd thrown my way ever since we met, nor the warm and friendly gaze I'd come to relish.

I'd noticed this same confusing-yet-enchanting look earlier in the living room. Goose bumps flared over my arms and traveled down my body as his unrelenting gaze burned into mine.

Finally, I mustered enough force to mouth, "Watch the movie." My lips turned up in the slightest smile, hoping to defuse the tension between us.

Logan simply smiled and turned his attention back up at the screen.

I dropped my head, staring into my tub of popcorn, but my nerves never left my hands; they trembled as I retrieved a handful. With a soft sigh, I tried to calm my racing heart.

As the movie made its way toward the climax, Oliver began to grow restless. Turned out he was still a bit too young to truly enjoy the holiday classic, no matter how funny it was.

Oliver squirmed in his seat. His hands ran through his recently refilled tub of popcorn, but instead of pulling out a kernel to eat, he tossed a handful to Scout, who was rolling around on the floor, equally bored.

"Oliver, Cassandra may not want Scout eating that,"

Logan said sternly, ending the silence. I hadn't heard his husky voice in over an hour; it was as sweet as ever.

"It's fine, although I think your dad might want some as well," I said, smiling at Oliver. I grabbed a piece of popcorn from my tub and held it up. "Open your mouth, Logan."

Logan cocked an eyebrow, but did as I asked. Oliver and I both laughed as I tossed in the popcorn, and with a swift move of his head, he caught it in his mouth like a pro.

"I want to try!" Oliver hopped down from the sofa and stood in front of us.

I laughed, tossing a popcorn kernel at his open mouth, but with no success. Oliver frowned, his brows pulling down.

"Try again." Oliver stomped his foot.

I tossed another and another, all of them failing to reach the goal.

"You're not very good at this, Cassie," Oliver pouted.

Logan dipped his head back, laughing. I shot him a look and he reached into his bowl, pulled out a piece, and held it up. "Let me try."

Oliver waited with his mouth open as wide as he could, a loud 'Ahhhh' sounding from his throat.

Logan aimed and tossed the puffy snack perfectly into his mouth. Oliver jumped up and down, giggling.

"Yeah! I did it!" he exclaimed proudly, then turned to me. "Must be a boy thing."

I huffed, offended, and grabbed a handful of popcorn. Catching Oliver off guard, I threw it straight at him.

Oliver shot me a stunned look, but within seconds had his full tub in hand and retaliated. Popcorn flew through the air in my direction from both Oliver and Logan.

I held my tub tightly and scrambled from my seat, ducking behind the row of recliners in the back. Oliver's laughter mixed with Logan's deep voice echoed throughout the room.

"Hmmm, where do you think she's hiding?" Logan taunted.

I could hear Oliver's snicker. My hand covered my mouth, silencing my own laughter.

Then all I could hear was Logan speaking in a hushed voice, but I couldn't make out the words. Oliver's footsteps were loud enough to hear coming up the back. With adrenaline racing through me, I belly crawled across the floor. Popcorn spilled out from my container, and I stopped at the edge of the recliners, waiting. My hand rested in my bowl, clutching a heaping amount, ready to fight back.

As if out of a movie, I heard Logan yell, "ATTACK!"

When I looked up, they were both standing over me, wearing smug grins. Popcorn rained down as I scurried to my feet. I threw my handful of popcorn at Logan and dumped the remainder of my tub over Oliver's head, giggling uncontrollably.

Logan laughed as I leapt over the recliners, adrenaline guiding me as I darted to the popcorn machine across the room.

I flung open the glass door and reached for the metal scoop just as I felt hands grip around my waist and pull me into the air.

My giggles poured out as my feet flung up. I tried with no avail to fight out of his grip as he chuckled. We'd been in this position twice before—and each time under different circumstances—but this was the first time I'd enjoyed myself in his arms.

"Surrender, sweetheart. You stand no chance against us West men." Logan's thick laughter caressed my ear.

I thrashed in his grip, refusing to lose. I reached out to grab the scoop in the popcorn machine, but he held me back, laughing harder. I needed some way for him to loosen his grip just enough so I could get the upper hand; I was less than a foot from the machine. Without another thought, I craned my neck back just enough to smack my lips down onto his.

Logan's eyes flew open in shock, and as I'd anticipated, his grip loosened.

Taking full advantage of his stunned and stiff demeanor, I plunged the scoop into the vat of warm popcorn and pulled his shirt open by the collar. My cheeks stung from the giant grin on my face as I tossed the buttery kernels down the front. *Payback!*

Pulled instantly from his stupor, Logan grabbed my hand just as I plunged the scoop in for more.

"You play dirty," he murmured. His thumb caressed my palm, sending electricity through it, but I was able to fight it off when I saw the stool behind him begin moving.

"I'm not the only one," I whispered, trying to keep a straight face.

Logan's body tensed as Oliver stood on the stool, held open his father's shirt, and dumped a full tub of popcorn inside. He released my hand, turning to find his son laughing hysterically.

"You little traitor!" Logan chuckled, shaking the kernels from his shirt.

Oliver stuck out his tongue in defiance.

Logan turned back to me, where I was waiting with the scoop overflowing with popcorn, held out over him.

"You win!" Logan shouted, holding his hands up in defeat. "I surrender!"

I dropped the scoop back in the machine and smiled at Oliver, giving him a well-deserved high five.

"Smart man." I giggled, helping Oliver down from the tall stool.

I followed Oliver back to the sofa, where he threw himself down onto the cushions. His giggles died down slowly as a yawn escaped his lips.

Logan pulled him up into his lap and sat back in his previous seat. I smiled, feeling at peace when Oliver rested his legs over mine. Quietly, we cozied up into the sofa, and the movie continued as if nothing had happened. The only evidence was the thousands of tiny pieces of popcorn that covered the room. The popcorn-machine, whose door was left open, was surrounded by more destroyed kernels.

Tiny pieces of popcorn fell into my lap when I ran my fingers through my tousled hair. I'd need a good, long shower before bed.

———◆◆◆———

Oliver had fallen asleep between Logan and me before the ending credits began to roll. I'd spent the rest of the movie wondering if Logan had thought twice about my kiss; it was quick and subtle, but it was a kiss nonetheless. It was just enough to tease my insides after the last one we'd shared at the farm. His lips were as firm and delicious as I remembered.

Glancing over at Logan, I found him staring straight ahead at the screen. His eyes were focused intently on Kevin McCallister reuniting with his mother.

"He was exhausted," I said, looking at Oliver. A loud yawn spilled from my lips.

"You seem quite sleepy yourself."

"Well, it's not like I didn't experience a bit of World War III."

"You?" Logan's eyebrows shot up, feigning hurt. "Might I remind you I'm the one that was attacked so ruthlessly?"

"You deserved it."

"Is that so? Why would that be?"

"You threatened to ruin my popcorn earlier."

"Ah, but my threats toward you are always so empty." His voice was warm and sexy, and all I wanted was for it to whisper in my ear for the rest of the night.

"Is that so?" I asked playfully, unconvinced.

"You know it is," he replied genuinely before adding, "I have to say, I am a bit surprised you would play so dirty. A kiss to force a man to relent? You could have done better than that."

"Would you have preferred an elbow to the gut?"

Logan shook his head, chuckling. "I'll always prefer your kiss, sweetheart."

My body sat rigid as my pulse picked up and raced through my veins, waking the one part only he could. I wondered if he could feel it, too.

He stared at me with the same sweltering look from earlier. I cleared my throat awkwardly and looked back at the screen. The end credits were still rolling, and John Williams' theme music filled the room.

"I should put him to bed," Logan said after a few short moments.

I could only give a shy smile and a nod. Logan lifted his son into his arms and pulled himself to stand. I followed him up the stairs that led out of the basement, Scout trailing behind.

"Cassie," Oliver mumbled through his sleepy fog. Logan stopped at the base of the second set of stairs in the foyer.

I was halfway to the living room to grab my bag, but stopped to walk over when I heard my name.

"I'm right here, sweetie. Go back to sleep. I'm going home to sleep, as well."

"No!" Oliver whined. "I want you to read me a book first."

I smiled. "Of course."

Logan glanced over his shoulder and gave me a grateful smile. I scooped Scout into my arms and followed Logan up the stairs to Oliver's room.

After pushing open the door with his elbow, Logan laid his son on the bed and pulled the covers over his tiny frame. I stood behind Logan, smiling at the dinosaurs covering the comforter. He stood and walked back to the door while I sat on the edge of the bed beside Oliver.

"What book would you like me to read?" I asked softly. Scout jumped from my arms onto the bed.

"The new book you gave me," Oliver murmured sleepily. His eyes struggled to remain open as he smiled at Scout. The pup had pushed his way under the covers, popping his head out the top under Oliver's chin.

I looked up at Logan. He nodded once and left the room to retrieve the book from downstairs.

"Can he stay with me tonight?" Oliver asked as his hands ran through the pup's short hair.

"I'm not sure your dad will be all right with that."

"Please? I know he won't mind."

Within moments Logan was back, book in hand.

"Please, Daddy, can Scout sleep over with me?"

"If Cassandra doesn't mind, then I'm all right with it as well."

I nodded. "I'll pick him up tomorrow afternoon."

"Thank you." Oliver yawned, pulling Scout closer into his arms.

I held up the book—*Green Eggs and Ham*—and began reading. I smiled; it was one of my favorite books from my childhood.

I read in a quiet voice while Logan stood listening in the doorway.

279

Oliver's eyes fluttered as he tried to stay awake. As the book ended, his determination slipped away. I closed the book and pulled the blankets up to his chest. He'd fallen asleep with a giant grin covering his innocent face, and Scout was sleeping soundly in his arms. As I pulled my tired body from the bed, I placed the book on his nightstand and clicked off the lamp.

My heartbeat began thrashing in my ears when I turned and saw Logan staring at me. In a matter of seconds, I'd be completely alone with him. It was nothing new—we'd spent plenty of time together alone—but after that day, something had changed. I wasn't sure what it was or when it'd happened, but I knew it wasn't just me who felt it.

With soft, cautious steps over the creaky wooden floor, I walked out of the room and closed the door halfway. Logan had moved to the side of the hall opposite me.

"He seems to have enjoyed the story. Thank you." Logan held my gaze as he leaned against the wall, his hands shoved deep into his pockets.

"It's my favorite." I shrugged, desperate to keep things light and natural. "I think I enjoyed it as much as he did." I puffed out an awkward giggle. Despite my efforts, the air between us grew thick quickly.

"I should get going," I said, unable to look away.

"Of course. I'll walk you out."

We walked down the hall and descended the steps, my head heavy with thought. Logan wasn't the same guy I'd met in August. He was sweet, funny, and extremely kind—everything I'd always wanted. After all the time I'd spent with him, I felt like we fit. He was my other half, and in that moment, I knew I couldn't resist him anymore.

His hand brushed against my lower back gently, and I closed my eyes at the sweet touch. My body was on full alert, calling out for his touch to never leave. I tried not to think about it, instead needing to focus on remembering how exactly to stay upright and walk at the same time.

I went to the living room to grab my bag before following him to the foyer, stopping at the front door. Hesitantly, I looked up at him, unsure what to make of his expression. His brows were lowered in thought as he dug his hands into his pockets, his shoulders tight.

"Today was a lot of fun," I said, unsure what he was thinking. "Thanks for inviting me over."

My bottom lip pulled in, and I nipped at it nervously while my hand ran up and down the strap of my tote uncomfortably. Why wasn't he speaking?

"Logan, is everything—"

"Cassandra—" We spoke in unison.

A soft but awkward laugh came from us both as we looked down shyly and then back at each other. Everything felt new and foreign, but I was ready for it.

"I heard you went on a date with Caleb's brother, Luke."

I stood dumbfounded. What was I supposed to say? That was the last thing I'd expected him to say.

My body tensed, shifting my weight from one foot to another. "I…um…it was just dinner with Hilary." I gave a small shrug. "Caleb and Luke showed up, but…it wasn't a…date."

I swallowed and chanced a look up at him. He was staring at me as if he were contemplating saying more, but instead he simply nodded, his lips pressed tightly together.

Without knowing why, I stepped forward. His eyes brightened and his posture softened. I needed just one touch—anything. Deciding a hug would satisfy my hunger, I took another step and stood directly in front of him. The closer I was to him, the braver I felt, so I reached out and folded my hand around his. It wasn't exactly the start of a friendly hug, but my body was leading the way. And judging by the look in Logan's eyes, there was no turning back now.

"Luke seems like a great guy," I whispered, searching for the right words—the words that would explain why Luke was nothing more than a nice guy. I held my gaze on our joined hands, unsure how to explain my feelings.

"Yeah, I'm sure he is," he murmured, then reached out with his free hand and lifted my chin. "You deserve a good guy, Cassandra."

I wanted nothing more than to lean in and close the gap between us, to wrap my arms around his neck and finally taste every inch of his inviting mouth.

As if Logan could read my mind, he released my hand and wrapped his arm around my waist. His other hand moved from my chin, his fingers brushing over my bottom lip. My eyes gave him everything I had—the approval I knew he was searching for.

He leaned in, and I closed my eyes. His warm breath caressed my cheek and lips, and I awaited the feeling of his.

"Merry Christmas, Cassandra." With that, his lips placed a tender kiss upon my cheek.

I swallowed, flushed and ready to give in to everything my body was demanding, but he stepped back and walked to the door. I stood there, dumbstruck at how much it hurt to move my legs forward.

"Thank you for the gifts, and for spending the day with us." His voice was smooth and sweet, but his eyes were filled with something deeper. "Can I walk you home?"

"No," I stammered, then looked down, trying to clear my thoughts and desires. When I looked back up, he was smiling more widely, and I felt instantly at ease. Only he could do that to me.

"Good night, Logan."

I ambled out into the chilly night air that did little to soothe the ache he'd awoken inside me yet again. Something had cracked in the armor around my heart, and I knew I couldn't resist the inevitable much longer. Logan West had somehow pulled me in, and I was finally ready to show him exactly what he was getting.

# Chapter Twenty-Five

## VULNERABLE

Christmas in the West home was one I'd never forget as long as I lived. Oliver and Logan were so in love with life and each other it left my soul utterly sated when I went home that night. Against all my reservations and reasoning, I was falling in love with them more and more each day. And as the holiday season came to an end, I couldn't deny my feelings any longer.

I wanted Logan West. No longer was the feeling simply a passionate seduction my body craved. There was an insatiable need growing inside me that only one man could fulfill. It consumed me in ways I'd never thought possible. He was all I could think of or dream about. He was it: everything I'd ever wanted.

"Come on, since when do you take this long?" Hilary complained.

Pulling myself from my daydream of telling Logan I wanted to try us, I took one last look at my reflection in the mirror. I felt like a new woman. I gave my hair one last tousle, smiling at the glitter Hilary had run through it minutes earlier.

With a confident strut, I stepped into the living room.

"Hot damn, girl!" Hilary smiled. She was sitting on the

armchair in my living room, slipping on black glittery heels. They added that extra sparkle to her red low-cut, body-hugging mini dress.

"You're sure it's not too much?" My nerves peeked through. I felt beautiful and sexy, but completely out of my comfort zone.

"It's freaking gorgeous!" Her smile grew wider. "You look stunning, and there's no way Logan won't be drooling all over himself when he sees you in that." She laughed. "Looks like the tables have turned, huh?"

I nodded with a smile, slinking down onto the couch across from her and slipping into my nude heels. "So you and Caleb are good?"

"I have never been happier. He's amazing. I mean, I always knew that, but he's so kind and loving and the most unbelievable kisser." She slumped back in the chair, swooning like a lovesick puppy.

"Yeah, I got it. You're falling in love."

She sat up, her eyebrows lowered. "No! I mean, no…I don't…oh my God."

I chuckled softly. "Why are you freaked about that? It's what you always dreamed about."

Hilary looked up at me, gnawing on her bottom lip. "I just…" She sighed. "I'm not falling in love with Caleb."

"Um…you sure about that?" I chuckled, bemused.

"Cassandra, I'm already in love with him." Her words came out slowly, as if she was realizing it while speaking.

"Oh."

"I know, right? We haven't even slept together."

My mouth fell open and I stared at her. Did I hear her correctly? Hilary was no virgin, nor was she a slut, but I couldn't think of a guy she'd dated more than a few times before sleeping with him.

"Stop looking at me like that!" she demanded. She stood up, glaring at me, and began pacing back and forth across the room.

I relaxed, smiling. "I'm happy for you. I always knew you and Caleb would end up together."

She stopped abruptly and looked over at me with disbelief. Slowly, a broad grin covered her lips. "Liar!"

I laughed. "Yeah, I honestly thought you'd never talk to him."

◆◆◆

Entering Haven just past ten that night, I felt like I was on fire. Every nerve ending in my body was lit and buzzing neurotically.

I knew Logan would be there. We'd been texting daily since Christmas—more so than ever before—about little jokes we'd heard, or something interesting we saw that just needed to be shared between us. Every time my phone sang the tune of a little chirping bird, I'd smile and rush over to check it. That'd be an issue once school resumed after winter break.

Logan had sent a text earlier that day, letting me know he'd be at Haven after nine and looked forward to seeing me. He also mentioned Oliver was spending the night with his grandmother. It was the perfect time to come clean about how I felt.

Caleb appeared and pulled Hilary into his arms. "Hey, baby. Where you been?" After a long and inappropriate public kiss during which I tried to look anywhere else, Caleb looked over at me with a smile. "Wow, look at you all sexed up. Did Hilary pick out that dress?"

I flushed. "Surprisingly, no—all me. I was feeling particularly brave." The black dress was snug against my body, with a deep, crystal-adorned V-cut down the chest. It revealed more cleavage than I'd ever shown in my life. The skirt blossomed out and fell mid-thigh. It screamed fun, flirty, and above all sexy.

Caleb nodded, squeezing Hilary more tightly and placing a quick peck on her forehead. They were adorable. "Good for you, Cassie. Logan's at the bar, by the way."

"Oh, I'll catch up with him later." I shrugged, playing it cool.

Hilary and Caleb both chuckled, giving each other a knowing look.

"Have fun tonight, but don't even think about stepping outside without Logan or me with you. Got it?" Caleb said seriously. I saluted, amused at his tone. "That means you, too." He glanced at Hilary.

I smiled, enjoying his big-brother protectiveness.

"I'm only allowed in the dark with Logan. Got it." She giggled.

He growled, pulling her to his chest. She giggled again, looking up at him. "You're a little smart ass tonight." He kissed her, ending her laughter abruptly. "I'm not as worried about you and Logan in the dark anymore. Seems he's got his eye on this one—and this one only." He winked at me.

I heard a fading "Have fun!" from Hilary as Caleb pulled her through the swarm of partygoers, leaving me standing there overanalyzing my next move.

*Go straight to the bar and find Logan, or play it cool a little longer?* Honestly, all I wanted was him holding me on the dance floor as soon as possible.

The thought alone got me weaving through the crowd toward the bar. After scanning the entire length of it and coming short of Logan, I frowned. Chewing on my bottom lip, I was debating sending him a text when a shiver shot up my spine, goose bumps flaring over my skin.

I closed my eyes, savoring the warmth of his breath along my neck.

"Happy New Year, sweetheart."

I turned, smiling, and wrapped my arms around his neck for a quick hug. It was something I'd never done before, but the most natural reaction tonight. His arms pulled me in closer for a brief second, and I could've sworn I heard him inhale a deep breath when his face hit my waves of hair.

I pulled back, hands still on his shoulders, all smiles. "Happy New Year."

He looked me up and down appreciatively. "Oh, Cassandra. Are you trying to kill me tonight?"

I giggled softly and leaned in. "You like?"

His tongue darted out, licking his lips. "I adore."

I flushed. His gaze held mine, and the intensity of his stare sent flutters straight through me. He made me feel brave and beautiful. I reached out and took his hand.

"Dance with me," I murmured.

Logan tightened his hand around mine and led us to the dance floor. Dozens of other bodies were moving and grinding to Beyoncé's "Single Ladies," which played from the DJ booth.

I laughed, dipping my head back and letting the fast tempo lead my feet. My arms snaked around Logan's neck as I moved my hips back and forth slowly. His hands gripped them tightly, holding me close.

We danced to song after song—all loud dance beats—and I felt a layer of sweat begin to cover my body from the hot, colorful lights flickering above us. After I twirled in Logan's outstretched hand, he grinned and pulled me into him, my back smacking against his chest.

His breath was intoxicating, tickling my ear as I ground my hips against him. I closed my eyes, losing myself in the moment, my hands reaching up above my head and back around his neck. His arms snaked up from my hips, fingers caressing my navel and making their way up between my breasts to my jaw. He turned me around, staring me in the eyes.

I knew what he was asking, and there was no need: I wanted it just as badly as, if not more than, he did. My hands ran down his forearms—all muscles through his thin white button-up shirt—and pulled him into me, crushing my mouth onto his.

With a heavy sigh, he pulled me flush against him, his fingers digging into my hair. My tongue ran across his bottom lip, and a growl escaped his throat as his lips opened. I took full advantage and thrust my tongue inside, my hands roaming over every inch of his body I could touch. I'd been starving for him, and I was now ready to quench my appetite.

After not nearly enough time acquainting his lips with mine, he pulled back. His long fingers caressed my cheek. I closed my eyes and leaned into his touch.

"Ah, Cassandra...tell me you want me as much as I want you."

Opening my eyes, I smiled, answering him with a wider grin. He returned an eager smile, gripping me tightly against him and closing the distance between us once again. This time, his desire for me was stronger. His hand slid down my back, blazing a trial in its wake, and gripped my ass. I shuddered, kissing him harder. His lips kissed down to my jaw then up to my ear.

"Let's—" he began.

"Ten, nine..."

We both pulled back, panting, instantly reminded we were not alone. He leaned in and kissed the tip of my nose, smiling, and joined in with the rest of the room.

"Four, three..." he mouthed, staring at me with an

energized grin. His eyes were bright and youthful, hair tousled from my passion for him. "...two, one!"

The room roared with a collective "Happy New Year!" and excited yelling, but the background noise fell silent as Logan brought me back into his arms and placed a soft, tender kiss upon my lips. It was unlike any kiss I'd ever experienced before, and the complete opposite of the ones we'd just shared.

He pushed me back gently, grinning, and twirled me in his arms. We danced through a couple more songs, kissing and touching, enjoying the new freedom to explore each other. It was past one in the morning when I kissed up his scruffy, five-o'clock-shadowed cheek and tugged on his earlobe with my teeth, earning me a pleased growl and tighter squeeze to my backside.

"Take me home," I whispered seductively.

Instantly, I was being pulled through the crowd toward the door, giggling.

"Wait—I should tell Hilary I'm leaving," I insisted.

"Text her," he replied quickly, grabbing my coat from the closet near the entrance.

I giggled more loudly. "Caleb will worry. It will only take a second." He held up my coat, and I slipped my arms inside before he took me in his arms. With a fierce, unforgettable kiss to my lips, he nodded.

"I'll get my car and meet you out front." He placed another kiss on my lips, unable to get enough—just like me. "Hurry."

I turned, giggling yet again when I felt the sting from his hand swatting my ass. With a seductive stare over my shoulder at him, I squeezed back through the mass of people all wanting the same thing as us: to make their escape into the new year with their lovers.

Finding Hilary and Caleb was harder than I'd anticipated. They weren't at the bar, and I was eager to get back to Logan. Filling with butterflies just thinking about him, I turned to look back at the door and froze.

He was talking to someone: a woman, who had her hands on his forearms.

My stomach dropped instantly. My feet turned me around and moved me back toward him, but I was all the way across the room. A swarm of laughing drunks stood in my way.

My gaze never strayed from Logan, and when he stepped back, I took in the sight of the woman. I recognized her from his painting: Oliver's mother. Logan's ex-fiancée.

My blood ran cold. She was back. What did this mean?

Before I knew it, I was directly behind him.

"Stay the hell away from Oliver and me. Do you understand me, Natasha?" he hissed, his hands balled into tight fists at his side. I stopped, suddenly aware of how this was affecting him. I only wanted to pull him away from her and hug him.

"I know you better than anyone, Logan." Natasha smiled with a cold look in her eyes. "You'll always love me, and in time, we'll be a family again."

With that, she placed a quick kiss on his cheek, which he instantly drew back from, and turned on her heel, strolling back through the door and into the night.

His hand wiped the spot her lips had touched, anger rolling off him in painful waves.

"Logan—" I began, placing my hand on his shoulder.

He flinched, then turned back, staring at me. The soft, carefree azure eyes from earlier were now dark and clouded.

"I can drive," I said softly. I reached for the keys dangling in his hand. He was too upset to drive; his body vibrated with rage.

291

His hand ripped back out of my reach, and his eyes narrowed at me. "I can drive!" he hissed.

His tone hurt, but I shook it off. "Fine. I brought my own car, anyway. We'll take that. I'm not letting you drive like this."

"Like what?" He was definitely pissed, and ready to unload on the first person to give him a reason. I didn't have anything to drink since I'd driven, and I knew Logan had had a few, so it made sense for me to drive anyway.

"Logan, please," I sighed.

"I'll drive, damn it!" he snapped, grabbing my hand and pulling me outside with him.

I followed behind him, gathering my composure. When we stepped onto the sidewalk, I ripped my hand from his, not wanting to go anywhere with him until he calmed down.

He sighed, running his hands through his short, wavy hair. "Damn it!" His voice rang out.

"Just let me drive you," I pleaded. I placed my hands on his cheeks, wanting him to forget all about Natasha and what her being in town meant.

"Kiss me," he murmured, and I obeyed with a smile.

The instant my lips touched his, he held the sides of my head and kissed me more deeply, his hands roaming wildly over my dress. He held me tightly, pushing me backward against the side of the building. As I became lost in my desire to hold him close, he whisked me around the corner so we were in the alley all alone, never once breaking the kiss.

I held him close to me, my lips attempting to wash away the past five minutes. His hand fisted my hair and the other moved from my ass, lifting my dress around my waist. The cold brick building stung my backside as his body pressed me roughly against it.

Logan's lips traveled from mine down my jaw and to my neck, nipping and licking, leaving behind a blazing trail in their

292

wake. I dipped my head back, resting it against the bitter wall. He tugged me up and pulled my legs around his waist, and I lost myself in the moment.

After what felt like both an eternity and an instant, he released me. His hands disappeared, and I lowered myself to the ground, gauging the expression on his face. He was tugging his wallet from his coat pocket, from which he pulled out a condom.

I recoiled, feeling suddenly cheap.

"Logan, I—" I adjusted my dress back down, covering myself. He watched me, bemused.

"What's wrong?" he asked, breathing heavily. Then he was kissing me again, pulling me back under his spell, until I heard the buckle of his belt opening.

Laughter from the parking lot filled the cool air, and I was expelled fully from my Logan-fueled haze. I tensed, moving away from the wall and out of his reach, finding my breath.

"Let me drive you home. You should get some sleep," I said, swallowing.

I frowned when a deep laugh rumbled from his chest.

"Sleep? You think I want to go to sleep!?" He continued laughing then took my hand, running his fingers over my knuckles. "You want this as much as I do, Cassandra. No more games. Admit it, and give me what I want."

I froze as I looked into his eyes, which were filled with nothing but lust. "And what is it you want?" I asked hesitantly. I knew what I wanted from him: I wanted everything. And someday, even sex in the back alley would be fun and exciting, but not our first time together.

"You already know what I want, sweetheart." A wicked grin spread over his lips as he placed a kiss on my neck, his hands tugging my hair. His tongue ran up to my ear as he whispered, "I want to fuck you, here and now. I'm tired of waiting."

I shoved him away, tears stinging my eyes. My chin jutted out as I struggled to remain strong, but it quivered from the pain of his words.

He'd spoken my worst fear—the one reason I'd kept myself guarded from him. But I wanted to believe what we shared was more than that. I looked down at the charm bracelet adorning my wrist, refusing to believe he didn't feel something more.

"So that's it?" I asked.

"Yes. You've known this, Cassandra—don't play coy. It's who I am." He stepped back, watching me. "But I've never wanted to fuck anyone more."

His words ripped the air from my lungs. I shook my head, not wanting to believe him. A tear slipped down my cheek.

"You're just hurt because of Natasha. But I'm not going to let you push me away." I moved to step forward, but his sharp expression stopped me. I looked down, fingers brushing over the gold Ferris-wheel charm. "I care about you. Please…let me drive you home. We can talk in the morning. You're just upset."

"Don't kid yourself." He looked straight through me. "I'll never want anything more from you than your body. So either give me what I want…" He threw the condom at me, and I watched it fall to my feet. "…or leave me the hell alone."

I couldn't hold back the gates any longer. Tears spilled from my eyes.

"Go to hell!" I ripped the bracelet from my wrist, wincing at the sting as it broke off, and threw it at his chest. I turned and ran to my car, my hand covering my mouth.

A loud sob escaped my throat, and the tears broke through harder than ever. My feet pushed me to my car as my pulse raced, my heart pounding through my ears.

I was such a fool, always wanting to believe the best in people—first Mark, and now Logan. I was never enough.

Slamming the driver's-side door shut, I tried unsuccessfully to control the frenzied sobs and even my breathing. But no amount of deep breaths seemed to ease the pain slicing through me. *Why did he have to do this to me?*

My head throbbed as I tried to figure out if anything over the past few months was real. Was it all some sick game to get me in bed—a city guy bored in the country? I was going to give him my heart—hand it over so freely—and all he wanted was…

*No.* I banged my hands on the steering wheel. I needed to calm down, or I'd never make it home.

Sniffing loudly and wiping away my tears, I turned on the engine and looked back once more at the alley where I'd left him.

There, standing in the shadows and staring at me with hooded eyes, was Logan.

Refusing to let him see me break down into a sobbing mess anymore, I rolled my shoulders back and jutted out my chin as I stomped down on the gas.

After pulling onto Main Street, I drove through town, passing two green lights before stopping at a red one about a half mile from Haven. My labored breathing finally began to calm. Glancing in my rearview mirror, I gasped. Long black streaks of mascara marred my swollen red eyes. I tried to wipe away the evidence of my hurt with the pads of my thumbs, but it was no use. It only looked worse. A loud honk sounded from behind me and I looked up to see the light had turned green.

I lifted my foot and placed it down on the accelerator slowly. The car had made it halfway into the intersection when a bright-white light blinded me from the side. I turned my head just as a thunderous metal-on-metal grinding sound took over the air. My body thrust forward, my seatbelt forgotten in the rush to flee Logan. I gripped the steering wheel for dear life as my hair flailed, blinding me as the car smacked down and then flipped up again as I lost my grip. A sharp stab slicing through my sides and down my legs followed the crunching of glass.

I hit something hard and landed on my back, warmth filling my head. In an instant, everything stopped, except for the deafening sound of a horn filling the night.

# Chapter Twenty-Six

## CONSEQUENCES

"Call 911!"

"Don't move her!"

"Oh God, is she alive?"

I whimpered. My throat was parched, lips dry. I couldn't breathe—something heavy was pressed against my chest. My ears rang as the muffled voices around me grew clearer.

"She's trapped!" a man's voice rang out.

"Help get it off her!"

"No, we could make it worse!"

I couldn't see anything or anyone, but I knew they were there. It did little to help calm the panic washing over me, though. I forced my eyes open and saw a shining ray of light hitting my face. I wasn't sure what it was—a flashlight, perhaps?

I winced, unsure what was happening.

"Can you hear us?" a woman asked, her voice cracking.

I felt something soft squeeze my hand, but my head betrayed my demand to move. I could only look straight up into the night sky, at the stars that filled the darkness.

"It's going to be okay," the voice said softly. "Help is on

the way."

I opened my mouth, "I…I…" Even with all my strength, I could manage nothing but a gurgling sound.

It hurt everywhere. My head was heavy and damp, and I could feel strands of hair matted against my cheeks. My body seemed to have disappeared. I tried to move my hands and legs, but there was nothing. Panic began to overwhelm me further, but the hand folded around mine gave it another tender squeeze, and I knew even without seeing it that my hands were there.

It was the most terrifying feeling I'd ever endured, and a thought I'd never dreamed I'd have; to be thankful to have your limbs still attached was heartbreaking. Warm liquid pooled in my eyes and spilled down my cheeks. I was left waiting there as the gasps and sobs of onlookers filled my ears. I focused on the positive, which was that I was not alone and was finding my strength anywhere I could as dull pain radiated through my chest.

The wail of sirens grew closer while the heaviness on my chest deepened and the darkness pulled me away.

"Cassandra!"

I struggled to open my eyes and keep them open as they fluttered, heat stinging them. Something was in my eyes, and the thought caused a terrifying shudder to rip through me. I raised my hand to wipe whatever it was away, but it was hopeless. My hand was there—I knew it was, I could slowly feel the tingling in my fingers—but the limb was too heavy to lift.

"Try to stay still, miss." A man's soothing voice relieved some of my torment. I closed my eyes, praying the pain would end soon.

Hands were on me, tugging something around my chest. Something stiff was wrapped around my neck. Fear bubbled up inside me; I wanted up—away from what was happening to my body.

"Cassandra!"

The voice from seconds earlier was back: Logan. I thought it'd been a dream. But it was Logan—he was there. I pushed up to go to him, but I couldn't move. Instead, a sharp pain tore through my back. My mouth fell open, and a pathetic ghost of a scream poured out.

"Cassandra!" Logan's voice was a deep growl—louder than before. I focused on it, willing it to come closer.

"Damn it! Let me through!"

"Sir, you need to stand back! Sir! *SIR!*"

A man yelled behind me, but all I wanted was Logan: his touch, his words, his everything. Nothing else mattered.

"Get the fuck out of my way!"

Someone dropped beside me on the pavement. I struggled to look out of the corner of my eye, but my vision was distorted. There was nothing to see other than the outline of a dark figure hovering over me.

"Cassandra…"

I felt his familiar cool fingers on my cheek, tender and soft, barely grazing my skin. Feeling peaceful, I closed my eyes. He'd make this better. He'd make the pain go away.

"What have I done?" he gasped, and suddenly all I could feel and smell was Logan. His trembling hand was in mine, squeezing it. Then, as if he could read my mind, I felt the soft touch of what I dreamed were his lips on my forehead.

"Sir, we need to get her to the hospital," someone said, and I used every ounce of strength I had to hold onto his hand. "I'm sorry, sir, but you can follow us."

I tried to reach my other hand out, not wanting him to go, but it remained limp at my side.

"I'll be with you. I promise you're going to be fine. I'm

going to make this right." His voice was broken and weak as he released my hand.

Hot tears slid down my cheeks as his reassurances faded slowly into the darkness that consumed me once again.

# Chapter Twenty-Seven

## — LOGAN —

## WAITING

"I'm riding with her," I demanded, watching Cassandra pass by me on the gurney and into the back of the ambulance. She was broken and bloodied, and I was to blame.

She was supposed to be with me, in my arms, safe and sound. Everything had gotten so far off course. I wanted to tell her how I felt tonight—to hold her and convince her I could be a better man: the man she deserved. Instead, I let Natasha get in my head. Just like old times, the damn woman knew how to knock me down.

I'd endured four years of hating her, and hating myself for ever trusting her and wanting to make her my wife. When she left, I wanted nothing more than to fuck and drink anything I could get my hands on—to forget the pain I felt over the fact that I wasn't enough for her.

And then in walked Cassandra: the fiery blonde who was as stubborn as she was beautiful. She threw my entire plan to the wolves, leaving me confused and bewitched. She meant something to me I couldn't describe, and I couldn't fathom

301

how deep it really was. Only Oliver had ever evoked those feelings from me. Not even Natasha could stand up against her.

Cassandra was sweet and loving, but also guarded, much like myself. She was so eager to live life, and just needed the right person by her side to help give her a push. I wanted to be that person, and now...now she was in the back of an ambulance, fighting for her life as the doors shut in my face.

I sprinted back to my car, adrenaline coursing through me as I ran every red light and blew through every stop sign on the tail of the blaring siren and flashing lights in front of me.

As I pulled up behind the ambulance, I watched Cassandra disappear inside and be taken straight to surgery. Slumped against the metal elevator door, I waited, praying for the first time since I was a young boy that someone was listening.

———•••———

As I paced across the dreary waiting room of the small hospital, every horrible outcome played through my mind. I wanted to fly her to the city to get her the best care possible, but it was out of my hands.

Hilary was there, crumpled around Caleb on a small, stiff-looking sofa. Occasionally, a sob would spill out from her direction of the room, but he'd only hold her more tightly, stroking her head and whispering into her hair.

The tender act filled me with envy. I wanted to be with Cassandra—holding her and helping her, not waiting.

A silver-haired doctor emerged from the double doors just past eight in the morning. All eyes flew up, watching him anxiously. I stopped instantly in my tracks and stared, my breath catching.

"Hilary Robinson?" he called out.

Hilary jumped from her spot, shoving away from Caleb, and crossed the room in one swift move. "Yes, that's me. Is Cassandra all right?"

"Follow me," he replied, his voice giving nothing away. He turned back to the doors he'd just appeared from and disappeared with her at his side.

An hour ticked by without word from Hilary. I continued pacing, unable to sit or think without the weight of the night crushing me. By noon, my body begged to piss out the booze I'd ingested, but I couldn't pull myself away from the room. The risk that I might miss an opportunity to speak to Hilary or see Cassandra was too great.

Caleb's voice broke through my silent wallowing.

"You should go get something to eat."

"I'm not leaving."

I didn't look up from the floor. *How dare he even suggest I step an inch from this room? Not without Cassandra.*

"I understand, but if Hilary comes out, I'll—"

"I'm not leaving!" I growled, shifting my gaze from the floor to him, closing the topic.

Caleb stood, holding up his hands in defeat. His expression was calm, and I knew if things were reversed, he wouldn't leave Hilary.

"I'll just go down to the cafeteria and bring you back something. Anything in particular sound good?"

I stared at him, scowling, not caring what he did. I just wanted the damn doctor or Hilary to give me an update— *anything.*

He nodded, understanding. "All right, I'll bring you whatever looks edible."

With that, Caleb walked in the direction of the elevators and I returned to pacing back and forth, wondering how many men had trudged over that same patch of carpet while they waited for news on the women they cared about. Out of all the men stuck waiting over the years in that room, I'd no doubt been the only one who deserved to be in those shoes.

"Damn," Luke said to himself.

I cocked my head to the side, watching him stare down at his phone.

When the yuppie had come in a little while after Hilary and Caleb, I chose to ignore him. I didn't know anything about him other than what his brother had told me, and I had no intention of getting to know him now. I did, however, overhear him trying to console Hilary. He told her Cassandra would be fine—that she was tough and would come out of this with a smile on her face, ready to take on the world.

I just shook my head at his comments. What the hell did he know about Cassandra? She was a fighter, yes—I saw it several times—but I also saw the scared girl hiding inside, holding her back. There was a woman in there desperate to break free, yet she chose to hide in her tiny house in the woods, reluctant to accept her true significance.

"I, um...I gotta go." Luke tucked his phone back into his pocket and stood. Throwing on his coat, he looked over at me as if I cared.

"Something came up at work. Can you tell Caleb I'll stop by later and to let me know if there's any news?"

I nodded once simply to avoid speaking to him, then turned my focus back to the floor.

◆◆◆

The day passed painfully slowly. I watched every second of every minute tick by with no news or return from Hilary. The growing frustration inside me built with each passing hour. Caleb had brought me a sandwich and coffee, but my stomach was too knotted to eat.

It was after six in the evening when Felicia barreled out of the elevator and raced over to Caleb, bracing herself against his forearms. Her eyes were bright red and swollen. She leaned into him, panting, looking like she'd run a marathon trying to get there.

"Where is she!?" she said, her voice broken.

"Still in ICU. Hilary went back this morning, and we haven't seen her since." He trailed off in a somber tone, but Felicia was walking toward the nurses' station before he could finish.

"Cassandra Clarke. I'm her mother."

"Yes, right this way, ma'am."

I watched as she disappeared behind the double doors, wanting nothing more than to follow her.

Hilary appeared several minutes later, and my entire body stiffened. I watched her walk over to Caleb and, defeated, she collapsed into his arms. She cried and beat against his chest as she rambled, but all I heard were muffled pleas.

Unable to stand there watching, knowing she had more information than me, I walked over, hands shoved deep in my pockets. I needed answers—now.

"How is she?" I asked, standing in front of her.

"Give her a minute," Caleb mouthed. His hands ran through Hilary's long, dark hair, trying to soothe her.

I needed to soothe Cassandra. I was tired of waiting.

"Damn it, just tell me how she is!"

Hilary pulled back from Caleb and wiped her sniffling nose.

"Please," I begged, my voice nothing more than a breath of air.

Hilary cleared her throat and dabbed at her eyes while I waited impatiently, desperate to hear anything.

"She's still asleep. The doctor said she should wake at any

time. They won't be able to get a full diagnosis until then."

"How did she...look?" I asked, relief washing over me. At the scene, I'd been terrified I was going to lose her; it was a thought I couldn't bear. I'd just found her, and she finally wanted to be with me—I could see it in her eyes as we danced and kissed. She wanted me as much as I wanted her. Oliver adored her, and would welcome her with open arms. She was the woman I never thought existed, and had given up dreaming about long ago. Losing her wasn't an option.

"She's pretty beat up. They said the biggest problem could be her—" Hilary swallowed and looked away. "—her legs. She hit the pavement hard, and the doctors say they won't know the extent of the damage until she's awake."

My jaw tightened, and I inhaled deeply through my nostrils. "I need to see her."

"Felicia is with her now, but I'm sure she'll let you see her later."

I turned and walked away, angry at the world. Cassandra didn't deserve this. I wanted to hit something, destroy everything in my way to get to her. It was harder to breathe, and my neck was painfully stiff. I needed some fresh air.

I rode the elevator to the ground floor and walked out into the parking garage. I rested my back against a cement pillar and pulled out my phone. There were two text messages from Julia, and a voicemail from an unknown number.

Julia's first text was at 1:32:

**Everything's fine here. Mom said she'd keep Oliver as long as you needed. I hope everything is going all right. Luv u**

I tried to smile, but my lips didn't move. I sighed, relieved I didn't have to worry about my boy, but devastated at the thought of having to explain this. He loved Cassandra.

Her next text was at 4:46:

**Just checking in. Let me know when there is any news. I'm coming back from the city now. I'm praying for her. Love u.**

Taking a deep breath, I scrolled to my voicemail and hit *Play*.

**"Hello, darling, it's me: Natasha. I know last night came as a surprise, but I really needed to see you. I miss you, and want to come back home. Please, Logan. I love you. I'll stop by later at your house."**

Anger ripped through me. I hung up, gripping the phone in my hands. I hadn't missed the fact that she hadn't even bothered to acknowledge Oliver, her own son. She was a manipulative bitch, yet I'd fallen for her. I blamed my young age. I was in my first year of college, on spring break, when she entered my life and turned it upside down. It wasn't love—I thought it was, wanted to believe it, but it was only lust. The only thing we did right was create our son.

Natasha was in for a real treat if she stopped by my house tonight. Julia was staying there over winter break, and from the sound of it, would be there soon. I finally managed a smile. Julia would tear her apart.

I slid the annoying device back in the pocket of my jeans just as it beeped. Frantically, I pulled it back out. There was a new text from Caleb.

**Hilary wants to go home. We'll be back in the morning. You need anything?**

It wasn't the message I wanted. Why couldn't someone just tell me she'd be fine? I leaned against the pillar and replied.

**No**

Exhausted, I rolled my head back, staring up at nothing. My legs grew heavy, pulling me down to the ground in agony. With my knees tightly against my chest, I rested my head and, for once, let go. Fat tears escaped for the first time in years. I hadn't been a crier since I was a child, and even then only when I broke my arm falling from a tree when I was eight. When Natasha walked away, I didn't cry once. I drank and made money. That was what I did: worked hard and fucked harder.

Well, before I'd met Cassandra, anyway.

—◆◆◆—

Looking up at the clock in the empty waiting room, I sighed. It was just after three in the morning, and my body was fighting my futile attempts to stay awake. My burning eyes began sliding shut, until the double doors opened and Felicia walked into the room.

I jumped to my feet and approached her immediately, gauging her expression. Her posture told me everything I didn't want to hear, but I refused to believe anything without seeing it for myself.

Cassandra was healthy and strong. She would fight with everything she had in her.

"Felicia," I said, pulling her attention away from her feet.

"Oh, hi, um… Logan." She attempted to pull on a smile, but it didn't stick. She frowned, barely holding herself together. Her bright-red eyes were surrounded by a pale-white face. "Have you been here this whole time?" she asked, tugging her purse up her arm.

"Cassandra and I have become…really close," I said, unsure what we were after everything that'd happened. "How is she?"

Felicia shook her head and looked away, sniffling. Tears were welled up in her eyes when she finally looked back.

"She hasn't woken up yet. I…I need to go home. I need to unpack, and—" Sobs poured out as she cupped her mouth. "I'm sorry. I just can't be here right now. I don't want her to wake up and see me like this. I'm always so strong for her, but I just need…oh…I don't know what I need. I don't want her to wake up alone, either, but—"

I stepped closer and Felicia wrapped her arms around me, holding me tightly for support. She needed comfort, and I wasn't going to refuse her. She was Cassandra's mother, and truthfully, it soothed me too. She loved Cassandra, and for that I felt instantly connected to her.

We stood silently, my hands around her back as she continued to cry. Once her breathing evened and her chest relaxed after a few long minutes, I finally spoke.

"I could sit with her," I offered, hopeful.

Felicia pulled away and took a tissue from her pocket.

I continued, more eager than ever in my life. "I'm staying all night, anyway." I sighed, wiping my hand over my forehead and running it through my hair anxiously. "Please. It would mean everything to me."

"Yeah, of course." Her voice was broken. She dabbed the tissue under her eyes and gave me an appreciative smile before walking back to the double doors. She pressed the buzzer and spoke too softly to overhear. After a moment, she turned around and gave a single nod.

The weight lifted from me. I'd see Cassandra soon—sit with her, hold her hand, and just be there for her.

"Thank you," Felicia said softly.

I watched as she waited for the elevator, then turned back to the desk.

"This way, Mr. West," the nurse said, pulling my attention to the double doors I'd waited anxiously to get through all day.

Walking through them made everything real again. My legs were heavy and my heart was ready to explode as we walked past another nurses' station.

"Cassandra's mother said you could stay with her until she

returns. Here you go." The nurse slid the glass door open and waited for me to enter.

My body grew instantly slack at the sight in front of me. Cassandra was still asleep, but through all the bruises and monitoring wires, I hardly recognized her.

Her beautiful, glowing face was marred with deep-purple bruises, but the blood that covered it at the scene had been washed away. A long bandage covered her arm, and blankets were pulled over her chest, covering her body.

"The buzzer is right here, if you need anything."

The nurse's voice faded to a murmur as I sat in the chair next to Cassandra and reached out to hold her hand.

"I'll leave you alone, then." The door shut behind me, but my attention was focused solely on the woman lying helpless in front of me.

Unsure where it was safe to touch her without causing her pain, I caressed my fingertips up and down her arm. I needed the connection, to feel her close to me. She'd been in my arms, her body nearly one with mine, lips demanding mine. And now here she lay.

With one hand holding hers, I brought the other up and brushed her cheek gently.

"Oh, Cassandra." I sighed heavily. "What have I done?" I leaned forward and lowered my lips to her cheek, but pulled back instantly.

I didn't deserve to kiss her. Once she woke, she'd throw me out of her room and never want to see me again. Tears stung my eyes as I rested my head on the bed beside her.

"Forgive me, Cassandra. Please. I never meant any of that shit I said. I was a fool, upset and confused. Christ, I'm worthless without you. Please, please, sweetheart. You have to fight. You have to come back to me." Tears streamed down my face, emotions taking over and leading the way for the first time in my life.

I continued with heavy sobs. "Please, Cassandra. Wake up. I'll do anything. I need you. You're all I've ever needed...all I've ever wanted."

I pulled away and stroked my finger across her chin. She was everything, and for the first time in my life, I knew I'd never want anyone else.

I caved and placed a small kiss on her forehead. My lips needed to feel her just once more. I didn't deserve it, but I wasn't ready to be a gentleman now. Pulling back, I looked down at her, my heart swelling in my chest.

"I love you," I murmured, my head resting next to her ear.

The words surprised me at first. I knew that I cared for her and was falling in love with her, but it was foreign on my tongue to speak it aloud. I once thought I'd loved Natasha, but it held nothing to what I felt for Cassandra. There was a bond—something within my soul that I'd never felt with anyone else before.

This was love—unconditional, all-consuming, mind-blowing love.

The thought of the future terrified me, but I'd never give up. No matter how much she fought against her feelings or how angry she was when she woke, I'd never give up on us.

I relaxed my head next to hers, our hands intertwined, and closed my eyes. She will wake *up*, I repeated in my head. Finally peaceful beside her, I allowed sleep to claim me.

# Chapter Twenty-Eight

## —LOGAN—

### WIDE AWAKE

I woke to the feeling of someone squeezing my hand. My head jerked up as I remembered where I was. A part of me had hoped it'd all been a bad dream.

"Cassandra?" I squeezed her hand, sitting up in my chair.

She moaned groggily, her eyes still closed but lids fluttering. She was coming back to me.

"Sweetheart, it's all right, I'm here."

Her eyes flickered open slowly, and my entire body flooded with relief.

"Cassandra," I sighed. Without releasing her hand, my other reached for the buzzer.

"Logan?" Cassandra murmured. Her voice was low and shaky.

"Shhh, don't talk. The nurse will be here any second." I smiled, thankful to see her bright, clear eyes and hear her beautiful, sweet voice.

Cassandra looked confused as her gaze shifted from me to her room and finally landed down on her own body. I watched painfully as her eyes grew wider, color draining from her face.

She tried to sit up, but winced when she could barely move. A loud yelp slipped from her throat as she stared at the ceiling, tears springing from her eyes. I ran my hands through her hair, wanting to soothe her.

"Relax. Try to stay still. Everything is going to be all right. Try to stay still."

Her head tipped toward me, her eyebrows lowering.

"Logan?" she murmured.

I smiled wider and nodded once. "Yes, I'm here."

I waited for her to say something, but she just continued to stare at me as if she didn't understand or recognize me.

"Why?" she breathed after a long pause.

"Why?" I repeated, not understanding.

"Why are you here?" Her voice was so low I could barely hear her, but the hurt behind it cut through me.

I stuttered, unsure where to start or how to explain just how sorry I was.

"You didn't want me then...you can't expect me to..." She coughed, clearing her throat. Her tongue slipped out, moistening her dry lips. "...to believe you want me now—like this."

"I'm so sorry." I sighed, my body slumping forward. I lifted her hand gently, desperate for more contact, and brought it to my lips.

I felt her attempt to pull away, but she was so weak.

"Please, forgive me. I didn't—" I began.

She let out a ragged breath and her head fell weakly to the other side, putting her face out of my view.

"I was wrong," she whispered, her voice broken. "I thought...I thought we were..." She sighed. "I can never be what you want. Just leave, please."

The sniffle that came from her broke my heart. I released her hand and brushed my fingers down her cheeks, desperate to see her face.

"Cassandra, you've always been what I wanted. I was angry when I saw Natasha was back. She has always made me doubt everything and everyone."

Her hand moved to her face slowly, wiping her cheek. I considered walking around the bed to see her, but I'd done enough. If she didn't want me to see her, I'd give her that. I'd give her everything I had.

I leaned forward, placing a chaste kiss to the nape of her neck. "I'll never forgive myself for the things I said to you. I was terrified—afraid of falling for you and having you leave me like she did. But you're nothing like her, and I'm ashamed I ever considered otherwise."

Between the occasional hushed whimper and her body's quivering, I knew she was crying.

It broke my heart. I did this. I always fucked things up, but this was the one time I'd never recover without painful scars—on both our hearts.

The nurse entered and I ran my hands down my face, wiping away tears I hadn't realized were there.

"P—please. Just leave." Cassandra was so quiet, so broken, I couldn't deny her. But I refused to leave her alone.

"You should go wait outside, sir," the nurse said, staring between us, gauging the situation.

It took everything in me to agree. I nodded and walked around the bed, bending down to come face to face with the woman I loved. Her eyes were swollen and red and tears streamed down her bruised face, but she was still as beautiful as ever.

"I'm not giving up on us." I traced the back of my hand gently up her cheek, wiping away the tears. Her eyes were so soft—so scared. "I'll never give up. You have my heart, my soul, my everything. When you're ready, I'll be here." I leaned forward, cupping her cheeks, and placed a tender kiss to her forehead before standing upright and walking out the door.

—◆◆◆—

The walk back to the waiting room was numbing. The double doors closed behind me, leaving me alone in the small room. My body rested against the window, and I stared out at the first snowfall of the year. I found myself wondering if Oliver was outside playing in it. He loved the snow. My mind couldn't shake the image of Cassandra and my son laughing as they stood outside, surrounded by a blanket of flurries.

The hustle and bustle from the morning shift change occurred around me, never once disturbing my state of despair. My forehead pressed against the cool glass as I stared out into nothingness.

"Logan?"

Exhausted, I lifted my heavy head and looked back, meeting Caleb's concerned expression.

"Felicia and Hilary just went back to see her. The nurse called and said she woke up earlier."

"I know."

"Felicia said you sat with her overnight. Were you there when she woke up?" Caleb asked, staring at me piteously. I despised it.

With a low sigh, I closed my eyes, pushing away the painful memory before finding the strength to mutter, "Yeah."

Caleb nodded as though he understood. I pushed away from the window where I'd stood for what felt like hours and ran my hands through my hair. The double doors leading to Cassandra opened, and I watched a nurse walk out and head toward the elevator. She looked at us and offered a small smile,

315

but my mind was focused in the direction she'd come from, its double doors separating me from the woman I desperately wished to hold.

The urge to rush inside and beg her to forgive me was overwhelming. I needed to hold her, kiss her, love her: all things I'd never have a chance to do now.

The thought sent a quake down my body that didn't go unnoticed by Caleb.

"You want me to get you something to eat? Some coffee or anything?"

With one small shake of my head, I gazed blankly past Caleb. "No. I have some business to take care of."

I strode past him, snatched my coat from one of the chairs, and stood in front of the elevators. I slipped it on and shoved my hands in the pockets, searching for my keys.

"I'll keep you posted if there's any news," Caleb said.

I could only nod. It took everything I had to walk away. When the elevator's steel doors opened, I stepped inside, a sense of alarm hovering around me. As I looked out at the waiting room, I frowned, realizing I knew every inch of it.

I forced my hand to reach out and press the button that would take me to the parking garage. I wouldn't come back— not unless she called for me. She needed time to sort through her feelings and focus on recovering. She only needed to heal right now.

Slowly, the steel doors closed.

The sharp breath I inhaled ripped through me, forcing me to brace myself on the wall. I was really leaving. My head reminded me it was for her own good and only temporary, but that didn't stop the tear that fell when the elevator stopped and opened to the parking garage.

—◆◆◆—

My house was quiet when I walked through the front door a few minutes before eight in the morning. Relieved, I headed straight to my bedroom and shut the door.

It took all my strength to remain calm. After slipping out of my clothes for the first time in two days, I took a hot shower, finally washing away the stench of New Year's Eve.

Once I'd pulled on a clean T-shirt and pajama pants, I sat on the end of my bed, holding my phone in my hands.

I spent the next few minutes calling my assistant and canceling every business meeting for the next two weeks. I explained it may be longer and that the older woman, who'd worked for me for over five years, should e-mail my clients immediately.

Next, I called my older brother Lawrence. I explained that I'd be unavailable to handle any business deals, and to expect any calls to be routed to him.

"Julia called last night," Lawrence replied. "I understand. Take all the time you need."

I tried to smile, thankful I had the support of my family while I sorted out what I could do to help Cassandra.

"Thanks," was all I could mutter before hanging up and climbing into bed.

—◆◆◆—

"I'll call the police!"

I woke with a start, muffled yells from downstairs pulling me from my blissful dreams of Cassandra wrapped around my body. Our limbs tangled together in my bed. Her sweet, familiar giggle filling my room. It was how the new year was supposed to begin: with the start of our future together.

But it was only a dream.

"You'll never see him again, you skanky bitch!"

I flung myself out of bed, recognizing Julia's voice, and

raced out of the room.

Skidding to a stop, I looked downstairs to find Julia standing toe to toe with a grinning Natasha.

"I want to see Logan—now!" Natasha hissed, starring Julia dead in the eyes. Her hand rested on her hip, and she tossed her long dark hair over her shoulder.

"Get the hell out or I swear to God I'll throw you out!"

"Logan and I belong together. You can't stand in the way, *sister.*"

"I'll never be your sister. You think I'm just going to stand back while you hook your slutty claws back into my brother?"

"You don't really have a choice in the matter. Now, if Logan isn't here, then I want to see Oliver."

"Wow, you actually remembered you have a son!" Julia feigned shock.

"Where is he?"

"Logan or Oliver? Which did you come back to see?"

"Both."

"Yet last night, when you tried to stop by, you never said a word about Oliver."

"I...I wanted to speak with Logan first."

"Bullshit. It doesn't matter, anyway—Oliver is with my mother and Jackson. And don't even *think* about trying to get his cell number; he hates you almost as much as I do. And Logan is—"

"Right here," I replied, irritated and still exhausted, walking down the stairs toward the two women staring up at me.

Julia grimaced and rolled her eyes while Natasha watched me with a smug grin.

"Leave us, Julia," I told her, staring straight at Natasha. I'd never hated anyone more. How could I have ever loved such a manipulative woman?

When we'd first met, we were both still so young. My financial situation was worth little compared to my accumulated wealth now, but I'd never thought that mattered to her—not until she ran off with the first old moneybags to catch her attention.

Julia mumbled under her breath and stomped out of the room, but not before shooting one last deadly glare at Natasha.

As I descended the last few steps, my hands kneading out the kink in my neck, I walked past Natasha toward the kitchen.

I was relieved Oliver wasn't home. I missed him, but this would be hard to explain; he'd been hoping and praying his mother would return one day. Every wish he'd ever made was for that one thing. And now here she was.

I poured a glass of orange juice and stood, resting my hip on the counter and waiting for her to explain herself.

"You look good, Logan." She licked her lips slowly and seductively as she began approaching me. She was too easy to read, and I was over it already.

I cocked my eyebrow at her brazen attempt to reel me in with sex and held up my hand to stop her.

"It's been almost four years, and *that's* what you have to say to me?"

"Well, I missed you. I forgot how delicious you were with messy bedhead and sleepy eyes."

"Cut the crap." I slammed my glass on the counter. "Why are you here?"

"I told you already: I want my family back."

"Why now, after four years? Run out of old desperate men to swindle?"

Her eyes grew just a hint, confirming the rumors that had swirled over the last few years.

I gave it no thought and continued. "Oh, yes, I heard all

about your little sexcapades. So tell me—did they finally catch on, or just drop from old age?"

She smiled. "You don't mean that, baby."

"Yes. I do." I stepped around her, glaring, and sat at the kitchen table. Resting my hand against my pounding head, I sighed. "I've spent enough time hating you, Natasha—regretting I ever met you. But you gave me the best thing in my life: Oliver."

"I want to see him," she replied quickly, moving to sit across from me.

"Not going to happen." I scoffed. "He barely remembers you, and I won't allow you to taint the few memories he does have."

Natasha's voice lowered. "He's my son—my own flesh and blood, Logan. You can't keep him from me."

"Watch me," I snapped. I stood from the table, unable to sit there any longer.

"He'll hate you."

I froze mid step halfway out of the room. Slowly, I craned my head at the brazen woman now standing behind me.

She stepped around me, my gaze following her. Her lips turned up, and I watched a malicious smile grow on her face. "He's going to grow up eventually, and when he does, he'll find me or I'll find him." She stepped closer, reaching out and brushing her hand down my chest. "I'll tell him you kept us apart, and he'll hate you forever."

I snatched her hand, which had been traveling down to the drawstrings of my pants. "Don't you dare come into my home and threaten me!" I released her hand, shoving it away, repulsed. "I'll make sure he knows exactly the kind of woman his mother is."

I walked around her and out of the room. My hands pumped into fists, my jaw clenched.

*How dare she.*

"Logan, please. I didn't mean to upset you." She came up behind me, her hands resting on my arms.

I shrugged her off, disgusted by her once-arousing touch. She stepped in front of me again, testing my patience. I could never hurt a woman, but Julia was in the next room, no doubt listening and waiting to throw Natasha out with one word from my mouth.

"I want you gone," I said, my voice hard.

"I'm not leaving town," she replied with ease, ignoring my threatening scowl, and walked to the front door. "I'm staying in a hotel nearby. Here's their card with my room number on it, as well as my cell number."

Natasha placed the shiny cream business card on the antique table beside the door.

"I want to make this work—our family. Please, Logan, for Oliver." Natasha opened the door, the cool night air reminding me of the reality waiting outside. "I'll be in touch." She closed the door behind her.

"Don't you dare say you're actually going to think about giving her another chance."

I turned to see Julia storming down the hall toward me.

"Not now." I sighed, running my hands down my face and around the back of my neck. I needed to think.

Her voice grew louder as I walked past her up the stairs and headed to my bedroom, where I slammed the door shut behind me. Without a single clear thought, I threw on a clean black shirt and dark pair of jeans and headed back downstairs.

"I'm going out."

"What?" Julia frowned, still standing where I'd left her minutes earlier. "The girl you care about is lying in a hospital bed because of a drunk driver, and you're going out? I know what that means, Logan!"

"I'm not going to drink—not this time. I just need..." I sighed, dropping my head. I had no clue what I needed. Slowly, I lifted my gaze back up at her.

The thought of getting drunk brought up nothing but bad memories. No, I needed fresh air and somewhere to think. Before Cassandra, I would've gone straight to Haven and screwed the first woman who greeted me with a smile, but now everything was different.

My body belonged to Cassandra, along with everything else. I ached for her in a way I never thought possible—not just for sex, but for her company, her bright smile, and her sweet laugh. I'd take anything she'd offer at this point.

I walked out to my garage, ripped the cloth cover from my vintage motorcycle, and pulled on my helmet. It'd been months since I'd gone for a ride, and I wondered if Cassandra would ride with me one day. The thought of having her that close, holding onto my body, her hands gripped around my waist, caused a shiver to race up my spine and shoot through my neck.

I could only dream of such a heaven.

Within minutes, I was on a backcountry road, cool air blowing against my face. The heaviness in my head lifted as I took every curve with slow precision. I was in no hurry.

Tightening my hands on the grips, I let my mind drift through all the ways I could persuade Cassandra to let me back in.

I would never give up. I was hers, and someday she would be mine.

# Pick up the next book in the Harmony Series now!

*Indulge, The Prequel,* available now.

*Irreplaceable,* Book 2, available now.

*Indestructible,* Book 3, available spring 2014.

# About the Author

Angela Graham is the bestselling author of the Harmony Series. She lives in Tipp City, Ohio, with her husband and three wonderful kids.

Visit Angela on Facebook for more info on future books:
https://www.facebook.com/angelagraham.author

# Acknowledgments

This story never would've been more than a rough draft of ideas if not for the constant support of a few very special people in my life.

To my children, who are my entire life and remind me every day why it's important to work hard for what you love. Dream big, and never give up.

To my sister and best friend, Michelle, who endured countless rants about characters she had yet to even meet, I am so incredibly grateful.

A special thank you to my father, Greg, for helping me take this story to the next level of a real book.

An enormous thank you to Stephanie, the best CP a girl could ask for. I can't say this book would be where it is today without your support through constant e-mails, texts, and long rambling phone calls. I look forward to the journey we're embarking on, and hope this is only one of many years of friendship and books to come.

To Sharon Graham and Bethany Shaw, thank you for your support and feedback.

To my editor, Jen, you have become one of the most important people on my team! I can't imagine writing a book without you there to pull it all together in the end. Thank you for putting up with my always-changing timelines and hectic schedule.

A HUGE thank you to my readers for taking a chance on me. Your encouragement and support is so greatly appreciated. Every time I receive an e-mail from one of you guys, I'm truly on cloud nine the rest of the day!

And last but certainly not least, to my husband. I love you, baby, forever and always. Thank you for helping out a little more while my head was preoccupied with writing.

*While you're waiting for*
*Book 3 of the Harmony Series,*
*be sure to check out*

# *Emerge*

### By S.E. Hall

No sooner than Laney Walker and her long-time best friend Evan Allen finally delve into romantic feelings for each other, college sends them packing, miles apart. Never the social butterfly, Laney is slow to adjust to life with a new softball team, crazy roommate and co-ed dorm. Without the support system of her Dad and her Evan, she's left to cope with diving into the real world on her own.

Just when she thinks nothing could tear her apart from her old life any further, she meets the mysterious, debonair Dane Kendrick and her heart is left divided.

The familiar love she shares with Evan has always been easy and sweet, but she can't help wondering what would happen if she let go and took a leap of faith into what she never knew she wanted? A jump that Dane seems more than happy to help her through.

CPSIA information can be obtained
at www.ICGtesting.com
Printed in the USA
FSOW01n1111231216
28789FS